TAXING COURTSHIP

The Hands of Destin 1

JAYCEE JARVIS

SOUL MATE PUBLISHING

New York

TAXING COURTSHIP

Copyright©2018

JAYCEE JARVIS

Cover Design by Anna Lena-Spies

This book is a work of fiction. The names, characters, places, and incidents are the products of the author's imagination or are used fictitiously. Any resemblance to actual events, business establishments, locales, or persons, living or dead, is entirely coincidental.

Published in the United States of America by
Soul Mate Publishing
P.O. Box 24
Macedon, New York, 14502

ISBN: 978-1-68291-741-1

ebook ISBN: 978-1-68291-713-8

www.SoulMatePublishing.com

The publisher does not have any control over and does not assume any responsibility for author or third-party websites or their content.

To Stony,

who shows me the true meaning of love every day.

Acknowledgments

A debut novel is a singular accomplishment that marks a much longer road of passion, dedication and learning.

Thank you to Romance Writers of America for all the support and educational opportunities. The writers in my local RWA chapter Rose City Romance Writers welcomed me from my very first meeting, so many years ago. A special shout out to the amazing Mermaids, Golden Heart class of 2016, and all the women in the Golden Network who are so generous with their time and knowledge.

Beyond teaching me the general craft and business of writing, I also have many people to credit for this particular book. It wouldn't have come into existence without my wonderful beta readers, especially Anne Applegate who encouraged and refined my early drafts. And the final draft would be a lot less polished without the expertise and guidance of my tireless editor at Soul Mate Publishing, Char Chaffin. It takes a village to create a book—I would be lost without my team.

Speaking of my team, a big thanks to Katherine Black and Meagan Johanson, the best of writing buddies who are my first sounding board when I get stuck or discouraged.

Finally, I want to give credit where credit is due to my amazing friends and family. Growing up with a writer means routines disrupted by deadlines, confusing dinnertime conversations about fictional characters and family vacations planned around writing conferences—challenges my children have always handled with grace and good humor. I am also blessed with the best, most supportive spouse imaginable. I appreciate all you do, Stony, from getting dinner on the table night after night, to weekend excursions with the kids, to a word of encouragement just when I need it most. I may not have a room of my own, but I have the next best thing!

Chapter 1

During the season of Ferel's descent in the first cycle of the Troika of Peace

On a night for making mischief, all decent people had long since closed themselves into their snug little homes to wait out the Earth God's day of the week. Only fools and outlaws roamed the streets of Trimble on Taricday.

Like any proper gentlewoman, Lady Emmanuella a'Fermena was tucked away in her room.

But she wasn't going to stay there.

The howl of a monkey echoed through the bamboo shutters covering the window. More concerned about the occupants of her father's estate than jungle animals, Em stared at the glinting strands of her bead curtain and strained her ears for sounds of movement in the private courtyard beyond. *Nothing.* Even her infant nephew had settled for the night.

Heart pounding, Em slipped out of bed, the silk sheet slithering over her bare skin. Goosebumps rose on her arms, though the sultry evening air held the day's heat. She stepped over to her bubinga wood wardrobe, but ignored the elegant saris folded on its shelves. Instead she knelt to reach into the deep shadows under the wardrobe.

The tile floor cooled her cheek as she pulled out a lumpy bundle of rough cloth. She extracted a dull chiton from the pile and slipped it over her head. Cinched at the waist with a leather belt, the coarse garment hung to her knees.

One shade lighter than her skin, the brown chiton offered no camouflage in the jungle surrounding Merdale, though it would help her blend into the shadows in Trimble. For the nearby town of Trimble was her destination. On Taricday.

Did that make her a fool or an outlaw?

The criminal part of her nocturnal activities was obvious and undeniable. She slipped a wrapped cloth containing lockpicks down the loose front of her chiton. She was going to Trimble to break into a government building. If caught by the city guards, they would clap her in the stocks without hesitation.

Em shivered. Beyond the suffocating torture of imprisonment, a day in the stocks would expose her sneak work and bring dishonor and shame to her family. If she were stripped of her noble title, all her sacrifices would be for naught.

She tugged her mother's silver ring off her finger and strung it on a leather cord. The ring brought her luck and reminded Em of her purpose.

When Mother's responsibilities had fallen onto Em's young shoulders, she'd traded her honor, and anything else of value, for the sake of Aerynet, a temple cared for by her family for generations. Em's sneak work supported her legacy, honoring her mother and protecting her dependents. She earned her cacao beans the only way she knew how, since she hadn't the skills to take in mending nor the temperament for prostitution. Besides, as a noble such honest work was also forbidden, because most temples had lands to sustain them. Unfortunately, as Em's Trilord father liked to remind her, Aerynet was too small for a parcel. So, every Taricday, she buried her misgivings and ventured into Trimble in memory of her mother.

Dropping the cord over her head, she nestled the silver talisman under her clothes, where it wouldn't glint and give her away.

Resigned more than resolved, Em strapped on a pair of hemp sandals. Cruder than her normal footwear, the sandals were finer than what a servant would wear and ruined her laborer's disguise. Going unshod would damage her feet, however, and so she made the compromise to protect her noble dignity.

She snorted. Her dignity had been traded with everything else.

She opened the shutters and swung a leg over the sill. Dropping silently to the ground, Em froze to listen for the sounds of any servants moving about the estate.

Hearing only chirping insects, she pulled the shutters closed behind her and slunk between the trees.

An hour later the walls of Trimble rose before her, black with sharp corners distinct from the layered shadows of the jungle. Clouds scuttled across the lone moon, visible for the first time in the clear sky above the river.

She crept along a footpath to a tunnel in the city walls, timing her entrance into the city to avoid the Trimble guards. Guardswomen, technically, since the men who served in the city watch honored Taric, the Earthen God of Strength, on his day of the week, leaving the women on patrol overworked and the city ripe for trouble.

Bypassing brick-lined streets in favor of dirt-packed alleys, Em prowled from the wall to the riverfront. Reaching her destination, she crouched in a shadowed passageway. Little more than a crack between two clay warehouses, her hiding spot offered ample concealment as a pair of guards marched by.

Em held her breath and counted to thirty. Once her pulse had calmed, she peered into the lane. The acrid tang of smoke hung in the humid air while a torch glimmered like a fallen star at the end of the street.

She retreated into the crack, the rough terra cotta wall catching at her clothes.

Soon.

The patrol would turn a corner on their route through the wharf district. Soon she could make her move on her target.

The Tribute Office squatted across from her hiding place. Square, brown, and featureless, it was nearly indistinguishable from the other clay-covered warehouses on the street. Only the cloverleaf emblem of Destin carved into its doors betrayed its official purpose.

Sneaking into a government building was risky, even on Taricday. But the pay was good and her criminal contact, Simon claimed the client was an auditor who worked there. He promised the door would be unlocked and unguarded. Getting in and out of the building should be quick and easy. Almost too easy. There was something fishy about this job, and it wasn't just the smell of the nearby river.

She'd been hired to add a medallion of The Water Goddess Marana to a locked trunk. The task stank of espionage and set her teeth on edge. She'd be more comfortable with straightforward theft. A smile twisted her lips. What had happened to her scruples?

Em's smile faded. Her scruples had died with her mother.

She kissed her mother's silver ring for luck. Fishy or not, she had a task to do, one that paid well enough to maintain Aerynet. Nothing else mattered, her conscience be damned.

In another hour, the patrol would march past again. By then she should be long gone, her fee for the night well earned.

Unease trickled down her spine as she approached the double doors of the Tribute Office and pulled on the bronze handle. Part of her expected the door to be barred, no matter what the client promised, but it swung open on silent hinges.

She slipped inside, taking her first easy breath since leaving Merdale.

Square beams of moonlight shone through windows set high on the walls of the echoing room. Stacked barrels and urns were little more than dark shadows, while the central floor was a maze of trunks and knee-high tables.

Careful not to stumble into any furniture, Em crept away from the door. When she was far enough into the room to be certain no light would leak onto the street, she removed a candle from the pouch on her belt. She pinched the wick between her fingers. Her lips moved in silent prayers to Fermena, Tarina and Marana, a deity for each of the three elements. With the help of the Goddesses, Em pushed heat and life into the candle. The wick sputtered into a flickering flame. She snatched her fingers back from the heat.

A sharp intake of breath echoed through the room, unnaturally loud in the stillness. "You're a woman."

Chapter 2

"Who's there?" Em gripped the comforting hilt of the knife strapped to her thigh. "What do you want?"

"I'm sorry. I didn't mean to frighten you." A young man wearing the loose brown kaftan of an auditor stepped into the ring of candlelight. The tax collector smiled tentatively, a few black curls escaping his fashionable queue to frame his earnest face.

Em narrowed her eyes. She wasn't naive enough to trust a stranger, no matter how guileless he appeared.

His kaftan billowed from his shoulders to mid-calf, leaving his bulk a mystery. His slender fingers and narrow wrists made him seem slight, yet he held a polished wooden staff expertly in his left hand. Two paces long, the staff reached from the floor to a foot above his head.

"You don't frighten me," she said, only half-bluffing. With her knife skills and speed, she had a good chance of escaping before he could summon the city watch. Only his staff caused her concern.

"I'm glad to hear it," he replied, his voice soft and soothing. A dimple flashed with his smile. "You're not what I expected."

She blinked. He expected her? "What?"

"Someone with certain specialized skills was hired for a job here tonight." A nervous chuckle escaped his lips. "I imagined some scar-faced ruffian sneaking through the door, not a lovely woman."

She drummed her fingers against the hilt of her knife. *I knew this job smelled rotten.*

"I don't work directly with clients."

"I'm sorry." His teeth flashed as he worried his lip. "You have to this time."

A muscle in her jaw ticked. The last time a client tried to oversee her work, he'd nearly brought the guard down on her head. Granted, silence wouldn't be as crucial for this task. Still, she had standards. "I could leave right now."

"You could." He tugged on a hank of wavy black hair. "But you won't get paid if you walk out."

The wooden hilt of her knife bit into her palm. She needed those beans. Mystic Patricia and the others at Aerynet depended on her. "If you hired an expert, why are you here?"

He yanked on his queue again. The nervous gesture spoke of his sincerity, weakening her resolve. "I need to add something to the trunk once you get it open."

"Why didn't you give the new materials to my contact?"

"The item is very sensitive. I need to do this personally."

Em sighed. She shouldn't let herself be swayed by his pretty face. In truth, he wasn't classically handsome, yet his wide-set eyes gave him an appealing, wholesome look. And she did need the payment.

"I won't get in your way," he added eagerly. "I can wait here while you work. Tell me when you get the trunk open and I'll do my part quick as a blink."

Reaching a decision, she released her knife. The dull fabric of her chiton fell back into place, covering the weapon. "There is no need for that. Can you show me exactly where this trunk is?"

He nodded vigorously, a black curl sliding free of his queue. Her fingers itched to smooth the strand off his face. As a Lady she was often surrounded by men too pompous and polished to ever have a hair out of place. The auditor's unaffected manner was refreshing. Almost enticing.

She jerked her mind away from such distracting thoughts. They had a job to do. "Lead me to it."

He folded his hands together around his staff and bent in a quick bow. "Thank you, most honorable thief," he said, his tone sincere and reverent.

Em waved her hand in a shooing motion to hide her surprise at the respectful gesture. *What kind of man honors an outlaw?* "We've wasted enough time."

He grabbed a coil of string from a nearby table before leading her to a doorway blocked by strands of wooden beads. The curtain rattled as he held it aside in another courtly gesture. After joining her in the office, he pointed at a trunk. "That's the one."

She crouched with the lock at eye level. The back of her neck itched. She'd never be able to work with him lurking behind her. "Willing to hold the candle for me?"

"It is an honor to serve." He leaned his staff against a wall and squatted beside her.

She pulled the packet of lockpicks out of her chiton and unfurled it on the floor. After selecting a pair of picks the appropriate size, she set to work. Moments later, her skilled hands felt the click as it gave way.

"Amazing," he murmured. "Could you teach me to do it?"

She raised her eyebrows. Was this his true motivation for intercepting her tonight? "You want to be my apprentice?"

"Certainly not." His eyes widened, charmingly scandalized by her wicked suggestion. Had she ever been so pure? "It's just a fascinating and useful skill."

Em felt a pang. His curiosity evoked memories of herself, when lockpicking had felt daring, a clever trick and not a dangerous, though necessary, occupation. She, too, had been flush with independence and eager for adventure, before six years of sneak work jaded her.

Part of her yearned to feed his interest and relive those simpler times.

"This is hardly the time and place for a lesson," she reminded them both.

He nodded, though his shoulders slumped.

Hiding her echo of disappointment, she pulled a gold medallion out of her pouch. "Do you want this in the trunk?"

"I'll do it." His fingers were a warm brush across her skin as he took the medallion. He fumbled and dropped the golden disk. Muttering an embarrassed curse, he scooped it off the floor.

Had he been so affected by their innocent touch? She rubbed her tingling palm against her scratchy chiton, fighting the temptation to touch him again.

He bent over the trunk and removed a familiar bundle.

She gasped. "Are those the offerings to the Novenary?"

As one of the three rulers of Destin, the Novenary oversaw all the temples in the country. Her religious orders were exempt from the ordinary taxes paid by other landholders. Instead, their titled patrons were expected to deliver lavish Allgoday gifts to the Novenary as a sign of their respect and loyalty.

While large temples and wealthy nobles sent their own messengers to present their annual gifts, most minor temples could not spare a devotee for the trip to the capital. Aerynet certainly couldn't, even before Mystic Patricia grew too frail for the long journey. Like many other Trimble patrons, Em had entrusted her tribute to the tax collectors. Her stomach rebelled at the betrayal.

This job got rottener all the time.

"What do you know about the tribute?" he asked, his voice sharp.

"I'm a thief. It's my business to know of any treasures in the city," she snapped back. Her face heated at her slip. She couldn't very well tell him she had spent the last year hunting parrots to make the headdress he so casually handled.

He frowned at her. "Well, we're not going to steal them."

"Good," she said shortly, trying to hide her relief. She

must not have succeeded because he sent her a quizzical look. She pursed her lips. "No sense in angering the gods."

"I quite agree." He tied the medallion to the end of a small skein of thread. The colorful knotted strands reminded her of the quipus her father used for his accounts, only in miniature. He placed the thread-wrapped medallion in the trunk and rearranged the tributes in the order he had found them.

"Now I'll truly earn my fee," she joked, trying to restore their earlier camaraderie. "Re-locking these things is a trick. Not every thief can do it."

He chuckled. "You needn't convince me of your skills."

She slid her tools into the lock. "You're welcome to come closer and watch."

He picked up the candle and leaned over her shoulder. The warmth of his body seeped into her like the sultry heat of the midday sun. His breath stirred the hairs on her neck. The scent of clean tallow soap mixed with something purely masculine coiled through her body.

Why was she so affected by him? Had she been too long without a lover? It had been nearly a season since her last, largely unsatisfying, tumble. Whatever the cause, it took all her professional skill to focus on the lock in front of her instead of the man behind her.

Finally, it clicked closed.

"Amazing," he said again.

Pleased with his flattery, she smiled up at him.

He inhaled sharply, interest flaring in his eyes. He swayed toward her, a curl of hair falling across his beguiling features.

Did he want to kiss her? Her tongue darted across her dry lips. *Fermena preserve her!* In that moment she would welcome his touch. It had been too long since she'd enjoyed a man.

He abruptly straightened and backed away.

She sighed, torn between relief and regret. Though she'd always been impulsive, wanting to kiss a stranger while on a sneak job crossed the line from reckless to outrageous. Her hands trembled as she returned her picks to their cloth sleeve.

He retrieved his staff from the wall next to the doorway. "Now we go?"

Not trusting herself to speak, Em nodded and stood.

Again, he held the beaded curtain aside for her. This time they walked side by side through the building, awareness throbbing in the space between them.

Or had she only imagined his attraction? In her best sari, she did not have the beauty to inspire unbridled lust. In her dull chiton, she blended into the shadows, as unremarkable as any servant or laborer. Her own fevered appetites had addled her wits. Why would he want—

He gasped and grabbed her elbow.

"What is it?" she asked in alarm.

"Someone's coming!"

Chapter 3

Han-Auditor Quintin nearly choked on his own panic. They were doomed. "The Bursar's coming!"

"What?" the lovely thief whispered. "How do you know?"

"We have to hide you," he told her, though he had no idea where.

She took a step back toward the room with the trunk.

"Not there." He dug his fingers into her elbow. "That's his office."

The sparsely furnished warehouse offered no better options.

Hurry! A thought belonging to another whistled through Quintin's mind. *Boss at door.*

The front door rattled ominously.

He froze like a rabbit spooked by an owl. This was a disaster. The Bursar was about to find him skulking around the Tribute Office with a professional thief. He would be dismissed in disgrace, his honor and standing as a Hand called into question. His friends would be shamed to know him and his mother—

The thief pushed him.

He staggered into a pile of goods and sat with a thump on a barrel. His staff clattered to the floor.

Before he could recover his balance, she straddled his lap. "Trust me."

He opened his mouth to speak.

She sealed it shut with her own. She grabbed one of his hands, and unceremoniously shoved it under her clothes.

The delicate skin of her backside filled his palm, softer and smoother than anything he had ever touched.

His mind swirled in confusion, his body instinctively reacting to the fierce pleasure of a beautiful woman in his arms. With a groan, he caressed the tempting flesh in his grasp.

She whimpered into his mouth and deepened their kiss. Her lips held the sweet zing of ginger, while a hint of jasmine teased his senses. The rasp of her tongue sent desire galloping to his groin. He had never realized how intoxicating a kiss could be.

Her hips rocked against the burgeoning ridge in his lap. A fever swept through him. He wanted—*needed*—more. Forgetting where they were and why, he strained closer to her heat.

"Ho, ho, what's this?"

The words were loud, the voice unwelcome. Unimportant. Nothing mattered but the woman in his embrace.

The beauty, however, wrenched out of his grasp and scrambled to straighten her clothing.

His body howled with need. Quintin stood and reached for her.

Bursar Fredrick held up an oil lamp, flooding the scene with light. "And here I hoped to do you a favor by breaking the monotony of guard duty."

Quintin squinted at his superior, trying to parse the Bursar's words over the pounding in his blood. *Guard duty? Oh, rotting hell!*

"You said no one would bother us here," the thief prompted in a stage whisper.

"It was pure luck I stopped by." Fredrick leered at her, his dark eyes gleaming in the light. "No wonder you were so eager to take Taricday duty, Quintin. You'd already planned a tryst with your lover."

His ears burned. "She's not—"

"This is awful!" his accomplice interrupted. She clung to him, hiding her face in his shoulder.

By Fermice's holy breath, he'd almost given them away with his instinctive honesty. As a Hand and a tax collector, he was duty bound to uphold the law. This subterfuge chafed like borrowed garments.

Thank the God of Wisdom for his ally's quick wits. He wrapped an arm around her. His heart continued to beat double time from her wondrous kiss. His cheek brushed against her silky hair. Their adventures had loosened her neat coils, and a braid drifted over her shoulder, the dark strands gleaming red in the lamplight.

"I'm shocked at you, of all people, using the warehouse for such a tawdry purpose." The Bursar clucked his tongue disapprovingly, his tone revealing his malicious pleasure. "What will the Luminary say?"

Known as the Mind of Destin, the Luminary managed all the taxes collected by the auditors throughout the country. As a Hand in service to the office, Quintin had been presented to the Luminary exactly once. The dour, imposing man would not be amused to learn of any shenanigans going on in a tribute office.

Quintin gulped. "You won't report me, will you, sir?"

"I should, you know." The Bursar wagged a thick brown finger at them both. "Taricday duty is serious business. An intruder could have snuck into my office while you were distracted."

"They'd regret it, I assure you," Quintin replied with complete honesty. He, at least, regretted this entire risky scheme, though his mystic friend Ophelia was desperate to contact the Novenary and they had no better plan.

The thief gripped his kaftan, her shoulders shaking under his arm. Surely, she was too much the professional to bark with laughter, though he sensed it might be a near thing.

The Bursar rubbed his chin. "If anyone finds out I let you get away with this—"

"I won't tell anyone." He squeezed his lovely accomplice. "She won't tell anyone, either."

Fredrick fondled the end of her loose braid. "I would hate to see such a pretty little thing in trouble. I'm sure she is entirely innocent."

"Entirely," Quintin agreed through gritted teeth as he fought the urge to swat his superior's hand.

"I'll let it go this time." The Bursar dropped her hair, his lips curling into a cruel smile. "You owe me one, Quintin."

Quintin flinched. His boss was sure to hold the debt against him. Despite the risks, he took the boon the Bursar offered. He had no other choice. "Yes, sir. Thank you, sir. If you'll indulge me, sir, I'll walk my, uh, friend home now."

"Yes, yes. Be careful. Who knows what dangerous outlaws are out there."

Quintin kept his arm around one outlaw's shoulders as they left the warehouse. He told himself he only wanted to perpetuate their romantic charade, but his body did not believe him. Desire hummed through him with every step as he tried and failed to banish the memory of their passionate kiss.

Follow you? The question slithered into Quintin's mind through his bond with his waccat, Elkart.

Yes. Stay out of sight, he replied in the same silent manner. Hallmarks of the Hands of Destin, waccats were a symbol of power and an emblem of trust. Beyond what they represented, waccats boasted wicked fangs and lethal claws. Even the hardiest outlaw would spook if confronted by one of the great cats. Fortunately, Elkart's dark coat and keen senses would allow him to keep pace without alerting the lovely thief.

"What happens now?" The woman at Quintin's side kept her voice low. "Will he follow us?"

"He won't leave the warehouse unattended, not on Taricday." Why had Fredrick come to the office at all? His story about relieving the tedium of Taricday duty did not ring true. Quintin shuddered. "I wouldn't put it past him to climb a barrel and watch us from the windows."

"Then I suppose we'll go our separate ways in a few blocks."

"Yes." His arm tightened around her. "But not yet."

"No, not yet." She leaned her head against his shoulder. Her body was soft and warm against his side and fit perfectly under his arm. The sheer rightness of holding her took his breath away.

With only one of the three moons risen, shadows filled the street, threatening to trip them with every step. By the grace of the Air God Fermice he could use his elemental air talent to help navigate their path. Quintin took a deep breath to fortify his connection to the firmament. Once he felt centered, he opened his mind to the air around them, giving him a kind of second sight.

The bronzed tip of his staff tapped the dirt road in rhythm with their feet as they strolled past slumbering warehouses. Any observer would dismiss them as a couple returning from a tryst. Sadness weighed heavy on Quintin as part of him wished their facade was the truth.

Their steps slowed as one when they reached a corner out of sight of the Tribute Office. If he were wise, he would disengage from her now, and return to the warehouse without a backward glance.

She eased away from him, her bottom lip caught between her teeth. The light of the moon threw the planes of her face into sharp relief. Her wide set eyes looked huge and luminous. She seemed very young for an outlaw.

He swallowed and tried not to remember how sweet she tasted. "You had nimble wits," he said, "back at the warehouse."

"Sometimes the easiest place to hide is in plain sight."

"You certainly demonstrated that tonight and saved us both." He held his staff between his palms and bowed his head in respect. "Thank you."

She nodded though he wasn't convinced she heard him. His heart pounded at the intensity of her gaze. Was she reliving their kiss as he was? Had it affected her half as much as it had him?

"This is far enough," she said. "It's time we parted company."

"Yes." Quintin licked his lips. "It was a pleasure doing business with you."

She planted a hard kiss on his mouth.

Before he could react, she backed around a corner. With a flash of red from her unusual hair, she melted into the shadows.

He touched his lips, staring at the spot where she had disappeared. He longed to pursue her though he had never been one to follow his heart into madness. What would he say to her if he caught her? He had no skill for flirtation. Besides, trying to engage in a romance with an outlaw went beyond foolish.

Marching footsteps thumped toward him. "Halt, who goes there?"

He spun to watch a pair of guards approach him. The silhouette of a large cat prowled between them. He held his staff out to one side for a deep bow. "Han-Auditor Quintin of Jardin. Is there some trouble?"

"Quintin? What are you doing out on Taricday?"

"Madi?" He peered around the blazing torch at Han-Triguard Magdalena, known as Madi to her friends. Selected by their waccats in the same season, Quintin and Madi had trained as Hands together and become fast friends. The rigorous training molded Hands into worthy agents of the Troika, ready to serve as everything from diplomats to healers. No one was surprised when stalwart, earthy Madi joined the ranks of the guard under the Mortarary.

Serious as ever while on duty, Madi frowned at Quintin. Tall and imposing at the best of times, her severe features were an ominous mask in the torchlight. "Do you need an escort?"

"Elkart is enough protection for me." He nodded to the side as a brown feline the size of a hunting hound slipped out of the shadows. His waccat stalked forward to sniff noses with Madi's waccat before settling on his haunches at Quintin's side.

Madi bowed her head respectfully at Elkart. "We had best continue on, then."

"How goes patrol?" he asked quickly, not wanting the guards to follow his thief too soon.

She shrugged. "It's Taricday. We've kept busy clearing the streets of lowlifes."

He kept his eyes fixed on her face, fighting the urge to glance at the corner where one such lowlife had disappeared. "I'm sure the citizens of Trimble sleep better for your vigilance."

The other guard snorted. "Not likely."

"I'm afraid the citizens of Trimble don't think of us much at all." Madi smirked. "Which is probably better than their opinion of you auditors."

He chuckled. "The citizens of Trimble always treat me with the utmost respect and courtesy. I'm sure they are courteous to you guards as well."

"Only because they don't want to end up in the stocks," Madi said, her teeth flashing in a feral grin.

"Who can blame them?" His stomach turned at how close he had come to such a fate. Thank Marana for his quick-witted thief.

The other guard cleared her throat. "We should get on with patrol, Han-Triguard."

Madi nodded. "Can you find your way without a torch?"

"Yes, my air gift gives me eyes as sharp as Elkart's." He bowed while the guards took their leave. His fingers tightened around his staff as he watched them walk away.

Elkart's thoughts whispered through Quintin's mind. *Task all finished?*

Yes. Ophelia will be pleased, he told the great cat. Like Madi, Ophelia was one of his year-mates, though the pretty Hand's gift for water led her to more peaceful work as a seer for Marana, the Goddess of the Future.

She be pleased you like her thief so much?

His face heated. *She doesn't need to know about that.*

When he sent a message to her temple in the morning to inform her of the quipu's safe delivery, he would leave out any details of the escapade. He shuddered at the thought of Ophelia, or worse yet Madi, knowing he had kissed an outlaw.

Quintin rubbed his fingers against his lips, disturbed by how much he wished to do it again.

Chapter 4

The next morning Lady Emmanuella rode to Trimble in a spacious palanquin. Wrapped from head to toe in an elaborate sari, her rank as a Lady of the Realm sparkled as brightly as the silver stitches on her hem. No one looking at her would guess she'd spent the night dressed as a laborer while sneaking around government buildings and sharing passionate kisses with strange men. Kisses that, try as she might, she could not quite forget in the light of day, when she dared not breathe a word about her nocturnal activities.

Hoping for a distraction, she pushed aside a gauzy drape and peered outside. Her brother Jonathan's riding okapi plodded alongside the palanquin, close enough for her to reach out and touch.

"A beautiful day for a ride, eh, Em?" Jonathan called down with a grin, his teeth flashing white against his brown skin.

She turned her head to hide her face from the other occupants of the palanquin and stuck her tongue out at her brother. With a laugh, Jon urged his okapi forward, giving her a nice view of the animal's broad striped hindquarters.

While she couldn't see him, she knew her oldest brother Gregory was also out riding and enjoying the sunshine. If only she could ride an okapi like her brothers instead of smothering in here with her father. Unfortunately, she was a Lady of the Realm. Proper Ladies wore saris and rode in palanquins, at least when headed to the Trimble market in the company of a Trilord.

Em suppressed a sigh. Sometimes she liked her role as Lady even less than her work as a thief.

Mistress Isabel, Gregory's wife, touched Em's elbow. Though Isabel wouldn't gain the rank of Lady until Gregory inherited their father's titles, she already had grace and poise to spare, along with a keen sense of fashion due to her Verisian heritage. "I do hope the latest shipment of fabrics are as impressive as I've been told. The new Verisian dyes are supposed to be very vivid."

Em dropped the curtain into place and settled against the pillows. While she tried to pretend interest, she doubted her attentive face fooled her sister by marriage. She offered a finger to the baby cooing and gurgling on Isabel's lap.

Isabel's dark eyes crinkled at the corners in a smile. "I'd like to buy some nice red linen for you. It will bring out the striking color in your hair."

"I don't know if I want Emmie wearing red." Lord Harold, Em's father, occupied the opposite side of the palanquin. Lounging on pillows, the Trilord puffed on a hookah. Sweet steam clouded the air around his head. The bejeweled rings on his fingers sparkled as he waved at Em. "I won't have my daughter looking garish."

Em bounced the tiny fist clutched around her finger and shared a smile with her infant nephew. "Why do I need a new sari?" she asked. "I've got two I've barely worn."

"Red is vibrant, not garish." Isabel smoothed the edge of her yellow sari on her shoulder. "As long as we wrap it properly, Em won't be provocative."

"Of course, you need new clothes." Lord Harold drummed his fingers against the bowl of the hookah. "The Reeve of Trimble bestowed a great honor on us by selecting Merdale to host the Allgoday celebration this year. We must honor him in return."

"If it's for Allgoday, then I should wear white or

lavender." Em pulled her attention away from the babe. "I am a Lady of Air, after all."

"That's what your mother would always say," Lord Harold muttered with a frown.

She glowered at him. Her mother probably always used to say it because it was true.

"Lavender cloth is too expensive." Isabel brushed a lock of Em's hair off her shoulder. "Besides, purple will do nothing for your hair, which is your best feature."

Em twitched away from Isabel's fussing hands. "I like white."

"All your saris are white." The bangles on Isabel's arm chimed as she dropped her hand. "It makes you look insipid. You'll never catch a man's eye wearing white."

"I don't want to catch a man's eye."

"Perhaps red isn't a bad idea," Lord Harold mused, taking a pull on the hookah.

"Papa!" She gaped at her father.

He raised his bushy black eyebrows and blew steam at her. "Do you want to pay for it? If you buy the fabric, you can pick the color."

She leaned back in her seat and crossed her arms. "I don't want a new sari at all."

"You'll be beautiful in red, you'll see." Isabel clapped her hands in front of the baby. He laughed and grabbed at her shiny silver bangles. "Your father is a Lord of Earth so there is nothing remarkable about you wearing earth colors. We should all strive to make Merdale proud at the Allgoday Feast."

Em sighed and held her tongue. In the three years since Gregory and Isabel had wed, Isabel had schemed and maneuvered to secure the honor of the Reeve's attendance at the annual holiday. Once the Reeve of Trimble selected Merdale, the Councilors and everyone of note in and around Trimble clamored for invitations. Heady with success, Isabel sent invitations as far away as the capitol. Even Isabel's parents planned to make the journey from the neighboring country of Verice for the first time since her wedding.

Though Em didn't understand the fuss of the holiday, she would do her best not to ruin Isabel's shining moment. Which apparently meant wearing red.

With a shouted command from the captain of Merdale's guards, the palanquin stopped outside the city wall. The conveyance swayed as the carriers maneuvered it off the trade road and out of a steady stream of encumbered merchants and braying beasts of burden. Since the day was cool, her family would enter Trimble on foot rather than pay the fee for bringing okapis and a spacious palanquin into the city.

Lord Harold took one last drag on the hookah before cupping the bowl in his hands. The steam dissipated as the bowl cooled.

Isabel wrapped her arms around the babe. Em braced herself. The captain shouted another command and the carriers lowered the palanquin to the ground in unison.

Lord Harold tucked his hookah between a pair of pillows while Isabel gathered up her child. They emerged in a shady spot under a canopy tree. Sparse trees populated the area next to the perimeter wall between the trade road and the river, leaving plenty of space for animals and palanquins. An unofficial track off the road ran down to the river for those who wished to pay water tariffs rather than the trade road fees.

The port town of Trimble had sprouted up around a bend in the river where the trade road veered close to the waterway. When the city had grown large enough to support a garrison and its attending Reeve, two perimeter walls had been built to give Trimble a lucky triangular shape, with the river forming the third side. The Reeve himself lived at the point of the triangle, far from the bustle of the riverfront and the sprawling market dominating the center of town.

While the Merdale captain organized their entourage, Em shook out her sari, careful to keep the pale fabric away from the dirt. Gregory climbed off his okapi to help Isabel load their infant son into a yellow linen sling matching her sari. Once the babe was secure on her back, two triads of guards fanned out around the family. The other half of the guards settled themselves in the shade with the okapis and palanquin.

With polished dirks strapped to their chests and feather headdresses making them appear taller, the guards easily cleared a path across the line of laden beasts and their handlers awaiting entrance at the main gate. Once on the other side of the road, their party joined the stream of humanity walking into Trimble through the tunnel in the wall.

Though the guards tried to keep the riffraff at bay, Em was jostled on all sides in the narrow tunnel. Voices echoed off the stones, assaulting her ears. While it was the same path, the teeming passageway had little in common with the deserted tunnel of the night before.

As they entered the city, the swaggering captain ushered them away from the crowded thoroughfare and onto the quieter streets of the Temple district. They would loop around and approach the market from the side near the Troika Hall.

When the street widened enough for them to walk two abreast, the captain fell back to consult with Lord Harold. Gregory slowed his steps to walk next to his wife, their dark heads canted together. She rested the fingers of one hand on his elbow while punctuating her speech with gestures from the other. The babe on her back waved a pudgy brown arm and gurgled.

Jonathan fell into step with Em and offered her his arm.

She took his elbow with a polite smile though she struggled to match his long strides. Her sari brushed the toes of her sandals, threatening to trip her at every step. The awkwardness of walking with her brother awakened the memory of how her body had moved in natural harmony with Quintin's the night before.

Loneliness stabbed her, even in the midst of her family.

"Why the dour face, Em?" Jonathan asked.

She pushed thoughts of the sweet auditor aside. "I've better things to do than dawdle at the market."

"Already spent your allowance, eh?"

She pursed her lips but did not reply. She purchased necessities for Aerynet with her allowance and had no use for the curiosities of the marketplace. The cacao their father gave her never went far, which was why she risked arrest for her Taricday earnings. Her belly twisted in apprehension. Simon hadn't shown at their rendezvous after the job last night. His absence wasn't unusual, though it was unfortunate. She sent up a silent prayer, hoping he had delivered her beans directly to the temple as planned. Otherwise Aerynet would be in dire straits.

Jon nudged her side. "If you see anything you like, whisper a word in my ear. The bones have been good to me this week."

Despite her worries, she managed to smile at her brother. "Thank you, Jon."

Her family bunched closer together as they approached the market square. The busy marketplace bombarded the senses. A cacophony of voices hawked everything from vegetables to furniture, while the smell of cooking food clashed with perfumes and spices. A tangle of colorful stalls filled the square, ranging in size from layered tents as big as a house to little more than a mat covered in goods.

Flags and banners in red, brown, and orange draped every awning. The colors honored the Earth Daemon Tarel, hoping to attract followers on their day of rest.

At a whistled command from the captain, the other guards in the party surrounded the family and managed the crowd so they could enter the busy square. Their steps slowed as they edged along in front of the Troika Hall. Three stories high and built of the same imported stone as the city wall, the impressive building stood as a testament to the rule of Destinese law in Trimble. Raised wooden platforms flanked it on both sides.

"Will you look at that?" Jonathan said.

Em tracked his pointing finger without thinking. Her breath caught, squeezing all the air out of her lungs.

"The stocks are full," Jon continued, his voice tinny and distant to her ears.

The nearest captive was a young man, nearly a boy. Dirty, thin, hopeless. The crude boards pinned him in a kneeling position. Trapped. Humiliated. Unable to move so much as an inch.

Cold sweat beaded on her forehead.

But for the grace of the gods, she could be the one imprisoned.

Jon bent to peer in her face, confusion and concern chasing across his features. "You feeling well, Em? You look like you're going to faint."

She dragged a breath into her lungs, calling on Fermena, the Goddess of Air and Serenity, to steady her mind. She had to stay calm in front of her family. No guard would arrest a Lady in the middle of market day.

"The stocks are horrible," she spat, hoping to wipe the solicitous look off Jon's face. "I hate to look at them."

Lord Harold snorted. "A little humiliation and thirst is no less than these cutpurses and trespassers deserve. Trimble is far too lax in my opinion. Thieves are branded in other towns."

Isabel shivered. "I'm so grateful we live at Merdale, safe from the treachery of outlaws."

Gregory tugged her forward. "Let's find the fabric merchant you're so excited about."

Jon patted Em's hand as they followed the others. "Well, a paragon of virtue like you needn't ever look at or think about the stocks if you don't wish to."

Em grunted in response. If her brother only knew. She lived with the danger of getting more than a look at the stocks every week. Worse yet, she couldn't tear her gaze away from the poor trapped souls she walked past.

She watched in horrified fascination as a devotee of Marana held a bowl of water out to a prisoner. The man bowed his head to lap up the water. Em repressed a shudder. To drink like a dog and be grateful for it—

As the devotee moved away, the prisoner raised his head.

Em's feet stopped.

Jonathan tripped as she pulled on his arm. "Watch it, Em. You're so clumsy."

"Sorry," she murmured. She forced her legs to move. The panic blooming in her heart was not so easily vanquished.

Simon was in the stocks.

Chapter 5

"Fermena's farts," Em muttered a few hours later as her family shuffled to a stop before a familiar two-story abode at the edge of the Reeve's district. Her father must want them to dine with her mother's family. It was only practical to take their aestivation in town rather than ask the guards to carry the palanquin home during the heat of the day.

"Em, such language," Jonathan scolded with a laugh.

A guard trotted up the wide stone steps and sounded a gong next to a pair of intricately carved double doors set in the colorful mosaic facade.

Dismay filling her heart, Em hurried to her father's side. "Father," she began, her words lost as the doors opened.

The Merdale captain ushered their party into the house. As she stepped over the threshold, she felt crushed by more than the press of bodies in the vestibule. She couldn't sit eating dainties and admiring Isabel's purchases for hours on end. Not with Simon in the stocks and her payment for last night's work locked up with him.

Itching to escape, Em squeezed through the crowd until she stood next to her father.

Aunt Florence crouched in the position of welcome before Lord Harold, not an easy task for a woman of her advanced years, but she was a stickler for the proprieties. Though not a lady herself, Florence had been raised by a Lady of the Realm with exacting standards. Holding a platter of cut fruit over her head at an inviting angle, she intoned the hospitality greeting.

Em waited until her father had selected an avocado dumpling to complete the ceremony, before tugging on his sleeve. "Father, I'd like to take my aestivation at Aerynet if I may."

Her aunt rose smoothly to her feet. "How is your temple?"

"Very well, thank you," Em replied by rote. She bit her lip, unsure what else to say.

When her noble grandmother had turned to ash, her father had petitioned the Novenary to pass Aerynet and its attendant title to Em's mother instead of Aunt Florence. While her aunt never breathed a word of resentment, and welcomed them into her home, Em knew her temple and title could have been her aunt's instead.

Lord Harold sniffed. "Aerynet is far too small for a party of our size and importance."

"I don't want to make anyone uncomfortable," she agreed. Her father had refused to set foot in the temple since her mother's death. Ordinarily, the snub would open old wounds. Today all she felt was relief. She expected Acolyte Lucy to be in a tizzy over the missing payment and didn't wish to expose Aerynet's troubles to the scrutiny of her family. "I can go on my own."

"Oh, Emmie," her aunt said, "this is only a sample of the fruits and dainties waiting in the courtyard."

"You are so kind," Em said with a polite smile. "I'm afraid I won't do your generous hospitality justice. I have a headache and need to rest in a cool quiet place."

"Well, an air temple is just the thing for a headache." Her aunt held out the platter. "At least take a couple pieces with you. I chilled them myself."

"Thank you, Aunt Florence. You are the most tolerant of hostesses." Her smile turned genuine as she chose a slice of icy mango. Since her aunt approved of her defection, her father would only look churlish if he forced her to stay.

"Take two guards with you," Lord Harold said as he followed Florence through an arched doorway.

"Yes, Papa." Elated by her reprieve, she stood against one wall and let the rest of her family leave the vestibule.

Violet, her only cousin on her mother's side, brought up the rear of the procession, bearing a second platter of fruit. "Aren't you coming, Emmie?"

She shook her head. "I'm going to Aerynet."

"Why? Isn't our repast fancy enough for a Lady of the Realm?"

Was Violet trying to make a joke? While they were of an age and looked enough alike to be mistaken for sisters, Em never understood her cousin. Their distinctive, auburn-tinted black hair was all they had in common.

Violet gestured at the icy mango in Em's hand. "You should eat it before it melts. You'll get mango juice on your lovely sari, and then won't your father be upset when he has to buy you a new one."

"I have a headache," Em said, too impatient to unravel her cousin's comments. She curled her fingers over the fruit. Her lips moved as she asked the goddesses to extract heat and energy from the juicy slice. Her hand might be numb before she reached the temple, but the orphan who lived at Aerynet would enjoy the frozen treat more than she would.

"A headache. Really?" Violet laughed. "Well, that's one thing your temple is good for." She turned and sashayed through the archway, her sari swishing with every step.

Shaking her head, Em collected a pair of guards and returned to the street. She focused on keeping the mango frozen as she traversed the brick lined roads of Trimble.

One of the guards walked in front of her to clear a path, though with the sun blazing overhead the wide avenues of the Reeve's district were nearly deserted. As they traveled toward the river, the streets narrowed and filled with vendors and laborers hurrying home or to the taverns and bathhouses which did brisk business in the heat of the day. By the time Em and her escort entered the wharf district, only beggars occupied the streets.

She stopped in front of a modest whitewashed temple nestled between a pair of muddy brown warehouses. Dedicated to Fermena, the Goddess of Air and Mistress of the Wind, Aerynet was a beacon of color and life in a sea of grim industry. A yarumo tree grew through the center of the conical building, emerging from its peak to brush leafy green branches against its neighbors.

Em frowned at the boughs of the tree. Its broad green leaves drooped in the noonday sun, some of them brown and curling at the edges. Acolyte Lucy had been saying for months they needed to hire an earthworker to replenish the soil under the building.

Her chest tightened at the thought. Good earthworkers didn't come cheap.

She took a fortifying breath before turning to the guards behind her. "Thank you for escorting me here. I'm sure you'll be more comfortable getting your own repast at a tavern."

The guards exchanged a glance before eyeing a tavern across the street.

"Yes, my lady." The younger guard pressed her palms together and bent at the waist in a low bow. Her red and black headdress fluttered with the movement.

The older guard mimicked the gesture. "We will return in time to escort you to the palanquin."

Em bobbed her head in an answering nod. Aware of the guards watching her, she forced herself to move with slow dignity to the base of the building.

Perched on pilings older than the retaining wall lining the riverbank, the temple had nine long steps from the ground to the sanctuary. A rune for each deity was etched into the wooden stairs, starting with the earth gods, then the water gods and finally the air gods, ending with Fermena's rune inscribed on the landing itself.

As she climbed the stairs, she recited the name of the deity on each step in a soothing ritual to keep her ascent slow and steady. When she reached the air deities, she could hear a low rumble of angry voices from inside. Though her heart pounded, she resisted the urge to hurry. She kept her head held high as she pushed aside strands of polished stone and faceted glass to enter the sanctuary.

Her shadow swayed and flickered with the movement of the beaded curtain behind her. The only other light came from a circular hole in the roof where the tree escaped the building to unfurl its leaves in the sunshine. Dim green light filtered through those leaves onto an ancient wooden statue depicting Fermena in her avian aspect. As her gaze fell on the carved face of the Goddess, Em raised her right hand to kiss her silver ring. Modeled after a long-ago ancestor, the life-like statue always reminded her of her mother.

A small body crashed into her side while a pair of skinny arms wrapped around her waist in a suffocating hold.

"Ben." She draped her arm across his thin shoulders. "Is Acolyte Lucy all right?"

The six-year-old shook his head, his black curls dancing.

"Well, I'm here to take care of it." She held out the frozen mango to the mute child. "I brought you a treat."

He grabbed it and flashed her a quick grin before disappearing into the darkness at the edges of the room.

Praying to the Goddess to give her clear thinking and ready wits, Em glided toward the alter and the pair of people arguing at its base.

"I'm not in the business of giving charity," a local fishmonger said, his voice bouncing off the curved walls of the sanctuary.

Acolyte Lucy's young face creased with a worried frown. "We're going to pay for the fish."

He slapped his wide-brimmed, woven reed hat against his knee. "Then why don't you give me the beans and be done with it?"

Em smiled to hide her sinking heart. "Robert the Fisher, how good to see you."

"My Lady Patron." Acolyte Lucy knelt with her forehead to the floor, her straight black braid trailing down her back.

Em ignored the obsequious greeting. Lucy only wanted to avoid dealing with the irritated fishmonger.

"Lady Emmanuella." He sketched a quick bow. "Have you come with my beans?"

"Oh, dear, weren't they delivered yesterday?" The stone bangles on her arms clicked together as she raised her hands to her lips and gave him a wide-eyed look. "There must have been some mistake. What a mess."

His thick eyebrows drew together. "Messes happen too frequently of late."

"We are most grateful for your forbearance." She clasped her hands together in front of her chest. "And here we are keeping you from your aestivation. Your good wife must be worried."

"She knows deliveries can take time."

"We mustn't keep you out in the heat when you should be resting at home." She pulled a stone bangle off her arm. "Here, give this to your wife as a token of our appreciation for her patience."

He frowned at the polished circle of stone. "I need my payment in beans, not trinkets."

"Oh, it's not payment for the fish." The remaining bangles on her wrist clicked as she waved his words away. "This is a gift for your wife with Fermena's blessing. Speaking of which, will you be joining your wife for services this week?"

"No, not likely." He took the bracelet and tucked it into a fold in his chiton. "Unlike some, I have to work for my livelihood. The fish don't catch themselves."

"A pity. You will be missed." Em placed a hand on the fishmonger's elbow to steer him toward the door. "We'll be sure to light incense for you and pray for your safety."

"I still need my payment," he said, though he moved with her down the aisle. "I won't be making any more deliveries here until I have it."

"Agreed. We'll deliver your cacao as soon as we can." She hoped her smile looked reassuring rather than desperate. "I'll send Acolyte Lucy to market with it. You needn't trouble yourself coming by again."

"See that you do."

After Em escorted the fishmonger out of the building, she turned to find Lucy behind her.

"Do you have the cacao, my lady?" Lucy asked. She looked older than she should, Em realized with a twinge of guilt. She would turn seventeen with the changing season, a full year less than Em herself. The worry and stress of the last six years had aged them both.

"We will," Em said with a confidence she did not feel. Simon arranged all her sneak work and found discrete buyers for any treasures she acquired on her own. How would Aerynet survive with him imprisoned?

"I didn't dare go to market today, not without any beans." Lucy sighed. "My brother never showed this morning."

Em bit her lip. "I know."

"How do you know?" The acolyte's brow puckered. "Why are you here?"

"I saw Simon in the stocks at the market this morning."

"In the stocks?" Lucy pressed a hand to her chest, her voice wobbling. "Marana have mercy. I wonder if his imprisonment is what upset Patricia last night."

"What do you mean?" Em asked. Though Mystic Patricia was nominally the spiritual leader of Aerynet, the elderly woman had suffered a series of falls and dizzy spells that left her weak and confused.

"While I was putting her to bed she became agitated, calling on the Goddess for wisdom and trying to stand up again. She wouldn't settle down until I promised not to go to market today." Lucy toyed with her braid. "I hadn't meant to keep my promise. We're out of fruit and need to pay the baker as well."

Em frowned. Patricia's illness had not diminished her connection to Fermena. If anything, the Goddess's influence on her had grown as she dwelt more and more in her own mind. "Do you think she had a vision?"

The acolyte nodded. "She probably knew Simon was in trouble and worried about me seeing my brother in the stocks."

Em narrowed her eyes. "Then there might be hope for us yet."

"What do you mean?"

"He was supposed to receive my payment around dawn this morning. If he was arrested at sundown then perhaps he never got paid."

"It's possible. Fermena is the Goddess of Now, and Patricia's visions have never predicted the future."

"Let's leave the prophesies to the water seers," Em agreed with a tight smile. Patricia's messages from the Goddess were stressful enough without throwing in the frustration and confusion of a foretelling.

"How does it help us if he wasn't paid? You can't go to the Troika Hall and ask him who owes you cacao."

"I don't have to ask him. I already know."

If the young auditor, Quintin, had not paid Simon for the job, then maybe she could convince him to pay her instead. Her palms prickled at the thought of seeking him out, but she could not pass up a chance to get her beans.

A slim hope was better than no hope at all.

Chapter 6

The trees of the jungle were little more than shadows around the edge of the garden as Quintin sipped his morning cup of tea the next day. The remains of a simple meal dotted the table in front of him, and his belly was pleasantly full. He loved this time of day, with the world still half asleep. He closed his eyes and listened to gentle birdsong punctuated by the sound of his mother Hannah shuffling in the house behind him and the soft crunch of Elkart gnawing on a bone.

Quintin took a deep, satisfying breath. Somehow the air smelled sweeter in the morning. He stirred a breeze with his gift and sent it wafting against his face. He filled his lungs again, and instantly regretted it.

The garden smelled of jasmine and brought to mind the woman he had held in his arms two nights ago. He groaned and rubbed his temple. Why could he not stop thinking about her? Her soft skin, how she smelled, the taste of her kiss . . .

"Willing to walk with me to market?"

Quintin started and nearly spilled his tea. He opened his eyes to peer up at his mother, a short sturdy woman with graying hair pulled back in a pair of no-nonsense braids with an expression to match.

"I've got a bumper crop of tubers and could use some help hauling them to town."

"Certainly, though we'll need to hurry. I don't want to be late for work." Quintin gulped the last of his tea while Hannah cleared the table.

Once the dishes were done, she handed him a heavy sack and balanced a towering basket on her own head.

He heaved the weight onto his back, grateful for all the hours he spent sparring and strengthening his body. He followed his mother down the dirt path from their homestead to the trade road, while Elkart wove between the trees. Soon enough they joined a steady stream of farmers and merchants heading into Trimble. Even with clomping oxen and snorting llamas, a sense of peace and anticipation clung to the crowd.

The quiet continued to the market square. Later the square would echo with the sounds of vendors hawking their wares. Now there was only the creak and rustle of unfurling tents, occasionally punctuated by sleepy conversation.

Quintin lowered the sack of tubers off his shoulder while his mother secured an awning over her modest stall. He pressed his palms together and gave her a short bow. "Have a good day at market. I may be home late tonight."

"I'll leave supper waiting for you in your room," she said, returning his bow.

He traversed the center of the market with ground-eating strides. Elkart ambled next to him with a freedom that would be impossible once the market was in full swing. While a few hardy souls were already trickling into the square in search of an early morning bargain, by and large the aisles between the stalls were deserted.

A woman laughed, reminding Quintin once again of his encounter with the thief.

Why can't I stop thinking about her? Desperate for answers, he silently sent the plaintive wail to his waccat.

Was she in heat? Elkart asked. *Most distracting, a female in heat.*

Quintin sighed. He knew better than to expect a cat to have any useful insight. While the kiss in the warehouse had been the most passionate embrace he had ever experienced, in truth the hard peck on the waterfront haunted him more. Their first kiss had been a ruse. The second was for him alone. He could not stop wondering what her kiss might mean.

A gentlewoman, trailed by a towering guard, crossed the aisle twenty feet in front of him. Before she disappeared behind a booth, the sunlight caught her dark hair. It glinted red.

His breath caught. He had only seen the like once before. *Could it be her?*

Elkart made a chuffing noise as he sniffed the air. *Not smell right.*

Knowing he was obsessed, Quintin hurried to the corner to watch her.

The woman wore a pink sari with matching flowers tucked into a loose braid falling to her waist. While she was short and slender like his outlaw, her clothes and demeanor marked her as wealthy, possibly nobility.

He had a hard time believing a professional thief would move in such rarefied circles, but the occasional glint of red in her hair held him mesmerized.

She was nearly at the end of the row when she turned to talk to a cloth merchant and her profile came into view.

His shoulders slumped as he swallowed his disappointment.

I told you. Elkart's tail twitched. *Smell wrong.*

Quintin was about to turn away when something in the merchant's expression caught his attention. He seemed less excited than he should be by a wealthy customer. Even at a distance he looked nervous as the gentlewoman in the sari leaned forward, her guard looming behind her.

Quintin took a deep breath and focused his gift. Careful not to stir a breeze that would alarm the speakers and distort sound, he caught the breath leaving their mouths and brought their words to his ears.

"I know you have some. Don't you dare lie to me."

"I don't sell such fine things, I swear to you. You'll have to try the Verisian traders."

"I don't like their prices. Besides, I know a bolt was given to you yesterday. I want it."

"I can't sell a bolt I've been commissioned to embroider! My reputation—"

"More than your reputation is at stake if you don't do as I say."

When those words reached Quintin's ears, he strode forward. His fingernails bit into his palms as he longed for the comforting weight of his sturdy mahogany staff. At least he had Elkart and his air gift to protect him if necessary.

The merchant reared back. "Are you threatening me? In the market square in broad daylight?"

"If I scream, my sentinel will have all the excuse she needs to cut you."

A blade glinted in the guard's hand.

Elkart, stop her!

Faster than thought, the waccat sprang forward.

"What seems to be the problem here?" Quintin called out as he trotted after the great cat.

The sentinel slammed her knife back into its sheath and relaxed into a less threatening pose.

The gentlewoman turned toward Quintin. Her lips peeled back in a smile. It did not reach her eyes. "Call off your cat, taxman. My guard can handle this. It's none of your concern."

Elkart sat down on the dusty bricks directly between the merchant and the guard. His snarl revealed teeth as long as a thumb.

The sentinel prudently retreated another step.

Coming to a halt next to his waccat, Quintin faced the gentlewoman. He pressed his palms together and nodded his head in a short bow. "Allow me to introduce myself. I am Han-Auditor Quintin. As a Hand of Destin any citizen in distress concerns me."

"How kind of you to care. I'm not in distress."

"I wasn't worried about you." His gaze flicked over her guard before landing on the merchant. "Is she bothering you?"

Watching the sentinel, the vendor edged closer to Quintin. "I would welcome her custom, if she were interested in something I can sell."

"Nothing you have is worth my time or my cacao." Head held high, she spun and stalked away.

Her guard made a move to follow her.

"Hold a moment," Quintin said, his voice soft but firm.

The guard frowned, her hand touching her dirk. "My mistress awaits."

A low growl rumbled through Elkart's throat.

Quintin stared pointedly at her knife. "Don't be a fool."

Her hand sprang away from the hilt. "I meant no disrespect."

"Let me give you a word of advice." Quintin stepped forward and crooked his finger, inviting her to bend down to his level. "Be a little less hasty with your knife. You'll be the one spending a night in the stocks if the city guards catch you roughing up vendors, while your mistress will sleep soundly in her cozy bed."

The guard straightened with a grunt, her gaze trailing after her mistress.

"Furthermore, I have connections in the market and friends in the city guard. I'll hear about it if you try this again. Whatever she's paying you, it isn't worth it. Do you understand?"

"Yes, Hand." She pressed her palms together and gave a low bow.

Quintin nodded and stepped back. He watched as the guard hurried after the woman in the sari. If he hadn't already lingered in the market too long, he would be tempted to trail them and try to eavesdrop.

"Many thanks to you, Han-Auditor." The merchant held out a folded square of deep green silk. "Please, take this as a sign of my appreciation."

"It is a very fine piece." Tempted by the vivid color, Quintin reached out to rub one corner of the soft silk between his thumb and forefinger. He could easily imagine adding texture and contrast to the fabric with a few well-placed stitches. He had the exact right thread at home.

Elkart nudged Quintin's hip, jostling him.

Quintin let go of the fabric and scratched his waccat behind the ears. "Thank you for the generous offer, but a Hand needs no reward for doing his duty."

With the merchant's praise ringing in his ears, Quintin hurried away from the market. He was sure to be late, and Tarinasday was always busy at the Tribute Office. He fought the urge to run. Though chancing tardiness, it was better to arrive with calm dignity, rather than panting and sweating.

When he reached the warehouse, he pulled open the door and was greeted by Bursar Fredrick's bellow. "The Inspectors are coming today. We don't have time for this nonsense!"

The Bursar loomed over the table of the newest auditor, a lanky young woman who always looked a little disheveled.

"I don't know what happened." Auditor Sarah trembled at the Bursar's feet, dark curls escaping the thick braid at her nape. She ran her fingers over the dangling threads of a quipu tied to a frame. "The knots are all wrong. I have to fix them."

"Silence!" Fredrick raised his staff of office, a polished black stick the size and weight of a thighbone, and brought it crashing down on Sarah's work table.

Sarah jumped, snatching her fingers back.

Elkart growled and pressed against Quintin's legs.

"If you bungled your accounts, you haven't got time to fix them now. You've got to work with what you have."

Fredrick used the staff to knock over the frame. Tangled threads spilled over the table like a colorful spiderweb.

As he hurried forward to intervene, Quintin silently cursed his tardiness. The only other Hand in the office was out overseeing tariff collections at the wharf, and no one else dared stand up to the Bursar.

"Pick it up!" Fredrick jabbed Sarah's shoulder with enough force to make her flinch.

Quintin cringed inside at her reaction since he knew from experience it was only likely to enrage the Bursar further.

"Why are you sniveling?" Fredrick roared, his heaving chest straining the bounds of his kaftan. His staff crashed into the table. "I said pick it up."

"What a mess." Quintin knelt next to Sarah. "We can get this straightened out, quick as a wink." He picked up the quipu frame and put it upright on the table.

With shaking hands, Sarah combed her fingers through the knotted threads, her eyes focused on the quipu.

"Quintin." Fredrick took a breath and bared his teeth in a smile. "How good of you to join us."

"A thousand apologies for my tardiness, Bursar." Quintin stood again to press his palms together and give Fredrick a proper bow.

"Tarinasday is a piss poor day to laze about." Fredrick tapped his staff against his leg in an irritated motion. While he would lecture or scold until Quintin wished his ears would fall off, he dared not rage at a Hand. Aside from the issues of prestige and influence, if Fredrick ever raised his staff at Quintin, Elkart would bite his arm off.

"I know, sir, and I am sorry," Quintin said sincerely, though he was really apologizing to Sarah. He placed a hand on Elkart's head, taking comfort from the waccat's warm strength. "We had to deal with a bit of trouble in the market this morning."

"At market? Why didn't you let the city guards deal with it?"

"It was during the shift change and no guards were about." Quintin shrugged. "A citizen needed us, and I had to help. Duty of a Hand and all."

As soon as the words were out of his mouth, he knew they were a mistake. Fredrick would not like the sharp reminder of Quintin's higher calling and duties outside the Bursar's purview. While Fredrick dared not assault the Hands under him, he did not hide his jealousy of their privileged position, nor his belief he should have been a Hand himself. As if a waccat would ever bond with such a grasping, temperamental peacock.

"Well, we wouldn't want the paltry arrival of the Luminary's Inspectors to interfere with your duty as a Hand," Fredrick said, sarcasm dripping like venom from his words.

"It was only a small delay," Quintin demurred. "Annoying yet unavoidable. I'm sure we'll be able to get Auditor Sarah's quipu straightened out in short order and have the tribute ready and accounted for before the Inspectors arrive."

The Inspectors toured the country every season, collecting all the tributes destined for the capitol. Unless they were delayed, they should descend on the Trimble office in the afternoon.

"She botched her audit and thinks to fix it now." Fredrick slapped his staff against the palm of his other hand. "I don't know what the Luminary was thinking, sending us a woman to be an auditor."

"Though Auditor Sarah is learning, she is perfectly competent at her job."

"I don't know what happened," Sarah said in a voice almost too low to be heard. "Somehow the knots slipped and now the numbers are all wrong."

Quintin placed a hand on her shoulder. "We'll straighten

it out. I know a couple of memory enhancing techniques. They might help."

Fredrick's chest puffed up. "You've got more pressing things to do than clean up her mess. She has to deal with what she has."

Was the Bursar truly suggesting they send on a known error? Was he trying to get Sarah dismissed? Quintin couldn't let it happen.

"The Luminary wants our accounts to be accurate," he said mildly. "It would be a shame to miss a chance to correct an error. I assure you, I can help the auditor and complete my other duties."

Fredrick scowled and huffed.

Before his superior could come up with another senseless argument, Quintin turned to Sarah. "How many knots slipped?"

"If you have so much time to spare, perhaps I should increase your duties next week," Fredrick interrupted, his frown slowly transforming into a nasty grin. "I haven't finalized the assignments yet. Why don't I have you audit a homestead, to remind you how it's done?"

"If you honestly think this is the best use of my time and experience, I will perform audits with all due diligence." Quintin bowed politely, though he seethed inside. For the past three years, he had managed the auditors working on properties inside Trimble, as well as helping Fredrick oversee other accounts as often as not. To go back to merely assessing homestead parcels was degrading.

"Oh, you'll also need to oversee the other auditors' work. Since you have such a surplus of time, I'm sure you can manage one homestead audit while performing your normal duties. I'll give you one of Sarah's. Hopefully with fewer audits to do, she can manage not to bungle them all."

"Whatever you think is best," Quintin said as calmly as he could. Auditing a homestead was a small price to pay for diverting Fredrick's wrath. Still, the expression on the Bursar's face filled him with misgivings.

"In that case, I have the perfect homestead for you." Bursar Fredrick's teeth glinted as he smiled. "Merdale."

Chapter 7

A few hours later Quintin paused in his other work to run his fingers over the knots of the quipu from the last audit of the Merdale homestead. He traced each rough woolen strand, the colors and types of knots telling him what to expect when he visited the estate in two days. His fingers would smell of wool and dye from all the time he had spent distracted from his other accounts by the Merdale quipu.

The quipu had taught him a lot about the Merdale estate. He now knew the owner was Lord Harold, a Trilord entrusted with two major temples and a minor one. He knew the prosperous homestead consisted of four parcels. He knew Lord Harold's wife was dead and his three grown children lived on the estate.

While the quipu was a wealth of information, it couldn't tell him why Fredrick had a queer smirk on his face every time he saw Quintin touching it.

Quintin scooped up the tangle of threads from his work table and hid it in the trunk next to his sitting mat. With the sun nearing its zenith, he would leave soon to relax at a tavern through the heat of the day. When he returned, he needed to focus on organizing the Trimble audits, and could waste no more time pondering what Merdale had in store for him.

Auditor Sarah stopped at his elbow. "I don't know how to thank you for your help."

"I'm sorry my assistance was necessary." He instinctively scanned the room for Bursar Fredrick. Being discussed by his underlings was the kind of thing to set the Bursar off again.

"He already left for his aestivation. I hope he returns in a better mood." Auditor Sarah let out a soft sigh. "I wanted to thank you, not only for diverting his temper, but for helping me straighten out my quipu. I don't know how it got in such a state since no one else had a chance to touch it." She laughed. "Unless you got bored during Taricday duty and fiddled with it."

Quintin frowned as he realized the Bursar himself could have altered the quipu on Taricday. Could the Bursar merely want to make trouble for Sarah or could he have a more sinister motive?

"Not that I'm accusing you of any such thing," she said quickly.

"No, I just realized—"

He cut off the thought. He had no proof the Bursar had tampered with the quipu. Such idle speculation was unworthy of a Hand. "It's not important."

"It was important to me." She bit her lip, her brown eyes shining with gratitude. "You saved me today."

He smiled and tried to sound encouraging. "Fortunately, your memory is very sound, so it wasn't hard to fix. You'll be a good Auditor, Sarah. Don't ever doubt it."

She clasped her hands together and bowed. "You are the kindest of men."

He waved away her words, his conscience nagging him for concealing the possibility of the Bursar's perfidy. "Any Hand would have done the same."

She touched his arm. "Perhaps, but you are special, Quintin."

His mouth went dry at the intensity of her words. Was she forming some kind of attachment to him?

"You've been watching out for me like a kindly uncle ever since I came here. I've missed my family terribly on this assignment. Knowing I can rely on you has been a great comfort."

"It is nothing," Quintin muttered, feeling oddly deflated. He had no romantic designs on the amiable auditor. Even so, it was disheartening to be relegated to the role of doting uncle by a woman scarcely younger than himself.

"Nevertheless, I wanted to thank you."

He nodded politely. "Tighten up those knots of yours and Fredrick will have less to shout about next week."

"I imagine it will be your quipu he's most interested in this time. I hope your audit goes smoothly."

"Knowing Fredrick, it'll be a tricky case."

"Which is also my fault."

"Think nothing of it." Quintin closed the lid of the trunk. "Now I should be off as well. It's too hot to breathe in here."

Auditor Sarah bowed again and took her leave.

Quintin left the warehouse, yearning for an hour free from thoughts of quipus or the Bursar's tricks.

Or how being called the kindest of men wasn't actually a compliment.

With his waccat at his side, he traversed the three short blocks along the waterfront to the Salty Dog Tavern to meet his favorite year-mates for their traditional Tarinasday meal. While twenty youths had trained to become Hands at the same time as Quintin, only the five of them had become closer than family.

A subtle tension left his shoulders as he stepped through a curtain of nuts and wooden knobs to enter the tavern. He paused to let his vision adjust to the dim interior before scanning the room for his friends and their waccats.

Most of the crude wooden tables were crowded with sailors and laborers enjoying a midday meal. Woven rugs added color to the clay walls, softened the noise of dozens of conversations, and held in the cool air given off by buckets of ice scattered around the room.

His friend Ulric waved an arm from a table near the wall.

At the movement, Quintin waved back, then picked his way between the cheap reed sitting mats covering the dirt floor.

Elkart pressed close behind him, like a furry feline shadow. Near the table occupied by three of Quintin's friends and their attending waccats, Elkart broke off to circle around and sniff noses with his pack.

Quintin chose a mat, careful to leave space for Madi, who had not yet arrived.

"Here." Ulric, a mountain of a man with a bushy black beard and mahogany skin, poured wine into a mug dwarfed by his huge hands.

"Thanks." Quintin sipped the cool watermelon wine. The sweet, tangy liquid washed away the stress of the morning. "I needed this."

"Really? Why?" Ophelia asked, her ethereal beauty enhanced by the green sari of a devotee of Marana, the Goddess of Water. While she looked as out of place kneeling on a wine-stained mat as a lily blooming in a mud bog, she seemed to enjoy their weekly gatherings at the rough and tumble tavern.

Elkart flopped down and rested his head on Quintin's knee. Quintin buried his fingers in the fur at the back of his waccat's neck. "The Tribute Office was a mess this morning."

"Oh?" Ophelia leaned forward, the silver threads woven into the pallu covering her black hair twinkling with the movement. "Any trouble getting the tribute out on time?"

"No, no." He gave her a reassuring smile, remembering she had one very important item tucked in among the offerings. "All the cacao beans, trunks, and offerings are packed and ready for the Luminary's Inspectors this afternoon. They're certain to be on their way to the capital by morning."

"Good." Her shoulders relaxed. "Very good."

"The Bursar was in fine form today, intimidating one of the new auditors." He rushed his words, hoping no one else noticed Ophelia's odd response. "He's incensed because I intervened, and I know he's scheming to get me punished. I just don't know how."

"Can't you get him fined or arrested or something?" Ulric asked.

"As far as I know, yelling and stomping and throwing tantrums isn't against the law." Quintin shot a look at Terin. As an advocate who dispensed justice in the name of the Troika, he was much better versed in the law than Quintin.

Terin lifted one shoulder in an elegant shrug. "He'd probably claim he was doing what was necessary to keep his underlings in line."

"Besides, I think Fredrick is the embarrassing younger son of a Trilord and a distant cousin of our own Reeve." Quintin tapped his fingers against the side of his mug. "I imagine they are quite happy to have him live out his days only causing trouble for an office full of auditors at a trade port town."

"How depressing." Ulric took a noisy swig from his mug.

"I was hoping to stop thinking about work for an hour or two."

Terin clapped a hand on Quintin's shoulder. "I know a way to take your mind off work."

He stared at Terin, refusing to ask the obvious question.

"What's that?" Ulric asked.

Quintin glared at him while Ophelia sighed.

"Don't encourage him," she said. "Next thing you know he'll be dragging Quintin off to chat up some strange woman."

"Oh, no, he won't."

"It'll be good for you," Terin said.

Quintin shook his head hard enough to loosen the leather knot holding his hair in place.

"What are you afraid of? She's not going to bite you." Terin grinned, a wicked glint in his dark eyes. "Not until she knows you better anyway."

Ulric jabbed his elbow into Quintin's side. "It'd do you some good to talk to a woman."

"I don't want to talk to any women." He plunked his mug on the table before reaching behind his head to tighten the strap in his hair.

"Excuse me?" Ophelia pressed a delicate hand against her chest. "I am a woman."

Ulric snorted. "Not in the way that matters."

She sat up very straight, every inch radiating annoyance. "And what way is that?"

"The sex way," Ulric replied, each word slow and deliberate.

"Why, you degenerate—"

Terin cleared his throat. "You must admit, Ophelia, after all these years it is exceedingly unlikely you are suddenly going to accompany Quintin home for a nice romp."

"I'm not taking anyone home for a 'romp' as you say." Quintin scowled, his fingers clamping around his mug. "What would my mother say?"

Terin's sculpted brows rose. "If your mother is preventing you from poking women then you need to move out."

"Has it occurred to you I might have no interest in poking some random woman?"

"Do you have someone specific in mind?"

Quintin hesitated for half a heartbeat as the sweet taste of the thief's kiss filled his mouth. Then he realized his friends were staring. "No, of course not."

"There *is* someone." Ophelia's copper eyes were as wide as a bushbaby's. "Who is she?"

The thought of lying to his friends sent Quintin's heart into a spasmodic beat. How could he tell them who haunted his thoughts? His mug twisted in his hands. "I don't know what you're talking about."

"Aw, don't be like that. We're your friends, we'll keep it quiet." Ulric leaned forward and lowered his voice. "You gotta tell us who you're poking."

Quintin met Ulric's gaze, relieved to give an honest response. "I'm not fornicating. At all."

"So you haven't gotten to that point yet." Terin nodded and took a sip of wine. "It can be an intricate dance. I don't blame you for not wanting to throw this lot into such a delicate negotiation."

Quintin dropped his gaze to his mug, his chest aching. If only he did have a woman to court and woo, someone he could introduce to his friends with pride. Instead, the first woman who had interested him in years was an outlaw whom he would never see again. "I'm not negotiating anything."

"But who is she?" Ophelia asked again. "We must know."

His shoulders slumped, suddenly too weary to dance around the truth. "I don't know."

"What do you mean, you don't know?"

"It was a chance encounter. She was nothing more than a pretty face." A pretty face that masked a quick wit and a distracting passion. He sighed. "I don't know her name. She merely came to mind when you asked who I might want to poke."

"We could find her for you." Terin rubbed his hands together, a gleam in his eye. "Trimble is not very big. If you give us some details, or Elkart shares her scent with the other waccats—"

"No, not a good idea," Quintin interrupted, appalled at how tempted he was by the notion.

"It's a great idea," Terin countered. "It should be easy for us to at least learn her name."

"Easy? Really?" Ophelia raised her eyebrows. "I can't imagine how you could pull off this mad scheme without utterly humiliating Quintin."

His palms prickled. She was right, no matter how much he might wish it otherwise. "I've already said too much."

"This is why Tarina invented prostitutes." Ulric slapped the table. "Everything is straightforward and simple with a prostitute."

Ophelia crossed her arms. "This is not the time to try to convince Quintin to accompany you on a trip to the stews."

He slapped the table again. "There was never a better time for it."

"I am not visiting a brothel with you, Ulric," Quintin said flatly. He had accompanied Ulric to the stews once, years ago before the rest of their friends moved to Trimble. The experience had been a disaster, leaving him not only with a distaste for prostitutes, but with his virginity intact.

Ulric grumbled into his mug, looking chagrined.

"Ulric has a good point, though." Terin stroked his smooth brown chin. "In my experience, the best cure for women troubles is another woman."

Ophelia heaved a sigh. "Men."

"That's my line," Madi said as she approached their table. Dressed in a flowing sarong, she appeared less formidable than in her guard uniform, though the dirk hanging from her belt dispelled any illusion of softness.

"Yes, only you usually sound more predatory and less disgusted," Terin said as he filled a mug for the late arrival.

She flopped onto the only open mat at the table and leaned against her waccat. "I've felt my share of womanly disgust at men."

Ulric chortled. "You've felt more than your share of men in all kinds of ways, Madi."

She raised her mug to him. "There, you see? Womanly disgust with a man."

"You don't have to be a woman to be disgusted with Ulric," Terin replied.

Ulric looked at Terin. "I have only one thing to say to that." He belched loudly.

Madi and Terin laughed, while Quintin and Ophelia exchanged a long-suffering glance.

"What kept you?" Quintin asked Madi, hoping the conversation would not revert back to his pathetic love life.

"I was waylaid by another guard. He has a gift for air and wanted to mind-share an incident at a goat farm this morning."

"On your day off?" Ulric protested.

"It's why he wanted to talk to me." Madi patted Verona, her waccat. "Anything outside the city walls is not part of our official duties, so he couldn't do much more than look around. He thought Verona and I might investigate on our own today."

Ulric grunted. "Did you tell him to go get burnt?"

"No, his concern is warranted." Madi pulled out a bronze dirk and ran her fingers over the blade. "The fence was all busted and the goat had been ravaged. The farmer's dog was mauled. I'm worried it might be a bogbear."

"A bogbear?" Ulric frowned. "What would a bogbear be doing this far north?"

She shrugged. "The last Circ troupe to come by packed up in an awful hurry."

A bogbear! Quintin's blood buzzed in his ears. Lightheaded and nauseated, he clutched the edge of the table. As a child, he'd sometimes paid a hard-earned cacao bean to see the oddities displayed by a passing Circ troupe. He would never forget the bogbear. The massive creature of earth had roared its displeasure and struggled against its chains, raking the air with claws like scythes, its open maw bracketed by wicked fangs. Even captured and controlled, the bear had set him trembling with terror.

To have such a monster loose in the jungle was a nightmare come to life. He swallowed hard and whispered, "If it escaped from the Circ then it will have lost its fear of people."

Madi nodded. "And it won't know how to hunt or forage properly, which explains why it attacked a goat farm."

"Do you think it will go after the goats again?" Terin asked.

"I don't know." Madi shrugged. "Such a beast can be very unpredictable."

Ophelia leaned forward, her knuckles white around her mug. "Will the guards help the farmer and his family?"

Madi sighed and put her dirk away. "Protecting his homestead is his own responsibility. The city guards will only hunt this animal if it threatens the trade road. The Trimble Reeve won't station guards at the farm or send a patrol to track it into the trees."

"It's not up to the guards," Terin said. "This is our duty as the Hands of Destin."

"Exactly." Madi glanced around the table. "I'm going hunting this afternoon. I would love more than my own waccat at my back."

Ophelia patted her golden waccat on the head. "Though I can't get away, Felice would be happy to join you."

"Maven and I can join you, too," Terin put in.

"Taric's balls." Ulric buried his hand in his beard. "We're doing a big aqueduct repair this week. Racon and I can only help after dark or if you're still hunting next Taricday."

"I don't want anyone hunting this thing after dark." Madi turned to Quintin. "What about you?"

"I have duties at the Tribute Office this afternoon."

Office boring. I go hunting.

"Elkart can go with you." He smoothed his palm over his waccat's head. *Be careful, fuzzface.*

I be with my pack. Four waccats beat one bogbear, every time.

His waccat was right. Madi's earthen gifts and the pack's ability to work together was more than a match for the bogbear's superior size and strength. Yet Quintin couldn't help worrying.

Ophelia toyed with her waccat's pointed ears. "What happens if you don't catch it today?"

Madi grimaced. "I'm back on patrol tomorrow."

The Tribute Office would be closed the next day, as all the auditors celebrated the day of the week honoring Fermice, the God of Air and Creator of Knots. Quintin drummed his fingers against the table and swallowed his fear. "I can go hunting tomorrow."

Foolish as it was, he would rather hunt with Elkart, than send his waccat off without him.

"I'm between circuits," Terin said, "so Maven and I can hunt this thing to the end."

Madi held up her mug. "With the gods' blessings the end will come quickly."

Chapter 8

Later in the evening, Quintin rubbed his forehead as he left the Tribute Office. He had made the best assignments he could for the coming week and had to trust the other auditors would do their jobs while he focused on the Merdale estate.

At the thought of the upcoming audit, the headache forming behind his eyes throbbed. He wished Merdale was managed by someone other than a Trilord. Dealing with nobles and all their needlessly complicated rituals was his least favorite part of an already unpleasant task.

Pinching the bridge of his nose, he stepped away from the warehouse to head home.

A hand reached out of an alley and touched his sleeve.

Quintin gulped in air, gathered his gift to defend himself, and spun to face his assailant. When he saw the features of the woman who had touched him, he blinked and wondered if his obsession with the thief had damaged his mind.

She was no illusion though, as she beckoned him down the alley.

Letting his breath out in a slow exhale, he followed the thief into the shadows. "What are you doing here?"

"The job's not finished."

"Not finished?"

"There is the small matter of payment."

"You didn't get paid?" He frowned. Why would Ophelia risk exposure by refusing to pay her contact? Or had the thief been cut out of the deal?

"No, and now I want my beans."

He glanced toward the entrance to the alley. "We can't talk here. Let's walk along the riverfront."

She frowned. "Won't the guards see us?"

"There is nothing untoward about taking a walk together under the rising moons." He smiled and offered his arm.

Resting her fingers on his elbow, she returned his smile. "Continuing our charade as lovers?"

"It's better than trying to explain skulking about in alleys together." They stepped out from between the buildings. Quintin nodded at the Tribute Office. "I'm not the last to leave, you know."

She bit her lip. "I see."

"I thought you would."

Worry tempered his excitement at seeing her again. A pity Elkart was out on the bogbear hunt. If there was ever a time he needed his waccat at his back, it was now, dealing with his pretty outlaw.

When a bend in the river caused the line of warehouses to end, Quintin led her over to a low wall overlooking the water. Only little Ferlune hung in the evening sky. He took it as an auspicious sign since the smallest moon was the legendary home of the Deities of Air who had always favored him. Though only half full, Ferlune bathed the scene in soft white light which sparkled and danced on the river.

Unable to resist the chance to hold his thief again, he slipped an arm around her waist. His cheek brushed her coiled braids. Her hair smelled exactly as he remembered. "Beautiful, isn't it?"

She let out a sigh and leaned against him. "It is lovely. Perfect camouflage."

He buried the disappointment her words evoked. She may have haunted his dreams, both awake and asleep, but she was not here to pursue a more personal relationship with him. "Yet it is deserted enough for us to speak freely. What is this about you not getting paid for your work? Is your contact holding out on you?"

"My contact is in the stocks." A shudder coursed through her body as she spoke.

"Fermice's breath," he muttered. Did Ophelia know?

"He was captured before we did the job, so he never got the cacao, as you well know. Now you can pay me instead."

"I wasn't in charge of arranging the job," Quintin said slowly. "Payment, or lack thereof, wasn't one of my tasks."

She stepped away.

He shivered, his side cold and empty without her.

She braced her hands against the wall behind her. Her chin tilted up in a challenge. "Are you refusing to pay me?"

He rubbed his lips, searching for a solution. If she was telling the truth, she deserved payment. If she was trying to swindle him, he didn't want to fall for it. "I could talk to my contact, the one who worked with yours, and verify your story. Then meet you here with your beans tomorrow night."

Her eyes widened. "You think I'm lying?"

"Listen," he began, then stopped in frustration. He didn't know what to call her. "I want to trust you, truly I do, but I don't even know your name. If what you say is true, then I'll have your cacao tomorrow. Will waiting one more day be so bad?"

"I was supposed to get paid three days ago," she said, her breath turning shallow. "I can't wait another day."

He flinched at the desperation in her voice. He wanted no part in cheating her out of her rightfully, if unlawfully, earned beans.

"Besides, you're asking for the very trust you won't give me," she said in a stronger voice. "How am I supposed to know you will come back tomorrow?"

"You know where I work." His lips twisted in a half smile. "And my name."

"Em."

"What?"

Her gaze searched his face as she tilted her chin up. "My name is Em."

"Em." He said her name like a benediction. Warmth filled his chest. He swayed toward her, his head descending for a kiss.

Something like fear flickered across her face.

He pulled himself upright without touching her. She wanted her payment, not him. The thought stung his heart. Worse yet, she might have allowed a kiss in the hopes of getting her beans. He pinched the bridge of his nose and focused on the problem at hand. "If I can verify your story, I might be able to get you at least some of your cacao tonight."

"I suppose I could take you to my contact in the stocks," she said in a doubtful tone. "Though it's pretty risky."

"I wouldn't trust your contact either."

"Then I don't know how to prove what I've told you."

"I do." He licked his lips. "I'm air gifted. I could link us mind-to-mind, where lying is nearly impossible. If you take down your air defenses."

Her eyes narrowed. "How will letting you control my thoughts prove my honesty?"

"I don't want to take over your mind, and I couldn't do it with you paying attention anyway." He let out a noisy sigh. She could light a candle which meant she was balanced, with small amounts of each of the three elements. Her only experience with air would be shielding her mind. She probably had heard all kinds of horror stories about coercion and deep mind reading, most of which were exaggerated or completely unfounded. "I want to have a conversation, nothing more."

She rubbed her temple. "We *are* having a conversation, though it seems to be going in circles."

"I want to believe you, Em. So much. Too much." Even frowning, she was beautiful, with her heart-shaped face and button nose. He'd pay fresh beans to see her smile again. "I can't trust myself to be objective around you. I would trust my gift."

"To do what?"

"To know the truth. It is very hard to lie in direct thoughts. The words and images flow too fast and clear. If you try to lie it slows everything down and makes it fuzzy. Lies taste bad, too."

"Thoughts have a taste?"

"To me they do. Probably because I also have a touch of water."

Her eyes narrowed. "So you want into my mind just to taste my honesty."

"I promise, I'll only be able to read your surface thoughts. Your mind and your secrets will remain your own."

Her brow furrowed in skepticism. "Unless I happen to think about them."

"Unless you think about them very hard and loud. My air gift isn't strong enough to delve into your mind. Linking mind-to-mind with a balanced person like you is going to be a strain as it is."

Her lips were pinched and bloodless. "Will you also be putting thoughts into my head?"

"Only if you want to know if what I say is true. I assure you, my thoughts will sound and feel as different from your own as the words you hear me speak."

She looked him in the eye. "You are asking for an awful lot of trust here, Quintin."

"I know, Em." He sighed. "If you don't want to do it, I understand. I swear I will meet you here tomorrow night. Maybe I could give you something of mine to hold in ransom of my return."

"No. I need the cacao tonight. I'll let you do it." She closed her eyes, her entire body a study of tension.

Quintin frowned. She looked like she was bracing for a bone-mending. This would not work if she was fearful or tense.

"Give me your hand," he said softly.

She opened her eyes, her dark brow knit in a frown. "What? Why?"

"It helps to be touching you, especially when establishing contact." He took her hand in both of his and let out a long, slow breath to remove his own air protections.

She might not realize it, but this was an act of trust for him as well. With his air gift he was more vulnerable to manipulations of the mind than she was, though he also had more ways to defend himself.

He breathed in and out to center himself and strengthen his gift. Then he reached out to her with his mind. The swirling whirlwind of her defenses brought him up short.

She turned her head to look over her shoulder.

"Your mind is still sheltered," he said. "The creepy feeling of being watched was me running into your protections. You can let them go now."

"Can't you break through them?"

"I could," he conceded with a nod. "Though it would wear me out and be a rather unpleasant experience for you. Not at all conducive to building trust and honesty. Take it down and then I'll do the rest."

"I'm not sure I remember how," she admitted.

"Don't spend much time with gifted folk?"

She tilted her chin up slightly. "Not any I trust to read my mind."

Yet she trusted him, or at least was willing to try. He raised her fingers to his lips and kissed them reverently. "I can help you."

Chapter 9

Em closed her eyes and focused on the feel of his hand clasped around hers. The warmth of his breath on her knuckles sent a shiver of sensation down her spine.

"Breathe out. Nice and slow. Let all the air flow out and away from you. Let your barriers scatter like the wind."

She emptied her lungs with every breath and slowly relaxed.

He rested his forehead against hers, his voice a soothing murmur in her ear.

Her defenses drifted away like a cloud, leaving her mind open and free.

Thank you.

The words echoed in her mind. They sounded foreign. Strange, but not alarming.

You're welcome, she replied mentally. She focused on the words, hoping he would not be able to delve deeper into her mind. *Do you have to be touching me?*

No, not since we've established contact, though it is less draining. He raised his head away from hers. *If you find my touch distasteful, I can try to maintain the link without it.*

She squeezed his fingers. *It's not distasteful.*

I'm glad. A tantalizing wealth of emotion lay behind his simple words. If lies tasted bad, the truth was delicious.

His fingers slipped from her grasp as he wrapped his arms around her, his smooth cheek pressed against her hair.

Closing her eyes, she breathed in the smell of cheap soap and warm male. She allowed herself to pretend, for only a moment, that she was safe, protected from the hard, cruel world by the strength in his arms.

Tell me about your payment.

She stiffened, as a memory of the fishmonger's angry face flashed through her mind.

Quintin's arms tightened around her.

Simon was supposed to deliver my payment, she thought with forceful clarity, banishing her worries. *He didn't because he was in the stocks before the job was done. You or your contact or whoever owes me twenty measures of good cacao.*

Twenty measures? he asked, though she could hear the echo of other calculations in his mind like a whispered conversation on the far side of the room.

Twenty measures, she thought with as much clarity and sincerity as she could muster.

He nodded, his chin rubbing against her braids. *I don't carry so much with me.*

I need those beans, she thought, helpless to disguise her desperation or avoid thinking of the fishmonger's ire.

I know. I understand. His words were clear and confident. She had no doubt he believed them. She knew better.

Tears stung the backs of her eyes. *No one understands.*

One of his hands came up to cradle her head. *We'll get you those beans tonight, I swear it. I have enough tucked away in my rooms.*

She sagged with relief and would have fallen if not for his arms holding her so close. *Where should we meet after you go to your rooms?*

Again, she got the sense he was thinking but could not discern the details.

His thoughts finally rang clear. *I live outside of town. It might be best for you to follow me home, rather than wait for me to return.*

You'll let me see where you live? she asked, oddly touched by his show of trust.

He chuckled. *Surely a woman of your talents could follow me home if you wished.* This thought was accompanied by an incongruous image of a stalking waccat. *Though not undetected.*

She leaned back to look him in the face. "Take me home," she said aloud. "I mean—"

He pressed a finger to her lips. *I know what you mean.*

His finger felt soft and warm. Something coiled deep inside her at the touch.

Are you married? Her traitorous mind flung out the question before she could stop it. Her face flamed. It was no business of hers if he was or not.

No, I am not married. His calm, firm answer broke through her scurrying thoughts.

She felt a subtle tension, a hidden apprehension, leave her body at his words.

"Are you?" he asked aloud, his breath warm on her face.

"Am I what?" she returned, mesmerized by his lips, suddenly longing to kiss him, caution be damned.

"Married."

She raised her gaze from his lips to his eyes and mutely shook her head.

"Good."

He leaned forward and softly pressed his lips to hers. Where their first kiss had been passionate and powerful, this kiss was sweet and tender. She wanted to weep at the pure beauty of it. Never before had she felt so fragile yet so safe in a man's arms.

"Halt, who goes there?"

Em reared back, the guard's voice shattering her sense of safety. Only Quintin's arms kept her from falling onto the bricks of the riverfront street.

Fermena's flatulence. His curse was sharp and clear, and mirrored her sentiments exactly.

As the sound of boot heels on bricks tromped over to them, they eased apart with reluctance.

Quintin pressed his palms together and gave a short bow. "Han-Auditor Quintin of Jardin. What seems to be the trouble?"

"Who's the woman?"

"Em," he answered.

"Em? Em who?"

"Em of Farbank," she said in a meek yet carrying voice. She mentally cursed Quintin for needlessly lying about his own title yet using her real name. With luck, naming the ramshackle slums clinging to the other side of the river as her home would be enough to protect her identity.

Quintin flashed a quick look of pity at her. Did he actually believe she lived on the wrong side of the river?

"Well, Hand or no, you can't loiter around here at night. Do you need an escort to an inn?" The guard looked askance at Em. "Or elsewhere."

"Your escort won't be necessary. My waccat is waiting for me." Quintin offered his arm to Em.

While she rested her fingers on his sleeve she held her body away from his as he led her through the sleeping city. When they approached the city wall, she tugged at his elbow. "Let's wait for the next patrol to pass. No need to inform them of our movements."

Annoyance nipped at her heels, as they passed through the tunnel out of the city with no further incidents. Soon the city faded behind them, and the shadows of the forest closed in. She could hear the distant calls of creatures high in the branches of the trees, though an eerie silence followed their footsteps.

"I'm really sorry, Em."

Em kept walking down the deserted trade road without looking at her companion. They were far enough into the forest to speak freely, though she had no desire to discuss his colossal mistake.

"I didn't mean to betray your trust."

"This is why I usually work alone," she said, not bothering to keep the disgust out of her voice.

They walked on. Chirping insects and croaking frogs filled the silence between them. Shrunken and waning, red Terlune had risen to join Ferlune in casting dappled moonlight on the hard clay road.

Quintin made a noise in his throat. "If it is any comfort, nothing is likely to come of my slip."

"Maybe, maybe not." Her gut churned at the possible consequences of his mistake. "Lying to the guards was a dumb thing to do."

"Wait." He stopped dead in the road. "I thought you were mad because I told them your name."

"That was a mistake, too." She spun to face him and planted her hands on her hips. "But telling him you were a Hand and then giving him your real name and position was beyond foolish. It will be easy enough for him to find you at the Tribute Office and then where will you be?"

"In trouble?"

"Yes!" She nearly hissed with exasperation at his confused tone. "Impersonating a Hand is at least a whipping offense. You are sure to lose your job and I don't want to think about what will happen if they start investigating Em of Farbank."

"It would be bad?"

"It would be a disaster!" Em thumped the back of her hand against his chest to knock some sense into him. "It was a pointless stunt. Reckless and poorly executed. If you are going to lie about your rank you had better lie about your name and everything else, too."

She thumped him again in annoyance, unable to shake the feeling he was laughing at her.

A soft low growl sounded behind her.

She spun around.

The moonlight filtering through the trees illuminated the shadowy outline of a waccat.

A scream partially escaped from her throat before she managed to stifle it with her hands over her mouth. "By Fermena's Holy Breath, one of the guards must have been a Hand and sent his waccat to follow us."

"No, it's only Elkart."

"What?"

He rubbed his chest where she had thumped him. "He wants you to stop hitting me and doesn't believe me when I tell him you're teasing. He, um, strongly suggests you stop it."

Her heart raced as the waccat prowled forward. While the great cats were as honorable as their bonded Hands, there was no denying the power in its feline frame. It was also strange and unnerving to see a waccat so far from a Hand. Em edged backward, though she knew running would be worse than useless.

"Stop it, Elkart." Quintin stepped directly between her and the cat. "You're scaring her."

"I don't understand," Em said slowly. Her ability to think trickled back, now that the menacing feline would have to dispatch Quintin to get to her. She knew it could overpower the auditor without breaking stride. Still his courage helped bolster her own. "How do you know its name?"

He glanced over his shoulder at her, though his face remained hidden in the shadows. "I didn't lie to the guards, Em."

Her stomach did a slow roll.

"My name is Han-Auditor Quintin of Jardin. I am a Hand and Elkart is my waccat."

She stepped away from him. He had to be lying. He was her client, not a Hand. "You can't be a Hand. Hands are above suspicion, honorable to a fault."

He turned to face her fully, the waccat a silent shadow at his side. "You think I'm dishonorable?"

"You worked with me. We broke into the Tribute Office together. You can't be a Hand." Hands did not kiss outlaws with tenderness or passion, let alone both. It had to be a trick, or some sort of mistake. "Hands don't hire thieves."

"Hands will do anything in service of the Troika and the people of Destin," he replied. "Even hire thieves if the situation calls for it."

She frowned, remembering the strange job at the warehouse. He had secreted a quipu into a trunk destined for the Novenary, the heart of the Troika and master of water. As an auditor, Quintin was an agent of air under the Luminary, also known as the mind of the Troika. So what business did he have with the Novenary?

Her eyes narrowed. "Are you a spy?"

He let out a short bark of laughter. "I'd be in a sad state if I were, needing to hire an outlaw every time I had a message."

She pursed her lips and swallowed her curiosity. She knew better than to ask questions about a job, though it was a novel relief to think her work had been in the name of a better cause than a jealous spouse, or a greedy troublemaker.

"Come on." He motioned at the road ahead. "Let's get your cacao."

She hesitated, eyeing his waccat. "Are you going to arrest me?"

"What?"

"It would be the proper, lawful thing to do."

"There is nothing proper, or honorable, in betraying an accomplice." He pressed his fist to his forehead, chest and navel. "By my word as a Hand, you shall come to no harm while with me."

Em felt her tense muscles relax, almost without conscious thought. Yet she had no reason to be comforted by the word of a man who made deals with thieves. With unscrupulous outlaws like herself. As a child Em had played Hands-and-Bandits with her brothers and dreamed of bonding with a waccat of her own. Then fate had intervened and forced her onto a different path, one devoid of such niceties as honor. Never had she imagined during those carefree days that she would end up as the bandit.

She stifled a sigh. If she could not trust the honor of a Hand, what good was there left in the world?

He held out his hand. "Please, Em, let me take you home."

She nodded and placed her fingers in his.

His hand was warm and soft. The palm pink, his brown fingers clean and free of calluses, untouched by heavy duties or common labor. It was a hand of privilege, and she wondered briefly if hers felt as soft, or if her years of sneak work had left their mark.

As she followed him deeper into the forest, she cast one look back at the waccat who followed behind them on silent paws.

Chapter 10

Quintin rubbed his thumb over Em's knuckles, amazed by the simple pleasure of holding her hand. Giddy relief bubbled through him. She wasn't mad at him for revealing her name. He'd nearly laughed aloud when she accused him of lying to the guards. Such subterfuge had never occurred to him. He was not cut out for the criminal life.

She not like Hands. Elkart jumped out of the bushes to land neatly on the road ahead of them.

She thought I was going to arrest her. He sighed, some of his joy escaping with the sound. Her reaction to his station was a stark reminder of how different their lives were. *You also gave her a scare, growling and showing your teeth.*

She hit you. Elkart's tail lashed. *Nobody hits my Hand.*

It was barely a tap. Madi hits me harder when we're sparring, and you don't growl at her.

Irritation nipped through the waccat's inarticulate thoughts. He jumped back into the jungle and disappeared with a rustle of leaves.

Quintin led Em a little further to an established path off the trade road.

The branches of the canopy met overhead, blocking out the red moonlight and leaving the narrow track in darkness. A choir of bugs buzzed in the night air. Her grip on his hand tightened and he could feel the warmth of her body as she pressed close.

He opened his senses to the air around him and used his gift to navigate. While it wasn't as good as true sight, it was enough to avoid leading Em into a tree trunk. With his senses on the alert, the jungle seemed full of mysterious shapes and odd movements.

Did you catch the bogbear? he asked Elkart.

No. Frustration colored the waccat's thoughts. *Bogbear hiding. We hunt again when light returns.*

Quintin stifled a groan at the prospect of heading off into the jungle with Terin at dawn. Putting thoughts of the morning aside, he tugged Em along the path to his home.

When the path ended at the edge of his mother's moonlit garden, Em gasped.

"Welcome to Jardin," he said in an undertone.

The house and garden were cradled in a ball of soft moonlight. After the darkness of the forest, the smooth clay walls of the house seemed to glow pink. He was glad to see its shutters were drawn and not a light could be seen inside. His mother must already be asleep.

He pulled Em beside him as he skirted the edge of the garden along a protective berry hedge. Even at the perimeter, the garden smelled of rich earth and green growing things.

He led her through a shadowy door at the side of the house and into his private chamber. The square room was cramped and furnished with the bare necessities. There was an altar against the far wall, a dark wooden credenza to one side of the door, and a trunk below a window on the other. It wasn't much, but it was all his. He closed the door behind them and plunged the room into darkness.

"If I hand you a lamp, can you light it?" he asked, his hushed voice loud in the stillness.

"Yes, I'm balanced," she responded in an equally quiet tone.

Elkart pranced in the center of the room. *Dinner now?*

Light first. He let go of her hand to shuffle across the room and retrieve a brass oil lamp off the credenza. He handed her the lamp and turned to attend his waccat. He had yet to take one step when light flared behind him. Then something hard and hot pressed into his back.

The lamp clanged to the floor as she swore.

He began to turn. "What—"

She clutched at his kaftan. "Stay there. I'll have this out in a moment."

The distinctive smell of lamp oil rose around them while the heat on his back was replaced with cold.

"What happened?" he asked.

"I tried to give you the lamp, but only succeeded in setting your clothes on fire and putting the light out."

He chuckled. "If I'm out of danger, I'll find you a candle."

Shrouded in darkness once more, he returned to the credenza.

"Are you hurt?" she asked.

"A little tender maybe." He fumbled in a drawer for a beeswax candle. "How are your hands?"

"Oh, fine. Takes more than a couple of sparks to blister a balanced woman."

He returned and gave her a candle. "This time keep the light for yourself. I can manage well enough with my air gift."

She nodded and focused on the candle.

He pulled off his ruined kaftan and examined the scorched spot on the back. It would need a patch. Candlelight brightened the scene, revealing an oil stain near the burn.

Em gasped.

Quintin turned quickly, expecting to find some new disaster. Instead she was staring at him with hungry eyes. Her gaze roved over his body, making him acutely aware of his bare arms and torso. Warmth spread through him in a confusing mix of embarrassment and desire. He was torn between holding his kaftan up like a shield and throwing it to the floor so she could look her fill.

"You're beautiful," she said, gliding toward him with one hand outstretched.

He dropped the kaftan.

She smiled. "You look like a devotee to Taric."

He let out a breathless laugh. "Still a follower of Fermice like all good auditors." Though being compared to the God of Earth and Flesh was a heady notion.

She brushed her fingers over his biceps.

His skin jumped at the touch. Desire raced through his body to the pit of his belly. He had never guessed his arm could be so sensitive, so erotic.

Her hand curled around him, testing his muscles.

So strong. Her thoughts drifted through the touch.

Fermice grant him wisdom, he had neglected to replace his mental protections, and she must have forgotten as well.

The candle's flame danced as she placed it on the credenza. She pressed her palm against his chest. An image of her lips closing around his nipple gusted through his mind. He captured her hand against his skin, her heat branding his heart.

He stared deep into her eyes, remembering their kiss on the waterfront. She had been so soft and sweet in his arms, filling his senses and leaving him dizzy with longing. He blew the memory into her mind but couldn't be sure how much she understood.

His air gift was a poor choice for conveying such an emotional experience. Water was the element of the blood, of the heart. Thin, cerebral air could only capture words and images.

Still her eyes widened. *Kiss me. Please.*

I want to do more than kiss you.

Good. She ran her hand up his arm. Her fingers slid over his shoulder to curl around the back of his neck and bring his head down. She tasted like spiced cider and smelled faintly of the jasmine haunting his dreams.

He wrapped his arms around her to pull her tight against his chest. When his lips parted, instead of plundering his mouth with her tongue, she shifted the angle of the kiss and sighed.

He drew her breath deep into his lungs, twining their air and minds more intimately together. Her thoughts swirled like flower petals in a gust of wind, bright and fleeting images of passion.

She pulled away from his mouth to lave the pulse point in his neck. His head fell back to give her better access. Her burning desire for their bodies to be entwined seared his brain.

Eager to please, he slid his hands down to cup her bottom. He lifted her up and pressed his knee between her legs. The feel of her skin against his was intoxicating.

She moaned. The breathy, needy sound propelled his passion higher. Her pelvis rocked against his leg in a rhythm as old as time. Erotic fragments of her thoughts flickered through his mind, merging and mixing, building on his own fantasies until real and imagined touches blurred into one.

When their mouths met again, he thrust his tongue deep, mimicking their shared desire. The vision of entering her was so vivid, his cock pulsed with need.

Her entire body shuddered as she scraped her teeth across his tongue.

It would feel so good to have you inside. Her thought was accompanied by a wave of frustration and a stab of loneliness.

His arms tightened around her. *We're together. Don't be lonely.*

Tonight is an illusion. Soon I'll be gone. Forever.

Pain and something akin to panic speared him.

She softened the kiss, subtly shifting away from him. "We have to stop, Quintin. This is madness and continuing will only lead to heartache."

From a deep reserve he found the will to let her go, though his heart howled and demanded he cling to her. "You're right," he said. "Of course, you are right."

Quintin turned away, taking deep cleansing breaths to establish his mind protections. He hoped she remembered to do the same. They needed no more accidental thought sharing. He pulled a folded kaftan out of his credenza, choosing one in a lighter shade than his usual auditor brown. The voluminous garment covered his body, hiding the lingering evidence of his ardor.

When he felt collected enough to look at her, he noted how she remained near the door, arms crossed over her stomach, her mouth a pinched white line.

"Why don't you sit down?" He touched her elbow to urge her toward a trunk doubling as a bench near the window.

She flinched and curled away from his fingers.

He dropped his hand and backed up.

All done kissing? Elkart asked.

Em shuffled over to the bench. She slipped off her sandals before pulling her feet up onto the smooth lid. She wrapped her arms around her legs and rested her chin on her knees.

Yes. All done kissing. If he were wise he would gather her beans and send her on her way before he made the mistake of touching her again.

Why you sad? Elkart sidled up to the trunk and sniffed at Em's feet. *You both sad. Don't humans like kissing?*

We like it too much. He nudged Elkart out of the way to squat down in front of her. She looked like a forlorn child, and guilt gnawed at him for putting her in such a state. "Would you like something to eat? My mother left a pot of curry here for my supper. There is more than enough to share."

One of her hands tugged at a loose thread on the edge of her chiton. "You don't have to feed me."

"I want to, if you're hungry." He placed a gentle hand over her fingers. "Let me take care of you, Em. Only for tonight."

She raised her gaze to meet his, and for one horrible moment he thought she might cry. Instead she managed a crooked smile. "Then, yes, please, I would like some curry."

"Good." He gave her an encouraging smile before standing and crossing to the credenza.

Elkart trotted after him. *Dinner?*

Let me feed our guest first. Quintin lifted the lid off a round ceramic crock, releasing a gingery cloud of steam.

The waccat sat down on Quintin's foot with a huff.

Ignoring the uncomfortable weight, he dished out a bowl of curry and yanked his foot out from under the waccat's rump to carry the bowl to Em.

The great cat bumped Quintin's knee with his head as he walked across the room. *Feed me.*

Patience, Elkart. Quintin managed to hand the bowl to Em without spilling it all over her, despite Elkart's interference.

Closing her eyes, she breathed in the curry's aroma. "This smells wonderful. Your mother made it?"

"Yes." Quintin gestured at a bead curtain in one wall as he returned to the sideboard with his waccat bouncing at his side. "She owns the house and grounds. I rent this room from her."

He uncovered a dish of meat for Elkart and set it on the floor.

Tail lashing, the cat crouched next to the bowl and devoured his meal.

As Quintin straightened, an odd pattern of shadows wavered across the wall. He glanced over at Em, to find she had moved to kneel in front of the low table opposite the door and was busy lighting the candelabra there.

She motioned at the floor next to her, the gesture oddly elegant. "Won't you join me for supper?"

"I would be honored."

Chapter 11

Quintin's hands shook as he hastily served himself a bowl of curry. He would have to take the dishes out to the garden and wash them himself to conceal Em's presence from his mother. A small price to pay for sharing a meal with a beautiful woman.

Setting his bowl down on the altar, he folded himself onto the floor next to Em. His knee jostled against her. Heat flooded him. He scooted away with a muttered apology.

"No harm done." She shifted to give him more room and took a bite of curry.

He fiddled with his spoon. He wanted to say something witty and charming but rhapsodizing about her beauty would probably make her uncomfortable. And it wasn't as if he could ask her about her life in Farbank.

"With a name like Quintin, you must have a passel of siblings," she said after a pause. "Do any of them live here, too?"

"No." A bitter taste filled his mouth at the thought of his so-called brothers. As if any of them would so much as set foot in such humble surroundings. He pushed aside old resentment and tried to be matter-of-fact as he recited his history. "My father had four other children from his first marriage, though I'm my mother's only child. This homestead belonged to my maternal grandmother. My mother and I moved back in with her after my father died. Later my mother inherited the homestead and so here we are."

"I'm sorry," she said softly.

He shrugged. "My mother has been quite happy to have this place to call her own, and it suits me well to live here, too."

"No, I mean I'm sorry your father has turned to ash."

"Oh." He poked his spoon at a carrot floating in the curry. "It was a long time ago. I was very young when he died and have few memories to haunt me."

"The pain never goes away, does it?"

Something in her tone caught his attention. "Is your father dead?"

"No, Fermena protect him." She pressed her thumb to her forehead, heart and navel.

Wincing, he mimicked her gesture.

She stirred her curry without taking a bite. "My mother died when I was twelve," she said at last.

"My sympathies."

"She had been ill for a long time. It was for the best."

"But the pain doesn't ever go away entirely." He echoed her words.

"I'm glad her suffering has ended, yet I still miss her." She fingered a leather cord at her neck. "My mother was gone from my life too soon. Sometimes I wish I had one last chance to talk to her, to ask her about all the things I was too young to understand before she died."

"Yes." He glanced over at the waccat pushing his dish around on the floor as he licked it with his broad tongue. "If my father had lived, my life would have been very different. I would have been different. Would I be a Hand?"

"Surely the traits and qualities that drew your waccat to you would not have been changed by the circumstances of your upbringing."

"Perhaps," Quintin agreed, not wanting to explain how eager, how desperate he had been to bond with Elkart. "My upbringing certainly was very different as an only child pampered by two lonely women, rather than a youngster scrabbling to keep up with four rough and tumble older siblings."

"What did happen to those children?" she asked, her tone one of idle musing. "With their father dead and their stepmother abandoning them?"

"My mother did not abandon them," he said sharply. He took a breath and continued in a more moderate tone. "They were much older and uninterested in her guardianship."

Which was a gross understatement. Though Quintin had been young when his father died, he vividly remembered the shouting, the tears and hateful insults that had preceded being expelled from the only home he had ever known. After they had settled at his grandmother's cottage, Quintin had finally dared to ask what 'whore' and 'bastard' meant, only to be firmly told such language was not welcome at Jardin.

"If she was half as good of a cook then as she is now, they were fools to let her go." Em pointed her spoon into her bowl. "This curry is delicious."

He smiled, appreciating how deftly she turned the conversation. "Cooking is one of the things my mother does best, as well she should since it is how she earns her living."

"Does she work at one of the taverns in town?"

"No, she sells produce at a stand in the marketplace. Mostly fresh herbs and spices which is why her food is so tasty. She'll sell vegetables, too, when the crops are bountiful."

"She can support herself by gardening?"

"She can. She also trades with her neighbors for eggs and milk and such. I help with expenses, as well. It isn't an extravagant life, but it is a good one."

Em's hair glinted red in the candlelight as she turned to survey the room.

Quintin followed her gaze. The furnishings were simple, the room unadorned since all his luxuries were tucked out of sight. Yet it was clean and dry and his alone. How did it compare to wherever she slept in Farbank?

She frowned down into her bowl. "I suppose an Auditor's salary can help a lot with the upkeep of a house."

"I do what I can, since she takes good care of me." He waved at the curry pot. "And I haven't even provided her with any grandbabies to spoil."

"Does she hound you for them?"

"Not exactly, though she occasionally drops broad hints about how I'm old enough to settle down and get married. I think she's concerned about my happiness."

Em sighed and stabbed her curry with her spoon. "Lucky you."

"What? Is your father itching for a babe to dandle on his knee?"

She laughed. "No, no, he already has a grandson." The humor faded from her eyes. "I don't think my happiness is at the forefront of his mind when he says it's high time I wed."

Why would her father pressure her to wed when she already earned her own beans, however ill gotten? He furrowed his brows. "What does he hope for? Someone to tame your wild ways?"

"Perhaps." Her lips curved in a rueful smile. "Mostly, he is looking for his own gain, not mine."

Her words reminded him she was not here to enjoy his company. He owed her cacao. He gestured at her nearly empty bowl. "Will you want more?"

"No, though your mother's cooking is superb." She scraped the last of the curry out of her bowl and licked the spoon.

His groin tightened as he remembered all the things they both imagined her doing with her tongue. He stood and picked up her bowl to cover his reaction.

"I could help wash up."

He held the dishes out of reach. "No, no. I'm taking care of you, remember. Why don't you relax here while I gather your pay?"

After he took the dishes to the credenza, Quintin opened his trunk and pulled out his best coverlet. As he spread the thin material over her, she gave him a wobbly smile. Tightness filled his chest. He forced his feet to back up a step to resist the temptation to stroke her glorious hair.

Perhaps gleaning some of his thoughts from his face, she dropped her gaze and ran a hand over the embroidered fabric. "You are the kindest of men."

"Did you bring your own sack to carry your payment or should I find one for you?" he asked quickly in an attempt to steer the conversation to safer ground. He did not want the memory of her passionate embrace tainted by any comments about his avuncular nature.

"If you have one to spare . . ."

He nodded and busied himself collecting the cacao he owed her. Twenty measures was a fair payment for her work, though the amount was nearly all of what he kept in his room. He pulled out the delicate scale he used to calculate his mother's tribute each season. As he weighed the beans, he was struck by how much risk she took for so little reward.

"Are the twenty measures your portion?"

"What?"

"Your contact takes part of your pay, right? For finding you the job?"

"Yes, the beans usually go through him."

"Then are the twenty measures what you were owed, or is it the full amount?"

"It's what I'm owed."

"How much is the full amount?"

"I'm not sure. We don't discuss it." She pulled the blanket close. "Whatever he's being paid, it's not enough."

"You run most of the risks."

"Do I? Yet here I am."

While her contact was in the stocks. Quintin poured twenty measures into a pouch, before piling more beans on the scales. "I'm going to give you five extra measures for your contact. You can give a little something to the Daughters of Mercy for his care if you wish."

Her eyes widened. "You are not at all what I expected a Hand to be like."

He laughed. "You should meet my year-mates. We're as varied as any other group of people."

"Perhaps." She traced a line of stitches with one finger. "The tales I remember growing up always painted Hands larger than life, heroes one and all."

"We're only human. Though we do try to do the right thing." He held out the pouches of cacao to her. "And isn't me giving you beans to help your friend the right thing to do? Isn't it what you would expect of a Hand?"

She had a queer look on her face as she reached out from under the quilt to accept the pair of pouches. "While I appreciate your generosity, I don't know if giving extra beans to an outlaw for her compatriot in the stocks qualifies as the right thing to do. Isn't helping outlaws and such against your vows?"

"Justice tempered with mercy is the way of the Troika," he said. "Some Hands are devotees of Marana. Giving them beans for their work is both just and merciful. It's not as if I'm offering to break him out or anything. That would be against my vows."

"More's the pity," she muttered as she pushed the coverlet off her lap. "Who knows how long he's going to be trapped there."

"I'd give you more for his care, if I had any extra."

She stood and carefully folded the blanket. "If you are ever hard up for beans, you should convince your mother to sell some of her embroidery." Her hand caressed the colorful stitches. "This, and the pillows, your kaftan. She's quite the artist."

Ears hot, he regretted the impulse to cover her with the cloth. "I wouldn't call it art."

"Her work is beautiful. Unique. Look at the detail on this flower." She presented the folded fabric with a yellow orchid facing him. "You should encourage her to sell it at market. It would probably pay better than growing vegetables."

He took the cloth and tucked it under his arm. "My mother doesn't embroider. She doesn't have the knack for it."

"But the pillows, the coverlet—"

He sighed. "They're mine."

"Yours?"

"Once my grandmother gave up any hope of having a granddaughter, she decided to pass her craft down to me. My mother was always hopeless with a needle. It warmed my grandmother's heart to have someone in the house take after her."

"So you made this?" Her fingers rested lightly on his cuff.

He nodded mutely, waiting for the mockery to begin.

Her thumb stroked the abstract blue design. "You have a gift." Her graceful brown fingers looked delicate and soft against the pale linen of his kaftan.

His body stirred, as he remembered how those fingers felt on his bare flesh. "It's only a hobby."

"One that requires a great deal of patience, not to mention nimble fingers." As he raised his gaze from her hand to her face, she snatched her fingers back and cleared her throat. "Your work is beautiful. You should be proud of your skill."

"You flatter me," he protested, though he grinned like a monkey. Better flattery than mockery.

"Not in the slightest, you have quite the gift." She bent to pick up the pouches of beans.

Panic rose in his throat at her movements. Any moment now she would take her payment and leave. He would never see her again. He licked his lips. "Would you care to barter?"

"Barter?" She straightened. "For what?"

"Put my nimble fingers to the test."

Her eyebrows shot up to her hairline.

"Not like that." His face heated. "Give me a lesson on how to pick locks and I'll let you have a pillow or kaftan or bolt of cloth."

"A pillow?"

He shrugged. "You said my mother could get a nice price for them in the marketplace. You could sell the piece instead and make a tidy profit. Unless you were flattering me."

She tilted her head, her eyes calculating. "Let me see your wares."

~ ~ ~

"Huzzah!" Quintin could not contain his exuberance as the lock finally clicked open. He turned with a grin on his face to share his triumph with Em. Then froze as he caught sight of her curled up on the floor next to the table.

She had fallen asleep with her head on a sitting pillow while he had been practicing with her picks. She rested so peacefully, with one hand curled under her cheek, and her dark hair shining red in the candlelight.

Elkart sidled up to Quintin and nudged his hand.

Quintin curled his fingers into the fur behind the waccat's ears. His gaze did not waver from Em's lovely face.

Lesson over. She go.

"Not yet," he murmured. He smiled softly at the sleeping woman. He stood up to spread the coverlet over her. "She can go in the morning."

Morning? The waccat's tail twitched. *Hannah not like it.*

I'll wake her up and send her home before Mother knows she's here. Let her rest easy for now. Who knew where she lived in Farbank? This might be the first decent sleep she'd had in months.

She sleep fine at her house. She smell like hot meals and soap. Probably has nicer bed than you.

A frown marred his brow. Elkart spoke true. She smelled of fresh jasmine, not day-old sweat. He pushed aside the sliver of doubt. There was no denying the desperation in her voice or the angry face which had flashed through her mind when she thought about getting her payment. Was that man her father, who put his own gain before her happiness?

Whatever the case may be, if he could shelter her from her daily cares for one night then he would.

I promised I would keep her safe. That I would take care of her.

In the morning she would be gone and out of his life forever. It almost didn't bear thinking about.

Chapter 12

Warm, moist air blew against Em's face. Half asleep, she opened her eyes to a gaping maw of sharp teeth. She screamed and jerked backward, smacking her head against a table leg. The pain brought her fully awake. Why was she lying on the floor with a waccat looming over her?

"Hush," Quintin hissed from a sleeping mat in the center of the shadowy room. "You don't want to wake my mother."

"What time is it?" Her neck prickled as she turned away from the waccat to peer at the shuttered window. She must have fallen asleep on his floor.

"Later than I intended." He groaned and climbed out of his sleeping roll. When he opened the shutters, the room was bathed in pearly gray light.

Her mouth went dry as she realized he had once again shed his kaftan and was completely bare from the waist up.

He turned from the window to glare at his waccat, who lingered over her. The great cat turned his attention from her to his Hand, giving her the uncanny impression they were speaking mind-to-mind. Quintin frowned and planted his fists on his hips, the corded muscles in his arms flexing with the motion.

She had not done his body justice when she had called him beautiful the night before. Flawless bronze skin gleamed in the pale glow of predawn light. A dusting of dark hair sprinkled over his chest and down his flat belly, narrowing to a line that disappeared into his trousers. She licked her lips. Her fingers itched to trace the line down past his hips.

The waccat slunk away from her over to his Hand, yanking her from her salacious thoughts.

Em scrambled to her feet. "Why didn't you wake me last night?"

"You were so peaceful. It seemed a kindness to let you sleep." He ran a hand through his wavy black hair, which was loose about his shoulders. "Though you should go now, before we wake my mother."

She eyed her things spread out on the trunk by the window. Stepping close to him and his tempting flesh struck her as deeply unwise. "You should get dressed," she muttered.

His eyes widened. He moved away from the trunk to pick up a kaftan folded at the foot of his sleeping mat.

She took his place by the window. Out of the corner of her eye, she watched the tantalizing planes and honed muscles of his torso disappear under the voluminous folds of his clothes. Sighing with mingled relief and regret, she turned her attention to the trunk.

Neatly laid out on its lid were her pouches of cacao, her open lockpick kit, and the embroidered length of cloth she had selected as her payment the night before.

Her face relaxed as she beheld it. The pattern of flowers and birds was even more colorful and enchanting in the ghostly light from the window. She touched one finger to a purple flower made of clever knots, before turning her attention to the lockpick kit. She removed her oldest pick, a versatile middle-sized one Simon had given her long before she went into the business. Flipping it in her hand, she held it out handle first to Quintin.

He slowly lowered his hands from tying back his hair, his brow knit in an expression of confusion.

The back of her neck prickled as if someone was watching her. She guessed he was testing her air defenses, but she dared not let him into her mind, not when she already felt so raw.

She stepped over to him and slipped the pick into his hand, then leaned forward to whisper in his ear. "For you. To practice with."

His fingers closed around the tool. Before he could speak, the sound of voices drifted through a bead curtain next to the credenza.

"Rotting hell." His curse was no less vehement, for all that it was said in a quiet undertone. "Terin's here. Pack up your stuff. Now."

She hurried back to the trunk. With practiced ease, she rolled up her lockpicks and slipped them into her chiton.

"I don't know if Quintin is awake yet," a woman said clearly, the voices coming closer.

The smaller bag of beans fit in her belt pouch.

"The aroma of your cooking should be enough to entice a dead man to rise," a man answered.

The other pouch of beans followed her picks down the front of her chiton. It had no sooner nestled against her belly above her belt than a man's head burst through the curtain.

"What's keeping you?" he asked before his gaze landed on Em. His classically handsome face slackened in shock as he stared at her.

She ignored him to pull on her sandals.

"I need to let Elkart out for a piss," Quintin said, his voice too loud and carrying.

She spun around to grab the folded cloth off the trunk and clutch it to her chest.

The handsome stranger blinked and seemed to recover. "Anything I can do to help?"

"No. I'll be out in a moment." Quintin waved his hands in a shooing motion.

The man grunted and gave Em a searching look before

pulling his head back through the curtain and asking Quintin's mother a question about their impending meal.

Quintin stepped over to the door and threw back the latch. "Stick to the hedge," he told her in an undertone. "And clear out quickly."

Elkart brushed past her as she stepped out the door. The brown waccat bounded straight into the garden, dodging between the neat rows of plants and flowers to join two other great cats already cavorting on the paths.

Em hurried around the edge of the clearing, staying as close to the berry hedge as she dared. She prayed the dark shadows hid her from anyone in the house, but there was no hiding from the waccats. She felt their gazes following her until she found the path and escaped.

"Stupid, stupid, stupid," Em muttered to herself as she hurried from the cottage to the trade road. Falling asleep and spending the night in Quintin's rooms had been an unforgivable mistake. A less honorable man could easily have taken advantage of her, and she was usually too smart to trust a stranger, even if he was a Hand.

Worse yet, it meant she had to traverse the streets of Trimble during the morning hustle and bustle while wearing her sneak clothes. Acolyte Lucy would be surprised to see her dressed this way, though her reaction would be nothing compared to what Lord Harold would do if he heard stories of his daughter dressed like a laborer.

She lowered her head as she arrived at the trade road and joined the workers and vendors trickling into the city. She had the wild urge to cover her face with the cloth she clutched in her arms, or to at least hide her distinctive hair. She tightened her arms around the fabric. Such an action would only draw unwanted attention as she hurried through the streets of Trimble.

When she reached her temple near the riverfront, she took the stairs two at a time, reciting the names of the gods in pairs. The crystal and glass curtain tinkled as she entered the sanctuary and breathed a silent sigh of relief. She was slipping off her sandals when Acolyte Lucy approached.

"May the blessings of Fermena blow through your life," she intoned. "How may I be—Lady Em! What are you doing here? And dressed like—"

"I've got the beans."

"What?"

Em shifted the folded cloth to under one arm and pulled the larger pouch out of her clothes. "I got the beans. We can pay the fishmonger."

Lucy took the pouch, though her face was a study of skepticism. "I shouldn't ask where these came from, should I?"

"It would be a long story," Em agreed, "and as you've noted, I need to change."

Leaving Lucy shaking her head behind her, Em skirted the tree and altar at the center of the sanctuary to enter a short hallway hidden behind the tree. She ducked through a simple bead curtain into one of two private chambers at the back of the building.

"Lady Maria? Is that you?" a shaky voice asked from a narrow pallet pushed against one wall.

"It's Lady Em, wise mystic." She crossed the room to stand next to the bed and smile down at the old woman.

"Lady Em. Foolish me, I keep forgetting." Mystic Patricia captured Em's hand with her knobby fingers. "You look more like your mother every day."

"You are too kind." She patted Patricia's hand with care. The mystic's skin felt as thin and fragile as dried leaves.

Patricia squinted, her face wrinkling like a walnut. "What are you doing dressed so strange, my lady?"

"I need to put a few things away, and then I'm going to meditate in the steamroom." Em pulled away from her mother's old nurse to open a trunk on the opposite wall. The trunk held her spare clothes, a bed roll, and any other odds and ends she might need at Aerynet.

Quintin's cloth spilled across her lap as she knelt next to the trunk. The fabric itself was unremarkable, a length of undyed linen, stiff and a little scratchy to the touch. His needlework was what transformed it into something special. She traced the wing of a bird so detailed it seemed ready to fly around the room. She could imagine Quintin creating those tiny colorful stitches, a line between his brow as his deft fingers applied the needle.

Em's hands tightened, clenching the cloth. She would never see him again. *Impossible.*

"I've brought you some tea," Lucy announced as she stepped into the room.

Em started, embarrassed to be caught mooning over a bunch of stitches. While the two holy women chatted behind her, Em buried the cloth at the bottom of the trunk. She had told Quintin the truth when she had said his work would fetch a good price at market, though she hoped to avoid selling it. The beautiful piece would be a fitting gift for the Novenary, better than what she usually managed for the Allgoday tribute, if only she could hang on to it during the coming year. While her heart ached a little at the thought of giving it to a stranger who might not appreciate it, the sacrifice was small on the scale of what she did for Aerynet.

Dwelling on her temple duties, she pulled a set of fresh clothes out of the trunk. A warm yellow accented with green, the kaftan and trousers were very different from the camouflaging grays and browns of her sneak clothes. Though informal enough to make her father frown, the kaftan was respectable and should deflect any awkward questions.

She removed the smaller pouch of beans from her work belt before storing her picks and other tools. She closed the lid and gave Lucy a nod. "I need to speak with you. I'm going to meditate in the steamroom. Please come get me when you are available."

The steamroom, a narrow chamber tucked between Lucy's and Patricia's rooms, had been designed for more intimate communion with the Goddess. Lined with balsa wood and other airy materials, it was supposed to help air talents focus their gifts, though as far as Em knew it had not been used by an outsider for generations. Lucy did not frequent the room much, for she needed Em's help heating the stones to create the steam that gave the room its name.

Em shed her sneak clothes behind a carved privacy screen in the tiny antechamber to the steamroom. She left her garments folded on the floor with the pouch of beans nestled on top.

Her skin pricked as she closed the folding door. Enclosed dark spaces often gave her a nervous turn, though the steamroom was less disturbing than most. Warped by time and moisture, the thin door no longer closed completely and couldn't be locked, leaving a clear escape route she found comforting.

She knelt next to a cold brazier and plunged her hands into the pile of porous lava rocks in the bowl, then bowed her head and prayed to the balanced trio of Goddesses, asking them to help her fill the rocks with heat and life. The rocks slowly warmed until it was uncomfortable to keep her hands buried in them.

Focusing on heat, she pulled her hands from the brazier and cupped them over the top of the pile. Once she judged the rocks hot enough, she poured tepid water over them. A billowing cloud of steam rose into the room.

Em breathed in the odorless steam and frowned. They had stopped adding costly perfumes and scents to the water years ago, though the plain vapor did little to honor the Goddess. In less than two weeks, the cycle would change and Fermena would begin her ascension. While Em had only turned nine at the last year of Fermena, she could remember the temple festooned with feathers and sporting a new coat of paint for the occasion. Her stomach twisted at the thought of how much more subdued the transformation would be this year.

She clasped her hands together and beseeched the Goddess to give her the wisdom and cunning to honor her properly, now and always.

The door squeaked as Lucy opened it. "Shall I join you, my lady?"

"We can speak in the antechamber." With one last prayer, Em left the hot, humid room. She picked up the pouch and opened it. Her nostrils wrinkled at the bitter smell of dried cacao. She pulled out one smooth brown bean and gave it to Lucy. "Take this to the devotees of Marana for your brother."

The acolyte rubbed the bean with her fingers. "You are too kind."

"He's earned it. I wish there was more I could do." Em sighed and cinched the pouch closed. "I don't dare risk associating my temple with Simon. As his sister you can afford to be charitable without raising comments."

Lucy raised her eyebrows. "The mystics of Marana are known for their discretion."

"I won't stake my reputation on theirs."

"You worry too much about your reputation."

"I worry too much, period," Em replied. "It's how you all stay fed."

Her acolyte pressed her palms together and bowed her head. "I wish we weren't such a burden to you."

"Being a Lady of Air and the patron of Aerynet is an honor, not a burden. I would never have it another way. Never." As proud as she was of her temple and title, supporting it did require struggle. She had sacrificed much in the last six years, including any sense of honor. The little pouch weighed heavy in her hand. She was sorely tempted to pocket the payment intended for Simon, but it hurt her heart to abuse Quintin's trust.

Before she could change her mind, she thrust the pouch at Lucy. "This is the rest of Simon's pay. Take it to his wife, as I'm sure she's at her wits' end."

Her acolyte squeezed the pouch. "How can you afford this?"

"They're not mine." Em stooped to pick up her clothes. "Those beans are for Simon. Since he's not available, giving them to his wife is only fair."

"It's uncommonly generous of you."

Em yanked the kaftan over her head, shaken by how close she had come to betraying Quintin's kindness.

"I like to think I have not sunk so low that I can't be trusted with a simple delivery." Her voice rang sharper than she intended.

"No, my lady." Lucy said. "I'm sure Jenny has been beside herself with worry, and these beans will mean the world to her, is all."

Em rubbed her temple in regret for snapping at Lucy, unsure how to mend the damage. "I should return home soon. Father worries when I spend the night at Aerynet. I don't want to worry him further by dallying here this morning."

The acolyte gave her a sideways glance, tactfully not pointing out that Em had not spent the night at the temple. "I'll get the beans to my brother's wife."

Em nodded absently, still thinking about her father. "I wish we weren't so dependent on him," she muttered.

"I've always felt it was risky, but what choice do we have?"

She frowned at the acolyte. "What?"

"He lives in a dangerous world and there are a lot of ways for it to go wrong, like it has." Lucy sighed, her fingers tightening around the pouch of beans. "I'm indebted to your mother for giving me a place as a novice instead of leaving me to fend for myself like my brother."

"Oh, I was talking about my father. I wish we weren't so dependent on his largess." Em smiled tightly. "Though it would be nice not to have to rely on your brother so much, either."

Lucy's brow wrinkled. "Your father's largess isn't very large though, is it?"

"No, but I don't know how we would ever manage without my allowance, and you're dressed in my cast-offs, too. It would be a long time before we could afford any new clothes if my father wasn't so foolishly intent on finding me a suitor."

"What if Isabel and your father are right?" Lucy asked. "Maybe you should think about getting married."

Em blinked, stunned by the suggestion from such an unexpected quarter.

Her acolyte shrugged. "It would free us from dependence on your father."

"And make us dependent upon my husband instead."

"Exactly." Lucy nodded. "Your mother didn't have to stoop to selling her jewels and all the other indignities you've endured, her husband made sure of it. Perhaps you can find a spouse to do the same for you."

Em jerked her chin up, a sour taste in her mouth. She had been too young to consider marriage when she first inherited. Now she was used to her independence and didn't relish the idea of entering a marriage like a beggar with her hand out. Besides, the secret of her sneak work would always be lurking, waiting to come to light and destroy her.

"While my father is miserly with his funds, he is generous with my time. If I marry, then my time will hardly be my own. I'll be too busy helping my lord husband run his estate, doing all the work Isabel does in my mother's stead."

"Please think on it, Lady Em. You're not a child anymore." Lucy bit her lip. "Working with my brother has always been chancy at best. We need a better, more reliable solution. For all of us."

Chapter 13

Near midday, Em entered the receiving room where her father lounged on a divan with his eyes closed. "You sent for me, Father?"

The air was heavy with midday heat, and she longed to be resting herself in her room. Careful not to tread on the hem of her sari, she glided over to her father. The soft carpet muffled her footsteps, though the silver bells of the payal around her ankle chimed with her movements. When she reached the divan, she pressed her hands together and bowed at the waist.

"We have a number of guests coming for the Allgoday celebration next week. The first of them will arrive today," her father said as he opened his eyes. The triple stranded deed chain around his neck clinked as he swung his legs over the side of the divan to sit up. "I want you to be the one to greet them."

"Me?" Such duties usually fell to Isabel as the wife of his heir.

"Isabel has enough to do preparing for the festival. I expect us all to help her in the coming week, especially you, Emmie. I sent for you now to make sure you weren't off hunting or dressed like a ragamuffin." Lord Harold inspected her from head to foot.

She struggled to exude the calm stillness of a Lady under his scrutiny, very glad she had taken the time to change into a sari when she received his strange summons. She wore it wrapped in a traditional style with the pallu covering the top of her head. Isabel might encourage her to show off her unusual hair, but Em knew her father preferred the old ways.

"You look nice, almost as pretty as your mother. You're as ready as you'll ever be to greet our guests." Lord Harold gave a short nod. "No need to dress quite so well tomorrow."

"Tomorrow?"

"We've got an auditor coming to inspect the estate, as if we haven't enough going on without a taxman underfoot. Ah, well, the Tribute Office in Trimble sets its own schedule."

Her stomach fluttered at this news. She'd had too many encounters with the Tribute Office of late.

"I expect you to take care of the taxman while he's here, since Isabel is so busy," Lord Harold continued.

"How long does an audit usually take?"

"Two or three days. Maybe longer if he's a real stickler."

"Fermenasday is in two days. I'll need to be at Aerynet—"

Lord Harold scowled. "We need you here. Your temple will have to get by without you this week."

"Can't Gregory or Jonathan greet the taxman? Surely he doesn't need to be honored by a Lady. One of your other children would serve as well."

"It never hurts to flatter the taxman, and I won't have my household accused of being rude. I certainly don't want to get on the wrong side of the Tribute Office."

"But—"

"No buts, Emmie. Your duty is here, and I don't want to hear another word about it."

"Yes, Father." Em bowed her head in acquiescence, though resentment bubbled in her heart. Once again, she wished she was not so dependent on her father's good graces.

"Our guests will be here any moment," Lord Harold said briskly. "Lord Evan a'Maral a'Tarina is a diplomat and one of my closest friends at court. He was widowed three seasons ago and will be coming out of mourning on Allgoday. I am very pleased he has chosen to spend such a significant holy day with us. I expect you to honor our house when you greet him and his daughter, Mistress Catherine."

"I will, Father." Her stomach pitched at her father's description. No doubt her father considered the widowed Lord Evan a potential suitor, though she had no interest in marrying a diplomat who lived in the capitol.

A gong reverberated at the front of the house, signaling the arrival of Lord Evan and his daughter.

"I'll return shortly with your guests." Em bobbed a quick bow to her father. She hurried to the entry hall and picked up a platter of delicacies set out on a side table. An assortment of nut cakes sprinkled with ground cacao, chilled fruits, and snake eggs cooked in the skin decorated the platter. Em's father clearly wanted to impress his friend from court.

As a guard opened the door, Em dropped into the pose of welcome. Her mother had patiently spent many an afternoon practicing the welcoming arts with Em before she got so sick. Even now, greeting a man whom Em would rather turn her back on, a slight smile curved her lips at those sweet memories. She crouched low with her feet crossed and close together while her knees stayed off the floor and her sari pooled around her. She held the platter above her bowed head, tilting it just so to display the delicacies at the most inviting angle.

A pair of dusty feet moved into her line of vision.

"Welcome to Merdale, Lord Evan a'Maral a'Tarina. We are most honored by your presence. For as long as you may grace our halls, our bounty is your bounty."

"It is I who am humbled and honored by your hospitality." Lord Evan intoned the expected response in a strong cultured voice. The platter shifted slightly as he selected a delicacy. "Your gifts are welcoming indeed to this weary traveler."

"We invite your daughter to also refresh herself with our humble repast," Em said, trying to keep her tone warm and inviting though her legs were beginning to ache.

"I am most honored." Mistress Catherine's voice was soft and hesitant. She jostled the tray as she selected a treat.

Em tightened her grip on the edge of the platter and rose carefully to her feet, grateful to have the formal part of the ritual complete. As she raised her head, she got a clear view of their guests for the first time.

Lord Evan appeared older than her father, with a brow as wrinkled as a nut and wispy gray hair pulled back into a thin queue. A pair of deed chains set with green and yellow stones were the only ornament on his brown kaftan.

Mistress Catherine's sari, on the other hand, twinkled with beads and shells sewn into the edges of the fabric. Her pallu draped over her shoulder, revealing thick black hair plaited around her crown. After a day of travel, some wispy strands had escaped to trail over her tawny cheeks. She looked older than her voice had sounded, possibly a year or two Em's senior, certainly no longer a child. She licked the juice from a chilled fruit off her slender fingers, until she saw her father's look. Her thumb popped out of her mouth.

"I am Lady Emmanuella a'Fermena." Em held the refreshments out with a smile, wordlessly inviting the young woman to help herself to more fruit. Travel was a thirsty endeavor. "It will be a great pleasure to have a woman my own age in the house and at the festival."

Catherine stared down at her bare feet. "You are too kind."

"Come, my father is eagerly awaiting your arrival." Em led the guests back to her father. As they traversed the short hallway, she could hear her father speaking sharply, though she could not make out his words.

"You will meet my eldest brother and his wife at the evening meal," she said in a carrying voice, attempting to warn her father of their arrival. "I'm sure Isabel will also be excited to have another woman in the household."

Lord Evan fingered the chain around his neck. "We are interested in visiting Trimble and seeing the sights while we're here."

Catherine's dark eyes sparkled. "I've heard you get the latest in Verisian dyes and patterns here, so close to the border."

"We are quite blessed in our market." Em held aside a curtain threaded with crystals and bowed the guests into the receiving room. Her father had been joined by her brother Jonathan and his friend Curtis, which explained the raised voices.

While Lord Harold rose to greet his guests and introduce Jonathan, Em headed across the room to intercept her brother's friend.

"Welcome, Curtis. Please share in our bounty." She crossed one leg behind her and presented the tray in an informal welcoming posture. While it galled her to bend that much for Curtis, she would shield Mistress Catherine from the scoundrel's attentions if she could.

"Good to see you, too, Emmie. I missed having you greet me when I arrived this morning." Curtis leaned forward, one dark curl sliding with artful carelessness over his forehead. He lowered his voice to an intimate purr. "Though I prefer you with feathers in your glorious hair."

"Perhaps Jonathan will be kind enough to wear feathers the next time you visit."

"Because you won't do the welcoming honors?" Curtis popped a boiled snake egg in his mouth with an insolent air. "Your cousin is never so inhospitable, and her hair is as pretty as yours."

"Would you be happier finding your entertainment at her house?" Em gestured toward the door. "I would be delighted to see you out."

"Oh, no. I knew this would be diverting when Jon was summoned here with all haste by your father. As much as I would enjoy a moment alone with you, Emmie, I find myself most intrigued by your other guests." He gave her a wink as he strolled around her to the knot of people on the other side of the room.

Em glared at his back as she followed him.

Curtis pressed his palms together and folded over at the waist in a deep bow. "May I have the honor of an introduction?"

Lord Harold glanced at Curtis, his wide nostrils flaring.

Curtis did not rise from his bow, and Em had to admit grudging respect for his careful use of the formalities.

"Lord Evan, this is Curtis of Trimble, Heir of Councilor Richard," Jonathan said quickly. "Curtis, this is Lord Evan a'Maral a'Tarina, Diplomat of Destin and Voice of the Luminary."

Curtis rose from his bow with a smile, his gaze fastening on Catherine. "And who is the lovely young woman?"

"My daughter, Mistress Catherine." Lord Evan's voice was as stiff as his spine.

"And my honored guest for the week," Lord Harold added, the warning clear in his tone.

Curtis slanted a glance at Lord Harold before smiling at Catherine. "You must be despondent about coming out to the sticks for Allgoday instead of celebrating in the capitol."

Catherine ducked her head. "I'm sure the celebration here will be lovely."

Lord Evan flashed an indulgent smile at his daughter. "And much more suitable for the sensibilities of a young woman."

"Our celebrations have their own charm," Jonathan assured her.

"I quite enjoy the bonfire," Em added.

Curtis smirked. "Come with me after sunset and I'll show you the most charming thing Trimble has to offer."

Catherine's brow wrinkled. Lord Evan puffed himself up and Lord Harold's hands twitched as if he yearned to strangle Jonathan's friend.

"Isabel is preparing some burning sticks to make a most impressive display in the bonfire." Em bared her teeth at Curtis in a smile. "I'm sure you'll enjoy those much more than whatever entertainments Curtis might have in mind."

"Hoping to keep my charms to yourself?" Innuendo oozed through his words, as sweet and sticky as warm honey.

Fighting the urge to gag, she curled her lip. "I'm hoping you'll keep your clothes on until you are out of sight of myself and all other decent women."

He pretended to yawn. "Decent women are so boring."

Jonathan started to laugh, choking it into a cough at his father's glare.

Lord Evan harrumphed. "You would probably enjoy some of the wilder parties at the capitol."

"I've been longing to celebrate Allgoday at the capitol for years."

Lord Harold raised his eyebrows. "Pity your father doesn't have the connections to get you an invitation."

Curtis straightened, the bored amusement washed from his face.

"Have you tried one of Cook's cakes?" Jonathan snatched one of the nut cakes off Em's platter. He shoved the crunchy sweet at his friend. "I don't know what she puts in them. They are the best I've ever tasted."

Curtis took a grudging bite, his eyes narrow slits of irritation.

Em held out the tray to Lord Evan and Catherine. "You should try one. They're quite satisfying after a long, hot journey."

Lord Evan's face relaxed as he took the offered treat. "You're a good girl, you are."

Em tried to keep her thoughts from her face as she wondered if he expected her to wag her tail and bark after his condescending compliment. Despair clawed at her throat as she remembered Lucy urging her to wed.

When her options were the patronizing friends of her father, or insulting charmers like Curtis, the prospect of marrying was grim indeed.

Chapter 14

Quintin had waited until Em's shadow had disappeared into the trees, before closing the door to his chamber. Echoing laughter from the main room of the cottage had indicated where his mother and Terin prepared trays of food. Quintin had joined them without comment.

As they'd carried the trays outside to eat, he felt an itch between his shoulder blades as if someone watched him. He glanced at Terin and the feeling intensified. His air gifted year-mate wanted to talk mind-to-mind. Quintin shook his head and then jerked his chin at his mother.

"What a lovely morning." Terin slid a tray onto the garden table. He nodded at Hannah. "Almost as lovely as the company."

Quintin stifled his guilty conscience as the itchy feeling disappeared. He hadn't exactly lied to his friend. He did detest the confusion of trying to carry on a normal conversation while also speaking mind-to-mind. If he were honest though, his mother's presence wasn't what stopped him from letting Terin into his thoughts. With his superior air gift and experience ferreting out the truth, Terin was sure to learn more about Em than Quintin wanted to share if they spoke mind-to-mind.

"It is a beautiful day," Hannah agreed. "Such colors!"

Sunrise pink clouds painted the sky while birdsong trilled from the jungle. Neither did anything to banish the dread churning in Quintin's gut. Keeping secrets from his friends was a new and uncomfortable experience.

He ate a piece of chilled mango without tasting it and had a hard time following the conversation between Hannah and Terin. Worst of all, he had only delayed the inevitable. Discrete and loyal, Terin would not breathe a word about the woman in Quintin's room to Hannah but as soon as his mother was out of earshot, an interrogation would begin.

"Those plantains were sublime, Hannah," Terin said a short while later as he folded his hands over his empty plate. "What is your secret?"

Hannah rubbed her callused fingers together. "I add a pinch of ginger. Gives it a little bite."

"Wonderful. Truly wonderful."

Hannah chuckled and reached for Terin's plate.

"Let me." Quintin picked up the plate and collected her empty dish as well. He carried the stack toward the house.

"I would love to eat like this every morning," Terin said. "You squander your talents on Quintin. You should come live with me—"

"My mother doesn't want to be your charmaid." The dishes clattered and splashed as Quintin dumped them in a water bucket near the door.

Terin raised his elegant eyebrows. "She'd be wasted as a charmaid. I'd make her my wife."

"I'll not be marrying you, you charmer." Hannah laughed and swatted Terin's arm. "I expect fidelity from my husband, I do."

Terin pressed his hands against his heart and batted his eyelashes at Hannah. "With cooking like that, I'll never look at another woman again."

Quintin splashed water over his feet and onto the ground in careless agitation as he scrubbed the dishes. "You're going to poke women blindfolded, then?"

"Shh, don't tell her my plan," Terin said with a mock glare.

Still grinning, Hannah wagged a finger at him. "I should be going, before I miss my best customers."

"Why don't Terin and I walk you as far as the trade road?" Quintin hastily pulled the plates out of the bucket and set them aside to dry. "If we're going to spend the day tracking a bogbear in the hopes of keeping citizens safe, I'd hate to have you run into it first."

"I doubt I have reason to worry, but I won't say no to the company." Hannah hoisted a towering basket of vegetables onto her head.

Terin whistled to the three waccats lounging in the shade of the berry bushes as he strode over to the narrow path to the trade road. The waccats dashed after him while Hannah picked her way to the trail.

Following his mother, Quintin pushed aside the occasional encroaching bush with his staff. He tried not to think about how good Em's hand had felt in his when they had traversed this same path the night before. He hoped she'd returned to Farbank safely.

When their company reached the trade road, Hannah turned toward Trimble with a cheery good-bye.

Quintin shifted his staff from one hand to the other as he faced his year-mate. "Where did the search leave off yesterday?"

Terin pointed with his own staff at the jungle on the other side of the road. "We went pretty far away from the road. Felice and Maven can show us exactly where."

The three waccats darted across the road and into the underbrush while the two Hands followed at a more sedate pace. Howler monkeys hooted in the distance, their rhythmic cry a challenge to all who would trespass into their domain.

Quintin suppressed a shiver and shoved his staff against the dense foliage. Moisture pattered on his head as he broke through the vines and into the jungle proper. The air was thick and warm, lit by rare sunbeams slipping between the leaves of the canopy trees.

The understory thinned as they moved farther from the road, letting the three waccats spread out while remaining in sight. They ranged all over, dashing ahead or to the side before loping back to the Hands.

Quintin grimaced as Terin moved to walk beside him. His friend kept pace in silence for a moment. Quintin knew his reprieve would soon end.

Terin clicked his tongue. "You're going to make me ask, aren't you?"

"I would rather you didn't." Quintin could feel his friend studying him, though he refused to meet his gaze. Whatever questions Terin had, he would not have good answers.

"There is only one thing I want to know." His friend knocked his staff against a passing tree trunk, bringing down a shower of condensation. "How did she convince you to part with the cloth?"

"She called it beautiful," he answered without thinking. Her eyes had glowed with desire when she looked at him. Terin, with his easy charm and handsome face, would not understand the allure of a woman who found him, plain old Han-Auditor Quintin, attractive.

"Madi thinks your work is beautiful, too," Terin said. "She raves about your use of color. She practically begged you to make her a wall hanging. If I recall she has offered to buy the very same cloth you apparently gifted to a stranger this morning."

"It was a trade, not a gift." Quintin winced at his own honesty.

Terin's eyebrows jumped and laughter danced in his eyes. "A trade, was it? After all your protests yesterday, I am shocked. Shocked, I say, to find you entertaining a prostitute in your mother's own house."

"She's not a—" Quintin forcefully bit his own tongue. He wanted to rap Terin's skull for casting aspersions on Em, though she would be safer if the advocate believed she was nothing more than a body for hire.

"She's not a prostitute?" Terin's gaze sharpened and he rubbed his chin. "Do you know her name now?"

Quintin sucked in a breath, envisioning Em on the waterfront, her ebony eyes wide and vulnerable. "Yes."

"So, you manage to both learn her name and get her into your bed in a single night." Terin whistled. "Quick work, even for a man of my experience and skills. You must have untapped powers of seduction. Who would have guessed?"

Quintin scowled and smacked a nearby bush with his staff, sending off a spray of water droplets. His belly twisted at the blunt assessment of his limited charms. Even worse, Terin grossly overestimated his skills since he'd done nothing more than exchange a few kisses with Em.

Terin your friend. Terin a Hand. Elkart's tail twitched. *Why not tell Terin truth?*

"It's complicated," he muttered.

His year-mate laughed, showing straight white teeth. "Obviously."

~ ~ ~

The late afternoon sun cast long shadows over the city of Trimble as Quintin, tired and frustrated, escorted Ophelia's waccat through the town after an unsuccessful day of hunting. Elkart and Felice stuck close to his sides in the busy streets, never hesitating until they reached the temple Ophelia and her waccat called home.

The Trimble High Temple dedicated to the Water Goddess Marana, Mother of Mercy and All-Knowing Seer, was a sight to behold. Rivara's smooth marble walls glistened as water trickled from the roof to splash into tiered ponds full of colorful fish and an array of blooming lilies.

The oversized wooden doors glinted with shiny stones and precious metals set amongst carvings of the Goddess in her many guises.

A smaller door, cleverly inset into the enormous double doors, opened and a stream of children tumbled out of the building and down the stairs. Quintin smiled through his weariness. As much as he craved knowledge, he could well remember his joy as a child heading home after a day of study.

Some of the children were diverted from their flight by the sight of a Hand and the waccats with him. One of the boys, about nine or ten years old, pressed his palms together and bowed. "Please, sir, Hand, sir. Why do you have two full grown waccats? Are you bonded to them both?"

"The bond does not work that way. Only one waccat per Hand." Quintin patted Felice, who was pressed against him in the crowd. "This one is bonded to a friend of mine and lives here. She was helping me with a job, and now I'm returning her to her Hand."

"May we pet them?" one of the younger children asked.

"Only until the path clears." The door to Rivara teemed with children so he had a moment to indulge the youngsters. "Those doors are locked at sunset, you know, and I don't want to be stuck inside."

The older children laughed while the younger ones jostled forward, eager to touch a genuine waccat.

Elkart and Felice wove between the children toward the doors. As soon as the last child exited the temple, the waccats bounded up the stairs.

Quintin shooed the stragglers home before following the waccats inside. He slipped off his shoes in the entryway and gave his staff to a bowing novice.

"May the blessings of Marana flow over your future," the novice intoned in a soft voice. "How may we be of service, Hand?"

He gestured at the golden waccat. "I'm here to bring Felice back to Han-Mystic Ophelia."

"Very good. The waccat can show you the way."

He bowed quickly before following Felice around the perimeter of the cavernous sanctuary. Flanked by the waccats, he nodded to acolytes as he passed but did not stop to speak to anyone. At the side of the sanctuary, they turned to walk under an arched doorway into a shadowed courtyard.

Scattered around the courtyard were a handful of children who lived at the temple, either as orphans enjoying the Goddess's Mercy or students whose homes were too far away to return to each evening. They ate a light meal under the watchful gaze of a pair of novices. Heads turned as the children tracked the waccats strolling across the courtyard.

A wave of chatter surged behind Quintin as they left the courtyard and headed down a cool dark hallway to Ophelia's room.

"How good of you to walk Felice home." A smile warmed Ophelia's lovely face as he entered her room with his waccat entourage.

"It was my pleasure, especially since I have something I need to talk to you about."

"Come and sit." She gestured at a pillow on the other side of the low table from her. "Would you like some watermelon wine? I'm afraid I have finished my repast. I could send a novice for more . . ."

"I'm sure my mother has supper waiting for me at home," he said as he folded himself cross-legged onto the pillow. "Though a goblet of wine would be most welcome."

She poured from a bronze decanter into a smooth clay goblet. "How went the bogbear hunt?"

"Not well. The waccats had a hard time picking up the trail this morning, and then lost it again in the afternoon. Terin is considering going out again tomorrow, though I don't see what good it will do if they can't find a fresher track." He thumped Elkart's side. "Waccats are no hunting hounds, able to follow a ghost of a scent through wind and rain."

His waccat flopped against his side. *Your nose worse.*

Yes, it is. We might need to try something different, is all.

Ophelia frowned. "Terin is welcome to take Felice with him again, though I'd be happier about her going out if she had more than the two of them for company. A bogbear is nothing to trifle with."

"He plans to talk to Madi tonight and see if they can come up with a better strategy than running around in circles in the jungle." Quintin took a sip of watermelon wine and let the sweet taste wash away the frustration of a day spent chasing a phantasm. "I imagine you'll know more about their ideas than I will since I have to return to work tomorrow."

She swirled the wine in her own goblet and cleared her throat. "Since you're here, I wanted to verify you had no trouble with the favor you did for me on Taricday."

His lips tightened. "I wouldn't say I had no trouble."

Her brown eyes widened. "The boy you sent assured me everything went according to plan."

"Our objective was achieved, which was all I dared share with a messenger." He sighed. Their complicated plan was worthy of Terin's twisted intellect, and much like Terin's schemes it had inevitably gone awry. "How did I let you talk me into such a wild scheme?"

"What went wrong?" she asked, her voice quavering. "The Troika must be alerted to Nadine's disappearance as soon as possible. I foresaw—" She pressed a hand against her forehead. "It was horrible."

"If the girl is going to die anyway—"

"I don't want her to die wretched and alone," Ophelia wailed. She clapped a palm over her mouth and glanced around her austere chamber as if someone might be hiding in the corners. Leaning forward, she lowered her voice. "If Nadine must die, no other children should suffer her fate. The matron had a hand in her disappearance, I'm sure of it, and if the temple is profiting off the sale of children . . ."

"The Novenary must be alerted," he agreed. There was little Ophelia could safely do to ferret out a slavery ring while living at Rivara. It was a job for the Novenary and her inquisitors, which was why he'd gone to such lengths to compose and deliver a quipu explaining Ophelia's concerns. Not everyone could decipher the colored strands and knots, but the Novenary would have scholars in her entourage up for the job. Now they must hold tight and wait for the inquisitor's arrival. Until then he needed to stop Ophelia from doing anything rash.

He covered her hand with his own. "The quipu went out with the tribute, this I swear. It is up to the Troika to respond."

"But you said there was trouble."

"Do you know your contact is in the stocks?"

"Yes, I saw him there a few days ago. I was most relieved to receive your message assuring me all was well." Her lush lips pulled down in a frown. "How did you discover his identity?"

"The thief you hired came and accosted me last night, demanding payment for the job."

"Oh, dear." Her hand flew to her mouth. "Did you get hurt?"

"No, no, I'm fine." While Em had tangled his emotions into a confusing knot of desire, worry, and gratitude, she hadn't hurt him physically.

"Do you need the beans, then? Have you arranged to meet the thief at some other time?"

"I already paid her, so replenishing my cacao would be most welcome."

"Her?" Ophelia's dark brows climbed toward her hairline. "The thief is a woman?"

"Yes." He licked his suddenly dry lips. "Not that it matters one way or the other."

"You paid her with your own beans? Without confirming her story?"

"She was desperate for the cacao, and I didn't want to be involved in cheating her."

She tilted her head and studied him. Her water gift splashed against his defenses in an attempt to taste his emotions. He took a sip of wine and declined to let her into his heart.

Her face tightened. "Is she the one?"

"The one?"

"The woman you were talking about at the Salty Dog."

The wine soured in his stomach as he tried to keep his embarrassment and lust from leaking through his water shield. Lying to Ophelia was impossible but confessing his attraction to a thief would be worse.

She refilled her goblet. "No wonder you said it was hopeless. Thank the Goddess you didn't tell Terin or Ulric any more about her."

"There's no chance I would. I have no desire for them to find her. Can you imagine what Madi would do if she thought I was poking a thief?"

Ophelia shuddered. "She would never forgive me for getting you involved in such a stunt."

Madi had sacrificed more than the rest of them to become a Hand, and she took her duties very seriously. "Hands or not, we could end up in the stocks alongside your contact."

Her shoulders shook with another shiver, before she took a sip of wine. She eyed him over the edge of her goblet. "Was she very beautiful?"

"Not as beautiful as you."

She plunked the goblet onto the table. "You are not going to distract me with empty flattery."

"It's the simple truth," he said with a shrug. With her gentle curves and luminous copper eyes, Ophelia had the kind of beauty praised in romantic ballads. While his desire for Em had more to do with her clever wit and intoxicating kisses than her pretty face.

"Yet it is not me you were sighing over at the Salty Dog."

He smiled tightly. He'd stopped sighing over Ophelia ten years ago. "While you may be lovely, we both know I'm like a brother to you. Affection and trust we have in abundance. Romance is out of the question."

"Romance should be out of the question with a thief as well."

"And so it is. Didn't I say as much at the Salty Dog?"

He would not admit how much he wished it otherwise. Em had disappeared back into the Trimble underworld, never to be seen again, and it really was for the best.

Now, if only he could convince his heart to forget her.

Chapter 15

The next morning Quintin ran an unknotted quipu nervously through his fingers as he strode down the avenue connecting the Merdale estate to the trade road. Imported gravel crunched under his sandals, with Elkart's footsteps echoing his own. Spaced wide enough for a palanquin and outriders, canopy trees lined the road like arboreal sentinels. High above the ground, where only monkeys dared to climb, their branches grew together to create a massive living tunnel through the forest.

When they reached the end of the tunnel, the gravel path split to curve around the edges of a circular garden nearly the size of an entire homestead plot. Since he was unburdened and on foot, Quintin abandoned the smooth gravel path to take a more direct route through the gardens to the manor house. While he admired the spiral paths and hidden grottoes casting a leisurely aura on the grounds, he was a vegetable vendor's son and knew most of the plants in the garden would add flavor and substance to the manor's table as well as being pleasing to the eye.

Elkart sniffed at a patch of mint. *Smell like home.*

The garden did resemble the one at Jardin, though his mother's plot was a fraction of the size, but any resemblance between the homesteads ended with the manor house. The cottage he called home peeked out from under the trees like a child hiding in her mother's skirts, while the manor house of Merdale lounged across the end of the drive like an elegant lady on a divan. In the soft morning sun, the sprawling structure sparkled with colorful mosaics. Lord

Harold spared no expense to keep the trees in check around the front of the house, insuring no shadows marred the jewel of the estate.

All in all, the place reminded Quintin far too much of his childhood home.

Elkart bumped his head against Quintin's hip. *Too much staring, not enough walking.*

Squaring his shoulders, Quintin wrapped the quipu around his left hand. The sooner he started, the sooner he would get this over with. He exited the fragrant garden and crossed the gravel road to a flight of stairs up to the door of the manor house. He struck the gong next to the door with the mallet hanging below. Its deep ringing tone echoed in his breastbone. When the door opened, he stepped inside with Elkart at his side.

A gentlewoman well practiced in the art of hospitality crouched in the center of the entryway, holding a tray of delicacies over her head. Her white sari pooled on the floor around her, while her head was bowed at the proper angle for a respectful welcome.

Quintin removed his shoes and nodded at the motionless guard holding the door. As he approached the woman, he mentally reviewed the steps of the ritual for entering a noble home.

"Welcome to Merdale, most honored Auditor, uh, Han-Auditor," she corrected herself as Elkart sat down next to Quintin. "We are honored by your presence. May your work here be swift and satisfying, as we hope our tribute is most pleasing to the Troika." There was something hauntingly familiar about her voice, probably from the rote cadences of her formal words.

"I thank you for your gracious welcome." He cleared his throat, hoping he remembered the correct wording for his response. He bent over to select a slice of plantain from her tray. "I am Han-Auditor Quintin of Jardin, Hand of Destin and—"

To Quintin's horror the platter trembled and began to tilt.

Elkart jumped out of the way as the bronze tray clanged against the tile floor. Bite sized pieces of food flew in all directions.

"A thousand apologies, Han-Auditor." The woman knelt on the floor, her careful pose abandoned as she tossed the food back on the platter.

"I'm sure it was my fault." His face hot with embarrassment, he squatted down to help her pick up the mess. "I've always been a clumsy oaf."

"No, no." She glanced at him and he got his first good look at her face.

The plantain he held was reduced to mush in his fingers. "Em?"

Her dark eyes widened. She jumped to her feet and brushed ineffectually at the stains on her sari. "I'll take you to Lord Harold now. I can clean this up later."

He followed her in a daze, his mind scrabbling for an explanation. She led him out of the house and into a courtyard. Her black hair gleamed red in the sunshine, reminding him of all the other times he imagined spotting Em. Perhaps he had been mistaken when he glimpsed her face.

I told you! She smelled of meat and soap. Elkart's thoughts were edged with a dark glee. *I told you. Her bed better than yours.*

She can't be Em. She just can't. Quintin licked the plantain off his fingers and studied the straight back of the woman before him. Her bleached white sari, now spattered and stained, twinkled with beads and shiny beetle wings cleverly sewn into row upon row of intricate needlework. His throat burned as he remembered Em admiring his simple stitches.

This could not be the same woman. *Maybe she's the spoiled woman from the market.*

Not smell like nasty bully. Elkart's tail twitched. *Smell like your thief.*

She walked through a tinkling curtain and bowed as a jowly older man rose from his seat at a table large enough for six. The room was appointed with trunks and sitting rugs, while the only decoration was a tapestry hung above the table that looked like a map of the Merdale estate.

Quintin's mind could not fully take it in as she introduced him to Lord Harold in a calm tone. There was no denying she was Em now. He watched the scene like a spectator at a farce, detached by a growing sense of outrage. She was a better actor than he had ever dreamed.

Lord Harold gestured at her. "My daughter, Lady Emmanuella a'Fermena, will see to your comfort during the audit."

"*Lady* Emmanuella?" Quintin asked with a sharp emphasis on the first word. Her deception got worse and worse.

"My daughter is a lady in her own right, though a minor one. She inherited a temple too small for even a parcel from her mother."

"I'm honored beyond words," he said with careful precision. It was a great honor to be attended by a genuine Lady, even one who spent her nights dressed as a laborer, breaking the law and kissing strangers. The impulse to speak to her, mind-to-mind, seized him. But as desperate as he was to ferret out the truth of her, he feared his own mental barriers were all that kept him from raging incoherently.

"Is something amiss, Han-Auditor?" Lord Harold asked.

Quintin blinked at the Trilord. "I beg your pardon."

"You seem distracted." Lord Harold frowned at his daughter, probably taking in her rumpled appearance and missing serving tray for the first time. "Has my daughter said or done something to offend?"

"No." Quintin slanted a glance at Lady Emmanuella, who at least had the good grace to squirm. He took a deep breath, further strengthening his protections and ordering his thoughts. "Your daughter is simply more lovely than I had imagined."

For once the lie flowed easily from his lips, perhaps because it had a kernel of truth in it. She had been pretty dressed in drab brown, and adorable curled up asleep on his floor. Those visions faded to nothing next to her current beauty. Her white sari accentuated her rich brown skin, while stone bangles made her limbs appear impossibly thin and graceful. The feathers in her hair softened the edges of her face. He could almost imagine them tickling his wrists as he cupped her face for a kiss.

Lord Harold laughed, though the sound was forced. "Emmie has always been a pretty little thing. Takes after her mother, she does."

Quintin stared at the Trilord and wondered how much of a fool the man was. "You underestimate her. She is exquisite."

"The auditor is far too kind." Lady Em's smile was as sharp and brittle as glass.

Lord Harold wagged a finger at Quintin. "Now Auditor, when it comes time for our aestivation, am I going to be able to leave her alone with you?"

"By my word as a Hand, she will come to no harm while with me," Quintin said, his tone harsher than he intended. Em flinched at the familiar words. Served her right. If only her word had meant half as much as his own.

Em of Farbank, indeed.

"Thank you, Han-Auditor." The Trilord gave a shallow bow. "I meant no disrespect."

"None taken. I am simply impatient to get to work," Quintin said, trying without much success to modulate his tone. He was furious, he realized, an unusual, uncomfortable state. It had been a long time since he had felt so thoroughly duped. "Your daughter, lovely as she is, will not distract me from my task."

Em gave a low bow, her movements full of unconscious grace. How had he not seen it before? Fredrick must have recognized her. No wonder he smirked in that nasty way whenever he caught Quintin studying the Merdale quipus.

The Bursar had put him in the untenable position of auditing his secret lover's family and would no doubt enjoy watching him squirm. By law Quintin was obligated to report the relationship and resign the case. Quintin shuddered. Doing so would cause a scandal and an investigation into their charade. It didn't bear thinking about.

If he continued with the audit, he risked blackmail or discovery. Add in his body's response to the mere sight of Em, and a banal penance had transformed into a treacherous nightmare.

Chapter 16

Em patted the velvety neck of her okapi and peered through the trees to spot the sun. Needing to clear her head, she had escaped into the forest surrounding the manor shortly after leaving her father alone with the Han-Auditor. While the familiar routine of hunting helped soothe her, soon she would need to return to the manor and face the auditor once more.

She carefully stowed her atlatl, a clever tool for launching arrows, next to the pair of partridges and single marmoset she had brought down with it. The meat would be welcome at Aerynet, though it would not quite make up for her absence during the holy day.

The calm she had gained in the forest proved all too fleeting. After handing off the okapi and giving instructions for her kills to be sent to town, she hurried through the manor to her rooms.

A secret smile curved her lips as she changed once more into a sari. Her father would be horrified if she presented herself to the Han-Auditor in the kaftan and trousers she wore for hunting. Little did he know Quintin had seen her dressed in much worse.

Em went to the kitchen to fetch a tray laden with their midday meal. Her heart pounded as she crossed the courtyard to her father's study. She would need all her skills at deception to keep her father from suspecting the effect the Han-Auditor had on her. She paused outside the curtain of glass beads and cut stones, barely able to see the forms of her father and Quintin seated across from each other at the long table.

A hot ball of conflicting emotions formed behind her breastbone at the sight of the Han-Auditor. His presence here spelled danger and disaster, yet her heart swelled with joy to see him again.

Schooling her features into a polite mask, she clasped the tray and pushed through the curtain.

Quintin and her father looked up from the table at the sound of the beads tinkling behind her. Something hot and dangerous flickered across Quintin's face before he assumed a distant expression.

Alarmed at the emotions he aroused, she presented the tray of food. "May the bounty of Merdale sustain and refresh you through the heat of the day."

"Merdale's bounty is great indeed. I thank you for sharing it." While the words were unfailingly polite, an undercurrent of irritation rippled through Quintin's response.

"It is you who honor us." She slid the tray onto the table between Quintin and her father, then knelt low with her forehead touching her knees. She held the posture perfectly, though her blood sang with a potent mix of desire and fear. For the first time in her life, she played host to a man who was worthy of the honor, yet also knew her secret shame and could betray her with one wrong word.

After Lord Harold and Quintin had selected their first choice of the array of dainties, her father waved a hand. "Join us in our meal, Daughter."

Raising her head, Em murmured her thanks and knelt at the table with the men. Well aware of her father's attention, she chose a stuffed mushroom without glancing at the Han-Auditor. As they ate, she strove to keep her expression distant and her conversation minimal and polite. Her father must never guess her powerful reaction to the auditor.

As the tray emptied, Lord Harold cleared his throat. "I am overdue for my aestivation."

Quintin scrambled to his feet to bow. "Please, do not let me keep you from your rest."

Her father sent Em a questioning glance, which she answered with a reassuring smile. Lord Harold stood and mirrored Quintin's bow. "Lady Emmanuella will attend to you now. I will return when it is time to resume our work."

Em kept her eyes averted as Lord Harold departed, though her body was acutely aware of Quintin towering over her. Once they were alone, she met his gaze for the first time since she had entered the room.

Tension transformed his amiable face. His eyes snapped with judgment, condemning her without a word.

A shiver of something—longing, regret—skittered down her spine. She gestured at the nearly empty platter. "If you have eaten your fill, I can escort you to a room where you may rest. Or sleep if you so desire."

His eyes darkened. "What if I desire something else?"

Rising to her feet, she licked her lips. Awareness throbbed between them. "That would depend on your request."

Stepping close enough for her to smell his soap, Quintin lowered his voice. "What if I want answers, will you grant me those?"

Her heart pounded at his words. "What do you wish to know?"

"Are we private here?"

"Reasonably so." Clear light twinkled off the beaded strands in the doorway, giving no sign of someone lurking in the hall. "Father will not want to insult your honor by being obvious about providing a chaperon, though I think you gave him a turn, gushing about my beauty."

He shrugged, some of the tension leaving his body with the motion. "I had to explain my shock somehow."

"It was quick thinking." Her lips curled in a tentative smile. "Though you did go a little too far."

"I was only being honest." His dimple flashed. "It seemed a better choice than kissing you, anyway."

She glanced at his mouth and let out a shuddering laugh. "Yes, kisses would not have been a good diversion this time."

His fingers curled into fists. "I'll admit, I was tempted."

Besieged by vivid memories of his embrace, her heart twinged. "I thought I would never see you again," she whispered.

"I certainly never dreamed I'd find you here." He gestured at the opulent room. "A Lady of the Realm. Here's a question for you. Do you realize your sari alone costs more than the payment I gave you?"

She smoothed one hand over the fine cloth. Beads and knots of embroidery scraped against her palm. "I am aware of that."

"So why not sell it instead of coming to me for cacao?"

"Am I supposed to walk around naked?"

Desire flared in his eyes, but his voice remained carefully controlled. "You have other clothes. I've seen them."

She snorted. "Those clothes aren't fit for a Lady and you know it."

"I felt sorry for you," he said, suddenly fierce. "I worried about you, wondering if my beans were enough to get you out of trouble and how you were managing in Farbank. I expected to see my embroidered cloth in the marketplace any day." He let out a bark of laughter, the sound ugly and raw. "Maybe I yet will, since you have much finer things all around you."

She twisted her mother's ring on her finger. "You have no idea what you're talking about."

"You lied to me. You aren't desperate, unable to wait a single night for your beans."

She jerked, stung by his words. "I let you into my mind, Quintin, to lay such fears to rest, and now you don't trust your own gift?"

He stepped back, confusion wrinkling his wide brow.

She spun the ring around and around on her finger. "My payment was two days late as it was."

"You shouldn't need to accost strange men for a piddling pouch of beans." Quintin scowled, the expression unnerving on his genial face. "Does skulking about at night give you a thrill?"

"I told you before, I needed the beans."

He pointed at the remains on the tray of delicacies. "Your family sprinkles ground cacao on food meant for the tax collector, and you're trying to tell me twenty measures means so much to you?"

"That cacao isn't mine." She crossed her arms, ashamed to think of how she had pilfered beans from the kitchen a time or two, before Simon found her regular work. While lockpicking was dishonorable, it was better than stealing from her own family. "Lord Harold a'Taric a'Fermice a'Marana prefers cacao with his midday meal and we were simply fortunate enough to dine with him."

"Then why not ask the Trilord, *your father*, to loan you some of his cacao?"

"And how would I pay him back without my sneak work?"

"You're his daughter. He wouldn't ask you to repay—"

"I tried asking my father for help." She took a shaky breath, rattled by remembered pain. "Fermena knows I did. I was twelve years old and hardly knew which way was up when it came to the temple. And then Patricia had her horrible fall. I was desperate. I asked my father for help. And do you know what he said?"

Quintin shook his head, his dark eyes serious.

"He told me to turn Mystic Patricia out. He insisted I demote her and replace her with someone more competent." Her arms tightened around her middle, her fingers squeezing her elbows. "Patricia ruined her health tending my mother through her dying days, and my father wanted me to cast her aside like a dried-up nanny goat."

"What did you do?"

"I refused. What else could I do? I couldn't betray Patricia after all she had done for my mother, though my father didn't agree. My mother sequestered herself at Aerynet at the end, letting us all pretend she wasn't dying. I think deep in his heart my father blames Patricia for my mother's death, which is ludicrous. When I refused to get rid of her, he was furious."

She jerked her chin up, resentment surging through her. It never stayed buried long. "He said if I wasn't going to listen to his advice, then he didn't want me crying to him for handouts. And so I haven't asked him for help, not ever again."

Quintin tugged at his ear. "He told you to fend for yourself? Inexcusable. A temple is too heavy a responsibility for one so young."

"I was twelve, fully grown in the eyes of the law, and my mother always wanted me to inherit. I'm glad the Novenary named me the next Lady a'Fermena in our line. Aerynet is truly my greatest source of joy, though I do wish Patricia had recovered more fully."

"How did she survive at all?"

"By the grace of Fermena, obviously. I spent a day and a night in my temple praying for help." Her legs had gone numb from kneeling on the steamroom floor as desperation and panic made it hard to push the prayers past her lips. Lucy kept vigil with her, proving herself to be more loyal and steadfast than Em's own father. "And then Simon came, a gift from the Goddess."

Quintin's eyes widened. "Your criminal contact is blessed by Fermena?"

"I've always thought so. As we were praying, he arrived at Aerynet." Simon had a habit of showing up at odd moments with gifts for his sister, though his help then proved far more valuable than a piece of honeycomb or a bent hairpin. "When he heard our plight, he offered to trade some valuables for cacao. I did sell some clothes and jewelry then, out of sheer desperation."

"I'm sorry."

She shrugged, not sure if he was sorry for his earlier pique, or for the general state of her life. "I'm much happier earning my beans than begging for charity. I am beholden enough to my father as it is, for saris and such." She waved at the remains of their meal.

"I'm growing less fond of your father by the minute."

"I shouldn't be so candid." She bent to pick up the tray. "It is difficult not to be honest, since you already know the worst of my secrets."

"I've never had much use for dissembling." Warmth flickered in his eyes. "I'm glad you can be honest with me."

Chapter 17

The rest of the afternoon passed in a blur for Quintin as he tried to focus on mundane accounting tasks.

Every time Lord Harold opened his mouth, Quintin's hands twitched with the urge to yank the breath from the pompous fool's throat rather than listen to him speak. If the Trilord had been able to put aside his grief long enough to help his daughter, then Lady Em would not have turned to lockpicking as a profession. Which meant Ophelia would not have hired her, and then Fredrick would not have caught them kissing.

Better caught stealing? Elkart's tail twitched. He lay on the floor at his Hand's back, where he had dozed away the afternoon.

No. Kissing is safer than stealing. Em was right about that, though their charade had led directly to their current dilemma. He suppressed a sigh. Despite the risks, he could not truly regret meeting Em.

"My daughter will be here shortly to escort you out," Lord Harold said as they concluded their tasks for the day.

With a nod, Quintin mentally braced himself for the encounter. His feelings for her were as tangled as an apprentice's quipu, though the effect she had on his body was as straightforward as it was alarming. Anxiety churned in his stomach, followed by annoyance.

By Fermice's Breath!

He was a tax-collector on a routine audit. The task should barely engage his mind, not swamp his heart with unruly emotions. Thank Fermena Em would be away at temple the next day, giving him a reprieve from his inappropriate reactions.

"Tomorrow I'll want to inspect your lands," he told the Trilord. "Perhaps Master Jonathan would be good enough to escort me."

"My daughter can show you around well enough."

Quintin paused in the act of wrapping a quipu around his hand. "Lady Emmanuella?"

"As I've said, she will see to your needs during your audit."

Aghast at the suggestion, Quintin choked on a protest. Riding around in the forest with her for hours would be pure torture.

She was utterly untouchable, he knew that. A lowly tax-collector did not go around mauling a Lady of the Realm. Even flirting with the daughter of the Lord he was auditing risked his position. But away from the prying eyes of her family it would be too easy to forget she was Lady Emmanuella. Over the course of a day alone together, he was sure to give in to the temptation of finding out if she still smelled like jasmine.

"Lady Emmanuella is quite familiar with the homestead lands and surrounding forest," Lord Harold said in a reassuring voice. "She won't lead you astray, I assure you."

Quintin took a deep breath to clear his mind and focus on the most salient argument against Lady Em leading him anywhere. He had expected to be spared her distracting presence the next day because she was a Lady of Air, of Fermena to be exact. He frowned and unwound the quipu to check his memory. "She is Lady Emmanuella a'Fermena, is she not?"

"She may be a Lady of the Realm," Lord Harold agreed, "but she is very comfortable on her okapi."

"I'm not questioning her ability to ride. I do wonder what she will be doing at Merdale at all tomorrow, on Fermenasday of all days."

"She has a duty to you." Lord Harold sniffed. "I will not have Merdale accused of dishonoring an agent of the Luminary."

"To be attended by such an esteemed personage is a far greater honor than a simple auditor has any right to expect." Quintin pressed his hands together and bent at the waist, the bow awkward in his seated position. "I assure you, I will take no offense if your son escorts me tomorrow. A patron's place is at her temple on its holy day. It would be passing strange to have her stay at Merdale for my sake."

A ruddy tone suffused the Trilord's leathery cheeks, but he waved a negligent hand, as if the matter did not concern him in the slightest. "Very well. Master Jonathan will greet you in the morning."

"Thank you." Quintin finished wrapping the quipu around his hand.

Elkart raised his haunches and stretched his forelegs out in front of him. *Trilord playing tricks?*

I'm not sure. While it was common for landowners to try to curry his favor by having an underling see to his needs during audits, Lord Harold's insistence that his noble daughter attend him was unusual. The Trilord might be hiding something and want Quintin distracted, or he might truly see nothing wrong with Lady Em missing the holy day of her temple. *Does he smell nervous?*

He smell like a deer in rut. On purpose. Elkart sneezed. *Human noses very broken.*

Quintin hid a smile and tried to pay attention as Lord Harold described what to expect riding the land the next day.

Lady Em appeared moments later.

He struggled not to look at her, since the Trilord had

yet to acknowledge her. Her presence pulled at him like a lodestone.

"Do you have any more questions?" Lord Harold asked.

"No, I expect the survey to go smoothly tomorrow." Quintin stood and bowed.

The Trilord returned his bow without rising and made a shooing motion at his daughter. "Show the auditor out."

Irritation flashed in her eyes before it was hidden by her bow. "It is an honor to serve."

Quintin's fingers curled around the cord encasing his palm. Dried flowers in a vase on the desk rustled in the breeze he stirred, but he harnessed his gift before it snatched the Trilord's air.

Em smiled a little too brightly. "Please come with me, good Han-Auditor."

Cursing his ridiculous reaction, he followed her from the room. He had plenty of experiencing dealing with arrogant nobles and knew better than to take offense at every little thing. In truth, Lord Harold was no worse than Quintin's own half-brothers. Em's perilous situation would unravel entirely if he didn't get himself under control.

In an effort to regain tranquility, Quintin inhaled slowly. The slightest hint of jasmine danced on the air, distracting him in a different way. Em's sparkling sari emphasized the graceful curve of her back and the subtle sway of her hips. From behind she looked like any other gently bred woman, but he would never forget her easy humor when teaching him to pick locks or the ardor in her reckless kisses.

Quintin felt like he should speak, though he had no idea how to talk to women under circumstances far less charged than these.

The bells of her payal chimed with every step as they crossed a courtyard.

When they reached the entryway, Lady Em turned and bowed low, one leg behind and her arms out to the sides.

"Thank you for your work here this day. May the Luminary be pleased with your efforts."

He frowned. Her flowery language offended his sense of honesty. He loathed the hidden meanings and secret barbs behind every word and gesture of the nobles. Trying to puzzle it all out was liable to give him a headache.

On the other hand, he didn't want to be rude, so he dredged up long forgotten etiquette lessons. "Your hospitality has been without equal."

"It has been my pleasure to serve."

Quintin cleared his throat, unsure if the spark of warmth he saw in her eyes was real or wishful thinking. He pressed his palms together and bowed deeply, before exiting the Merdale estate with Elkart at his side.

He rubbed his thumb against the rough threads wrapped around his hand. Should he take the quipu to Trimble tonight? Jardin was off the trade road between Merdale and Trimble, which meant he would have to walk nearly past his home on the way to the Tribute Office, adding more than an hour of travel to his evening.

If this had been an ordinary homestead audit, he would head straight home without question. Unfortunately, nothing about this audit was ordinary.

Should we go home or should we go to the Tribute Office? he asked his waccat. While he did not expect Elkart to have a satisfactory answer, the conversation might clarify his own thinking. At least he could trust his waccat to be honest.

Elkart's tail lashed in agitation. *Go home. Eat dinner. Office boring, useless.*

Fredrick is probably waiting for us, hoping to gloat.
Let him wait.

Quintin stroked the strands of the quipu. *I don't want him to think I'm avoiding him, that I'm afraid of him.*

You not afraid. He wrong twice.

Yet I am afraid. Quintin's feet slowed to a stop in the middle of the trade road. Fear lurked under his sympathy for Em, his irritation with her father. Even his lingering distrust because of her deception held an edge of fear.

Afraid of Fredrick? You Hand. He only weasel.

I'm not afraid of Fredrick. There was only so much the Bursar could do to him without appealing to the Troika and exposing himself. *I am afraid of what he has set in motion.*

Ever since Quintin had recognized Em in the Merdale vestibule, he had been stalked by the feeling something vital was lost or possibly gained. Somehow the foundations of his life had been altered, and deep in his heart he was terrified.

~ ~ ~

The sun disappeared behind the canopy trees surrounding the Merdale manor as Em positioned two low tables for the evening meal. She moved them close enough to the fountain for the diners to enjoy a refreshing mist while being far enough away to hold a polite conversation over the noise of tinkling water. The delicate balance would only get more complex as more guests arrived.

"Is supper ready?" Jonathan asked as he entered the courtyard.

"Not quite. I'm not done arranging the place settings."

"You didn't put me next to Gregory, did you?"

"I hadn't planned to. Why?"

"He's on a tear again, and I'd rather not have my appetite spoiled with lectures."

"What have you done this time?"

Jon gave her a wounded look. "Why do you assume it's my fault?"

Em shrugged. "Because it usually is."

"Gregory's in a snit about how much cacao I owe Curtis."

"I thought the bones were being good to you."

Jon waved a hand. "That was days ago. The bones are quite fickle, you know."

Em didn't know, not firsthand, and was glad of it. Her life was precarious enough without adding a penchant for gambling to the mix.

"Is Curtis here?" she asked. "Do I need to find a place for him at the table?"

"No, I chased him off as soon as he collected his beans. He was saying the most outrageous things to Mistress Catherine."

"He says the most outrageous things to me all the time and you just laugh."

"It's not the same. I've seen you practice knife fighting with the guards. You could eviscerate Curtis if you wanted. Catherine is different." Jonathan pulled an iris out of an arrangement in a nearby urn. He twirled the stalk between his fingers. "She's a shy and delicate flower. I don't want Curtis making her uncomfortable."

Em plucked the flower out of Jon's hand and returned it to the urn. "You're sitting there," she said shortly, pointing at a pillow at one end of the table. "Conveniently far from Gregory."

"Bless you, Em, for getting this all straightened out," Isabel bustled into the room with her babe on one hip. She made a few adjustments to the seats while the rest of the family trickled in to the courtyard.

Soon Em was seated on a pillow next to Lord Evan with her father across from her.

Once everyone was served, Lord Harold leaned forward to address Em directly. "I wanted to let you know, Emmie, the auditor does not want you attending him tomorrow."

Em stilled, torn between relief and regret. "Did he say why?"

"He gave me quite the lecture about how you should be at your temple on Fermenasday. As if a mere tax collector knows more than a Trilord about the duties of a patron."

"What nonsense," Lord Evan exclaimed. "A well-run temple has no need of its patron's attendance every week. The Novenary herself doesn't live in the same town as most of her temples and she is a fine patron."

"Nevertheless, there is no need to antagonize the taxman." Isabel pushed her plate out of the baby's reach. "I have enough to do without a triad of inquisitors underfoot while we prepare for the Allgoday festival."

"You are quite correct, Isabel." Lord Harold picked up his goblet and gestured at Em. "I'm afraid you're going to have to go to Trimble tomorrow."

"I am delighted to be at Aerynet tomorrow," Em said, with a genuine smile. "It is what I wished all along."

Lord Evan patted her hand. "I'm sure your temple is very nice, and your devotion to it does you credit. But it is only a minor temple. Not a nobleman himself, the taxman has no comprehension of the scope of your duties or how your time is best spent."

Lord Harold laughed. "You have the right of it, Evan. If I visited each of my temples on their holy days, I would spend a third of my time in prayer, and my temples are much larger and more influential than Emmie's little air shrine."

Her chin tilted up. "Aerynet may be small, but it does important work."

"I'm sure it does. It just doesn't need you there to do it." Her father tapped his fingers on the edge of the table. "You are old enough to do something more meaningful with your life."

Em took a sip of wine, swallowing the urge to argue in front of their guests.

Mistress Catherine cleared her throat. "Maybe we can

all go to Trimble tomorrow. I would like to see if the Verisian fabric vendor stayed in town."

Jonathan leaned forward with a grin. "Trimble offers a number of delights."

"Which you will have to miss." Lord Harold pointed at Jonathan with a gnawed curassow leg. "The Han-Auditor requested your escort specifically."

"What?" Jonathan gaped. "This is outrageous. I'm stuck squiring the little twerp around because Em doesn't know how to flirt properly?"

Isabel's shoulders moved in a languid shrug. "Maybe the auditor prefers the company of men. Perhaps Jonathan will be the one who needs to practice his flirting."

Em snorted at the ridiculous suggestion. "The Han-Auditor does not prefer men."

Isabel cocked her head. "How would you know?"

Em twisted her ring. Heat coiled in her belly at the memory of his kisses and the passion they shared mind-to-mind. "He called me lovely," she said quietly.

Gregory swirled the wine in his goblet. "From the gossip in the servants' quarters, his flattery was probably to cover his embarrassment after you tossed the welcoming tray on the floor."

"You threw the tray at him?" Jon rolled his eyes. "Taric's balls, no wonder he doesn't want you to greet him tomorrow."

"Language, Jonathan!" Isabel scolded.

Jon's gaze darted to Mistress Catherine as he muttered an apology.

Em's face heated. "I did not throw anything. It just slipped."

Lord Harold grunted. "Em's clumsiness aside, I have no doubt the auditor found her attractive. I saw the way he acted around her."

"He didn't find her attractive enough to spend time with tomorrow," Jonathan grumbled.

She glared at her brother. "Attraction has nothing to do with it. The Han-Auditor happens to recognize the importance of my duty to my temple."

Her father sighed. "Come now, Emmie, don't be naive. The taxman doesn't care about your temple. He's probably worried that if you wander all over the estate with him, he won't be able to control his lust."

Em's lips compressed into a hard line. "Are you doubting the honor of a Hand?"

Lord Harold eyed their guests, as if suddenly aware of their audience. "Not at all. I'm merely pointing out the lengths a Hand will go to for the sake of his word."

"Just because Jon cannot come doesn't mean we shouldn't enjoy a trip to town tomorrow," Isabel said, smoothly turning the conversation to what the Trimble market had to offer.

Em stopped attending their chatter. She lifted a glazed dumpling to her lips. Its gingery flavor evoked the taste of the simple curry Quintin had fed her. The dumpling turned to paste in her mouth as a wave of sadness washed over her. How she longed for that meal. Not only because it filled her belly, but because Quintin had offered it to plain old Em.

Knowing the worst of her, he treated her better than those who only saw her at her best.

Chapter 18

The next morning, Em knelt on a prayer rug in a place of honor at the front of Aerynet's sanctuary. The smell of incense and the sound of a dozen voices singing praises to Fermena wrapped around her like a favorite blanket. One voice in particular filled her with joy.

Mystic Patricia stood before the altar, her wrinkled face a mask of exaltation as Fermenasday hymns flowed from her lips. For the other eight days of the week, Patricia's mind was clouded and confused, her movements slow, her voice quivering and uncertain. She was as likely as not to spend the entire day abed, dozing and disoriented. But every Fermenasday she rose from her pallet and joined them in the sanctuary. There she shined, lifted up by the rituals and routines of a lifetime devoted to the Goddess.

Em swallowed past the ache in her chest and gave thanks to Fermena for Patricia's weekly transformation. She spared a prayer for Quintin, too, grateful his respect for her duty to her temple allowed her to be there.

As they began the final hymn, Patricia raised her arms in a reflection of the outstretched wings of the statue of Fermena hung above the altar.

Em closed her eyes, unable to bear the idol's uncanny likeness to her mother, and the disappointment she imagined on its carved face. Shame scrabbled at her throat.

Nine generations of women had made Aerynet prosper, while Em struggled to keep her acolytes fed. She did not know how her sickly and often bedridden mother had managed it. Though back then Patricia had the strength and wisdom to care for Mother, while her current infirmary left Em caring for the mystic instead. Em was alone in a way her mother never had been.

Perhaps Lucy was right, and it was time for Em to find a husband. She squirmed at the thought of being trapped in holy matrimony with a man like Lord Evan. He would expect complete devotion and obedience in return for feeding her acolytes. If she failed to please her husband, Aerynet would pay the price. She shivered, unwilling to take such a risk.

"May Fermena's wisdom guide you to your highest self."

Em opened her eyes to find Lucy standing at her elbow with a platter of sliced partridge meat. As patron of Aerynet, Em was offered the first morsel. She murmured her thanks, though part of her wished she could politely turn down the meat she herself had provided.

Ben followed behind Lucy with a tray of steaming tea.

Forcing a smile, Em accepted a cup. She sipped her cinnamon tea and tried not to think how much it cost. It was the sacred duty of all temples to provide sustenance and rest to any who asked for it. As her father never failed to remind her, her temple was a minor one. Their petitioners were a shrinking group of devoted followers whose offerings to the Goddess barely covered the expense of their weekly repast.

The beads at the entrance rattled. Whispered conversations sprang up like flames. She heard the words "outlaw" and "stocks" before she saw Simon kneel on a prayer rug off to one side near the door. Her heart lightened with relief at his freedom, though she kept her face impassive as she cast a quelling look at the other petitioners. The whispers died as quickly as they started.

She turned back to the altar where Patricia waited with her head bowed in silent prayer. Simon's presence pressed on her nerves, distracting Em from her prayers. He never came to Aerynet on Fermenasday. It boded ill for him to do so now.

After an interminable wait, Lucy and Ben joined the mystic at the front. The holy women led the devoted in a final song before Lucy stepped forward to dismiss the congregation. "Those who wish to stay and rest or meditate are welcome to do so. If you require a private blessing or desire to release a bird, please come to the altar."

As murmured conversations swirled through the sanctuary, Em selected a cage of songbirds. Simon's presence behind her was an itch between her shoulder blades she dared not scratch until the parishioners departed.

A couple dressed in wedding finery approached Patricia. The bride lifted her left hand which was tightly bound to her husband's right with a braided ribbon. "We ask for Fermena's blessing on our union."

The old mystic frowned, confusion clouding her eyes.

Lucy picked up Patricia's hand and laid it over the couple's clasped fingers, leaving her own on top. "May you live fully in each moment together, forgetting your past mistakes and your future hopes, for Fermena is the Goddess of Now."

Patricia's face cleared and her voice joined Lucy's for the rest of the traditional air blessing.

Em's throat tightened. There was so much hope and love shining in their eyes, she had no doubt they would relish each moment together. A blade of jealousy stabbed her. Such a joyful union was not what her father had in mind when he told her to wed. The knife twisted. Aside from her father's wishes, the needs of the temple denied her the choice to marry for love.

As the blessing drew to a close, the man handed Lucy a small purse with his thanks.

"Would you like to release a bird for luck?" the acolyte asked, gesturing at the cages.

Remembering her manners, Em cleared her throat. "Ben managed to catch a pair of love birds if you would like them."

The bride smiled. "How lucky!"

Careful not to acknowledge Simon in any way, Em led the bridal couple and a few other devotees to the narrow landing outside the door. Ben squeezed through the group and stood on the top step, a giant macaw perched on his forearm. He tossed his arm into the air, and the huge red bird took flight, soaring in circles around the yarumo tree.

Em opened her cage and shouted, "Blessed be, Wise Fermena."

Her words were echoed by the other parishioners, as they opened their cages. The landing was alive with flapping wings and squawking as half a dozen birds flew into the air. Em stomped her foot, sending the bells on her ankle jangling. The bride joined in, while none of the other women present had payal adorned with bells. As the birds disappeared over the top of a neighboring building, the congregants slowly dispersed down the staircase.

Em returned to the sanctuary where Lucy was leading Patricia back to the steamroom. Ben followed after her to release the rest of the caged birds. A lone petitioner, a pilgrim who subsisted on the scant offerings from temples each day, was deep in meditation on his prayer mat, while Simon sat silently in the shadows by the door.

Beckoning Simon to follow, Em headed to Lucy's room, where they could speak privately. Once they were alone she allowed herself to show her relief. "Would you like more tea?"

"Please." He sank down next to Lucy's low table with a sigh. His normally golden skin had a sallow tinge. "Jenny told me not to come. Begged me not to, but I wanted to tell you in person. Figure I owe you and my sister that much at least."

Em handed him a cup of tea, wishing she had something more to feed him. He had always been thin. Now his clothes hung off his shoulders.

"Tell me what?" she asked, though she wasn't certain she wanted to know.

"I'm leaving Trimble. You heard the crowd when I came in, whispering about me." His face tightened, his cheekbones sharp as knives. "There's no place for me here now."

"But, but . . ." Her throat closed, choking off her words.

"I know you'll be in a bad way without me." He gripped the cup with two hands. "I'm sorry I didn't get you the payment for your last job."

"I got paid."

The teacup rattled as he placed it on the table. "Impossible!"

"The *job* was impossible! You don't want to know how many ways it went wrong, though I did get paid, and got a few extra beans for your wife as well. It might not be as much as you were owed—"

"Anything at all is more than I'd hoped for." He closed his eyes. Wrinkles fanned out from the corners of his lids, tired creases that hadn't existed a week ago. "It doesn't matter. The stocks ruined me. I've gotta leave. Jenny's uncle has work for us, away from the city and all its troubles."

"What will I do without you?" she whispered, barely registering his words over her growing panic. She was doomed. With her one source of independent income wiped out, she would have to rely ever more heavily on her father. Not only would she have to find her own sneak work, she would have to sell her own goods. Quintin's fine cloth couldn't help Aerynet survive if she didn't get a good price for it. All she had worked for was collapsing around her.

"A Lady like you can find a better way to get beans." Simon sighed, regret making him look older than his twenty years. "I never should've dragged you into the sneak business in the first place. Now you can marry some fine Lord like you've always wanted."

She closed her eyes, fighting tears. Simon had offered to marry her once, more out of obligation than affection. She'd turned him down flat, ending their tenuous affair. He'd had an inflated sense of her prospects ever since.

"I'm sorry it has to be this way." He stood and bowed. "Fare thee well, Lady Emmanuella."

Lucy cleared her throat from the doorway. "May I accompany my brother home?"

Em nodded, holding on to her composure by the thinnest of threads. "May Fermena watch over your travels, and Marana guide your future, Simon."

He bowed again and left with his sister close behind.

While Lucy would try to change his mind, Em doubted she would succeed, nor should she. Simon and his wife were moving on to a better, safer life. Em's dependence on him did not change the wisdom of his decision. Simon had always been her salvation, though it had cost him dearly. He was right to end it.

How will I manage without him?

~ ~ ~

The afternoon was well advanced when Quintin turned his okapi away from a banana grove and rode deeper into the forest. The sounds of laborers calling to each other and the thwack of blades separating the fruit from the trees faded behind him to be replaced by the screeching of birds and monkeys. He took a deep breath and used his air gift to recall Lord Harold's map of his lands.

"Are we finished yet?" Jonathan asked from the okapi behind him. "We've been wandering around all day and this path leads to trackless jungle."

Quintin's mouth tightened with irritation. Master Jonathan had spouted one complaint after another since they left the manor. Would he have been better off in Em's company? For all that she was a dangerously tempting enigma, at least she wouldn't fuss about the trials of missing her aestivation.

"This is the last section. Once we finish here we can head back to the house." Quintin closed his eyes to focus on his mental map.

"With all its winding trails, this section will take hours." Jonathan heaved out a sigh. "I swear to you, it's only suitable for tapir hunting and my sister's jaunts."

Quintin's eyes snapped open. "Lady Emmanuella enjoys riding in the forest?"

"Em loves hunting. She's always riding off with her atlatl and coming back with monkeys or birds. When she's not at her temple, she's out here in the trees." Jonathan chuckled. "I think she likes the excuse to escape Isabel and her matchmaking."

Without acknowledging the painful bit of gossip, Quintin urged his okapi forward onto a narrow track between the trees. A clever man could hide an illegal cacao tree or two in an overgrown area like this. The Novenary controlled the sacred plant, only allowing its cultivation on lands dedicated to the support of temples and holy orders.

The primary purpose of an audit was to catch any landowners growing the forbidden beans. "Let's get started on those winding trails. It is my duty to inspect all the land and I won't have it said I was negligent."

"Oh, negligent you are not." Jonathan's okapi plodded after Quintin. "I can attest to it."

"You'd better," Quintin muttered. Fredrick was sure to scrutinize the accounts of this particular audit for any hint of favoritism. True to his intentions, Quintin scanned the surrounding vegetation for hidden trails. He stretched mental fingers into the jungle, attuned to the gnats attracted by cacao flowers.

The underbrush rustled as Elkart ranged away from the trail to sniff out water sources for cacao trees. *Bogbear!*

Quintin yanked his okapi to a halt.

Jonathan cursed as he struggled to control his mount at the sudden stop. "What are you doing?"

"Silence." Quintin made a slashing motion with his hand. *Is the bogbear here?*

No. Scent old. Elkart moved deeper into the jungle. *From before goat attack.*

Quintin's tense shoulders relaxed. He nudged his heels into the okapi's side to get it moving again. "My waccat scented a bogbear," he said over his shoulder by way of explanation to Jonathan.

"Are you certain? We're too far north for bogbears."

"Some wild animal attacked a homestead upriver. Our best guess is a bogbear. Elkart says the trail here is old."

"By Taric's Bones, I would hope so. Running into a bogbear would be about the only thing to make this day any worse."

Quintin twisted around to face his companion. He had let any number of complaints slide, but the spoiled noble went too far. "Is my company so distasteful? Or is it doing your duty for Merdale that you find objectionable?"

Jonathan shifted in his saddle. "I meant no offense, honored Han-Auditor."

Quintin grunted and turned his back on the man.

"You're a good sort, especially for a tax collector." Jonathan sighed. "It's just we have some very special guests visiting right now, and I'm most aggrieved to miss a day of their company."

"Understandable, but duty comes first."

"I know," Jonathan grumbled. "I'm here, aren't I? Though I don't know why you'd prefer my escort to my sister's. Even if she's no great beauty, she's better company than I am."

"She is a Lady of Air," Quintin said, torn between amusement and disgust. "It is an affront to the gods to have a Lady of the Realm attend an auditor on her holy day."

"Lady or not, she has a duty to Merdale as well."

"Which she fulfilled yesterday, and I imagine will fulfill again tomorrow when I am assessing your father's stores, while you are given plenty of time to visit with your diverting guests."

Jonathan grumbled, not arguing the point.

Given her family's blatant disregard for her temple duties, why did Lady Em stay in residence at Merdale? Perhaps she had no choice. Quintin shivered at the memory of the angry man who haunted Em's thoughts. Desperation had led her to risky dealings with such criminals. He could understand why she would not want to stretch her resources further by feeding and clothing herself. Even if the price was her pride.

Worry washed over him, a familiar feeling where Em was concerned. Strange how learning she was a Lady of the Realm only heightened his confusion, without reassuring him at all. He wished he could spare her the need for her nocturnal activities. All he could do was keep her secrets and protect her from the worst of the Bursar's schemes.

Hours later, they exited the winding trails through the jungle and entered Merdale's more cultivated lands.

Elkart leapt out of the underbrush. Mud caked his paws and spattered over his flanks. *All done?*

The survey is finished. Quintin pulled a twig out of his hair. *And no cacao to be found.*

Eat soon! Elkart dashed down the trail toward the manor house. His waccat's boundless energy made Quintin feel even more tired by the day's work. Scratches from overhanging branches stung his arms, while sweat trickled down his spine, providing no relief in the muggy heat.

As the path widened, Jonathan urged his okapi up to ride abreast.

Quintin slanted a glance at his escort. "We've finished in plenty of time for your evening meal."

Jonathan brushed a leaf from his shoulder. "I hope I have time to change."

Quintin quirked his brow. "Hard to impress your important guests when you smell like okapi."

"Exactly so." Jonathan grinned. "You may care more about honoring the gods than spending time with a charming woman. Not all of us have your admirable priorities."

"Must be my fine temple education," Quintin said in an attempt to needle the Trilord's son. He had never met a noble who didn't scorn those so poor and desperate for learning that they turned to the temple schools.

Jonathan's only response was a quiet snort.

They broke through the trees between the house and the stables, giving them a clear view of the gardens and circular lane.

Jonathan stopped. "The palanquins have arrived."

A hundred feet ahead, two dozen guards lowered a pair of palanquins to the ground while outriders led okapis away. Elaborately dressed nobles emanated from the silken boxes.

Quintin held his breath, waiting for Em to appear. While he gladly avoided spending the day with her, he longed for a glimpse of her face.

The party of nobles swelled. Lord Harold laughed with another older man who held himself like a Lord of a similar rank. Finally, a head crowned with Em's distinctive reddish hair emerged.

Quintin held his breath.

The woman straightened.

His air escaped in a hiss. "It's not Em."

Jonathan turned sharply, his eyebrows arched. "No, not *Em*," he said with a slight emphasis on the name. "I'm surprised you could tell the difference at this distance. Our cousin Violet has been mistaken for my sister more than once."

Quintin pressed his lips together, grudgingly grateful to Jonathan for not making a stink about his use of a pet name for Lady Emmanuella. "Your cousin cannot be the charming woman you were referring to earlier."

"You'll never hear me deny Violet's charms. I'm wise enough to stay on her good side." Jonathan pointed at the man standing next to his father. "Our interesting guests are Lord Evan a'Maral a'Tarina, a diplomat from the capitol, and his daughter Mistress Catherine."

"Mistress Catherine does look lovely. The other gentlewoman must be your brother's wife, Mistress Isabel."

"Correct."

Quintin frowned. "Where is Lady Emmanuella? Didn't she go to town to visit her temple?"

"Yes." Jonathan snorted. "She would spend every waking minute at that temple if Father let her. At a guess I would say she will ride an okapi home, or a palanquin will fetch her later. Father will be vexed if she spends the night when she needs to attend you in the morning."

"Does she sleep at her temple often?"

"More often than is probably wise." He rolled his eyes. "She was there at least once this week. It is safer for her to stay at her temple than to venture through the city after dark, especially on Taricday."

"Only fools and outlaws roam the streets on Taricday," Quintin murmured, falling back on the old adage to cover his embarrassment. His misguided gallantry had left Em sleeping on his floor rather than at her temple as her family believed.

"Exactly so," Jonathan agreed. "Though she should learn to plan better and not get caught in town so often.

Father wants her to wed and start a family, and I'm sure Lord Evan won't want his wife devoting so much time to a minor temple."

Quintin's okapi pranced as his hands clutched the reigns. "Your sister is betrothed to Lord Evan?"

"Well, not officially. The Lord is in mourning until the new year. It wouldn't be seemly for him to pursue a courtship yet."

Which meant she hadn't broken any vows with their wild kisses. Why wasn't the knowledge more reassuring?

"My father would be delighted with the match," Jonathan continued. "Lord Evan is wealthy and connected and I've heard he was very indulgent with his late wife. He'll certainly need a lot of patience dealing with Emmie."

Johnathan's words landed like a punch in the gut. Quintin had felt so benevolent giving her a bit of undyed linen. Lord Evan could shower her with silk and jewels.

He should not be upset she had a Lord for a suitor. It didn't matter if the man was rather old. Quintin's own parents had a similar gap in their ages. Such a match was only fitting for a Lady of the Realm. In fact, Quintin should be happy for her, especially if the marriage freed her from her sneak work.

So why did the thought of the Lord flirting with her make him want to retch?

Chapter 19

"Now don't let him run amok when it's time to eat." Quintin wagged one finger at Terin after breakfast the next morning. He joked to hide his nervousness at letting his waccat out of his sight. "He should only kill it if he's going to eat it. Except for the bogbear, obviously."

Elkart bumped his head against Quintin's hip. *I be fine. Hunting fun.*

"I appreciate you lending him to me today," Terin said, his tone devoid of his usual banter. "Ophelia needs Felice with her this morning, and I don't like my chances against a bogbear with only Maven at my side."

Quintin drummed his fingers on his leg. "The sooner you get that thing caught, the better."

"If I don't catch it soon, I'll need to try a new tactic. We can't have it running around on Allgoday when drunken revelers might stumble into it."

"I might be able to help you tomorrow. Today I need to take an account of Merdale's stores."

Have fun with knots.

You be careful and come back in one piece. Quintin gave his waccat one last pat, bowed to Terin, and headed down the road. He tried to enjoy the solitude of the early morning walk to Merdale though part of him longed to join the trio in their hunt. Chasing a phantasm through the woods sounded downright relaxing compared to a day dodging temptation with Em in the dusty corners of the sprawling villa.

He arrived at Merdale without incident and managed to

accept a bite from the welcoming tray without spilling it all over Lady Em.

She rose to her feet with a strained smile. "My brother tells me you want to tour the storerooms this morning."

"I need to record your father's holdings before tabulating a proper tribute. Do you have the keys, or will someone else be escorting me?"

"I am attending you." Her face tightened. "The manor is very thin on diversions this morning, so my brother and cousin will be accompanying us as well. My cousin has the keys."

His brow furrowed. By law and custom, landowners could have as many witnesses as they wished to the accounting, but Quintin didn't relish an audience. "Your family finds watching the tax collector tabulate accounts entertaining?"

"My brother is convinced you are sweet on me, and my cousin hopes to catch us flirting." She toyed with a simple silver ring on her right hand. "They've probably laid bets on whether you'll kiss me before noon."

He sniffed. "I would like to think my self-control is strong enough to prevent me from groping you in front of your family."

She looked up at him through her lashes. "That's why I accepted their company. To bolster my own self-control."

His body warmed while his treacherous mind teased him with memories of her wild kisses.

Turning away abruptly, she strode down an arched breezeway. The swaying feathers in her hair beckoned him to follow.

She led him to a storeroom set between a courtyard and a cooking area. From the open door he could hear laughter inside. The sound stopped the moment Quintin stepped over the threshold.

"You've already met Master Jonathan." Em gestured at her brother and a woman standing close together in one corner of the storeroom. "This gentlewoman is Violet of Trimble, daughter of Mystic Marcus a'Fermice. She is our cousin and guest for the week."

Violet's face wrinkled as if she smelled waccat droppings. He recognized her as the woman with the overzealous guard in the marketplace. From the expression on her face, she remembered him as well. She gave a bow shallow enough to border on rude.

Quintin precisely mirrored the gesture as Em completed the introduction.

"These are the common stores, mostly staples and foodstuffs for use in the kitchen." Em waved a hand around a room larger than his chamber at home. Shelves loaded with clay jugs and lumpy sacks reached to the ceiling, while barrels crowded the floor.

Quintin nodded curtly and stepped over to the nearest barrel. "Are spirits kept here?"

"Those are in a separate storeroom," Em replied.

He unwound the quipu from his hand before making his way methodically around the room, sniffing at spices, estimating amounts, counting jugs and recording everything on the quipu.

Through it all Em stood by the door, poised as a practiced Lady.

Jonathan lounged against one wall, grinning at Violet as she whispered and tittered behind her hand.

Not bothering to use his gift to eavesdrop, Quintin went to work. He needed no distractions from his accounts. The sooner he finished this mundane task, the sooner he would be done with the assignment.

Once he finished tallying the goods, he turned to Em. "I'm done here. Where to next?"

Violet twirled a ring of keys around one finger. "Since you were so interested in spirits, let's go there."

Frowning, Quintin trailed behind the sashaying woman. He would have been happier following Em's lead.

Violet unlocked a door not far from the first storeroom and flung it open.

Jonathan sauntered in to peruse the shelves as Violet latched on to Em's arm and dragged her into the room. "Which ones will your father serve at the celebration, do you think?"

"I'm sure I don't know." Em extracted her arm from her cousin and backed away, nearly colliding with Quintin in the doorway.

His fingers made knots with practiced ease as he moved around the room counting bottles and jugs. It was a good thing the tally needed little of his attention, since Em was so distracting, and not in the way he had expected. She froze on the threshold, her hands clenched and her breathing shallow. What frightened her so?

When the tally was done, Violet shooed him out and locked the door behind them. They visited three more storerooms in much the same manner, with Violet leading the way and Em waiting in the hall, unwilling or unable to enter any of the cramped rooms.

"I'm done here," Quintin announced after accounting all of Lord Harold's linens. "Let's go to the cacao vault."

"Why don't you lead the Han-Auditor to the cacao stores, Emmie?" Violet tapped a finger against her lip. "I'm quite sure I don't know where it is."

Quintin offered his arm to Em, glad not to be trailing after Violet for once.

Her body felt as stiff as a marionette beside him, nothing like the easy harmony they had shared during their other walks together. He covered her cold fingers with his hand.

Keeping his gaze fixed ahead, he gave her a quick squeeze and sent his air gift out to brush against her defenses.

She bit her lip and let out a quiet sigh.

When he breathed against her mind a second time, he felt no resistance. He formulated his thoughts carefully and blew them through their linked hands. *What's wrong?*

I don't like storerooms. There was a complex mix of thoughts behind her simple statement.

How can a thief not enjoy a treasure trove?

I always like knowing how I'll get out again. Her fingers tightened on his sleeve. *Three people is too much. The exit isn't clear.*

Violet brushed passed them to unlock a door and throw it wide.

I certainly wouldn't trust your cousin to get out of your way. Quintin stepped into the room, unconsciously dragging Em in with him.

She struggled to disengage from his arm, before stumbling forward and crashing into him.

The door banged shut. Yawning darkness filled the room.

Em yanked out of his grip. Flesh slapped against wood.

"Have fun counting beans with the Auditor." The thick door muffled Violet's words.

"Jon? Violet?" Em cried, her voice keening into the black void. "Let us out."

Fading laughter answered her.

A vise closed around Quintin's lungs, while disjointed images of a dying woman invaded his thoughts. The nightmare wasn't his own, yet it dug into his mind with blood-soaked claws.

Em banged her fists against the door. Her rasping breath echoed in the tiny room.

Desperate to fight off the horror spilling from her mind, Quintin slapped his hands against his chest. His gift dragged air into his lungs, granting him the focus needed to sever the mind-to-mind connection. The nightmare images faded.

Fear, thick and choking as smoke, remained.

He swallowed hard to fortify his water. Usually his weak water gift did not allow for such potent emotional sharing. He did not want to think of what it might mean to have his heart tied so closely to hers.

Opening his mind to the air around him, his gift penetrated the darkness. Em scrabbled at the door, her breath little more than sobbing gasps. He needed to break through her fear before she injured herself. He gripped her shoulders.

She jumped and squeaked.

"We're fine, Em."

"We're trapped in here," she choked out. Her body swayed toward his.

Trying to give her strength, he wrapped his arms around her waist. She pressed more fully against him, their bodies fitting together like two halves of a whole. His face nuzzled her hair. The smell of jasmine tickled his senses.

A shiver wracked her frame. "It's so dark."

"There is a candle in front of us. If you touch it, can you light it?"

"How do you know where it is?"

"My air gift. I can see in here, though not well." He guided her hand to a sconce by the door. "There. Can you light it?"

"Yes, thank Fermena, Tarina, and Marana." Relief chased some of the strain from her face.

The candle sputtered to life under her fingers. While balanced folk took such acts for granted, to him the fires they lit always seemed like a tiny miracle, as mysterious as the spark of life.

He felt more than heard her sigh. "I've been trapped in here before."

"Your brother has locked you up before?" Rage flooded through him. He wanted to rip the last breath of air from her brother's body for terrorizing her so.

"No, no. It was an accident and had nothing to do with Jon. My mother collapsed across the door and I was too little to move her out of the way. It was the first time I realized how sick she was." She shuddered. "I know the vault is not to blame for her death, yet I can't stand the way it smells in here."

Quintin turned her to face him, his blood pumping fury. "All the more reason your brother shouldn't play mean tricks."

"Violet was the one who locked us in here. My brother just goes along with her nonsense."

"He's a coward." Quintin's voice was little more than a growl. "If I had a sister, I wouldn't let anyone scare her."

Her face softened. "I'm sure you would make a very good big brother."

He winced, his anger receding. "Yes, that's me. Good old brotherly Quintin."

"You say that like it's a bad thing."

A dark and heavy pause lingered after her words. "Quintin?"

He closed his eyes, blocking out her curiosity. "Do you want me to tell you a story?"

Her hand pressed against his chest. "Please."

He covered her hand with his, trapping its warmth against his heart. "At the beginning of my training to become a Hand, I fell madly in love with one of my year-mates. She was a beauty, sweeter than a glass of watermelon wine. She liked me, too. Soon I was one of her dearest friends, her closest confidant."

He paused, surprised at the rawness of the old wound.

Em's fingers curled into his kaftan. Her breath fanned over his face.

Inhaling deeply, his lungs filled with her air. "She liked me so much that when she decided to seduce one of our mutual friends, she trusted me to sneak her into his room, into his bed. And when he broke her heart, who should she turn to but good old Quintin, always ready to dry her tears."

Em's free hand cupped his face, her thumb brushing across his cheekbone.

"I was like a brother to her, Em. Still am. And I'll be damned if I'll be like a brother to you, too."

"You are nothing like my brothers," she promised.

Quintin opened his eyes. What did she mean?

Her fingers slid into his hair. Rising on tiptoe, she covered his lips with her own.

Chapter 20

Her kiss was everything Quintin remembered and more. He opened his mouth, welcoming the invasion of her tongue. She tasted like spiced cider, and smelled faintly of jasmine and something else, something uniquely Em. The rasping slide of her tongue made him forget everything but the way she felt in his arms.

Desire swept through him. He clung to her, reveling in how her curves fit against his body.

With a groan, he buried one hand in her hair, mussing its neat coils. Feathers brushed against his fingers, a stark reminder he kissed Lady Emmanuella, not Em the outlaw.

Quintin raised his head, gulping air and trying to regain his sanity.

"I've dreamed about your beautiful body, aching to touch you again." Trailing kisses along his neck, she whispered the words against his skin.

He moaned and grasped her shoulders, lacking the will to push her away, though he knew he should.

She gripped the fabric of his kaftan and hauled the edge past his hips. Her hands slid under his clothes, caressing his back, his sides, his stomach. "How did an air-gifted auditor end up with such a perfect body?"

"I was a sickly child," he began, hoping to distract her with words and distance himself from the pleasure of her warm hands against his flesh. "Scrawny, prone to chills. When I came into my gifts, I was all air and water with nothing left for earth. Such an imbalance isn't healthy. My instructors insisted I strengthen my body to compensate. I work hard every day to keep my body strong."

"And then you hide all your efforts under a shapeless kaftan." She lifted his clothing out of the way to feather kisses over his stomach and chest. "I like knowing your secret strength. Others might see a scrawny auditor, while I know the truth."

She swirled her tongue over his nipple.

He arched his back and moaned. How could one touch send pleasure reverberating all the way to his toes? "Ferel's breath, that feels good."

"I can make it even better." She hooked her fingers into the top of his trousers.

"No." He gripped her hands. He could imagine Violet returning to find him with his trousers around his ankles. Her caustic laughter would be the least of their troubles, but that vision alone ruined the mood.

He raised Em's knuckles to his lips. "I'm not going to lose my virginity to a Lady of the Realm in a cacao vault while on an audit. The Troika would take turns roasting me alive."

"I know. You're right." Smiling sadly, she squeezed his fingers. "It's impossible to think when I'm touching you."

To avoid kissing her again, Quintin dropped her hands and backed away. He focused on straightening his kaftan and fixing his queue.

She adjusted the feathers in her hair. "Are you truly a virgin?"

His ears burned. "Yes."

"What about the friend you mentioned?"

"I was only twelve at the time. She's a few years older. Our age difference is unimportant now. It seemed vast nine years ago."

"Surely in the time since then you've had opportunities—"

"Opportunities, yes. Inclination, no." He had tried visiting a brothel once with Ulric. Reeling from some falling out with a woman, his year-mate had taken to drinking and whoring nightly. Finally, Ulric's agitated waccat refused to accompany him on his destructive path to the stews.

Quintin had gone instead, his head turned by a half-baked plan to keep Ulric out of trouble and maybe gain a little experience with women for himself. But the whores had not been what he expected. Harsh and jaded, they had filled him with pity, not desire. They reacted to his discomfort like piranhas on a dying fish, their crude flattery shifting to cruel mockery in a heartbeat.

Always on edge those days, Ulric had exploded in his defense. Quintin barely managed to drag him from the brothel without bloodshed. After that his inexperience seemed more a blessing than a curse.

"Being slightly younger than my friends has given me a unique perspective on all their wretched attempts at love. It has not been hard to resist temptation."

Until now.

He crossed his arms over his chest to stop himself from reaching for her. "What about you? Are you virginal?"

She tucked and straightened her sari, restoring her appearance as a proper lady. "I'm not as strong as you, able to turn away from a moment's release and a spot of comfort when it's offered."

He felt a pang. "I didn't mean to deny you comfort."

"Have no fear, you've been a great distraction in this vile place." She smiled ruefully. "I wouldn't want you to think I'm always jumping on men in the dark. As a Lady, my opportunities have been somewhat limited."

"Not all of your suitors are to your liking?"

She snorted. "I never touch potential suitors. I wouldn't want to raise their expectations of marriage."

He twitched, stung by her blunt assessment. She was far above his station, undeniably so. Yet it hurt to be so summarily dismissed from the ranks of possible suitors.

"My first lover was a street urchin and a longtime friend." She smiled fondly. "He was the one who taught me how to pick locks after I conceived a terror of enclosed spaces. He thought it might calm me to be able to break my way out whenever I wished."

"Do you wish to break out now?"

"I don't have my tools."

"You have me."

"You're too big to fit in the lock."

He chuckled, glad her humor had returned. "Well, I happen to be carrying a very precious gift from a beautiful woman." He reached into a pouch attached to his belt and pulled out a worn pick.

She threw her arms around him in a hug that made him stagger. "Oh, thank Fermena."

He clasped her to him briefly, before edging away. "I take it you don't want to wait for someone to have mercy on us."

"My cousin's sense of mercy is distinctly warped." She snatched the pick and pressed it against her chest. "Or do you want to do it? To practice?"

"I think we should let the best in the business get us out of here."

She nodded and faced the door. Head bent over the tool in her hand, she muttered, "You know all my secrets."

He almost laughed aloud. He'd never met anyone who surprised him as much as this woman. "Surely you have one or two left for me to uncover."

She cast an annoyed look over her shoulder before tackling the lock.

Wispy black hairs curled around the exposed curve of her neck, tempting him to lean over and kiss her soft skin.

He cleared his throat. "I must know a few more of your secrets than your cousin though, if she thought it would be a worthwhile trick to lock you in."

Em paused. "How will we explain the unlocked door?"

"Your family doesn't know about your street urchin friend?" No wonder she thought he knew her so well, when the people closest to her knew nothing at all. "Never mind. We can pretend your cousin fumbled and didn't lock it properly."

In short order the door swung open, spilling light and fresh air onto their faces.

"Thank Fermena's Sweet Breath." She stepped into the hall, her shoulders straightening.

He plucked the pick from her unresisting fingers. Her smile made his chest ache. He pressed a kiss to her mouth so quickly he ended up catching more teeth than lips.

She reached for him, but he ducked back into the cacao vault. "You stay out here, while I make my tally."

She followed him into the vault. "Quintin—"

He pressed a finger to her lips as the sound of raised voices in the hallway caught his attention.

"Really, Jonathan, I cannot believe you would play such a rotten trick on your sister," an unfamiliar feminine voice remonstrated. "She has been the soul of kindness since we arrived."

Quintin shooed Em out of the cacao vault in time to see the woman Jonathan had identified as Mistress Catherine turn the corner and stop.

"I swear to you, Em's as up for a prank as anyone," Jonathan said as he appeared next to her.

"Or maybe the joke is on me." Mistress Catherine crossed her arms. "Since you didn't actually lock your sister in with the Han-Auditor."

Jonathan gaped at the open door. "How did you get out?"

"You're lucky Violet doesn't know how to lock a door properly. Why did you allow her to try it?" Em planted her hands on her hips. "Do you have any idea of the trouble we'll be in if word of this gets back to the Troika? Father will kill you—"

"Calm down, Emmie. We were coming to let you out. Where's your sense of humor?"

Quintin's blood roared in his ears as all his anger at Em's feckless brother flooded back. His hands twitched. He wanted to yank the air out of the pampered noble's lungs until he felt as trapped and frightened as Em had in the vault.

"Imprisoning a tax collector in the middle of an audit is not amusing, Jonathan!"

"Apologize to your sister." The words came from deep inside Quintin, from a place he scarcely recognized. A gust of wind swirled around Jonathan, ruffling the loose sleeves of his kaftan.

Em stared at Quintin in openmouthed horror.

"And me," he hastily added. After putting a halt to her kisses in the vault, it would be the height of foolishness to expose his tender feelings to her family. "Make your bows and your apologies, and then you may go," he told Jonathan, proud of his officious tone.

The gentleman's face puckered like a child facing a medicinal draught. "What?"

Quintin closed his hand in a beckoning gesture, pulling enough air from the miscreant's nose to trigger a coughing fit. "The words you are looking for are, 'I humbly beg your pardon for dishonoring a Hand and through him the Luminary of Destin. Though I am unworthy, please have pity on me for disrupting your work and frightening my sister.'"

Em's lips curved in a polite smile, though her eyes flashed a warning. "The Han-Auditor is far too kind, to show such concern for the unseemly reaction of a stranger."

"You were terrified," he snapped. "What's unseemly is to have your own flesh, breath, and blood treat you so poorly." He wanted to growl and snarl like a waccat protecting a cub. Jonathan reminded him all too much of his own noble brothers, who would do as they liked to anyone in their power and never suffer a consequence in their lives. Still, the intensity of his anger frightened him a little. He drew a calming breath, struggling to rise above the storm of emotions swirling in his heart.

Mistress Catherine shoved Jonathan's shoulder. "You are better than this, Jon."

Jonathan touched his throat and eyed Quintin before pressing his hands together and bending at the waist in a deep and respectful bow. "In the name of the Troika, please accept this apology from their most humble and unworthy servant. I swear to you, I meant no disrespect."

Quintin narrowed his eyes. "I should report you to the Reeve, you know. You and your cousin could use a day or two in the stocks."

"No." Jon's knees buckled. He knelt with his forehead nearly touching the floor. "Please, no."

"Have mercy, good and honorable Hand." Catherine clasped her hands together. "What Jon did was thoughtless and cruel. He sees the error of his ways."

"If his sister can find the grace to overlook his grievous transgression, then perhaps I can be lenient as well."

Jonathan shuffled until he was on his knees at Em's feet. The sight filled Quintin with an unholy satisfaction. "Dearest sister, please forgive me for my part in your distress. It was unworthy of me as your brother. I am sorry, Em."

She wiped at her eyes, her voice trembly with tears. "I forgive you, Jon."

"Next time," Quintin warned, "you'd better risk getting on your cousin's bad side instead."

Chapter 21

A few hours later, Em waited outside while Quintin tallied the contents of a root cellar. Her stomach gurgled at the smell of frying onions from the nearby cooking area. The morning was nearly over. She turned her face up to the sun, enjoying the warmth on her skin, though the midday heat wasn't enough to chase the ice from her bones.

A chill had settled over her ever since speaking with Simon. She'd spent a restless night, worrying about the future of Aerynet, which left her raw and vulnerable to her fear of the dark storerooms. While kissing Quintin had been foolish and weak, at least she had felt warm for those few moments in his arms.

"I'm finished."

She smiled as Quintin emerged from the underground storeroom. The morning had passed swiftly but uneventfully since their adventure in the cacao vault. "What would you like to see next? Do you tally our personal effects?"

"Not usually, no." He unrolled the quipu and stretched it out before him. Knotted strands dangled from a thicker cord down to his knees. His eyes moved up and down as he inspected the threads. A dark lock escaped his queue and curled over his cheek.

She crossed her arms over her stomach to stop herself from pushing the errant curl back in place. He appeared so serious and self-contained, but she knew a dimple formed in his cheek when he smiled. She knew the planes of his body under his shapeless clothes. And the taste of his kiss. Her fingers bit into her elbows.

He wrapped the quipu around his hand. Something, desire or despair, flickered in his eyes. "I am done with my audit. The new Merdale quipu is complete. It's time for me to go."

"Oh." She licked her lips. "Can I escort you to the lane?"

His mouth curved in a smile too small to bring out his dimple. "Please do."

She walked next to him through the gardens at the front of the house. Bees buzzed in lazy circles above flowers drooping in the noonday sun. A dove cooed in a fig tree, the mournful sound mirroring Em's mood.

Her lips tightened with annoyance at her melancholy. She should be relieved he had completed his task without revealing her secrets and be glad to see the last of him. Instead, a mantle of loneliness settled over her shoulders at the thought of saying good-bye.

At the edge of the garden, he pressed his palms together and gave her a deep bow. "Thank you for your hospitality."

Her heart swelled. A simple bow was not enough to convey the depth of her emotions. She dropped into a modified version of the welcoming pose. "You have honored us more than we deserve, good Han-Auditor. We humbly hope our tribute is a worthy reflection of our esteem for the Luminary."

Gravel crunched as he shuffled his feet. "You may tell your father I will return in the new year to collect."

She bit her lip and straightened. "After Allgoday, Mistress Isabel will return to the welcoming duties."

"It is probably for the best," he said quietly.

"Agreed. Good-bye, Quintin." She fled before she embarrassed them both. The bells on her ankles jangled with her hasty steps. A pair of doves flew from the fig tree with a drumming of wings at her approach. She slowed as she reached the tree. When she returned to the house, she would be expected to join her family for their repast.

Em leaned her forehead against the smooth bark of the tree. She should not have touched the Han-Auditor. Everything only seemed so hopeless because the taste of him clung to her lips.

"Surely a Lady, so young and pretty as you, has no cause for distress?"

She jerked her head up to find Lord Evan sitting on a bench in the nearby shade.

He stood and moved close enough for her to see the concern in his watery eyes. "A taxman can chill the most festive atmosphere. Will he deny you the pleasure of your aestivation today?"

She pushed away from the tree and straightened her sari. "No. The audit is complete."

"Good. It's been a shame to have you occupied with other duties during our visit." Lord Evan's face crinkled in a smile. "I look forward to seeing more of your lovely face."

"It is an honor to serve."

"Are you headed in for the midday meal?" He offered his arm. "Let me walk with you."

As much as she wanted to politely refuse, Simon's desertion forced her to consider marriage as a solution to her financial woes. She placed her fingers on Lord Evan's elbow. Panic clawed at her throat at the thought of charming a proposal from the older man, but she dared not snub him either.

He patted her fingers as he towed her through the gardens to the house. "Give us a smile now. You're so pretty when you smile."

She forced her face to obey, though her stomach twisted in rebellion. A lifetime with the old Lord would grind her soul into dust.

He frowned as they entered the central courtyard. Two tables stood on opposite sides of the tinkling fountain, each with only one seat empty.

Relieved at the reprieve, Em extracted her hand and pressed her palms together for a polite bow. "I'm sure my father will want you to sit with him. I'll join the other young people."

Lord Evan returned her bow. "I hope you'll walk with me again sometime."

She nodded in silent acknowledgment before approaching the table of her peers. Since the group included Violet and Jonathan, who had been joined once more by Curtis, she would rather eat at a table full of snakes. Unfortunately, she had no excuse to flee and couldn't leave Mistress Catherine to face the vipers alone. Missing Quintin more than ever, she sat and filled her plate.

"What did you do with your pet auditor?" Violet asked.

"The audit is over. Han-Auditor Quintin has left the estate."

"So soon?" Jonathan snorted. "He dragged me all over yesterday. Why, we didn't stop for a proper aestivation or anything."

Em tore a dumpling in half. "I think he found our hospitality somewhat lacking today."

Violet selected a date from the serving dish. "If he didn't enjoy his time here, the fault is entirely yours, Emmie. We gave you the perfect opportunity to kiss him."

Curtis made a gagging sound. "Why would anyone want to kiss a taxman?"

"Hush, Violet." Jonathan glared daggers at his cousin. "He threatened to have us put in the stocks, and I think he would have done it, too, if I hadn't groveled for leniency."

Curtis tossed a frown between Jonathan and Violet. "What are you up to now?"

Laughter erupted from their parents' table on the other side of the fountain.

Catherine shot a look in their direction before leaning

forward. "Violet and Jon locked the auditor in the cacao vault with Em. Or at least tried to."

Curtis's jaw dropped. "Are you insane?"

Em swirled the wine in her goblet. "You don't think the idea of trapping me in a windowless room with a man is amusing?"

"When the man in question is a tax-collector? No." He waggled his eyebrows at her. "If I were the lucky man, then it would be most entertaining."

She gave an exaggerated shudder. "I can think of no worse fate than being locked in a closet with you, Curtis."

Violet leaned forward. "Did you enjoy your time with the taxman, then?"

Em's pulse picked up as she remembered her mindless terror, and the heady comfort of Quintin's voice in the dark. She gritted her teeth and met her cousin's avid gaze. "The Han-Auditor was not amused."

"I imagine not." Curtis clicked his tongue. "While I've no great fondness for your father, Jon, trying to bring a trio of inquisitors down on his head is going too far. You'd better pray to Marana the auditor feels forgiving when it comes to tabulating Merdale's tribute."

Violet pouted. "If Em was a better flirt, Uncle Harold's tribute would be less, not more."

Curtis snorted. "If Han-Auditors were so easy to sway, every landowner in Destin would prostitute their sons and daughters."

"Not every auditor is sweet on Em." Jon swiped a dumpling through the curry on his plate. "You should have heard him talking yesterday. I figured he'd be delighted for a moment alone with you."

Em sniffed. "A Hand would never take advantage."

Violet cocked her head. "So you didn't kiss the taxman while you were alone?"

"Absolutely not." Em took a sip of wine to banish the salty taste of his skin.

"I knew you were hopeless about men, Emmie." Violet's tone dripped with malicious delight. She held out a hand to Jon. "Pay up."

He grumbled as he removed a ring from his pinky and gave it to Violet.

A frown wrinkled Catherine's forehead. "What are you doing?"

"Jon and I made a little wager." Violet's lips curved in a satisfied smile as she tucked the jewelry away. "I knew Em didn't have it in her to seduce the taxman."

Em's fingers tightened around the stem of her goblet. She glared at her brother. "Is that why you came to unlock the door? Did you hope to catch us in an embrace?"

"No, I didn't." Jon's tone was defensive as he slid a sideways glance at Catherine.

She frowned back at him. "He wouldn't have let you out at all, if I hadn't insisted."

"At least one of you has some sense." One corner of Curtis's mouth quirked up. "You are far too good a woman to be wasting your kisses on the likes of Jon."

Catherine blushed while Jon gaped like a fish.

"We haven't been kissing," he sputtered.

Curtis lifted one black eyebrow. "Then you are doubly foolish for proving yourself a knave before you've had the pleasure."

"Maybe Mistress Catherine isn't interested in Jon's kisses," Em protested, though from the look on the young woman's face, the opposite was more likely to be true.

"Most of us aren't afraid of a little kissing, Emmie," Violet huffed. "We don't all want to die a virgin like you."

Curtis laughed. "So, who are you hoping to catch alone on Allgoday, Violet?"

She lowered her eyelashes. "Is anyone interesting going to be here?"

As the pair turned to flirting, Jon leaned closer to Em. "I am sorry, you know. I shouldn't have gone along with it, either the wager or the vault."

"Let's pretend it never happened and hope the Han-Auditor does the same."

"You're a good sort, Em." Jon gave her arm an affectionate squeeze. "Thanks for forgetting it."

Em feared her responding smile looked pained. She would never forget those soul-shattering moments in Quintin's arms.

~ ~ ~

Quintin spent his midday break practicing his staff forms. With fresh kisses from Em to distract him, he knew rest would be impossible, and hoped the exercise would burn the tension from his body. His attempt was only half successful. Even as his body dripped with sweat from his exertions, his mind continued to dwell on their time alone in the vault.

He wished Elkart had not gone off hunting with Terin. While the waccat had little of use to say about Em and kissing, at least he could distract Quintin from his own circling thoughts.

When the afternoon shadows stretched across the yard, he stopped putting off the inevitable and headed to the Trimble Tribute Office. Relief washed over him when he found the Bursar out. Quintin sat down at his work table and hung the new Merdale quipu on a frame. He spread the old one over the table and soon was lost in the painstaking work of comparing the two.

"Is that the quipu for the Merdale estate?"

His mind on accounts and tributes, Quintin blinked up

at Bursar Fredrick. "I wanted to compare my quipu with last year's and tighten my knots."

"Are you done then?"

"I need to do some final tabulations, but I won't have to go back to the estate until it is time to collect."

Fredrick tapped his staff of office against his thigh. "How was the audit? Was Lord Harold hospitable?"

"Lord Harold was as welcoming as anyone is to a taxman." Quintin decided not to report Violet's ill-advised prank. The Bursar was likely to salivate at any stories involving Em.

The Bursar smirked. "And was his daughter friendly as well?"

Quintin stared his superior in the eye, trying not to think about the feel of her lips on his skin. "Lady Emmanuella was most gracious."

"Gracious, huh?" Fredrick rocked back and forth on his heels. "She's quite pretty."

"She is as lovely as any lady," he answered in as bored a voice as he could manage.

"I always enjoy the look of a woman in a sari." Fredrick's thick tongue smacked over his lips. "Like a present waiting to be unwrapped."

"Careful, Bursar." Quintin's fingers clenched around the strands of the quipu as he battled his temper. There was nothing to be gained by rising to Fredrick's bait. "I'm sure the Novenary would not approve of you speaking of a Lady of the Realm in such a manner."

Fredrick's eyebrows shot up. "I'm only talking about it. You're the one doing it."

Quintin's face felt tight. "I beg your pardon?"

"I forgot. It's our little secret." Fredrick leaned forward and lowered his voice. "You had better hope I don't forget in more auspicious company than this."

Sweat prickled along Quintin's back. He wouldn't give Fredrick the satisfaction of seeing him squirm. "I'm sure you'll remember playing games with the Troika's tribute is no laughing matter. Especially in auspicious company."

Fredrick narrowed his eyes. "Make sure you get your quipu nice and tight. We wouldn't want you to slip up like Sarah did."

"I am always careful with my knots." Quintin turned back to the strands dangling from the frame. He would have to be extra diligent when tabulating the tribute so the Bursar had nothing to complain about. "You're right. I had best get back to work."

Fredrick stalked away, slapping his staff against his palm with every step.

Chapter 22

The next morning Quintin carried a steaming bowl to the table at the edge of the garden.

His mother followed close behind him with her own morning dish of curry. "Are you done with the audit?"

"Almost. I have some accounting to do."

"I was hoping you could help me carry watermelons to town today, but maybe tomorrow would work as well. It is good business to have melons on the water gods' days."

"I can walk with you into town. I won't be going back to the estate." He tapped his spoon on the edge of the bowl. "Ever."

Hannah stirred her curry. "You sound very . . . grim about it."

"It is simply fact. I can do the rest of my work from town and so I will."

She put down her spoon and leaned her forearms on the table. "You've been distracted during this whole audit. Is something amiss?"

Quintin took a bite as he considered his answer. He could tell her about Fredrick's likely blackmail, though the story was complicated and exposed secrets that weren't his to share. Part of him longed to confide how he felt about Lady Em, if only to help him sort out his own thoughts. His mother would understand his dilemma better than most. "The Lord of the estate has a lovely daughter. She's been attending me these last few days."

"Ahhh." She leaned back. "So you are reluctant to see the audit end."

"It is for the best. An audit is no place for romance."

"Romance? You want to court this gentlewoman? There must be more to her than a pretty face."

"There is. Oh, there is." More than he could ever explain to his mother. "It doesn't matter. The audit is over and I'll never see her again."

"Well, why not? In a month or two, you could try to find her at her father's temple."

"I'm not going to court her." He blew on a spoonful of curry to cool it. "She's not merely a gentlewoman. She's a Lady in her own right."

"There is no law against a Hand marrying a Lady."

"Is that truly your advice? Because as I recall, loving a noble didn't work out so well for you."

"It did, actually." She smiled, the tender expression softening her careworn face. "I had many years of happiness with your father. I wouldn't trade them for anything."

"You weren't always happy." He had a vivid memory of his mother weeping before a major festival because his half-brother had ruined her only sari, leaving her with the humiliating choice of dressing as a commoner or begging off hosting duties. It was one of the few times Quintin remembered hearing his father yell. What rankled most, even after all this time, was his father blaming Hannah for dishonoring their guests. He never did find fault with his unruly sons.

"The good times more than outweighed the bad."

"Until he died and you lost everything."

"I was devastated when your father died, undeniably. But not because he was a Lord. Do you think I would have missed him less if he were a goatherd? That the widows of tailors don't grieve as much?"

The wooden handle of his spoon bit into his fingers. "The widows of tailors don't get kicked out of their homes."

"If your father had been a goatherd, he would have left his homestead to his eldest and I still would have come home to my mother. Edward had an obligation to his children and wanted to provide for them after his death. I respected his wishes."

Quintin studied his tight knuckles. "He didn't provide for me."

"Yes, he did." Hannah turned her bowl in her hands. "Your portion was only smaller because you were so young."

"And a bastard."

She dropped her spoon. "You know I don't like such language."

He gritted his teeth. "It's the truth."

Her shoulders hunched. "We said our vows before all nine gods as any wedded couple should."

"Which would have been enough if he hadn't been a noble." Nobles needed the approval of the Novenary to wed. Though his parents' union had been blessed by the gods, Quintin and his mother were shunned at his father's burning. When his father died, he'd lost not only his home but his very identity. Never again was he introduced as Master Quintin, son of Lord Edward a'Marice. "The way Father's family treated me, I might as well have been a bastard."

Hannah sighed as she dusted the crumbs on the table into a pile. "It's true your brothers never approved of Edward's relationship with me. They were embarrassed by my low birth and youth, though I think our happiness was the bitterest draught of all for them." She swept the crumbs to the ground. "Once your father died, I was glad to leave their petty anger behind."

His mother may have been glad to escape the arguments and insults, but he remembered listening to her cry at night during their long trek to Jardin. Though he tried to match her brave face during the day, her nightly misery had terrified him. "And you don't think any of your pain had to do with my father's title?"

"There are sad and jealous people in all walks of life." She touched his arm. "Don't reject this Lady because of her title alone."

He pushed his bowl away, his appetite gone. "She is being courted by a diplomat from the capitol."

"Oh." His mother's hand dropped back to the table. "Well, if her heart is engaged elsewhere, there isn't much you can do. Water flows where water will."

A warbler landed on a flower stalk in the garden, bending it nearly to the ground. The bird snatched a seed before flitting back into the trees. While Em's interest in Quintin was as fleeting, her caresses in the vault had not been those of a woman in love with another man. "I don't think she's in love with him."

"Then I guess the question is, are you in love with her?"

Quintin's breath caught painfully. "Yes," he hissed.

His mother gripped the edge of the table. "You must try to see her again, without an audit to inhibit you. Go to her temple."

He could barely hear his mother over the blood pounding in his ears. He was in love with Em. No, with Lady Emmanuella a'Fermena and he would be wise never to forget it. He'd known since he was a child that love led to heartache, doubly so with a noble, yet somehow he'd managed to fall for a Lady. How could he be such a fool?

Dishes clattered as Elkart jumped to his feet.

Quintin grabbed at the table to steady it. *What is it? Bogbear!*

What? The birds twittered merrily in the bushes, giving no sign of a predator nearby.

Not here. Maven has the scent. Elkart danced in place. *Time to go hunting!*

"What's happening?" Fear in her voice, Hannah scrambled to her feet. "What does he smell?"

"He says Maven's found the bogbear out in the jungle."

Go now! Elkart butted Quintin in the shoulder, rocking him.

Quintin sprang to his feet. "He wants to leave. I was going to carry watermelons—"

"Forget the watermelons." She made a shooing motion. "Go do your duty as a Hand."

~ ~ ~

"This sounds like a very agreeable marriage settlement."

Em froze in the hall outside her father's study. Why was Lord Evan talking about marriage with her father?

"A father does what he can to provide for his children," Lord Harold replied.

Em's fingers cramped around the edges of the serving tray she carried. Were they discussing her future without her?

"I think we should hold off until after Allgoday to make any announcement," her father continued. "I don't want to get in the way of Isabel's festivities."

The platter in her hands trembled as fury coursed through her veins. If she stepped through the curtain, she would end up throwing their refreshments at their heads.

"Oh, I quite agree," Lord Evan said. "The new year is a lucky time to make such changes, and besides I am officially in mourning until then."

A wave of despair washed over her anger. As infuriating as their presumptuous discussion was, it did offer salvation for Aerynet. She shuddered. There must be some other solution, but until she found it, she could not risk scorning the wealthy Lord.

"Do you have a plan for talking to the Novenary?" her father asked.

Heart pounding, Em slowly backed away. She slid her right foot along the floor to keep her payal quiet. While she understood the wisdom of controlling her temper, she did not have the fortitude to serve their meal with ladylike dignity.

"I can't imagine the Novenary will have any objections." Her father's odious friend chuckled. "I'm more worried about the bride's reaction."

She continued inching away, making it difficult to catch her father's response, though his laughter grated on her nerves. When Lord Evan joined in, she judged it safe to walk at a more normal pace. Perverse glee filled her as she absconded with their midday meal. Hunger pangs were a petty retribution for their machinations, but somehow made her feel better.

Moments later, she encountered Jonathan and Mistress Catherine in the family courtyard. She thrust the tray at her brother. "Here. Enjoy your aestivation."

"Thanks." Jon picked up a plantain dusted in cacao. "Fancy!"

Em bowed to Mistress Catherine. "Merdale offers the best to our honored guests."

"You're too kind." Catherine smiled and ducked her head. "Won't you join us?"

"I'm not hungry. I'm going to rest." Em hurried to her chamber, though she had no intention of trying to sleep. Alone in her room, she shed her sari and pulled on her hunting garb. Time in the jungle would help her think.

"Here you are, Em. Did you deliver your father's meal?" Isabel stepped through the beaded curtain and narrowed her eyes. "What are you doing dressed like a commoner?"

Em ran a hand over her soft kaftan and trousers. While her garb was more casual than a Lady's usual attire, it was a perfectly respectable outfit. "I'm going out hunting. A sari isn't practical in the forest."

"Going hunting?" A frown wrinkled Isabel's forehead. "Whatever for?"

"A little extra meat is always welcome at Aerynet."

"You'd be better off wearing a sari and hunting for a husband. Let him worry about that temple of yours."

"I can't trust Aerynet to someone who marries me for my limited earthly charms." Her heart ached. Lord Evan had no interest in her beyond her pretty face. How could she expect him to respect her opinions about her temple when he failed to ask her opinion on their marriage? There had to be another answer. She couldn't think with the walls of the house closing around her.

Isabel tapped her foot. "You're prettier than you give yourself credit for."

Em suppressed a sigh and reached for her atlatl.

"You are. You could shine like a jewel at the feast if only you attended to your appearance."

Em eyed the space in the doorway and considered squeezing past Isabel. "I'm sure my new sari will be very beautiful."

"Don't pretend you care." Isabel braced an arm across the doorway. "It will be the most beautiful sari you have ever owned, and you haven't tried it on."

"Why would I try it on? Does it need to be folded differently?" Fermena protect her from Isabel's latest fashions.

"No, no." Isabel waved a hand impatiently. "Have you no curiosity about how it will look? You have no desire to be beautiful? Fine. Then I will make you beautiful for your father, for your brother my husband, so they will be proud at the festival, and people will not whisper at you behind their hands as if you are a poor relation. Will you at least try to help me in this? Can you try not to embarrass us all?"

Em's face felt hot. "I always do my best to make my family proud."

Isabel raised one imperious eyebrow.

She gritted her teeth. "I will be the very model of a Lady at the festival, I promise."

"Well, you needn't be quite so demure." Isabel's eyes sparkled. "It is an Allgoday celebration after all. A little license is allowed, and you need to practice the fine art of flirtation."

"Jonathan's friends don't need any encouragement from me." The only man she wanted would not be invited.

"I think some of Jonathan's friends are quite charming. And if they are not to your taste, we have guests coming from all over Destin. If you try, you are sure to find someone fun to flirt with." Isabel leaned forward with a wicked smile. "An Allgoday festival is a fine time to test out a suitor, as it were, to make sure you are compatible in all aspects of married life."

"What if I'm not interested in marriage? I wouldn't want to raise expectations."

"It's all in good fun on Allgoday. You aren't going to break any hearts, I assure you."

Em tucked a quiver of arrows under her arm. "Scampering off into the bushes after sunset doesn't seem like the best way to find a nice man who respects me."

Isabel laughed. "Who wants a nice man? Especially on Allgoday! You need a man who fills you with fire."

"Nice men can be full of fire, too." The memory of Quintin's touch sent heat spiraling through her belly.

Smirking, Isabel wagged a finger at Em. "If you find such a paragon—a man who both respects you and fills you with fire—I suggest you hold on to him with both hands."

Em's stomach turned to stone. Isabel was right. Men such as Quintin were a rare treasure, but he had wisely resisted her seduction and would never come courting. He was a Hand, a man whose honor was above reproach, while she was a thief whose honor was for sale. The world would think she had set her sights too low if she accepted a mere auditor. She knew better and so did he.

Suddenly she felt sick.

"The best we can hope for is a man or two for you to have some fun with at the festival," Isabel teased.

Em's fingers tightened on her atlatl. "If you'll excuse me, I need to go now if I'm to return in a timely fashion."

"You persist in hunting? My parents are due to arrive today."

Biting her lip, Em swallowed a rude response. She needed the solitude more than ever if she was going to face their guests with any kind of decorum. "I'll be back in time to welcome your parents with the respect they deserve."

Isabel tapped her fingers on the door frame. "Promise me you won't let any of our guests see you."

"I won't embarrass you, or my father. I promise."

"Very well." Isabel stepped aside to let Em pass.

As Em entered the stable, she waved away the groom who jumped up to attend her. She picked up a light riding saddle, slipping the atlatl and arrows into the saddle bag.

Her okapi peered at her from over the door to his stall. Built for looks and speed, he was a beautiful animal, with a long graceful neck and intelligent eyes. He snuffled at her as she approached, his purple tongue flicking out to snatch a leaf off her shoulder.

She smiled and scratched the sensitive skin between the short horns on his wide forehead. Shifting her grip on the saddle, she opened the half door to his stall. She smoothed the blanket covering him from sloping shoulders to swishing tail before swinging the saddle onto his broad back. With one hand gripping his halter, she opened the door to lead him outside to the mounting block.

As she settled into the saddle and headed into the jungle, her spinning thoughts slowed. While Quintin's kindness and kisses were too sweet to forget, she needed to move past them. More important to her immediate happiness was finding a way to support Aerynet so she could refuse Lord Evan with a clear conscience.

It would break her heart to marry a man who neither respected her nor filled her with fire.

Chapter 23

Shadows carpeted the jungle floor even as the sun rose to its highest point. The air was heavy and still, filled with the whistles and twitters of birds flying through the tree tops, unperturbed by the intruders below.

Quintin shivered, feeling insignificant in the vast, trackless jungle. Struggling to keep Elkart's russet brown tail in sight, he pushed aside a sapling with his staff. *We're lost, aren't we?*

Not lost. The waccat's tail twitched. *Maven and Terin this way.*

Quintin ducked under a low branch. *And once we find Maven, will we be able to find our way home again?*

When we find Maven, we kill bogbear, not go home. Elkart's ear swiveled around as a twig snapped under Quintin's foot. *Unless bogbear hear you first.*

The large cat slipped between a pair of bushes with a soft rustle of leaves.

Scowling, Quintin followed. Branches snagged his clothes in three places at once. He flailed around with his staff in an ineffectual attempt to free himself, before crashing after his waccat in a shower of leaves.

Elkart waited on a narrow track, every line of his body radiating displeasure.

I'm taller than you. Quintin brushed a twig off his shoulder and frowned at a tear in his kaftan. *I can't move as quietly.*

The tip of the waccat's tail flicked against the ground. *Bogbear big. Not noisy like you.*

If we follow the path, I can be quieter.

Maven not on path.

Then what do you want to do? Quintin knocked his staff against the undergrowth, breaking more twigs. They had been tramping around for hours with no sign of Maven or the bogbear. He was hot, tired and irritable. Hauling watermelons for his mother would have been more satisfying. *I can't bushwhack through the jungle in silence.*

You go home. I hunt. Elkart jumped into the bushes and disappeared.

Be careful, Quintin mentally called after him. He received a wordless reassurance in reply.

The track cut through the forest in both directions with nothing to distinguish one way from the other. He shrugged and started walking. The path was sure to lead back to the trade road eventually, or to someone who could point him in the right direction. His footsteps squelched on fallen leaves, the sound small and lonely in the jungle. Bird song and the distant howl of a monkey grew louder and more ominous in his solitude.

He hadn't gone far when the tromp and rustle of something heavy caught his attention. His heartbeat kicked up a notch. Was the bogbear behind him?

He shifted to a two-handed grip on his staff.

An okapi and rider appeared around a bend in the track. "Quintin? What are you doing here?"

"Lady Emmanuella." Her name was little more than a sigh. His tense body relaxed, while his traitorous heart sang. "By Fermice's breath, am I glad to see you. I'm lost."

"Lost? Why are you on Merdale lands?"

"My waccat led me on a crazy hunt and then abandoned me, dratted cat." He peered past her. "What are you doing all alone, Lady Em? And in such casual garb."

She laughed. "Why am I ever out on my own and dressed below my station? I'm providing for my temple."

"Your temple?"

"I'm hunting." She patted the feathers of a curassow carcass tied to her saddle. "The fishmonger is vexed with us, so there will be no meat on the table this week unless I provide it."

"Your temple offended a fishmonger? Doesn't he want Fermena's blessing?"

"Maral is the patron of fishermen, and those who want an air blessing usually prefer Ferel to Fermena these days, more's the pity." She dismounted and gestured down the path. "Merdale is back there, if that is an acceptable way to get unlost."

He grimaced. "I'd rather not parade my foolish self in front of the manor house if it can be avoided. Do you know a more direct route to the trade road?"

"I think the trail along the ridge on this side of the garden is passable." She looped the okapi's reigns around her hand and murmured to turn him around.

The narrow path made it impossible to walk abreast. Quintin fell in behind them, his view dominated by the okapi's brown and white striped hindquarters. The plodding animal occasionally stretched out its long neck and nibbled the overhanging vegetation. The distant sounds of the jungle closed in around them, but this time the bird song felt more cheerful.

Em turned the okapi off the path onto an overgrown trail. The land sloped up before leveling off. Soon they were skirting the edge of a hill, with tantalizing glimpses of the manor house visible through the trees.

They paused where a fallen tree blocked the trail. Its massive trunk crushed the underbrush along its length, leaving a clear view of the Merdale gardens.

"Isn't it beautiful?" She made a sweeping gesture at the majestic garden beds, laid out like a tapestry below.

"It's lovely," he agreed, though his eyes were on the woman beside him. While he longed to express his admiration for her, his swollen tongue would never find the right words.

"It will look magical on Allgoday, with torches everywhere and the big bonfire in the middle."

"Looking forward to throwing your flowers on the fire?"

"I certainly don't begrudge the gods my thanks. Fire is a blessing to us all." She sighed deeply. "This past season has been challenging, especially of late. Yet the gods have not forsaken me or Aerynet. I must have faith Fermena will continue to take care of us. After all, she delivered you to be my salvation."

"I'm not sure if I've been a blessing or a curse," he muttered, thinking of Fredrick and his threats.

"You have been a blessing." She touched his arm. "Never doubt it. We'd have no provisions at all if it weren't for your beans."

Her hand warmed his skin, sparking memories of her touch on other parts of his body. He narrowed his eyes and tried to focus past his distracting response. Her words didn't make any sense. "You used my cacao to buy food?"

"And pay off the fishmonger." She let go of his arm to fiddle with the reins. "He was incensed about getting his payment late."

His bafflement grew. He'd assumed the man threatening her had something to do with her sneak work. He had a hard time imagining a food vendor terrorizing a Lady. "The man you were so afraid of was a fishmonger?"

"I'm not afraid of him." She bit her lip and wrapped the leather cords around her fingers. "I just don't want him spreading tales around the marketplace. We've enough trouble paying for food and supplies as it is."

He frowned. Why was she purchasing food for Aerynet? Was there something wrong with her temple lands? How many devotees did the place support? He opened his mouth to ask and grunted instead when her okapi sidestepped into him.

The animal snorted and tossed its head.

Em gasped. "What's that?"

The nightmare visage of a bogbear emerged from the side of the path. Dagger sized fangs bracketed a muzzle wide enough to crush a watermelon. Branches snapped as powerful shoulders pushed through the underbrush.

The okapi bleated.

"Get out of here," Quintin told Em.

The shaggy brown body squeezed between the trees and turned to face them. On all fours, it was as tall as a man.

Quintin braced himself with his staff at the ready. *Elkart!* he called mentally. *Bogbear here.*

His waccat's reply was a distant echo of acknowledgment, too far away to help.

Eyes rolling, the bogbear snuffled in their direction.

"Go away," Quintin shouted, shoving the words into the beast's brain, though the mind command had little chance of working against a wild animal at this distance.

The bogbear snarled, exposing a row of sharp teeth. It lowered its head and charged, shaking the ground with bounding strides.

Quintin's heart pounded. He held his stance until the beast was an arm's length away. Ducking to the side, he swung his staff. It thunked against the animal's skull.

The bogbear yowled. Curved claws swiped at Quintin.

He dodged the massive paw. Swung again with his staff. *Missed!*

The beast retaliated. Sharp claws slashed deep into his forearm.

He gulped, instinctively using his water gift to keep his blood in his body. The other end of his staff thwacked the animal's snout.

The bogbear snorted and shook his head.

Desperate for room to maneuver, Quintin stumbled back. He tripped and fell. Agony shot through his arm. He dropped his staff.

The bogbear roared.

Quintin saw his own death in the beast's eyes.

I love you, Elkart. he mentally shouted, praying his waccat was near enough to understand his final thoughts. He wished he could do the same for his mother. Wished he'd had the courage to tell Em how he felt. Regret burned a hole in his heart. He would die a virgin, too shy and scared to have taken a chance on love. *What a waste.*

The beast charged.

Without much hope, he yanked at the air in the bogbear's lungs. Though wind ruffled its fur, the beast didn't cough. A feeling of doom gripped Quintin.

He was about to try again when a stick sprouted from the creature's thick neck.

Yowling, the bogbear reared onto its hind legs.

Another stick sprouted from its belly.

The beast bellowed in rage.

Kicking up leaves, Quintin scooted away.

A third arrow appeared in the animal's side.

Quintin staggered to his feet, cradling his wounded arm against his chest.

With a final howl, the bogbear turned and crashed through the undergrowth.

This time he saw the dart before it struck the fleeing animal. Following the path of the arrow, he spun back to the clearing by the fallen tree.

His breath caught.

Em stood in the stirrups on her okapi, the length of her atlatl extended from her last throw. She looked like an avatar of Tarina, more mythical beast than mere rider, the coat of her okapi shining like her sunlit hair.

Quintin had never seen anything quite so beautiful in his life. "Magnificent," he breathed.

Her face split with a fierce grin.

Despite the pain in his arm, he grinned back, dizzy with sheer joy from being alive. Or perhaps blood loss. He gritted his teeth and yanked his blood back into his body where it belonged.

"That *was* magnificent, wasn't it?" She plopped back down in the saddle and nudged her okapi with her heels. The animal snorted and pranced but moved closer to Quintin. The sounds of the bogbear's retreat faded as she slid from the okapi's back.

"You are magnificent." He smiled shyly. "Nice shooting, too."

"You were the magnificent one, facing the monster on foot." She threw her arms around him and gave him a smacking kiss.

He flinched slightly at her enthusiasm. Her grip loosened. Quintin slipped his uninjured arm around her waist to stop her from stepping away, pulling her close enough to see the brown rings in her dark eyes. A gentle breeze stirred the soft hairs framing her face.

Her breath caught. Something warm and welcoming flickered across her face.

He tilted his head. On the verge of kissing her, he whispered, "I love you."

"What?" She jerked her head back. Her chin knocked into his nose.

He let go of her to rub his nose. "I love you," he said again, his voice nasal and distorted.

"You're only saying that because I saved your life."

"It's true I couldn't say it if I were dead." His heart pounded, straining his underused water gift. "When I was lying there and the bogbear came at me . . ." He struggled to contain his emotions, the wounds in his arm threatening to gush and bleed. "I was sure I was dead, and all I could think about was how I'd never told you how I feel. I love you, Lady Emmanuella a'Fermena."

"You hardly know me." She crossed her arms over her stomach, her face pained. "It's merely lust you feel."

"I do lust for you." He swallowed hard, fighting for control of his water gift. His arm throbbed with each beat of his heart. He fought through the pain and fear, his emotional strength strained along with his gift. "I desire you in a way I've never experienced before in my life. But it's more than lust, Em. So much more. I wanted you to know, come what may, I hold you in my heart."

"Oh, Quintin." Tears sparkled in her eyes as she pressed her fingers to her lips. "You are so sweet. I don't—"

"Nothing can come of it. I know that," he said, his voice harsh. He couldn't bear to hear her rejection cloaked in false compliments about his kindness. He knew she didn't see him as a suitor, yet he had hoped for so much more than this embarrassing response. "I don't expect you to return my feelings."

But oh, how he had hoped. Foolish, foolish hope. The back of his eyes ached with unshed tears. His control slipped, and a warm wetness soaked the sleeve of his kaftan.

Her eyes widened. "Quintin, your arm."

He slapped a hand over the wounds to staunch the bleeding. His gift was too weak. His water talent collapsed, and blood welled up between his fingers.

"I think I'm losing it," he murmured as the world went gray and fuzzy at the edges.

Chapter 24

Em grabbed Quintin as he swayed. His brown sleeve turned black and shiny with blood. She eased him into a sitting position next to the fallen tree. Muttering curses and prayers under her breath, she grabbed a knife out of her saddle bags and cut a long strip off the hem of her kaftan.

She knelt next to Quintin, pushing his sticky sleeve up past his elbow. And suppressed a gag.

His forearm was a mess of gore, with at least three deep gashes. He needed stitches, which meant summoning a healer from Trimble.

She anchored her makeshift bandage at his elbow and began winding it down his arm.

"Sorry," he mumbled, his voice little more than a slur. "I'm gettin' blood all over you."

"The only thing you have to be sorry about is hiding how badly you were hurt," she said, grateful he was able to speak at all. She pulled the cloth tight at his wrist before winding it back up his arm. "We should have tended your wounds immediately, instead of wasting time on kisses and . . ." Her voice faltered at the memory of his words. Love without hope tasted so bittersweet.

His head thunked against the log behind him. "Water gift had it under control."

"Obviously not." She jerked the end of the cloth harder than necessary as she tied off the bandage at his elbow. "Anyway, aren't you air talented?"

"Gotta touch of water. Enough to keep my own blood in my body. Most of the time."

Em sat back on her heels. He hadn't fainted, though it was a near thing. He slumped over as if too woozy to hold himself up.

"I'll fetch you a drink." She stepped over to her okapi and patted the animal's neck. He had done well holding steady in the presence of the bogbear. Murmuring praise, she untied a water-skin from the saddle.

The okapi tossed his head and sidled away from her.

The forest went quiet, all birdsong silenced.

Em dropped the water and grabbed her atlatl and arrows.

She did not expect the bogbear to return. Even with her short arrows, she had gotten in four good hits. The bogbear should have stumbled into the forest to die. She cursed softly. With Quintin too weak to stand, she couldn't take any chances.

Something massive crashed closer.

Her hands shook as she fitted a dart to her atlatl. Only three left.

A flock of birds burst from cover in a noisy flurry of feathers.

She cocked her atlatl over her shoulder, arrow at the ready.

A brown waccat rounded the bend, sliding as it took the turn.

"Elkart!" Quintin cried with joy.

Em let her arm fall to her side, her knees weak and wobbly.

The okapi snorted and tossed his head at the predator bounding toward them. Em grabbed the reins and pulled the okapi away from the Han-Auditor.

The waccat barreled straight into his Hand. He butted his head against Quintin's shoulder, nearly knocking him over.

Grinning, Quintin thumped and scratched his waccat with his uninjured hand.

Stroking the okapi's neck, Em moved him as far away from Elkart as the clearing would allow. She looped the reins around the branch of a sapling before retrieving the water-skin.

She returned to Quintin and pulled the cork. "You need to drink something, Quintin."

Elkart flopped on the ground, his back pressed against his Hand's leg.

Quintin trembled as he reached for the water.

She kept a grip around the bag to steady it. Their hands moved together to raise the spout to his bloodless lips. Her entire world narrowed to his hands and mouth.

After a couple of sips, he sat a little taller. "Thank you," he murmured.

"It's my pleasure," she replied, shaken by the truth of her words. Caring for him, being with him, it was always a pleasure. Something cracked inside her as she remembered his heartfelt words . . .

Come what may, I hold you in my heart.

As he raised the water-skin once more, she let her hands fall away.

Nothing can ever come of it. She would be a fool to forget it.

"If I gave you a boost, do you think you could ride?" she asked.

He handed the water-skin back to her. "I'd rather not go to the manor house."

"I don't see what choice we have." Her mouth tightened. Her promise to be presentable for Isabel's parents was as good as broken. "You need a healer and stitches, and the best way to get them is by sending a messenger to town from Merdale."

"You could take me home," he said in a quiet voice.

She sighed, surprised at the allure of his suggestion. She longed to climb on her okapi with him and ride away. Away from Merdale and her family and Lord Evan's unwelcome suit. Forget about being Lady Emmanuella and become plain Em. But it would mean turning her back on Aerynet.

Besides, Quintin was in no condition to ride off with her. Already blood seeped through the bandage on his arm.

"Please, Quintin, let me be the one to take care of you now."

~ ~ ~

A little while later, Em clambered down the hill holding the okapi's halter. She tried to keep the animal calm as they abandoned the path to cut straight to the lane.

Quintin flinched with every jostling step. Though she had torn another length of cloth from her kaftan to fashion him a sling, the support was not enough for his injured arm.

"Soon we'll reach level ground and be done with all the bumps." Trying to hide her fear, she gave him an encouraging smile.

He grimaced in response.

The okapi slipped, jerking as it caught its balance. Quintin hissed, his lips losing all color.

Em stroked the okapi's nose to calm him. He didn't like this steep descent either. The sooner they reached the bottom the better.

Elkart bounded down the hill with ease. He trotted along the lane toward the manor house, while Em and the okapi picked their path more carefully.

With the blessings of the gods, they reached the manicured lane without incident. "Do you need another drink? Or to rest a bit?"

"I need something stronger than water," Quintin muttered.

She patted his leg. "I'll get you some of Father's finest honey spirits as soon as we're back at the house."

"I don't think your father will want to share his finest with the taxman."

She slanted a glance up at him. "My father will have so many other things to bluster about, he won't miss the spirits."

He grunted, a ghost of a smile touching his lips.

She clucked at the okapi to get him moving again. Some of the tension left her shoulders as his hooves crunched on the gravel drive in smooth steady steps.

"By Fermice's foul flatulence," Quintin groaned.

She stopped the okapi. "What's wrong?"

"I forgot about Terin."

"Terin?" Unease trickled down her spine. "Wasn't he the man who saw me at your house?"

"Yes. He's a Hand, one of my year-mates." He rubbed his temple. "He's in the jungle nearby."

Her jaw dropped. "What?"

"He was hunting the bogbear, too."

"Is he going to come here?"

"Elkart told his waccat about my brush with death. He will want to help."

Her fingers twisted around the reins, while a strange buzzing sound filled her ears. "He can't come here."

Quintin leaned forward, pressing against the okapi's neck. "I assure you, Terin is the soul of discretion. He won't breathe a word of his previous encounter with you to your family."

She swallowed, her hands trembling. "What did you tell him about me?"

"Practically nothing. He thought you were a prostitute paid with the cloth. I somewhat disabused him of the notion and left him with the impression we were lovers."

"He won't say a word to my family?"

"Not one word." He gave her a crooked smile. "He'll tease me later for seducing a Lady, but he won't be so crass as to embarrass you. It's also possible he won't recognize you. It was pretty dark in my room."

Taking a deep breath, she banished the panic induced by the thought of getting caught. She rubbed the coarse cloth of her kaftan between her fingers. Between the bloodstains and the sacrifices made for his injuries, she was in a sorry state. "Once you're settled, I'll go put on a sari. It should help to look like a Lady. And if he lets something slip to my family, we'll manage."

"You want your family to think you're poking the taxman?"

She snorted softly. "Our charade is better than the truth."

As they approached the stable, a boy ran out to take the okapi. He stopped before he reached them and instead ran toward the house.

"Wait," Em called. Too late. He was already shouting for help.

Quintin grimaced. "So much for subtlety."

"We'll be getting you those spirits very soon now," she said with another pat on his leg. She led the okapi past the stables to the front of the manor.

Guards, most with their headdresses askew or missing entirely, boiled out of the barracks on the far side of the manor house. The front door crashed open. The head guard stepped out, his short sword at the ready.

"I am well," Em called up to him. "There is no need for alarm."

Eyes wide, he hastened down the steps. "What happened, my lady?"

"Em, is that you?" Isabel said from inside the house. "My parents will be here any minute." She appeared in the doorway. "You need to—Marana preserve us, is there blood on your face?"

Em's fingers flew to her cheek. "There is a bogbear in the woods."

"A bogbear!" Isabel pressed her hand to her chest and slumped against the door frame.

The head guard scanned the surrounding trees. "Where?"

"It is injured. Possibly dead," Em said. "It veered off the ridge path a little north of the fallen tree."

"I'll send two triads to bring it back."

"Please send a messenger to fetch a healer as well," Em instructed him.

"Yes, my lady." He gave her a hurried bow before heading to the barracks.

"Why do you need a healer?" Isabel clutched the edges of her sari as she fluttered down the steps. "Are you hurt?"

"I am unharmed. The Han-Auditor needs stitches." Em turned to Quintin perched on the okapi. "Do you need help getting down?"

"I can manage." Face tense, he swung his leg over the back of the okapi and slid to the ground.

"What is the Han-Auditor doing here? I thought the audit was over."

"The bogbear attacked a nearby farm," Quintin explained. Swaying slightly, he clung to the okapi's saddle. "My waccat and I foolishly went hunting for it and didn't realize we had crossed into Merdale lands."

Isabel frowned. "How did—"

Em stepped over to Quintin and offered him a shoulder to lean on. "I want to get the Han-Auditor inside and settled while we wait for the healer."

"Certainly." Isabel flitted back up the steps ahead of them.

"I think there is something else wrong with the arm," he told her in an undertone as they navigated the stairs. His fingers bit into her shoulder and more of his weight shifted on to her. "It hurts too much."

"The healer will figure it out," she assured him. "Until then, we have plenty of spirits."

Isabel held the door open for them. "Why don't you take him to the receiving room?"

Quintin and Em staggered into the vestibule in tandem.

Isabel slammed the door and spun to Em. "You need to go change. Now."

"After I get Quintin settled," Em bit out, surprised by the shift in Isabel's demeanor.

"There's a palanquin in the drive." Isabel's hands fluttered over her hair and down her sari, smoothing the fabric into place. "My parents have arrived."

Ignoring her fussing, Em steered Quintin toward an arched doorway to one side.

"Isabel? Do you know where—" Lord Harold entered the vestibule from the courtyard and stopped. "Taric's bones, Em, what happened to you? And what is the Han-Auditor doing here?"

Quintin straightened, dropping his arm from Em's shoulders. "A bogbear attacked—"

"You can explain everything in the receiving room." Isabel made frantic shooing motions. "I am about to welcome guests and I can't do it properly with you standing here bleeding."

Her stomach churning, Em tugged on Quintin's good arm to lead him out of the vestibule.

"Lord Evan and I have been awaiting our repast," Lord Harold told Isabel.

"Well, you are going to have to fetch it from the cookfire yourself or wait until my family is settled," Isabel said, her tone as tart as an unripe plum. "Em is in no condition to serve anyone anything."

Chapter 25

When they reached the receiving room, Quintin balked, unwilling to step on the carpet. It would be impossible to get bloodstains out of the lush wool.

Tightening her grip, Em towed him over to a pair of padded leather divans. "We can make you comfortable here."

"Mistress Isabel is not going to want me bleeding all over the cushions."

"Mistress Isabel should bite her tongue." She helped him settle on one of the soft seats. "My father knows better than to turn away a Hand in need."

He held himself stiff and straight, not daring to lean back for fear of aggravating his arm.

Elkart jumped up on the divan and pressed his head against Quintin's leg. *Rest here. Stop bleeding.*

I'll try. While the room was appointed for relaxation, with a number of floor pillows in addition to divans, the very opulence of it left Quintin ill at ease. "This is much nicer than the aestivation room you let me use."

"It's also closer." She scooped a pillow off the floor and tucked it behind his back.

As she leaned over him, he caught the scent of jasmine hiding beneath the sweat and blood. Their eyes met.

She hesitated, her body canted over his.

He reached out with his air gift, desperate to know what flickered behind her serious gaze.

Her ebony eyes widened for an instant, then her face softened.

He held his breath, sure she was going to kiss him.

"You should go wash up," Lord Harold said from the doorway.

She jerked upright. "I need to attend the auditor until the healer arrives."

"You shouldn't be attending anyone looking like that." Lord Harold's brows drew together. "What are you doing in such ridiculous garb?"

"I was hunting for my temple." Her chin tilted up. "A sari would have been most impractical."

Her father snorted. "You are supposed to be attending my guests, not spoiling your acolytes with extra meat."

"I will thank Fermena until the end of my days for giving her an excuse to be out in the jungle today," Quintin said mildly, reminding the Trilord of his presence before the pompous fool said something unforgivable.

Lord Harold stiffened, as if a brooch had poked his bottom. "Whether or not she was fulfilling the will of the gods, the fact remains she needs to go change." He jerked his head toward the door. "Put a sari on."

"The Han-Auditor—"

"I will attend the auditor." Lord Harold's wide lips flattened into a thin line. "An injured man will be better off without the kind of attentions you were giving him anyway."

She flushed and opened her mouth.

"I would like to take your kaftan with me after the healer fixes me up," Quintin said quickly. "I would be grateful if you'd go wash up now."

"Take it with you?"

"My blood's all over it, isn't it?" He felt a little dizzy looking at the red stains on her clothes. "I would rather not leave it behind if I don't have to."

Lord Harold puffed out his chest. "We would never use your blood to curse you."

"I'm sure you wouldn't, most honorable Trilord." Quintin gave him a respectful nod. "However, you can't speak for every charmaid on the estate. I'll be more comfortable taking it home with me, unless Lady Emmanuella doesn't wish to part with it or is likely to wear it again."

Em held out the skirt of her kaftan displaying bloodstains and the ragged edge where she had cut off bandages. She shuddered.

"She won't be wearing that again. You may take it with you."

Eyes flashing, her head jerked up.

"Besides, the bloodstains will alarm my year-mate," Quintin said, in case she had forgotten Terin's arrival. "Much better to meet him in a clean sari."

Em's eyes widened. "I'll return shortly."

She graced her father with a respectful bow before sweeping from the room with all the poise of a Lady despite her tattered garments.

"Willful chit," Lord Harold muttered, the bejeweled curtain swaying from her passage. "After she washes up, she should be attending to my other guests, not returning here."

Other guests not bleeding. Elkart's tail beat an irritated tattoo against the cushions. *Other guests not Hands.*

Quintin raised his eyebrows. "My deepest apologies for throwing your household into disarray with my injuries."

"It is an honor to serve," the Trilord muttered, though his peeved tone belied the polite words.

"I'm sure the Luminary will be glad to hear it." Quintin stroked Elkart's head. As a tax collector, dealing with irritated nobles was nothing new, though usually he did more to annoy them than dare to bleed in their presence. "As I said, my year-mate will be here soon. He'll escort me home after the healer stitches my wounds. I'm afraid I'll have to impose on your hospitality until then."

"I welcome you to make yourself comfortable in my home," the Trilord said graciously, either overcoming his irritation or hiding it better. He settled onto the other divan and picked up a hookah.

Quintin nearly groaned aloud. His arm throbbed with every beat of his heart, and his emotions felt scraped raw by his brush with death. The last thing he wanted was a cozy chat with Em's father.

"Has a healer been sent for?" Lord Harold asked as he cupped his hands around the glass base of the hookah.

"Your daughter took care of it." Quintin rubbed his waccat's back, taking comfort from the great cat. If only he could pretend Lord Harold was nothing more than a man he was auditing who he now had to impose upon. "I expect my friend to arrive first, since he was also in the jungle hunting the bogbear."

"Is that why you were on my lands?"

The leather cushion squeaked as Quintin shifted in his seat. Was the Trilord accusing him of trespassing? "Well, I'd given up the hunt and was trying to find my way home. Praise be to Marana for protecting my future and sending Lady Emmanuella to help me."

Lord Harold's eyebrows lifted skeptically. "So you claim my daughter encountered you by chance?"

"I beg your pardon?"

"You seem an honorable man." Lord Harold took a pull on the hookah and blew out a puff of steam. "May I be blunt?"

Say no, Elkart urged.

Quintin buried his fingers in the waccat's fur, tempted to follow Elkart's advice, though it probably wouldn't stop the Trilord from speaking his piece. Instead Quintin dipped his head in a nod. "Honesty is always valued by the Luminary, my lord."

Lord Harold tapped his fingers against the bowl of the hookah. "Whatever games you are playing with my daughter, I'd like them to stop."

Quintin's body froze, though his heart raced. What had the Trilord discovered? "I'm not sure what you mean," he said carefully.

"From the first day, you eyed her like a treat to be gobbled up, which was bad enough." Lord Harold sighed. "I let it go. I figured it was no bad thing to have the tax collector enamored of my daughter as long as he kept his hands to himself. But you haven't kept your hands to yourself, have you?"

Quintin licked his lips. "I won't deny your daughter is a lovely woman—"

"Do you take me for a fool?" Lord Harold's hand slapped against the leather seat. "She neglected her duties to meet with you in the jungle."

"You mistake the situation, sir," Quintin protested, his pulse rising in agitation. "It was sheer good fortune she found me when she did."

"And did I mistake what I saw here?" The Trilord's voice dripped with scorn. "She was crawling all over you in a public room, where anyone could have walked in. If you are going to dally with my daughter, at least have the decency not to do it in my own house!"

A low growl rumbled in Elkart's throat. *No yell at you! I bite?*

"Peace, Elkart." Quintin pressed his palm against the top of the waccat's head, trying to soothe them both with the gesture.

Lord Harold leaned back and took a drag off the hookah. "I apologize for my outburst. I'm very worried about her."

"We were not touching," Quintin pointed out, struggling to keep his tone calm. Guilt gnawed at him. If the Trilord had arrived a moment later, he would not be able to make such a claim.

Lord Harold's expression was flat and humorless as he

blew out a stream of scented fog. "I ask you again to not take me for a fool."

Quintin toyed with the loose end of the bandage near his wrist. By Marana's tears, his arm hurt. "The bogbear attack was terrifying. Dangerous. Peril can stir the blood, the passions."

"That's what I'm afraid of." Lord Harold waved the end of the hookah. "Emmie is going to turn eighteen with the new year, entering her third cycle, and the full flower of womanhood. It will be an auspicious year for her to wed, but she won't consider our eligible guests this week if she's pining for an injured Hand. While heroics are all well and good, my daughter needs a husband who can provide for a Lady."

"Your daughter knows what makes a good suitor." Quintin winced at his loose tongue. Em's father did not need to know she only dallied with ineligible men. Grieving anew for impossible dreams, Quintin sighed. "She would never contemplate marrying me."

"She's never contemplated anyone else either." The Trilord took a drag on the hookah, steam curling from his mouth as he spoke. "My Emmie has always had a fascination with Hands. It's a pity the Reeve is already married."

Though Quintin wanted to gag at the thought of Em wedded and bedded by anyone else, if he loved her then he had to hope for her ultimate happiness. He struggled to match the Trilord's blasé tone. "Perhaps she would have better luck finding an eligible Hand in the capital."

"An excellent idea. Important Hands always gather when the new trainees are presented to the Troika. Perhaps someone there will catch Emmie's fancy. A Han-General or a prince, someone suitable for an alliance with a Lady of the Realm. Yes, a trip to the capitol will be a just the thing." The Trilord nodded at Quintin. "Thank you for suggesting it."

"It is an honor to serve, my lord," he answered by rote.

Lady not go, Elkart protested. *Lady stay here with you.*

Quintin's heart wept, echoing his waccat's sentiment. His high emotion threatened his fragile water control. He pressed a hand against the sling on his arm and contained his blood.

"You're a good sort, Han-Auditor." Lord Harold offered the end of the hookah to Quintin.

He waved it away, not trusting himself to speak. He wished the Trilord would leave him to suffer in peace.

I scare him away?

No, Elkart, we're not chasing him out of his own receiving room. Quintin slumped against the waccat, grateful for his support, even with his temptingly impossible suggestions.

Lord Harold took a long pull on the pipe. "I'm sorry my daughter has put you in such a spot. Must be embarrassing to have a Lady fawning over you, with no hope for the future. You'll be better off not seeing her again."

Quintin's fingers clenched around his sling. The Trilord's attitude reminded him of his eldest brother's protestations that he and his mother would be so much happier and more comfortable living in Gramma's cottage as he threw them off his lands. His brother had been correct, just as Lord Harold was now. Yet the truth of their words did not mask the contempt behind their hollow concern.

Elkart rubbed his head against Quintin's lap. *Healer come soon?*

I hope so. He wasn't sure how much longer he could keep his blood in check.

The sound of laughter in the hallway preceded Em's return. She glided into the room with one hand on Terin's elbow, her smiling face turned up to him.

Quintin's stomach lurched to see her looking so elegant and at ease with his charming friend. His wounds cracked and bled as his control slipped.

Elkart's tail lashed. *Not funny.*

Lord Harold rose to his feet, his face grim. "You must be the Hand the auditor is expecting."

Terin dropped Em's arm and bent in a low bow. "Han-Advocate Terin d'Outcounty at your service."

"You'll excuse me for staying seated, Terin," Quintin murmured woozily.

Bells jangled as Em hurried to his side. She splashed pungent amber liquid into a chalice. "I brought you those promised spirits."

He tried to smile at her, though he was afraid it came off more like a grimace. His fingers were red and sticky as he pulled them away from the sling to accept the liqueur. "Did you fetch it yourself?"

"All on my own," she said with a hint of pride.

"Brave Em," he murmured. His hand shook as he sipped the potent liquid. It burned sliding down his throat but failed to warm him.

Her hand flew to her lips. "Oh, Quintin, you're bleeding again."

He peered down at his arm, lacking the focus to control his blood.

A woman in a sari appeared next to Em. "Let me help."

"Ophelia." He said her name like a prayer. "Thank Marana you've come."

Elkart jumped down from the divan and Ophelia settled into his place. She wrapped an arm around his shoulders and rested a hand above his injury.

He sagged against her, grateful to relax his water gift and let her take over the complicated job of keeping his blood in check.

He could hear Terin talking to Lord Harold and Em on the other side of the room. He watched them through his lashes, his eyelids too heavy to open properly. Terin's teeth glinted in a charming smile as Em served him honey spirits.

While neither Lady Emmanuella nor her father would find a landless advocate any more eligible than a mere auditor, Terin would not have any qualms about dallying with a Lady, especially one as beautiful as Em.

Quintin closed his eyes, unable to watch his friend flirt with the woman he loved.

Chapter 26

Blue ribbons of predawn light framed the edges of Quintin's door the next morning. His injured arm rested across his chest, pinning him on his back. Between the ache of his wounds and his spinning thoughts, he doubted he would get another moment of sleep. He lurched to his feet.

Elkart raised his head off his paws. *Too early.*

I can't sleep. Quintin dumped some meat in a dish for the waccat. Usually when he awoke early, he ran through forms with his staff, calming his mind by working his body. With his injury, such exercise wasn't possible.

Feeling restless and irritated, he served himself a bowl of curry lefthanded. His cumbersome motions annoyed him further. He gripped the edge of the table and hung his head. What an ungrateful wretch he was to curse his injured arm when he was lucky to be alive. *I'm going to visit Em's temple before work.*

The waccat stretched, his mouth gaping wide in a yawn. *Hope to see lady thief?*

She probably won't be there. Quintin put their dishes on a tray and managed to pick it up with just one hand.

Grumbling, Elkart rose to his feet to amble outside. *Why visit if Lady not there?*

I want to show my appreciation for her bravery yesterday. Em would like a gift for her temple more than anything for herself, which was good since he owned precious little fit to impress a Lady. Besides, there was something about Aerynet that didn't add up. He wanted to visit it in person to see how it fared.

Quintin was attempting to wash his dish one-handed when his mother awoke.

"I'll clean up," she offered, taking the bowl from him. "I could have warmed something up for you, too."

"I didn't want to wake you."

She tutted at him as she dunked his bowl in the bucket. "What will you do today? Should I stay home from market?"

"I'm going in to work since I'm behind from yesterday."

She frowned at his sling. "Are you sure?"

"I'm sure the Bursar is annoyed with me for skipping work. I'm not going to ask for special treatment today."

"Well, take a long aestivation, at least. Maybe sleep a little."

"Yes, Mother." He gave her a kiss on the cheek before heading to Trimble.

Quintin rested a hand on the head of the great cat at his side, comforted by his warmth. Elkart pressed closer than usual. Quintin had the feeling his waccat would never let him out of his sight again.

The early morning streets were sparsely populated, making for a quiet walk. The solitude refreshed Quintin, giving him new energy as he roamed the riverfront in search of Aerynet.

Tucked between towering warehouses, the tiny temple was a relic of a bygone era when the spiritual needs of the people were served by intimate community shrines. Now most pilgrims seeking Fermena's wisdom visited a larger sanctuary in the fashionable Temple district on the other side of the market.

Small. Elkart's muzzle wrinkled. *And stinky.*

I think it looks cozy. Perched on top of pilings, the whitewashed cone reminded Quintin of a dove brooding on a nest. Audible over the drone of the river, colorful parrots cackled and cawed from the branches of a yarumo tree sprouting from the tip of the cone. *The riverfront always stinks.*

Elkart chuffed. *Smells extra bad.*

The flock of birds probably added to the assault on the waccat's sensitive nose. *You can wait for me here*, Quintin suggested.

With wordless disagreement, Elkart loped up the staircase.

Quintin stepped through the bead curtain and stooped to store his sandals under a bench beside the door. When he straightened, a woman dressed in a white sari that looked suspiciously like one of Em's stood beside him.

"May the blessings of Fermena blow through your life, honorable Hand." The acolyte bent at the waist with her palms pressed together. "How may we serve you?"

"Your patron, Lady Emmanuella, did me a great service yesterday." He held out a cloth pouch, tied at the top with a colorful ribbon. "Please accept this small token of my gratitude."

"I'm sure our Lady was pleased to serve." The acolyte held the pouch to her nose. She inhaled deeply, a smile lighting her face. "Kapok tea. This is a worthy gift. Lady Emmanuella will be honored."

"Your Lady spoke most fondly of this temple. I thought to visit since I have never been here, though I have always favored Fermena." He stepped past the acolyte to peer around the conical room. The wooden planks of the floor chilled his feet, while birds cooed in the boughs of the tree. A feeling of peace settled over him as he stopped before the altar.

A brown leaf drifted past a statue of Fermena, then down from the high table to the floor, where it joined a dozen or more other fallen leaves.

Elkart sat at Quintin's feet, his tail wrapped around his paws. *Tree dying?*

I don't know. Quintin frowned at the curling leaves, his sense of peace shaken by how little he knew. In a less than a week, the year of Fermena would begin, yet this sanctuary bore no signs of preparation or celebration.

Elkart's lips curled. *Still smells bad.*

Quintin sniffed, disturbed by the faint odor of stale urine. The temple and its holy tree needed earthworking badly. The sole acolyte had disappeared, making the place feel deserted, neglected. He shivered. What was Em spending all her cacao on?

Lady here! Elkart bounced to his feet, sending birds squawking.

"Quintin?" Em emerged from a hidden hallway behind the tree. "What are you doing here? How is your arm?"

Elkart nudged his head against her hip, leaving a sprinkling of brown hairs on her cream-colored kaftan.

"Lady Em." Quintin pressed his palms together and gave her a deep bow, his wounds twinging with the motion. He envied Elkart's freedom to touch her. "Though my arm is better, it wasn't allowing me to sleep past sunrise. I came to repay your service to me yesterday with a gift to your temple. I didn't expect to find you here."

She scratched the waccat's pointed ears, then pushed his head away from her skirts. "I'm delivering the curassow I caught yesterday and spending a moment in peace here before the Merdale household wakes up."

"Was your gift well received?"

"Oh, yes." She beamed and took his arm. "Let me show you around a bit before I return to Merdale."

Bemused, Quintin watched her face as she enthused about the history of Aerynet. Her eyes danced, free of the tension and worry usually veiling her features. "You must love it here."

"This is my home, more than Merdale ever will be." She gazed in rapture at the altar.

If she cared so much, why was she letting the tree die?

Struggling to understand, he glanced around the sanctuary. "What is your favorite thing here?"

"The statue of Fermena has always had a special place in my heart." She gestured at the carved relic above the primary altar. "It dates back seven generations. Aerynet itself has been in my family for nine, longer than Trimble has been a proper city."

"It passes from mother to daughter?"

"With the Novenary's blessing." She waved around grandly, but with a rueful chuckle. "Someday my lucky daughter will inherit all this."

He pushed his lips into a smile, suddenly struggling to breathe. He could imagine, with painful clarity, Em showing the temple to a bright-eyed little girl, and he wanted, more than wanted, burned with yearning to be there, holding her other hand.

You want to mate? Elkart sniffed at Em's legs. *She not in heat.*

Quintin flushed at the images his waccat's comments brought to mind. *Making a family doesn't work the same for humans. While I want more than sex, it is impossible.*

He would love her to his dying breath, but even if she loved him back, he could never subject her daughter to the uncertainty of being denied the Novenary's blessing.

He cleared his throat, banishing all thoughts of her future children. "Do you have many devotees?"

"Only two, Acolyte Lucy and Mystic Patricia."

He frowned. Wasn't Patricia ill? No matter how small, a temple needed more than a lone acolyte to tend it properly.

Footsteps pounded on the temple steps, sending vibrations through the wooden floor. A woman clutching a baby burst through the beaded curtain. A pair of children tumbled after her.

"You must help him!" The woman ran to Em and thrust the infant at her. "Please! He's not breathing."

The baby exhaled a raspy wheeze followed by a squeaking gasp.

"Come receive the blessings of the Goddess." Em waved at the altar, before dashing away. "I'll go get Acolyte Lucy. She can help."

Frozen under the statue of Fermena, the woman rocked the hapless babe. Her sniffling children cowered against her legs. The babe's labored breaths mingled with her fervent prayers.

Drawn by the pitiful sound, Quintin stepped closer. "I have a gift for air. Can I try to aid his breathing?"

"Oh, please, can you do something?" She shifted the babe away from her.

His thin wail of protest degenerated into a barking cough.

"Help me hold him." Quintin cuddled the babe with his left arm while shaking off his sling. Ignoring the pull of his stitches, he rested his right hand on the infant's back behind his lungs.

The mother stroked her son's hair, soothing him as his coughs faded into wretched gasps.

Quintin exhaled completely to disperse his air shield. Using his gift, his will infused the ether twisting and swirling around them.

As the child gasped, the air moved toward him.

Quintin moved with it, easing life-giving air past pinched tubes and tightened passages down into the babe's lungs.

When the boy exhaled, Quintin pushed the foul stale breath away, so his next breath was pure and sweet.

He gasped again, and again Quintin followed, drawing more air deep into his lungs.

In and out. Deep and pure. In and out.

Quintin soon lost himself in the rhythms of the child's breath.

Chapter 27

Em sent Lucy to the main sanctuary, then hurried to the steamroom. The inner sanctuary focused the gifts of the Goddess and would help strengthen the babe's weak air. She shed her clothes and scurried into the cramped room. She prayed to all the Goddesses and heated the stones as quickly as she could. She was pouring water over the stones to make steam when Lucy entered the room alone.

Em frowned at her. "Where's the babe?"

"There's a bit of trouble bringing him in here." Lucy held a hand over the brazier to feel the heat. "I can tend this now if you can help the mother."

Was the mother having trouble getting undressed? Her brow wrinkled in confusion, Em squeezed through the door to the antechamber.

The babe's family filled the space. The mother stood with her arms around the older children, pulling them tight against her sides, while a man cradled the babe against his chest, their heads tucked together. A waccat squeezed between the man's knees and the wall.

Em blinked, realizing the man was Quintin, not the child's father. She inhaled sharply as she noticed something else. Those painful gasps had stopped. Quintin had somehow eased the little boy's breathing.

"The Hand won't give him up," the mother said in a warbling voice. "The holy woman was able to push him here. He doesn't seem to hear us. I don't want to yank Joseph out of his arms, especially now he's breathing so nice."

"I see," Em said, though she did not actually understand at all. Quintin must be using his air gift to help the boy breathe. Perhaps the task was so difficult he needed all his attention on it? When similar cases had come to the temple before, Lucy took them to the steamroom only to pray. As far as Em knew she did not directly influence their air.

Ben appeared in the doorway. Beckoning the other children, he held out a pair of macaw feathers.

Em smiled at him and then at the mother. "Ben has a gift for your children and would like to introduce them to his favorite bird. Then maybe they can meet Mystic Patricia while you take the babe into the steamroom."

As the children disappeared, the mother began to disrobe.

Em touched his shoulder. "Quintin, it's time to let go now."

Eyes closed, he did not so much as twitch at the sound of his name.

She bit her lip, hesitant to shake him for fear of jostling the babe.

"Maybe he can carry Joseph into the steamroom as he is," the mother suggested.

Em bit her lip. "I don't think this state is good for him. It must be depleting his air, and his water was severely taxed yesterday. Such imbalance isn't healthy."

Elkart whined and nudged her hip. She got the distinct impression the waccat was asking for help.

Out of her depth, but determined to try something, she motioned the mother closer. "Come support the babe, in case I startle him."

The woman stepped over and took hold of her son.

Em took a deep breath and then exhaled fully, scattering her mental protections as she did so. She placed her hand against the side of Quintin's face, hoping skin to skin contact would be enough to get her thoughts to him. *You've done well, Quintin. Now let the babe go to his mother.*

Em? How did you . . . What is happening?

You helped the babe. He's breathing well. His mother wants to take him to the steamroom. She stroked a thumb over his cheekbone, her heart aching. *Open your eyes now, Quintin. Let the boy breathe on his own.*

His lids rose, though it took a moment for his eyes to focus. He lifted his head away from the babe.

Em let her hand fall to her side.

The mother pressed her palms together and bowed deeply. "My sincere thanks to you, most kind and generous Hand."

Joseph shifted and sighed, no longer struggling for air.

"It is my pleasure to serve," Quintin said quietly. With gentle care, he handed the babe to his mother.

A hard lump formed in Em's chest. She could not imagine Lord Evan showing such tenderness to his own child, let alone a stranger's.

The mother removed her son's nappy with a practiced motion and carried him into the steamroom.

Once they were alone, Quintin's heated gaze roved over Em's body. A kaleidoscope of images invaded her mind, ending with a vision of her draped on a bed with her hair spread across the pillow. *By Fermena's breath, you are glorious.*

Her body warmed with equal parts embarrassment and desire. Regretting the lack of privacy in the temple, she snatched her kaftan off the floor. *Now is not the time.*

I'm well aware of that. He turned his attention to easing his injured arm back into its sling. The tantalizing images faded as his focus shifted.

No matter how inappropriate the urge, she longed to kiss him. Instead Em yanked on her clothes. "Let's get you a hookah or a bit of curassow meat to restore your air."

He rubbed his forehead as he followed her out of the antechamber. *Did you send your thoughts to me?*

Tried to. I'm glad it worked.

How did you? You don't have an air gift, do you?

No, but your mind was gone, lost in air. She held aside the curtain to Lucy's cell. *I couldn't think how else to reach you.*

It is passing strange you were able to. He gingerly sat at the low table.

I remembered what you said about only detecting loud and clear thoughts. She rubbed her temples. A headache throbbed behind her eyes.

"We should speak aloud and save our air."

She laughed. "I don't have any air. I'm a balanced and ordinary woman."

"Being balanced doesn't mean having no air. You have the proper amount, while I have too much."

"I'll wager that mother doesn't think you have too much," she said, opening an icebox set against the wall.

He grunted. "Put the meat away. I'm not eating your curassow."

"You are a talented guest who exhausted your air aiding a parishioner. We should be able to help you recover."

"You should," he agreed. "I know better."

Her face burned with shame and the sinking feeling she was doing it all wrong when it came to her temple. Em did not remember her mother struggling so, but perhaps her mother's ease had been an illusion. She fought the urge to protest and hide Aerynet's poverty. Pretending was pointless. He knew the truth, and the truth wasn't pretty.

She closed the icebox. "At least let me warm a hookah for you."

"Very well. Thank you." He leaned back against his waccat with a weary sigh. There were purple smudges under his eyes and lines of pain on his face.

Em bit her lip, wishing she could do more for him. She

cupped her hands around the base of a hookah and warmed the infused water within.

Beads clattered as Ben entered the room. He pointed at the icebox and tapped his lips with his fingers.

"Are the children hungry?" Em asked.

He nodded and touched his head in his gesture for Mystic Patricia.

"Lucy should be available to cook Patricia a proper meal soon. For now, take some dates and nuts to share with her and the children."

Silently he filled a bowl. Then he bobbed a bow to both Em and Quintin and disappeared back through the curtain.

Aromatic steam began to waft out of the hookah. Em offered it to Quintin.

He accepted with a tired smile. "Is the mute boy a temple novice?"

"Not yet, though Lucy plans to train him when he's old enough. He was working on a trading ship and had a horrible accident. Nearly drowned. His shipmates brought him here to have his air restored." She sat down across from Quintin, filled with mingled frustration and affection as she often found herself when she thought of Ben's history. "They paid us generously for his care, or so we thought until they never returned."

"Isn't an abandoned child the province of Marana? It's clear Aerynet can't afford another mouth to feed."

"Ben does his part to earn his keep. He's positively gifted with birds." She fiddled with the hem of her kaftan. "Besides, I shudder to think what would happen to him at Rivara once he came of age."

Some of the color had returned to Quintin's cheeks as he blew out a stream of vapor. "Wouldn't the matrons find a place for him?"

"Maybe. If he's lucky." Lucy had been one of the lucky ones, sent to Aerynet as a novice at the first sign of her air gift, though her training with Patricia had been sadly cut short. Lucy's balanced brother had fared much worse, let loose on the streets to fend for himself. Simon turned to thievery to survive, a risky and lawless life, one he was fortunate to finally escape.

Em would protect Ben from a similar fate if she could. She sighed. "While grounds-keepers and temples alike will pay fresh cacao for the chance to hire gifted temple orphans, I don't think a mute would be much in demand."

He gaped at her. "How do you know about this?"

Her forehead crinkled at his reaction. "Any landowner knows a temple raised orphan will show uncommon loyalty if you treat them right. They're knowledgeable, too, and trained in their gifts as soon as they emerge."

Quintin's mouth tightened like he tasted something sour. "Does your father engage in this practice?"

"Occasionally." She shrugged. "I've been blessed a time or two myself to overhear a landowner or patron's wishes for new talent. Lucy remains friendly with the matron at Rivara and arranges to take in the appropriate novice long enough for us to introduce them to their new employer."

"You!" He gasped, his face pained. "You sell children, too?"

"Nobody is treating people like chattel to be bartered and sold," Em snapped. He made it sound so awful. Those youths could do much worse than the steady employment of a position on an estate. She knew what it was like to be deemed adult enough to fend for herself while woefully unprepared for the responsibilities. "The Goddess of Mercy's duty to unwanted children ends far too soon. We give those youths a chance at a good life where they will be valued and appreciated. If my father's friends are grateful for our assistance and express their gratitude in beans, well, those donations mean a great deal to Aerynet, too."

An uncomfortable silence stretched between them.

Quintin stared at the hookah as if the simple device confounded him.

Had she said too much? He acted like he understood the extent of her financial worries. Maybe he hadn't realized exactly how bad it was.

He raised his gaze to hers, his dark eyes troubled. "Will you trust me?"

"I do trust you," she said immediately. It was true, she trusted him more than anyone else in her life. She knotted her fingers together and hid them in her skirts. What would she do when she no longer had an excuse to see him?

He cleared his throat. "Where is all the cacao going? Are you being blackmailed?"

"What? No." Em twisted her mother's ring. "All my money goes to Aerynet."

"Then why is it in such poor shape? Why are you hunting for temple offerings? Why is your tree dying?"

She turned the ring back and forth. "I'm doing all I can," she whispered, shame and guilt closing her throat. "Saving up enough for an earthworker is impossible."

"Do you need to petition the Novenary for a larger portion?"

She frowned. "The Novenary doesn't give me an allowance."

She had been presented to the Novenary as a child though she had not spoken two words to the formidable woman, nor seen her since. The Novenary had sent a messenger after her mother's death, confirming Em was a Lady of the Realm, and nothing more.

"I meant, she should be notified if your lands are inadequate."

"Unfortunately, my temple is too small to have any lands."

His brow puckered with a puzzled frown. "All temples have lands, Em."

"My father always says my temple is too small for a parcel."

"It doesn't matter what size it is. They all have lands."

Her heart stuttered. Could it be true? Surely she would know.

"A little temple like this might be attached to a quarter parcel. Maybe a half, given its age," Quintin said. "You should have enough for a garden to feed a few acolytes and room for some cacao plants, maybe a beehive. Ordinarily, you'd have to manage it very wisely to pay for new repairs. With your extra income an earthworker should be well within your means."

She gazed at the wall, almost able to picture it. It sounded as lovely as a dream. "I don't have anything like that."

"You must." He bit his lip. "Perhaps your father managed it for your mother, and kept doing so after she died?"

"He pays me an allowance." Her skull felt tight, like her head was too small to contain this new information. "I thought it was from the goodness of his heart. Maybe it comes from temple lands."

Quintin tapped a finger against the base of the water pipe. "I hate to say it, but he might be robbing you. The allowance he gives you can't be enough for Aerynet, or you wouldn't have turned to sneak work. And other things."

A pensive look on his face, he took a long drag from the hookah.

She had to talk to her father. Confront him with this new information. Her stomach churned at the thought, though there was also a lightness in her chest. Maybe she could safely put her sneak work behind her. Maybe she wouldn't need an unpalatable marriage to save her temple.

For the first time since her mother died, Em felt hope.

Quintin blew a cloud of aromatic steam across the table. "When was the last time?"

Em blinked at the change in subject. "What?"

"How recently have you matched up a talented orphan with a grateful landowner?"

She frowned. "Less than a month ago I found a home for a water gifted girl called Nadine. Why?"

"Ophelia did a foretelling on that child, the last to leave Rivara. Her fate is dreadful."

"Misfortune can befall any of us," Em protested. A worm of doubt wriggled in her heart, leaving room for guilt and uncertainty. While she had never heard rumors of cruelty from the lords and ladies she worked with, how well did she know any of her family's friends? "Did she . . ." She swallowed hard. "Did she foresee abuse?"

"I don't know the details of her foretelling. I just know she's desperate to find the girl."

"I can give you directions to the estate easy enough. Merdale could spare a messenger to make an introduction if you like." She leaned forward and touched his hand. *I would never intentionally put children in danger. You know that, right?*

He turned his hand over and clasped her fingers. *Yes. I know.*

The sincerity in his words warmed her heart, even as his very real concern chilled her.

"Ophelia has been dreadfully worried," he said aloud. "If she can go visit Nadine, then perhaps there will be no need for the inquisitors."

Em gripped his fingers, suddenly lightheaded. "Inquisitors?"

"You remember the quipu we put in with the Allgoday gifts? Ophelia was begging the Novenary to send a trio of inquisitors to investigate the missing children."

Panic clawed at her throat. "I can't have inquisitors here!"

"I'll talk to Ophelia." He let go of her hand to rub his forehead. "I'm sure once she sees Nadine safe, she'll be happy to call the inquisitors off."

"She'd better," Em muttered. It would be a disaster to have inquisitors snooping around Aerynet, reporting all her failings to the Novenary.

Chapter 28

An hour later, Em tossed her reins to a Merdale groom. The morning sun sparkled off the front of the house, reminding her of how long she had lingered at Aerynet.

Entering without fanfare, she hesitated as she approached the family courtyard. There were masculine voices up ahead, revealing her father to be awake. She had hoped to change before speaking to him. An elegant sari could act like a shield, reminding her father and herself of her position as a Lady.

Now she couldn't get to her room without passing the men. There was no help for it. She took a breath and stepped into the courtyard. Her father and brothers broke off their conversation to stare at her.

"What are you doing in such a getup?" Her father brushed a hand over his own glittering kaftan. "Do you spend all your days dressed like a common boy?"

Her face heated. "I had errands in town and took an okapi."

"Well, you'd better not let Isabel see you." Jon laughed. "She'll take a whip to anyone who dishonors her parents."

"My wife is doing the work of three people with the preparations for Allgoday," Gregory pointed out icily. "The least we can do is not embarrass her in front of our guests."

"I quite agree." Lord Harold's rings flashed as he dismissed Em. "Go change into a sari and join us in the main courtyard for the meal."

Em licked her lips and swallowed hard. "I need to speak with you today."

His brows drew together. "What about?"

"It can wait until you have a moment in private."

He huffed. "I don't expect a moment's peace all day. If you have something to say, you'd best say it now."

All too aware of her brothers listening, she spun her mother's ring around her finger. "It's about my allowance."

Her father raised his eyebrows. "You think now is the best time to ask for more cacao?"

Her chin tilted up. "I want to know where it comes from."

"It is a gift from my personal stores, so you may comport yourself as befits the child of a Trilord." His gaze raked over her clothes. "Not that you or Jonny ever use it properly."

Jonathan gasped. "That's not fair. Gambling is a time-honored tradition for nobles."

Lord Harold's eye twitched. "You keep this up, and I'll regret my generosity to both of you."

Ever the peacekeeper, Gregory cleared his throat. "I'm sure Isabel and our guests are waiting to break their fast."

"I only started receiving my allowance after Mother died," Em continued doggedly, refusing to be cowed by her father's threat. If her allowance came from her temple lands, he had no right to cut it off.

"It was a little before her death, actually." Some of the anger left his face, replaced by sorrow. "The Allgoday you turned twelve, if you recall."

"Oh, you're right." The season a child turned twelve was supposed to be a grand affair marking their transition into adulthood. With her mother so sick, their Allgoday celebration had been a somber event. She scarcely remembered her father pressing a purse into her hands and droning on about her new responsibilities. "I had forgotten."

He clasped his hands together. "What is this all about, Emmie?"

"Perhaps I'll go tell my wife we'll be there shortly." Gregory beckoned at Jon, but their lackadaisical brother waved off the gesture.

Ignoring her brothers' antics, she tried to formulate her thoughts. "I thought the cacao might be coming from my temple lands."

Could Quintin be mistaken? Her father always said Aerynet was too small for a parcel. "Do I have temple lands?"

"Certainly you have lands. How else are your acolytes supposed to eat?"

"By my hunting skills," she said with slow precision. Quintin had known the truth of it. She had lands. She could hardly believe it. "And very careful purchases with my allowance."

Her father barked out a laugh. "Your allowance isn't enough to support a temple, even a tiny one."

"I've also gotten fairly good at gleaning scraps from the kitchen." Her smile felt like a rictus mask as anger sparked through her veins. "Did you know your gardeners will throw out perfectly good produce merely because of a few worms?"

"Disgusting." Jon gagged. "Remind me never to visit your temple on its holy day."

"If the Novenary ever found out . . ." Gregory's voice trailed off, his eyes wide in horror.

"Are you trying to disgrace us all?" her father thundered. "What in rotting hell happens to the cacao and produce from your own temple plot?"

"A very good question." She curled her fingers into fists to keep her hands from shaking. Fermena's breath, she'd been a fool. "One I'd hoped you could answer since I didn't know I *had* lands."

"How could you not know you have a temple plot?" Her father's voice rose with every word. "All temples have lands. What did you think your deed chain was for anyway?"

Her face flushed hot and then cold. "I don't have a deed chain."

"What? Of course, you do."

"No, I don't."

"Did you lose it?" Gregory asked weakly. He looked ill, as if he wanted to faint or throw-up and couldn't decide which.

"I didn't lose anything," Em growled at him before glaring at her father. "You always said my temple was too small for a parcel."

"Yes, yes, it only has a half parcel." Her father waved a hand as if the lands didn't concern him. "The deed chain is a little short. Strange looking on account of its age. Perhaps you didn't recognize it."

"I know what a deed chain looks like, Father."

"Your mother kept it buried in her jewel box. You do remember receiving her jewelry?"

"There was no deed chain in with her jewels."

Jon made a pained sound.

Her father heaved himself to his feet. "Let's go look."

"It's not in there." There was precious little left in the jewel box she inherited from her mother. The best pieces had been sold to pay for one thing or another over the last six years.

Her father strode to her room. "You must have overlooked it."

"I never had it," she protested as she followed her father. Her brothers trailed after them, an unwelcome audience she didn't have the wits or energy to banish.

She stood stiff with mortification as her father opened the box on her vanity and stared at the contents.

"What happened to your mother's jewels?"

"You are quite right. My allowance was inadequate for the maintenance of Aerynet," she said, each word clipped and clear. She wouldn't apologize for selling her mother's treasures for the sake of the temple.

Her father spun, the box clutched in his hands. "You sold your deed chain? How did you find a buyer?"

"I am not an imbecile." Her voice sharpened with denial. She had never felt more stupid. Aerynet could have been cared for without any of her struggles and sacrifices. If only she had known. "There was never a deed chain in the box."

"Impossible!"

She waved at the box in his hands. "Did you check? Before you foisted the box off on me, did you peek inside to see if it was there?"

"Where else could it be?"

"I don't know! Maybe Mother was wearing it when she died and it turned to ash with her."

Gregory gasped. "Is that possible?"

"Don't be ridiculous. Your mother never wore her chain. It was uglier than a slug and I couldn't stand the thing." Flecks of spittle flew from Lord Harold's mouth as he shouted. He shook the box. "She always kept it in here. Always!"

"Then where could it have gone?" Gregory asked.

"I know." Jon cleared his throat, his face tight. "I know who took it."

"What do you mean?" Em asked, her anger draining away into sick dread. "Why would anyone steal a deed chain?"

"Over six years ago, I snuck Violet into Mother's room and let her pick a jewel from the box."

Gregory's eyes widened, disbelief written across his face. "You helped our cousin steal from our mother?"

Lord Harold's face turned purple. "Of all the lowdown, irresponsible—"

"I didn't know she took a deed chain," Jonathan sputtered. "I stood guard at the door, and she hid the piece in her sari."

Not sure she wanted the answer, Em asked, "Where was Mama?"

His gaze skittered away. "She'd moved to her temple."

Feeling small and sad, Em closed her eyes. Her brother had been sneaking around stealing her inheritance while their mother was on her deathbed. "Oh, Jon. How could you?"

"We'd been rolling the bones and I lost. Violet offered to take jewels instead of cacao. It seemed like a deal to me."

Anger blazed through her, burning away her despair. "The deed chain wasn't yours to gamble away."

"I told you, I didn't know what she took." Jonathan spread his hands wide. "I figured I deserved one piece for my inheritance, since Maral knows Mother didn't set anything else aside for me. She gave Gregory a necklace set for his future bride, and Em got everything else in the box. I got nothing when she died."

Em snorted. "She probably realized you'd lose it on the next roll of the bones, which is exactly what happened, isn't it? Only instead of gambling away a treasured heirloom, you gave Violet my deed chain."

"I never guessed she'd be so greedy." Jon raked his hand through his hair. "Why did Mother keep something so valuable in an unlocked box anyway?"

"A deed chain is a holy trust, but it isn't valuable on its own," Gregory said slowly. "The stones in it aren't big or fancy enough to sell and only our mother could use it intact."

Lord Harold stirred a finger through the contents of the jewel box. "Your mother had much more valuable pieces in here. Or at least she used to."

"Why would Violet want it then?" Jonathan asked.

"She used it to impersonate me." Em pressed a hand to her pitching stomach. "All these years, the cacao from my plot has been going to her."

Gregory nodded. "It would be a clever scheme, and our cousin is bold enough to pull it off."

Em's whole body felt hot and itchy. When she thought of all the desperate risks she had taken, of all the times Lucy had gone without. Without food, without clothing, without proper schooling. Patricia might have gotten better care and recovered if Em hadn't had to struggle to keep her fed. All the while her cousin dripped jewels and made snide remarks about her useless temple. "I'm going to kill her."

Lord Harold snapped the jewel box closed. "Don't be ridiculous. You're not killing anyone."

"Give me one reason why I shouldn't."

Gregory pinched the bridge of his nose. "Aside from murder being a burning offense, the last thing we need is a scandal."

Jon moaned. "My reputation will be in tatters."

She paced the narrow space between her bed and her vanity in short jerky steps. "As well it should be for robbing your dying mother."

"I didn't have to tell you," he snapped. "I'm trying to be a better person and atone for my past. It's hardly worth it if this is the thanks I get. Will you repay my honesty with a scandal to ruin me?"

Em waved her arms in agitation. "I don't give a fig about scandal."

"Do you give a fig about your temple?" Lord Harold slammed the jewel box onto the vanity. "The Novenary is likely to strip you of your title if word of this gets back to her."

"What?" Em gaped at her father. "Violet is the one who has been stealing."

"It won't go well for Violet nor for Jon, it's true. But a temple is a holy trust. The Novenary can't sit idly by and let you shatter her trust." He wagged a fat finger at her. "Mark my words, she'll make an example of you so other Lords and Ladies don't get any ideas about selling off their temple lands."

"I didn't *sell* anything. It was stolen from me!"

"A theft you conveniently didn't report for six years."

"I didn't know—"

"If Violet runs to the Reeve with your deed chain in hand, you will not be spared the consequences," Lord Harold warned.

Gregory looked faint again. "We have a houseful of important guests and a major feast in five days. Let's not do anything rash until we have some chance of keeping this family affair private."

Her back stiffened. "You cannot expect me to dine with Violet and pretend she isn't a lying, traitorous snake."

"Given that you barely comport yourself like a Lady on the best of days, I suppose it is too much to ask for civilized behavior after such a shocking upset." Lord Harold sighed, sounding old and weary. "Why don't you go for a ride? Or better yet, head over to your temple for a day or two. Prayer and meditation can bring great clarity of thought."

Gregory frowned. "Won't our guests wonder at her absence?"

"It will cause less talk than if she dunks your cousin in the fountain." Lord Harold rubbed his forehead. "I'll make your excuses, Emmie. Given my new understanding of the state of your finances, I imagine there is much to be done before your temple will be ready for the year of Fermena."

Not trusting herself to speak, Em nodded sharply.

"I'll get you some cacao and see if Cook can spare you supplies. You'll need to return on Taralday. Try to calm yourself by then."

Chapter 29

The next morning before work, Quintin entered Trimble in a pensive mood. Em and her troubles preyed on his mind. Instead of heading directly to the Tribute Office, he cut through the quiet market square to the house Ulric shared with Terin and Madi. Maybe he could persuade his friends to arrange some assistance for Lady Em. It was also Ophelia's day off, so she might be at the house, giving him an opportunity to convince her the inquisitors were no longer needed.

He stroked Elkart's head as he wove through the early morning market, dodging vendors setting up for the day. His steps slowed as he neared the stocks. A half dozen people knelt behind the heavy wooden contraptions, their heads and hands poking through snug holes. The stench of nervous sweat and desperation hung in the air around them.

"Please, sir, have pity," one woman begged Quintin, her voice little more than a croak. "A bit of water, sir, please."

But for the grace of the gods, it could be Em trapped there. He shuddered. "I'll get a mystic for you."

Elkart whined and pressed against Quintin's legs. *Stocks nasty.*

Flagging down an acolyte of Marana, Quintin pressed all the cacao he had on him into her hands. "I'd like to buy water and gruel for as many as this can feed."

The acolyte nodded, her eyes soft with sympathy. "It's hard to watch them, isn't it?"

"I know they have done wrong, yet who among us has not erred?"

"And so, we have justice tempered with mercy." She tucked his offering into a purse hanging from her waist before bowing with respect. "Your generosity will be appreciated by these poor souls. May the blessings of Marana flood your future."

He bowed in return before hurrying away from the marketplace and the pitiful prisoners. A short while later he climbed the steps of a two-story clay house in the Three-Fountain District.

Ignoring the gong, he pulled open the door. "Is anyone home?"

"We're in the gallery," Terin called.

Elkart bounded through an arched doorway toward the voice.

Quintin followed him into a long room with polished wooden floors and high windows. All manner of weapons covered the walls, except where an altar to Tarina honored the warrior goddess. Elkart chased Ulric's and Terin's waccats in circles, while their Hands stood close together at the center of the room.

"I've been giving Terin a nice set of bruises." Ulric swung a staff in a showy maneuver. "Do you want some?"

Quintin's fingers itched for a staff of his own. Instead he gestured at his sling. "Not yet, I'm afraid. If I tear my stitches, this will never heal."

Ulric grunted. "A pity. Terin's not much of a challenge."

"I'm done for the day." Terin leaned against his staff, breathing heavily. "What brings you here, Quintin? Skipping work to go whoring with Ulric?"

"I'll leave that to you. I wanted to ask Ulric a favor."

Ulric grunted encouragingly as he strode across the room to a bucket on a stand and pulled out a dipper.

"I visited an old temple down near the river yesterday, and its yarumo tree is in dire need of some earthwork."

Ulric took a gulp of water and wiped his mouth with the back of his hand. Droplets splattered the floor. "What were you doing there?"

Terin watched Quintin, a wicked gleam in his eye. "The lovely Lady Emmanuella wouldn't be its patron, now would she?"

"She is, actually. I went to pay my respects."

"Showing your fair savior the depth of your appreciation?"

"Yes, though a pouch of kapok tea is hardly a balanced exchange for my life." He fiddled with his sling. Had Terin recognized Em or was his teasing more general? "Lady Em has been very gracious. She insists I owe her nothing, but I thought she wouldn't turn down earthwork for her holy tree."

Ulric tossed the dipper back in the bucket. "You want me to head over there and fix it up?"

"This morning, if you're willing."

Ulric shrugged his massive shoulders. "I'm willing to earn the blessings of the gods."

"I'll go along to introduce Ulric to your fair savior." Terin waggled his eyebrows at Quintin. "Unless you want the pleasure of seeing her yourself."

"She probably won't be there, otherwise I'd be sorely tempted." As much as he wanted to help Em, he also needed to keep his distance or risk giving the Bursar more fodder for his attacks.

"We can't let Ulric go alone. He's likely to offend someone before he's so much as stated his purpose." Terin rubbed his chin. "This scheme needs grace and charm to smooth the way."

"Hey, I can be charming," Ulric protested. He lifted an arm and sniffed his pit. "Though maybe not right after besting you in staves."

"Neither of you needs to charm anyone. All I want is help for her tree."

Terin smiled knowingly. "If you want to be the one to flirt with her, you should go with Ulric."

Ulric pointed at himself with his thumb. "Since I'm the one saving the tree, I get to flirt with the Lady."

"You don't know the first thing about flirting." Terin made a disgusted noise. "Especially with a Lady."

"Who's flirting with Ladies?" Ophelia asked as she stepped through the archway.

"I am." Ulric tousled Quintin's hair. "As a favor to Quintin."

"Moving up from your usual Taricday entertainments?" Ophelia asked, her voice heavy with disapproval.

"I'll get to those later." Ulric clapped a hand on Terin's shoulder. "Coming with me?"

"Certainly." Terin sniffed. "I'm your only hope of success."

Quintin waited until he heard the outside door close behind them before turning to Ophelia. "I need to talk to you."

"What is it?"

"I know what happened to your missing orphan."

Ophelia gasped. "Where is she? Does she yet live?"

"She's working on an estate upriver. A messenger from Merdale will stop by Rivera today to take you there if you wish."

"However did you arrange this?" She clasped her hands together, her eyes wide and eager. "Merdale? Isn't that where you got injured?"

"Yes, and it's how I arranged this." Quintin explained about his conversation with Em, while carefully leaving out any hints of her secrets. "Once you're satisfied Nadine is safe, it would be a great favor to the Lady if we could call off the inquisitors."

"Oh, it's too late for that."

"What?"

"They arrived last night."

Chapter 30

Em lit an incense cone on the center of the altar at Aerynet. "Blessed Fermena, blow your holy breath upon my mind so I may find a solution to this predicament."

Stiff from a night praying in the steamroom, her body protested as she knelt before the altar. Her vigil brought back painful memories of her first months as a Lady. Then, as now, her desperate prayers were caused by Violet's greed. The injustice of it all infuriated her.

She breathed deeply, grappling with her rage. The Goddess of Air had no use for strong emotion.

"Holy Fermena, mother of wisdom, please help me." She needed the wisdom of the Goddess to see a way out of her dilemma. While her brother's revelation about her cousin's theft changed her understanding of her whole life, she was helpless to set things right and prevent Violet from continuing her damaging deception.

The beaded curtain at the door rattled. Em twisted around, her aching body crying out at the motion. Lucy had gone to market, supplied by Lord Harold's largess, and Em did not expect her back so soon. Had something gone wrong?

Instead of Lucy, Quintin's handsome friend Terin stepped into the sanctuary. "Lady Emmanuella, what a delight to see you here."

Em stood and delivered a respectful bow. "Welcome to Aerynet, Han-Advocate."

A massive stranger loomed next to Terin, his face obscured by a bushy black beard. Though too large for a munto, he had the dark coloring of the reclusive mountain people. His brows drew together as his eyes studied her with unnerving intensity.

She smoothed her hands over the skirt of her kaftan and curved her lips in a polite smile. "Have you and your friend come to receive Fermena's blessing?"

Terin's teeth glinted as he smiled. "We've come to *earn* her blessing."

The large man snorted. "You're just here to look pretty. I'm doing the work."

"Pretty manners are necessary to the task."

Em's stomach pitched. Between the problem with her deed chain and the threat of an inquisition, she couldn't handle another surprise. "I don't understand."

"Pretty manners, my arse." The stranger cuffed Terin's shoulder with a beefy fist. "Introduce us."

Terin gave his companion a narrow-eyed glare, before shining a smile at Em. "My deepest apologies, for I have been remiss. My lady, allow me to present Han-Builder Ulric of Furpass, Hand of Destin and Artificer for the Mortarary. Ulric, this is Lady Emmanuella a'Fermena."

Ulric bent his barrel of a body in a jerky bow.

"Ulric is earth talented. Quintin thought your tree might be in need of his skills."

She licked her lips. While her father had placated her with a purse of cacao, the paltry amount would insult an earthworker. Besides, Lucy was out spending those beans on other supplies as they spoke. "It was very kind of Quintin to think of me, and you were quite obliging to visit, but really there was no need for you to come."

Ulric snorted and jerked his head at the tree's yellowing leaves. "You shoulda had this done months ago."

She flushed, unable to deny it. "Your visit has caught me by surprise. I'm not prepared to properly repay you for your work. It would be best—"

Terin waved an elegant hand in dismissal. "Consider it a gift."

She forced herself to laugh, though the sound was breathy and raw to her own ears. "I cannot accept such a valuable gift from a stranger."

Ulric's dark brows drew together in a fierce scowl. "It's not a gift."

Terin face tightened though he continued to smile at her. "We're not going to charge her, Ulric. Remember, let me do the talking to avoid offend—"

"It's *not* a gift." The beefy man pointed a thick finger at her. "Quintin says this little bit of a thing saved his life. True or not?"

She bit her lip. "Well, yes, but—"

Ulric's head jerked in a nod. "An hour of earthwork is a piss poor trade for my year-mate's life. I'll come out every season for a cycle or two. Fair?"

She tilted her chin up. She had saved Quintin simply because it had been the right thing to do, a first in her lawless life. Her soul rebelled at twisting her honorable act into yet another way to make ends meet. "I didn't help him in order to extort his friends."

"We wouldn't dream you did, my lady." Terin pressed his hands together and bent low. "We are indebted to you nonetheless. Quintin thought this might be one thing we could do to repay you. Please be gracious enough to accept this meager work as a token of our gratitude."

"Today." Ulric crossed his arms over his chest, his massive biceps bulging. "And once a season for a whole cycle."

"Yes, yes." While she had enjoyed feeling honorable and good while it lasted, as always Aerynet came first. To have the tree tended twice a year for nine years might restore it to full health again. "As you noted we are in dire need of it."

"Show me the roots, and I'll get to work."

Em led Ulric back down the steps and around the pilings at the base of the building.

He ducked his head to avoid the beams supporting the temple floor, and brushed cobwebs away from his face. He gagged as he moved deeper into the gloom. "This is terrible. Have you never had earthwork done?"

"It's been years," she admitted in a small voice, torn between shame at her own failures to provide for Aerynet and renewed outrage at her cousin's theft.

Ulric muttered curses in response.

Terin cleared his throat. "We'll leave you to it then, eh, Ulric?"

"Yes." Ulric's booming voice echoed strangely from under the building. "This will take at least a couple hours."

Terin offered his arm to Em. "Shall we go for a walk?"

"While I'm needed here, you have no obligation to stay." She held her breath against the hope he would leave. She wanted to return to her meditations, not spend two hours in idle chatter.

"Abandon a beautiful Lady? Perish the thought. Why do you have to stay?"

She climbed the steps back up to the sanctuary, slowly reciting the names of the gods in her head to soothe her disappointment. "Acolyte Lucy is out running errands, so I'm in charge of greeting any visitors."

"Is Aerynet too minor for a single Mystic?"

"Mystic Patricia is resting." Em held aside the sparkling strands curtaining the entrance. "Have you been on a job like this with Ulric before?"

"Quintin isn't in the habit of risking life and limb, so this situation is unique. I've only seen Ulric replenish the soil for Quintin's mother." Terin swept into the temple, his black and white waccat trailing behind him. "If you've got some good earthen food ready for him afterward, he'll appreciate it."

"My father sent down a smoked bogbear haunch for my acolytes. I could warm some of it for him."

"Meat from the bogbear that nearly killed Quintin?" He flashed a perfect smile. "Ulric will relish it."

"What about you? Would you like some tea or refreshments?"

"It is not you who should be serving me." Terin bent low at the waist. "The question is, how can I best please you?"

Em's brow knitted. Did she imagine the innuendo in his tone? "I beg your pardon?"

"I am also in your debt for my year-mate's life." Terin stepped closer, lowering his voice to a sultry purr. "I don't have Ulric's gift, but I do have other, more personal, skills you might enjoy."

"Since we're all alone with a couple of hours to fill?"

"Exactly." He smiled, slow and sensuous as a snake.

Too bad she'd never cared for reptiles. She skipped backward and pinned on her brightest smile. "How are your skills with a broom?"

He staggered slightly, as if her move away had surprised him. "A broom?"

"Yes. Fermena is ascending in less than a week, and we need to prepare for the celebration." She cocked her head, abandoning all plans of polite yet tedious chatter. If this charmer wanted to hang around until Ulric finished his task, he could make himself useful. "The best way for you to repay your debt is to help me scrub this place from top to bottom."

"Oh, so that's the way it is." His seductive smile grew into a grin. "Shall I entertain you with stories of Quintin in his youth, then?"

"No," Em said quickly, an ache in her heart. His offer was more tempting than it should be. There was no future in learning more about the Han-Auditor. "Let's get to work."

An hour later, Em was covered in dust and well satisfied

with the progress they had made. Terin had convinced young Ben to climb into the rafters to string garlands and bunches of feathers around the ceiling. The sanctuary had a festive air unlike any time since her mother's death. It was enough to give Em a thin ray of hope.

The glass beads tinkled at the entrance. Em turned, expecting Lucy or Ulric. Instead a trio in the black and red tunics of inquisitors strode into the room.

Her heart plunged to her stomach. Still she hurried forward to greet them, snagging a bundle of feathers as she went. There was nothing to be gained by appearing rude. She sank into the welcoming pose, the feathers held above her head. "Welcome to Aerynet, good inquisitors. A thousand pardons, I do not have a proper repast prepared for you. Please accept these feathers as a token of our esteem."

The trio stepped forward, making introductions and accepting the feathers.

Em rose to her feet. "How may we be of service? Do you seek the blessing of the Goddess?"

"Who does not wish to be blessed by the gods?" One woman asked. She appeared older than the other two and stood slightly in front of them. "Though our task here today is more specific in nature. Are you Acolyte Lucy d'Fermena?"

"Acolyte Lucy is out at the moment. I am Lady Emmanuella, patron of Aerynet. May I help?"

The lead inquisitor frowned. "We have questions only the acolyte can answer. When will she return?"

"Bartering at the market is an unpredictable task. She could be gone for hours yet." Em tried not to twitch as the other two inquisitors drifted away, their keen eyes studying the interior of her temple. Quintin had been able to deduce the state of their finances within minutes. Would these inquisitors also see beyond the paltry decorations?

"You say you're the patron?" The older woman raked a contemptuous glance over her dusty kaftan. "You don't look like a Lady. Show me your deed chain."

Em's stomach dropped to her toes. "I don't have it on me," she stammered. "I'm cleaning in anticipation of the new year and left my finery at home."

The inquisitor sniffed. "Your deed chain is not some bauble to be cast aside on a whim."

"Certainly not!" Em replied, trying to sound offended. "But I wouldn't want it dirtied or damaged."

The inquisitor's face tightened.

Fearing she'd gone too far, Em bent in another respectful bow. "Shall I get you some tea while you wait for Acolyte Lucy?"

"Or you could help scrub the sanctuary," Terin suggested from his perch on a table against one wall.

Em suppressed a flinch at his voice. She had forgotten he was there, witness to her humiliation.

"Who are you?" the lead inquisitor demanded.

"Han-Advocate Terin, at your service." He hopped down from the table and bowed deeply. His black and white waccat appeared from the shadows and sat at his feet.

"What's a Hand doing scrubbing floors?" the nearest inquisitor asked.

"I'm happy to help my friend, Lady Em, while I'm between circuits. Besides, even Hands benefit from the blessings of the gods." He waved a dirty rag at the inquisitor. "How about it? Want to earn some divine favor?"

The inquisitor reared back, her nose wrinkling in disgust.

"No, thank you," the lead inquisitor said firmly. "Since you are busy here we will return to question Acolyte Lucy later."

"Shall I send word to the Troika Hall when she returns?"

"Yes, I would appreciate it." The inquisitor pierced Em with a gimlet glare. "I expect to see your deed chain when I return."

Em swallowed hard to conceal her panic. "Yes, ma'am."

Chapter 31

After Ulric completed his task, Em sent him and Terin on their way as quickly as good manners allowed. She needed her deed chain and there was only one way to get it. She rode her okapi to Merdale as fast as possible, not slowing to a walk until they entered the gardens.

Her okapi snorted, his hooves crunching on the gravel drive.

"Thank you, Fermena for your blessing and guidance," Em murmured as she spotted Violet sewing under a fig tree at the edge of the garden. She had to talk to her cousin before her father realized she was back. The Goddess must approve of Em's plan to let her find her quarry so quickly, and all alone. She climbed down from her okapi.

Violet squinted against the noonday sun as Em stood over her. "Where have you been?"

"Preparing my temple for the coming year."

"Hoping the year of Fermena will be auspicious?" Her cousin slid a needle into the cloth and pulled the thread tight. "Well, you should scurry to your room before an important guest sees you dressed like a beggar."

"This year of Fermena is going to be a good one." Em looped the okapi's reins around and around her palm. "Everything is going to change, starting with the management of my lands."

Violet's hands stilled, and she cocked her head at Em. "Your lands? Does your tiny little temple have lands?"

"It does, though I've been remiss in my management of them."

Violet bared her teeth in a mocking smile. "I'm sure you've been doing a fine job."

Em's fingers tightened, the leather straps biting into her flesh. "Jon told me what you did, Violet."

Violet stood, her embroidery crumpling in her fist. "I don't know what you're talking about."

"You've had your fun. Now the time for games is over. You need to return my deed chain and put things right."

"Put things right?" Her cousin laughed. "My mother should have inherited the title years ago and you know it. I'd rather give the chain to the Reeve than back to your cheating family. I'll take it to him as soon as I get my hands on it again. You see if I won't."

"You don't know where it is?"

The okapi shied at Em's shout.

"I haven't lost it," Violet snapped. "The deed chain is safe, hidden where you'll never find it. Once this stupid Allgoday celebration is over, I'll take it to the Reeve and laugh when the Novenary strips you of your title. Your whole family will be disgraced, and you can forget about marrying Lord Evan."

"You're a thief and a fraud, Violet." Em's voice shook. "Are you eager for the Reeve to throw you in the stocks?"

Violet's dark eyes narrowed. "Your brother will be the one in the stocks, I'll make sure of it."

"If you show up with my deed chain in hand, the Reeve is not going to believe you are some innocent bystander."

"Wanna bet?"

"No, I do not want to bet. I won't be drawn into such foolishness." Em climbed back on her okapi. "Mark my words, Violet. This will not end well for you."

She nudged the okapi into a trot back the way they had come.

"It will end worse for you, Emmie," Violet called after her.

Em rode away from the estate as if to outrun her cousin's words. She let the animal have his head as he barreled down the lane with no clear destination. Anger and fear churned in her belly like eels, surging up her throat and battering at her clenched teeth. Not knowing if they would come out as screams or vomit, she locked her jaw and rode out the wriggly, writhing mess.

She couldn't go back to Aerynet while in such a state. Returning to Merdale was equally impossible. She needed time and space to regain control. To be herself without all the masks of duty and obligation.

Only one person dealt with her so honestly.

Reining her okapi to a calmer pace, Em turned off the road toward Jardin. Even if Quintin wasn't home yet for his aestivation, his peaceful garden and the memory of his kindness would soothe her soul. A few moments alone there would be almost as good as his understanding ear.

Her okapi's hooves clopped against the smooth packed ground. Distant birdsong echoed through the branches of the trees. A bright green lizard scampered around a tree trunk. How could the world carry on in such a prosaic fashion when she felt so undone?

The path opened up into a pool of cheerful sunlight. While the cottage had been welcoming in the moonlight, it fairly glowed with cozy comfort in the sunshine. A riot of vibrant flowers and darting warblers brought life to the garden.

Breathing deeply, Em climbed off her okapi. Her thoughts spun in angry circles around her dilemma, but she no longer felt on the verge of vomiting.

A stout woman emerged from a shadowed lean-to next to the house. Her eyes widened as she caught sight of Em walking into her yard.

Em's stomach tightened. She had forgotten about Quintin's mother.

The woman's face crinkled in a smile. She casually plucked a leafy stem from a nearby plant and strolled over to Em. Her long yellow chiton flapped around her calves, a line of dark embroidery dancing at the hem.

Em fought the temptation to jump back on her okapi. Riding away would be unpardonably rude.

Quintin's mother dropped into an approximation of the welcome pose and held out the plant. "Welcome to my humble home, Lady Emmanuella. I am Hannah, Mistress of Jardin. A thousand apologies for I have no vittles prepared for your visit. Please take this simple mint as a token of our hospitality."

"How do you know my name?" The question burst from her lips, bypassing her better sense. Her stomach threatening to rebel again, she wrestled with her manners and took the herb. She was in no mood to impress a stranger. "I mean, many thanks for your welcome. You are too kind."

"It wasn't hard to guess who you are since not many of our visitors arrive on okapis." Hannah's eyes twinkled as she rose to her feet. "Quintin has spoken highly of you and your beauty."

Em could only imagine what Quintin might have told his mother about her, and none of it featured her looks. The smell of mint rose from her fingers as she crushed the stalk in her hand. "Is Quintin home?"

"Not yet, though with his injury I hope he won't work long today. Please come in and sit for a spell while I prepare our repast."

"Your hospitality has already been more than I have any right to expect."

Hannah raised her eyebrows. "Especially from a no-account vegetable seller?"

Em straightened her shoulders. "Your manners are every bit as pretty as a Lady's."

Hannah cackled. "As well they should be since I was married to a Lord for nearly a cycle."

"Quintin's father was a Lord? He never mentioned it."

"He wouldn't." Quintin's mother shrugged, though there was warmth in her voice. "He's not one to puff himself up."

"Being a Hand is a greater honor than having noble relatives anyway," Em muttered, thinking dark thoughts about her own relations.

"Exactly so." Hannah gestured at the house. "Please, won't you come in until Quintin returns?"

"You don't need to feed me, a stranger dropping in unannounced." Em twisted the stalk of mint, releasing more of its pungent aroma. Her nerves skittered through her veins like minnows. She'd been seeking Quintin and his soothing acceptance of her complicated life, not the banal torture of trying to make polite conversation. "I should go."

"If you'd rather wait out here, I could set you to work weeding the garden. I find burying my fingers in the soil quite clears my head." The lines around Hannah's eyes deepened with her smile. "Ripping up a few offensive plants can be a satisfying change from the restrictive duties of a Lady."

"It's not my duties causing me grief."

"Then what do you want Quintin's help with?"

Em's fingers stilled. "Am I so obvious?"

"A Lady is not likely to visit a humble homestead purely for pleasure."

She knew she should protest but couldn't push a polite fib past her throat. Sick to death of lying and pretending, how could she explain the impulse that had led her to Jardin?

"I question only whether helping you would get my Quintin in trouble."

"No, no," Em assured her. "I'm hoping he'll talk me out of making trouble."

"Oh, my son's good at calming the roughest waters. He's got a level head on his shoulders." Hannah waved a hand at the garden. "In the meantime, let me show you the worst of the weeds. You can rain death and destruction down on their heads with no fear of the consequences."

Em's face cracked into a smile for the first time in hours. "A little harmless destruction would be lovely."

Chapter 32

Quintin hissed in pain as he tied off a knot on a quipu. His stitches pulled with each movement of his fingers, and he could only manage a loose, clumsy knot.

He wiped sweat off his forehead with the back of his wrist. The sticky midday heat added to his discomfort.

Elkart nudged his knee. *Go home now?*

Not yet. Quintin gritted his teeth as he tied another knot. *I want to finish this so we don't have to come back. I'm going to drink myself silly and maybe get some sleep this afternoon.*

The outside door swung open, letting in marginally cooler air. A private guard wearing the Merdale colors strode into the warehouse.

Quintin stifled a groan and slumped in his seat. What now?

The guard banged the butt of a ceremonial spear against the floor. All conversation among the auditors ceased.

"I seek Han-Auditor Quintin of Jardin," the guard intoned, his voice echoing through the hot, heavy air.

Wooden knobs rattled as Fredrick burst from his office. "What is the meaning of this? We're busy preparing for the end of the year, and don't have time for any nonsense."

The guard stood as straight and stiff as his spear. "I have a message for the Han-Auditor."

Bursar Fredrick tapped his staff of office against his thigh. "I'm the Bursar here. I'll see your message delivered, if I deem it important enough."

The guard's gaze lit on Elkart before jumping to

Quintin's face. Looking him in the eye, the man pitched his voice to carry. "Lord Evan a'Maral a'Tarina, Voice of the Luminary, requests the honor of Han-Auditor Quintin of Jardin's presence at a feast hosted by Lord Harold a'Taric a'Fermice a'Marana, Trilord of Merdale."

The bursar's staff tapped faster. "I have heard Lord Harold is hosting a great many notable persons for Allgoday."

"The invitation is not for Allgoday." The messenger sniffed. "My lord plans a feast tomorrow—"

"Tomorrow?" Fredrick squawked. "Impossible."

"The Troika will honor Lady Emmanuella a'Fermena for her bravery in vanquishing a bogbear and saving the life of a Hand. It is only fitting the Hand in question attend."

Fredrick's fat tongue traced his lips. "If it is important, perhaps I can attend in his stead. Mind you, it won't be easy for me—"

"Do not trouble yourself. Lord Evan has no interest in a proxy."

"Then your lord will be disappointed. The Han-Auditor is unavailable."

The messenger made no move to leave and merely raised his eyebrows at Quintin.

Fredrick noticed where the man was staring and gasped in outrage.

"It is as my Bursar says," Quintin said quickly, hoping to head off an outburst. "My deepest regrets. I'm afraid I cannot attend."

"I will convey your message to my lord." The messenger bowed and left the building.

The Bursar's raspy breathing echoed in the silence the guard left behind. Fredrick stalked over to Quintin's worktable and planted his hands on the surface.

"Don't try to make me look like a fool."

"I wouldn't dream of it, sir."

Elkart raised his head off his paws. *He not look like fool. He is fool.*

"Let me tell you something, Quintin." The Bursar leaned over, giving Quintin a face full of his wine soured breath. "Nobody likes a martyr. You think you can impress a Trilord by saving his daughter from some wild animal? It won't work. Lord Harold knows his daughter is too good for you, and nothing you do will ever change that."

With a touch of his gift, Quintin circulated the foul air away from his face. "I'm well aware of our respective stations, sir."

Fredrick lowered his voice. "You should have resigned the case when you had the chance."

Quintin met Fredrick's gaze without flinching, though his stomach tried to crawl out his throat. "My audit was honest and true."

Fredrick slapped his hand against the table. "I'll be the judge of that."

Elkart's tail lashed. *Drunken ass.*

"Get back to work," the Bursar growled to the room at large before swaggering out the door to the street.

Quintin tried to return to his knots, but nerves shook his hands, rendering the painful task impossible.

Auditor Sarah sank onto the mat next to him. "Go and get some rest."

"I've got too much to do."

"I can finish up for you. Though my knots are a little loose and wobbly, they're as good as the ones you're doing."

Quintin wiggled his swollen fingers, frustrated anew at his injury.

"I don't know why you came in today." She made a shooing motion. "You don't need to return after your aestivation."

"The Bursar won't like it."

"The Bursar is likely to be too soused after his own repast to notice."

"Or he'll be even more belligerent." The Bursar was not a happy drunk. "He might take it out on all of you if I'm not here."

"We can manage for a day." Sarah sighed. "If you don't give yourself time to heal, you'll make the damage worse, and that'll be no good for any of us. Go home, Quintin, and take care of yourself for once."

Elkart nudged Quintin's knee. *Tax-woman speaks truth.*

"Fine, fine." He clambered to his feet and eased his arm back into its sling. "My thanks, Sarah."

His arm throbbed with every step as he made his way out of the warehouse and down the street. The walk home passed in a hazy blur. Only the promise of a chilled cup of wine kept him moving. Maybe if he drank enough, he could actually sleep.

About halfway down the narrow path from the trade road to the house, Elkart lifted his nose in the air. *Okapi.*

Quintin straightened his shoulders and stitched a polite smile on his face, though his mood darkened at the thought of minding his manners in front of important visitors when all he wanted was a drink and a nap.

He reached the end of the path and his swollen fingers twitched.

Lady Em knelt in the garden not far from his mother. She tugged at a recalcitrant weed, digging her knees into the dirt, and doubtlessly ruining her trousers. She said something to his mother, who laughed easily in response.

His chest ached. He would treasure the memory of Em smiling in the sun with his mother for the rest of his days. Even as he drank in the sight, he knew he would pay for the treasure ten times over in heartache.

Elkart bounded forward and circled around the women.

"Quintin, you're home." Hannah clambered to her feet, her face bright with a welcoming smile. "And here I haven't prepared our repast. You will be staying, won't you, Lady Emmanuella?"

"I would be honored."

"I'll holler when it's ready. Maybe you can take a little walk around the garden while you wait."

Quintin watched his mother bustle into the house. "I'll be fielding questions about you for a season at least."

"I'm sorry." Em stood, batting a hand against the dirt on her knees. "I shouldn't have come."

"I'm glad you did." Seeing her while knowing he shouldn't touch her was a bittersweet torture. Still, any time they spent together was limited, and he would treat each moment like a gift from Fermena, the Goddess of Now.

She licked her lips. "I wanted to thank you. For sending your year-mates to Aerynet."

Elkart sniffed at her hand. *Lady scared.*

She patted the waccat's wide brown head. "Your earthworking friend's scolding was both embarrassing and well deserved."

He flinched. "I hope Ulric wasn't too much of an ass."

"He was very sweet actually, insisting on coming back for a full cycle in exchange for your life." She scratched Elkart, who stretched his chin up with an expression of bliss. "You're very fortunate in your friends."

"They're more dear to me than family."

Her mouth twisted. "They're better than my family for certain."

"Did you talk to your father about your temple lands?"

Pain, perhaps sorrow, flickered across her face as she nodded, her attention fixed on Elkart.

Quintin stepped close, his pulse drumming in his ears. "Is he robbing you? You don't have to suffer his greed. We'll take your case straight to the Novenary herself."

"It's not so simple." Her breath stuttered, and her voice cracked. "Can we go on a walk? I don't want to shock your mother with my tears."

"While you needn't worry about my mother's sensibilities, a private conversation is probably for the best." He offered her his elbow. "There is a nice little trail into the jungle over here."

She rested stiff fingers on his sleeve. Tension radiated off her body, as if she were holding herself together by the sheer force of her will.

He tugged her through a break in the berry hedge. The shadows of the jungle closed in around them, smelling of rich earth and decaying leaves. Loose, loamy soil muffled their footsteps, while a lone parrot cawed in the distance.

Slowly her hand relaxed against his arm. Her body lost its tension and swayed closer.

The side of her breast brushed his sleeve. Desire pulsed through him. His mouth hungered for her taste. It would be so easy, so right to turn and kiss her. As he started to reach for her, agony shot through his arm.

"Quintin." Her grip shifted from sweet to supportive. "What's wrong?"

He pulled away to rub his forehead. "I need to sit down."

"Of course." She looked left and right.

There were no logs or rocks nearby. Too tired to search for a better spot, he plopped down in the center of the trail.

Elkart slipped behind him and laid down to create a back rest.

"You should be taking your ease at home." She paced the trail in agitated steps. "You were injured two days ago protecting me, and now I've dragged you off into the jungle again."

He barked out a laugh. "If a bogbear stumbles upon us here, I will be most annoyed."

I kill it. Elkart promised.

Quintin ruffled the waccat's ears. *You aren't a match for a bogbear alone, my brave friend.*

Em stopped pacing and crossed her arms. "I have no excuse for being so selfish."

"Then make it up to me."

Her brow wrinkled.

"Come here." He patted the ground next to his uninjured side. "You've already got dirt all over your trousers."

She bit her lip and gingerly sat where he indicated.

He slipped his arm around her shoulders, inviting her to lean against him. Her hair tickled his nose as he breathed in her scent. "Better. Does more for the pain than a good cup of wine and is twice as sweet."

She pressed a hand against his chest and tilted her head back. "I don't want to hurt you."

"My arm will be fine." His heart, on the other hand, might never recover. Not wanting to dwell on such depressing thoughts, he moved on to the reason for her visit. "Now tell me, is your father robbing you?"

"Not my father. Violet."

"Your maniacal cousin?"

She shivered and pressed against his side. "She stole my mother's deed chain. Then after Mother died, she impersonated me and took over the lands. She probably expected to get away with it for only a few months. I'm such an ignorant fool it's been six years."

Nasty woman. Elkart bared his teeth. *Should have bitten at market.*

Silently agreeing with the cat, Quintin rubbed his hand up and down Em's arm. "Ferel's flatulence, what a mess."

"My father won't help me get it back. He's terrified of a scandal and says the Novenary will punish me if word of this reaches her." Em's voice shook slightly. "Do you think the Novenary would strip me of my title?"

"She might. She would have to do something in recompense for such an abuse of her trust." He sighed. He didn't want to scare Em but she deserved the whole truth. "I'm more worried about what might happen if she launches an inquisition into your temple and finds out what you've actually been doing to support it."

"It might be too late," she said quietly. "A trio of inquisitors came by looking for Lucy, and one of them noticed my absent deed chain."

His stomach plummeted. "You didn't tell them your cousin has it?"

"No. I went straight to Merdale to confront Violet, and she laughed in my face. She said she'd rather give the chain to the Reeve than to me and plans to enjoy it when the Novenary humiliates me."

He raised his eyebrows. "If she admits to bilking your temple lands for most of a cycle, she'll be lucky to escape execution."

"I think she's bluffing." Her fingers clutched his tunic. "My cousin is a dedicated gambler, and I'm sure she expects to frighten me into leaving her alone."

"Then you must call her bluff."

"Yes, but how?" She sighed, a world of despair in the sound. "Fighting the bogbear was easier than this."

"Only because bogbears are simple creatures, whereas your cousin is a devious fiend." He rubbed his cheek against her hair. "You need to start by getting your deed chain back and ending any speculation by the inquisitors. The missing chain is the only advantage Violet has. As it is, she's free to gossip about you bartering away your holy trust without implicating herself. If you have the deed chain, then she has to divulge her own fraud in order to harm you, which is much more dangerous for her."

Her eyes narrowed. "And how do you propose I force Violet to give me the chain?"

"The finest lockpick in Trimble has to ask such a question?" Quinton's mouth twisted in a smile. "You steal it, obviously."

Chapter 33

Em sat up slowly, hope blooming in her heart. "Do you think it would work?"

Quintin's shoulder moved behind her as he shrugged. "I don't see why not. She can't report the theft of something which wasn't hers to begin with. You don't want to be caught in the act, so you'll need to find the right time to go through her room at Merdale."

She tapped her lips, considering. "She said she didn't have it with her at our house."

"Even better, as long as you know where she lives in town."

Em nodded, dizzy with the possibilities. She grinned at Quintin. "This is brilliant. Oh, I could just kiss you!"

He ducked his head, a shy smile on his lips. "I wouldn't mind. If you want to."

Heat coiled in her belly at the memory of their other kisses. While she had intended her words as a jest, now she longed to kiss him properly. She rucked up her kaftan and swung a leg over his outstretched limbs, so her knees bracketed his lap.

His thighs tensed under her, though he made no move to hold her, letting her control their contact.

Heady with power, she framed his face with her hands. She ran her thumb along the edge of his bottom lip.

His breath hitched.

Dragging out the anticipation, she leaned close. She angled her head, their lips nearly touching. Her breath fanning over his face, she spoke slowly and deliberately.

"Thank you, Quintin, for giving me hope."

His lips parted, a sound of inarticulate need emerging from his throat. His uninjured hand gripped her hip.

She pressed a kiss to the corner of his mouth. Her body hummed with tension as she held herself over him, allowing only that single point of skin to skin connection.

He slid his hand around her waist, urging more contact.

Smiling against his mouth, she resisted the pressure. Instead she leisurely nibbled his bottom lip.

"Oh, Em. I want you so much," he murmured, each word laced with longing.

Unable to hold out a moment more, she fused their lips together in a passionate kiss. Her tongue plundered his mouth, stroking deep before swirling against his teeth. At the same time, she undulated her spine to press her breasts and pelvis against him.

He groaned, deep and raw, while his arm squeezed her tight.

From their sizzling kiss to her legs bracketing his lap, their bodies fit together like a key in a lock. Never had an embrace felt so right, so perfect. Her pelvis rocked against his, frustrated by the layers of cloth between them. The rigid proof of his arousal sent her desire spiraling to new heights. Scheming to get rid of their pesky attire, she sat up and broke the kiss.

A smile full of joy and innocence danced across his face. "I ought to have good ideas more often."

She stroked his cheek, her heart breaking a little. He would no more want to lose his virginity to her now than in the cacao vault. "You deserve it. And so much more."

He did deserve more. He deserved kisses from a woman of honor and integrity. He deserved the love of someone as pure and good as himself.

Instead, the only one here was her, an outlaw with a checkered past.

Unable to resist, she leaned down. "Your idea was so good, it might warrant a second kiss."

"Oh, yes, please," he moaned. Then his body tensed as if in pain.

"What's wrong? Did I hurt you?"

"No." He tugged at his queue. "Elkart hears my mother calling. If we don't head back she might come looking for us."

Elkart heaved himself to his feet. Deprived of his waccat's support, Quintin flopped onto the path, his head hitting the ground with a thunk.

Em winced in sympathy. She scrambled off his lap and offered him a hand up.

He staggered to his feet and shook out his kaftan. The voluminous garment did a reasonable job hiding his arousal. He gave her a wry smile. "My mother's timing is abysmal."

"Or fortuitous. Much longer and I might have had my way with you." She smiled to show it was a joke, only it wasn't, not really. Her need for him ached like a wound. She patted her hair. "Do I look respectable, or is she going to nag you for another month?"

"You're lovely." He stepped close enough to brush some dust from her skirt. "Which is why my mother will nag me for a month."

She studied his beloved face, before capturing the back of his neck and pulling him in for one last kiss.

Elkart whined and pranced down the trail.

He sighed and offered her his arm. "Elkart is right. It is time to go convince my mother we are utterly indifferent to each other."

"I don't know if I'm up for such a task. Can't we pretend to be friends?"

He smiled, though sadness clouded his eyes. "Oh, yes. I'm very good at being friends."

~ ~ ~

Evening shadows stretched long hands across an avenue in the Reeve District. Em twisted her mother's ring around and around on her finger. Her nerves hummed as darkness fell. She rarely took sneak work in this area and had only done so before on Taralday, when the private guards were tired from their vigilance on Taricday. To pull a job in the wealthy district on Taricday itself was pure foolishness, but she had no choice. Em had to get the chain before the Allgoday festivities ended and Violet returned home. Tonight was her only opportunity.

Dressed once again as a nondescript laborer, she tried to walk with the casual confidence of someone who belonged. Dread drummed in her veins as she navigated a route she normally traversed in the daylight. Darkness transformed the familiar streets into a strange and sinister maze. She sagged with relief when she spotted the fountain across from her aunt's house.

Slipping down a side alley, she circled around the house to the back and crept along the wall, carefully counting windows. When she reached Violet's room, she pushed on the shutters. *Locked.*

She slid her knife between the panels and drew it upward until it met resistance. Easing the blade higher, she unlatched the shutters. This time they swung open easily at her push.

The shadowy room contained only silent furnishings. With a final glance along the alley to make sure she was unobserved, she scrabbled up the wall into the room.

Once inside, she froze and listened. Footsteps shuffled in other parts of the house, accompanied by the low murmur of voices. With the family at Merdale, Violet's private room would not be used at night, yet Em dared not light a candle. Her search had to be entirely silent. Any sign of activity would arouse suspicion.

She sidled over to the wardrobe and eased its door open, then made quick work of checking the shelves and drawers.

No deed chain. Though she tried to leave the neatly folded saris and sashes as she found them, Violet would know someone had been through her things.

At the back of one drawer, she found a lumpy purse the size of a mango. She tugged on the drawstring, releasing a pungent aroma of cacao. After a moment's hesitation she slid the purse down the front of her chiton and closed the drawer.

The gentle sounds of a household going to sleep faded. All the servants had retired to their quarters for the night. Even the guards were likely to be snoozing at their posts soon.

She knelt before a trunk at the foot of the bed and lifted the lid. Inside were more stacks of clothes and bedding. Em sorted through it all, searching for a jewel box, a lumpy sari, or the deed chain itself.

Nothing except a smaller pouch of beans, which she tied to her belt.

Swallowing disappointment, she rubbed her sweaty hands against the rough fabric of her chiton. She replaced the contents of the trunk as carefully as she had the wardrobe before soundlessly lowering the lid.

Em crept over to the vanity to check its drawers. Nothing. Painted boxes and glass bottles littered the top of the vanity. The boxes were the type to hold jewelry and hair pieces. Would Violet keep the deed chain with her other jewels? Her cousin might think such pieces made the best camouflage.

Slowly and methodically, Em opened the boxes. She found only cheap beads and bedraggled feathers until she tried the largest box.

It was locked.

Her pulse sped up. She pulled her lock picking tools from the pouch at her waist and laid them out on the vanity. With practiced fingers, she went to work on the jewelry box.

When the lock clicked, the rush of satisfaction was

headier than usual. She paused a moment to calm her nerves before opening the lid and removing the top tray.

In the dim light, she sorted the jewels as much by feel as by sight. Her heart plummeted. A deed chain did not hide on the tray nor in the box.

She fingered a glittering necklace, sorely tempted to slip it into her belt pouch. Simon had always handled such sales for her, though, so she was unlikely to get a good price for it. Besides, jewelry could be identified and traced.

With a stifled sigh, she returned the necklace to the tray. She was about to replace the tray when she realized the depth of the box.

There was a second tray.

She removed it as carefully as the first. This time she was rewarded. With a shaking hand, she pulled a deed chain from the bottom of the box.

Blue-gray pumice disks set in silver marked it as a deed chain for an air temple, while crystals smaller than the tip of her pinky added some sparkle to its length. Even with the airy stones, the chain was heavy in her hand, and she could understand why her mother rarely wore it. It was not a pretty piece of jewelry, but the freedom it represented was beautiful indeed.

Slipping the chain over her head, Em replaced the trays in the jewel box. When she tried to relock the lid, her fingers trembled too much to manage it. It didn't matter. Violet would know she'd been robbed soon enough.

Em crept back out the window and pulled the shutter closed behind her. Her heart thumped like it always did after a successful job, though tonight's task was far more important than an ordinary theft.

She leaned against the wall next the window and raised her mother's ring to her lips. "Finally, Mama, finally."

Praise Fermena! She would be able to claim her lands and no one, not her cousin, not her father, could stop her.

She was free in a way she had not experienced for the past six years.

A bubble of laughter escaped her throat.

She clapped her hands over her mouth and straightened away from the wall. Now all she needed to do was return to Aerynet and shed her sneak clothes for good. The task would be simple enough if she could stop herself from giggling like a drunken idiot who had never been on a job before.

As she left the alley, she clutched the deed chain in her fist. The links pinched her neck with the force of her grip, but she needed to cling to the tangible proof of her freedom.

In the morning she would talk to her father, or maybe Gregory. She would rather ask her brother for help than her father. She would rather never ask her father for anything ever again. Gregory could help her select a grounds-keeper and survey her land with her.

She would need to dress and act like Violet when she fired whomever had been working with Violet and replaced them. Did any buildings grace her land? It would be wonderful if she could move out of her father's house entirely. She should not allow her dreams to spin too far ahead. Though in truth, her heart overflowed with hope, spilling joy through her whole body. She felt better than she had since her mother died.

"Halt, who goes there?"

Em froze. Between one heartbeat and the next, her light and bubbling heart sank like a stone to the pit of her belly.

"I said, who goes there?"

She glanced over her shoulder, her feet poised to run. A waccat prowled alongside a pair of city guards. Em's shoulders slumped as she slowly turned to face them. Running was hopeless with a waccat ready to chase her. She would have to talk her way out of this. "My name is Molly," she said. "Molly of Farbank."

"Farbank, huh?" The guard nearest the waccat stepped forward, her eyes narrowed to slits. "What are you doing here then? And in the middle of the night?"

"I'm heading home." Em licked her lips. "I worked late."

"What do you do?"

"I'm a charmaid." She could fake those skills well enough.

"For what house?"

"For Councilor Richard," Em answered quickly. At least Curtis's home was occupied, unlike her aunt's residence. "I was only hired on for tonight, for a party."

"A party?" the second guard muttered from the shadows. "On Taricday?"

Em shrugged, striving for a light tone. "Nobles have all kinds of odd notions."

The first guard leaned closer. The torch in her hand cast ominous shadows over her sharp cheekbones. "What are you holding onto there?"

The blood drained from Em's face as she realized she gripped the deed chain around her neck like a ninny. "It's mine," she whispered.

A muscle ticked in the guard's cheek. She held out her hand. "If you're telling the truth, I'll be sure to return it to you."

"It's *mine*." Em clutched the chain tighter. Her other hand rose up to cover it, instinctively protecting it. Her mind scrabbled like a lizard in a pot for excuses. "It's my payment for tonight."

The other guard snorted. "Councilor Richard pays his charmaids with jewelry?"

"All right, I admit it. I wasn't cooking and cleaning tonight." She was talking too fast and she knew it. "I was hired to provide a bit of entertainment for the Councilor's son. He gave me a necklace for my services. It's the prettiest thing I've ever had."

The first guard made a beckoning motion with her fingers. "Give me the necklace and we'll see if your story checks out."

"I doubt Curtis will admit to hiring me." Em handed the chain over to the guard, since protesting further would only raise more suspicions.

"We'll see what he says."

Em held her breath as the guard dangled the chain in the torchlight. Maybe she wouldn't recognize it as a deed chain.

"In the meantime—" The guard clenched the chain in her fist. "You're going to the stocks."

Chapter 34

Sleep eluded Quintin as he stretched out on his bedroll in his dark room. His stitches itched, and his nerves jangled with every creak and moan of the wind. His ears strained for the sound of an okapi's hooves on the path outside. By now Em should have finished the job. Though she'd made no foolish promises about reporting on her escapade to him, he hoped she would come to end his suspense. The night would be a long and torturous ordeal if he had to wait until morning to find out if she had been successful.

He closed his eyes and practiced breathing deeply, determined to quiet his mind. He needed to sleep and heal.

Lady! Trouble! Elkart's paws scrabbled against the floor as he jumped to his feet. A disjointed image of Em struggling with a pair of guards flashed through Quintin's mind.

Where are they? Quintin threw off his blanket and dashed to the door, grateful he had chosen to sleep in his kaftan. He yanked on his sandals. *How are you seeing her?*

While Elkart liked Em, a waccat could only bond so tightly with one person.

Verona there. Elkart shoved his head against Quintin's back, pushing him out the door. *Madi trap Lady.*

Quintin cursed under his breath. Dedicated and diligent, Madi wouldn't let Em talk her way out of trouble. He only hoped he could find a way to help. Trotting across the garden, he tightened his sling as he went. When he reached the trees, he broke into a run. Though his lungs burned by the time the walls of the town came into view, he didn't slow his pace.

Where are they now? Quintin asked Elkart as they entered the city.

Market. Stocks. Elkart's tail lashed. *Verona not fight them.*

Quintin grunted in response, saving his breath for running. While he wished Em did not have to endure the stocks, he could not fault Verona for letting it happen. Madi had no air, which made communication with her waccat unreliable, and the possibilities for misinterpretation were far too great for Verona to fight the arrest.

He slowed to a walk, since he would need to talk without gasping to the guards. What was the best approach? He could tell Madi about Em being a Lady and possibly win her freedom, though not without risk. Nobles were not immune to the consequences of the law and the last thing Em needed was her questionable behavior coming to the attention of the Novenary. He would have to find out what evidence they had and work from there. His stomach cramped at the thought of lying to Madi, but he would do whatever he had to in order to free Em before the sun rose.

As they approached the market square, an eerie keening filled the air.

Elkart broke into a run.

Compelled by the horrible sound, Quintin dashed after him.

There were a half a dozen people trapped in the stocks, most of them quietly weeping or slumped in exhaustion. The prisoner closest to the building writhed and thrashed in her bonds. Her head banged with repetitive thumps against the rough wood.

Elkart streaked across the square and leapt onto the platform next to her.

All thoughts of rescue strategies and persuasive arguments fled as Quintin ran to Em. He clambered onto the platform and knelt before her. Pushing the hair out of her face, he tried to give her some reassurance. "I'm here, Em. It'll be fine. I'll get you out."

She twisted as if she could somehow wiggle through the holes in the boards. A horrible panicked whine emanated from her throat. She didn't seem to see him or know he was there.

Help! Elkart prowled next to them, his tail lashing. *Lady scared.*

I'm trying. Ignoring the ache in his arm, he held his forehead to hers and pressed on her air shield, trying to break through her terror. "I'm here, Em, I'm here," he repeated both aloud and against her mind.

Her protections whistled with a thousand holes.

He blew calm promises through the cracks. "By my honor as a Hand, I will get you out of here."

Quintin. She stopped thrashing, her breath coming in panicky little pants. *Help me.*

I will. Tell me what happened.

They caught me outside the house.

Did you get the deed chain?

They took it. I'd just gotten it back and they took it! She twisted her arms, scraping the skin on her wrists as she tried to squeeze her hands through the narrow holes. Her thoughts edged into panic. *They got my picks, too, and are going to talk to Curtis about my lies. Everything is ruined, and I'll be trapped forever.*

Elkart whined and licked at her fingers.

We'll get you out of here. Quintin kissed her forehead.

Her eyes fluttered closed. *Did you bring your lockpick?*

That won't work this time. The pick she gave him felt hot and heavy hanging from his belt. *I haven't the skill to use it, and we'd be sure to get caught.*

What am I going to do? Her desperation made his own heart thump with fear.

"Quintin? Why are you here?"

Em whimpered and flinched at the sound of Madi's voice.

You will be safe. Quintin clasped her hand and looked over his shoulder at his friend. "Elkart alerted me to Em's distress. I came as quickly as I could."

Madi stood on the ground next to the platform, her hands on her hips and a frown on her face. "Come down from there."

"I can't leave her. She's terrified."

His year-mate's powerful gray and black waccat jumped onto the platform next to Elkart.

Madi's scowl deepened, though her attention was on her waccat. "You know this woman? And how did Elkart know she was in trouble?"

"Verona told him. Elkart has taken quite a liking to her."

"What? Why would Verona—"

"I have no idea what horrible misunderstanding led to this situation." He nodded at Em imprisoned by the stocks. "This is intolerable."

Em whimpered and pulled against the boards. Her panic scrabbled at him like claws.

He squeezed her fingers. *I'm here, Em. You will be safe.*

Madi crossed her arms over her chest. "She was skulking around the Reeve's district."

"There is nothing wrong with walking down a public street."

"Then why did she lie about what she was doing there?"

Let me go! Em twisted her arms again as images of her mother and the cacao vault flashed through her mind. *I have to get out.*

He held tight to her hands, trying to prevent more damage to her wrists. "I will get you free, I promise."

Her head drooped as a stream of prayers passed through her mind.

Quintin turned back to his year-mate. "Please, Madi, can't you let her out of this thing? I'll answer any questions you want. You can put me in instead if you need to. Please, please, let her go."

His friend snorted. "I'm not putting a Hand in the stocks."

Em's fingers bit into his.

"Please. She's hurting herself."

"Who is this woman?" Madi's expression was harsh in the dim light. "Why do you care if some housebreaker gets scraped up?"

"She's my . . ." Quintin's stomach churned. He had to push the words past his lips. "She's my lover."

"Your lover is a thief?"

Em whimpered again and twisted in his grip.

"She's not," he protested. "Please, Madi. I can explain everything after she's out of this thing. I give my word as a Hand, we won't run away."

Madi let out her breath in a huff. "I'll go get the keys. We'll need to talk mind-to-mind about this before I can let her leave."

"Yes, yes. Anything you need. Thank you, Madi."

She tromped away, her boots ringing on the bricks. Her waccat flopped down on the platform while Elkart paced in circles around them.

Quintin smoothed Em's hair back from her face. *Hold on a little longer. We're getting you out.*

She blinked at him. "I'll be free?" she asked, her voice raw and scratchy.

"Soon. Madi went to get the key." He ran a thumb over her cheek. "We'll get you out, then I'll talk to Madi for a bit and then we can go."

Her lips trembled. *What if she locks me up again?*

No! Elkart's intruding thought was accompanied by a growl. *No more traps. I stop her.*

Quintin shuddered at the thought of Elkart brawling with Madi. *I'll talk her into letting Em go.*

Elkart's ears flattened. *Madi like trapping thieves.*

Em did nothing wrong tonight. He would cling to the thought like a drowning man. With the difficulties of lying mind-to-mind, he would need every truth on his side. *Em is my beloved and she did nothing wrong. All I need to do is convince Madi there is nothing more to it.*

Footsteps echoed on the platform as Madi returned. Silently, she stuck a big bronze key into the lock holding the boards together. The key rattled as the lock fell open. Quintin stood to help Madi remove the top board.

Sobbing quietly, Em scrambled out of the stocks as soon as her neck and arms were free.

Quintin tensed, worried she would bolt. Instead she slumped onto the platform. He fell to his knees next to her and pulled her into a hug.

She crawled into his lap, her position a heartbreaking parody of their embrace in the woods earlier. She shook like a leaf in his arms, a far cry from the powerful, sensual woman who had kissed him with such skill.

"You're safe now. I've got you," he muttered into her hair.

While her thoughts flitted about like terrified birds, her soul-crushing panic receded. She trusted him. He had to find a way to keep his promise and secure her freedom.

Elkart nuzzled Em, his very presence a guarantee of bloodshed if anyone tried to lock her up again.

Madi clapped a hand on Quintin's shoulder. "You owe me an explanation."

"Agreed." His stomach flopped like a dying fish. Uncomfortable truths tended to knock around in his brain and out of his mouth whether he wanted to speak them or not. Keeping all his thoughts sorted while speaking mind-to-mind would take a degree of cleverness he wasn't sure he possessed. Trying to calm himself and bolster his gift, he took a deep breath. He inhaled the jasmine scent of Em's hair. His mind sharpened and his nerves quieted.

He could do this. For her.

Keeping one arm around Em, he took hold of Madi's callused fingers.

His gift gusted against his year-mate's mind. Even with her protections gone, he strained to blow his thoughts through her thin air. *I may not be very coherent,* he told her honestly, wanting to set a tone of confidences shared rather than an interrogation. *This has been very upsetting. And all my fault.*

Your fault?

We've been sneaking around. Memories of their stolen kisses flooded his mind. He reveled in the images, though he couldn't be sure Madi could see them. He'd forgotten how much focus it usually took to speak mind-to-mind.

She was coming to see you?

I wanted her to. Guilt stabbed at him. *It was my idea and it all went terribly wrong.*

He squeezed the woman in his arms. "I'm sorry, Em," he murmured into her hair.

"Why do you need to sneak around?" Madi said aloud, either forgetting about the mind-to-mind contact or uncomfortable with the strain.

Em raised her head and licked her lips. "My father's a Trilord."

"I'm only interested in Quintin's answers," Madi said sharply. "I've had enough of your lies."

Em shrank against him. "Yes, sir," she murmured, her voice full of tears.

Quintin dropped his year-mate's hand to stroke Em's hair. "Really, Madi, that is outside of enough."

"Sorry, Quintin. All she's done is told us one lie after another."

"Would you have believed her if she'd told you her father was a Trilord?"

"If her father is a Trilord, why does she look like a laborer?"

"Exactly so." He nodded shortly. "You wouldn't believe her, or would want to talk to her father, which would be awful since he thinks she's tucked safely in bed."

"You never did explain the reason for this midnight tryst."

"Isn't it obvious? Her father doesn't approve of our relationship."

"Why not? You're a respectable Hand."

"I'm a vegetable seller's son. He has higher expectations for his daughter."

"Is she the one who told you that?" Madi jerked her chin at Em. "She's been playing you for a fool, Quintin, probably hoping to use you as an alibi to get her out of the stocks. She's a thief, not a Trilord's daughter."

"You're wrong." Not knowing how else to convince her, Quintin focused his air and pressed his thoughts into Madi's mind. *She is a Lady of the Realm. Her Trilord father told me to my face to keep my hands off his daughter.*

If she's not a thief, how do you explain these? Madi held out Em's packet of lockpicks.

Quintin licked his lips, his stomach dropping. "It's a game we play—"

"Mind-to-mind please."

"Sorry." He took a breath to steady himself and strengthen his gift. *She's been teaching me, for fun.* He envisioned her laughing in his rooms as he struggled with his chest. She'd been so beautiful and lighthearted then, nothing like the woman shivering in his arms now.

"How does a Lady know how to pick locks?"

Em tensed. He rubbed her back, trying to soothe her. "She's afraid of tight places, of being trapped. Knowing how to escape a locked room calms her," he said, blowing the words into Madi's mind as he spoke. *The stocks were a nightmare.*

Madi tapped the picks against her palm. *I'm sorry.*

I'd like to take her home now.

To your house or hers?

Her choice. Though he had a sudden longing to see her curled up safe in his room again. He cleared his throat. "Will you have to tell your captain? This has been horrible enough. I'll never forgive myself if she's subjected to nasty rumors on my account as well."

"I'll talk to my partner and keep it quiet. We're no more eager for the Reeve to hear about this than you are, believe me." Madi handed him the picks. "I'll go get her other things."

Quintin helped Em to her feet and down from the platform. Elkart leapt easily to the ground beside them.

"Thank you for freeing me," she said.

"I'm sorry it was necessary and glad it worked."

Her whole body trembled. "I can't imagine spending a week there."

Madi cleared her throat behind them. "Here are her beans and the deed chain she was wearing."

"Thank you," Quintin said simply as he took the pouch. Em curled into him again at the sound of Madi's voice.

Madi frowned at her. "It was an honest mistake."

Quintin sighed. Madi had only been doing her job, but he could not pretend no harm had been done. Em felt as tense and fragile as a thread pulled too tight. "We will be more circumspect in the future," he said.

If there is a future.

Chapter 35

"Where should we go?" Quintin asked the woman tucked against his side as they left the market square behind. Part of him never wanted to let Em go again, though his practical side knew he needed to get her to safety and then return to his own lonely bed. "Do you have an okapi outside of town?"

"I can't go back to Merdale. Not dressed like this."

"I could take you to my house, though I don't relish hiding you from my mother."

"I planned to spend the night at Aerynet. I've a change of clothes there and can head home in the morning."

"As you wish."

They walked together through the dimly lit wharf district, their bodies moving in a harmony that made him ache inside. Laughter boomed from a nearby tavern. Em started at the noise.

Elkart nudged her hip. *Lady free. Why scared?*

It has been a very rough night.

When they reached the stairs to her temple, he bent into a low bow of deep respect. "I'm glad your work tonight was successful."

"Please." She touched his cheek.

"Yes?" He held his breath against the hope she would kiss him.

"Please. I know I have no right to ask for anything more."

He silently cursed his lascivious thoughts. She was clearly too distressed for kisses. "What is it, Em? What can I do?"

"Come with me." Need and fear swam in her eyes. "I don't want to be alone."

"Isn't your acolyte already here?"

"I don't want to wake her. I'll feel like a ninny, crying about my close call with the stocks when her brother spent half a week in them."

"Her brother was your contact for jobs?"

"Not anymore. He left town." Her voice dropped to a whisper. "One stint in the stocks was enough for him."

He rubbed her arms. "I'll stay until you're cleaned up and settled."

Elkart bounded up the stairs and batted at the door.

"Hush." Em brushed past the waccat to slide the panel aside. She lit a candle and paused for a moment under the statue of Fermena. The flickering light cast harsh shadows over her tense features. Yet, despite the tracks of her tears shining on her cheeks, a holy serenity infused her face. "Praise Fermena for her wisdom and guidance."

Quintin shook with the impulse to erase her tears with his lips. She needed comfort, not passion. Not knowing how to give one without the other, he curbed his desires and rumbled out his own prayer of thanks.

The birds in the rafters cooed, adding their sleepy sounds to the prayers. After a final bow to the avatar of the Goddess, Em tugged him behind the alter. "The steamroom won't be as good as a bath, but it's the best Aerynet has to offer."

He cleared his throat as they stepped into the alcove leading to the steamroom. "I probably shouldn't go in there with you."

"Why not?"

He licked his lips. How could he explain without sounding depraved? "I don't know if I can take the torture of seeing you naked again. My injured hand is useless for relieving these kinds of tensions, you know."

She chuckled. The sound coiled through him. Thank Fermena she could laugh.

Her wicked smile chased some of the shadows from her eyes. "I'm very good at relieving tensions, and both my hands work fine."

Quintin forgot to breathe as his cock surged to life. He tried to hold on to his sanity in the face of her suggestion. "The steamroom is a holy sanctuary."

"Fermena is a Goddess of the Now. I doubt she begrudges anyone a moment of comfort or pleasure."

Would she take comfort from touching him, or was she offering him pleasure because she was grateful, as with her kiss in the jungle? He didn't want her thanks.

Her belt slithered to the floor.

He did want her, though. More than breath.

Her chiton joined her belt.

His mouth went dry. She was so beautiful. How could he think when she was standing there naked? When every fiber of his being yearned to touch her?

She cocked her head at the door. "Coming with me?"

He shrugged off his sling. "Getting undressed with one hand is a slow business."

"I'll help you." She peeled his kaftan off over his head, being careful of his wounds.

He fumbled with his trousers, until she took over the task with unnerving ease.

She pulled him by the wrist into the tiny chamber. After lighting a candle on either side of the doorway, she sat down cross-legged in front of the brazier. Murmuring prayers, she buried her hands in the rocks.

Quintin knelt on the wood floor next to her and tried not to shiver. His body hummed with anticipation, while his mind scampered in loops like a lizard circling a tree branch. He breathed deeply in an attempt to capture the spirit of the holy place. He needed all the help he could get to live in the Now and let go of his worries and doubts for the future.

Em pulled away from the heat rippling off the brazier. As she poured water over the rocks, hissing steam glowed gold in the candlelight.

"I am forever in your debt, for everything." She leaned toward him, her head tilted for a kiss.

He shifted away. He wanted her desire, not her gratitude. "You don't owe me anything."

"You lied for me. To another Hand." Her eyes narrowed. "You knew her, didn't you? She called you Quintin."

"Madi is one of my year-mates, a friend." He mentally stirred the air, distributing the heat around the room. "We're lucky she's the one who caught you. I might not have been able to convince another guard to let you go."

"Is she one of your friends more dear than family?"

"Yes. Now you've met all four of them."

"You lied to one of your closest friends. For me."

"Claiming a beautiful woman as my lover isn't much of a hardship."

"Shall I make it up to you by turning your lie into a reality?"

"You don't have to—"

She pressed a finger against his lips. "I want to."

Her mouth replaced her finger. Her questing tongue chased the doubts from his mind. Did it matter why she was kissing him, as long as she didn't stop?

Passion sparked through Quintin's veins, flaming to life everywhere she touched. She slid her hot hands over his shoulders and down his back. When she reached his hips, one hand drifted into his lap.

His cock twitched, pulsing and hardening as she explored his length. His head fell back with a moan. "Marana have mercy, that feels so good."

How would it feel if she explored him with her tongue? He'd heard of such things, dreamed about them, but never experienced them. As if reading his mind, she trailed kisses over his neck and down his chest. Her fingers caressed his cock as her lips drifted over the planes of his belly.

His fingers tangled in her hair. He should stop her. A few thankful kisses were one thing. This was too much.

"I am honored to serve," she purred before her lips closed over him.

Any protest he might have given drowned in a flood of ecstasy. His entire body pulsed with each stroke of her tongue.

He made a keening noise as her fiery, wet mouth transported him to paradise.

Chapter 36

Paradise.

Em's heart bubbled with satisfaction, though her mouth was too busy to smile. Quintin's thoughts whispered at the edges of her mind, only one word clear in a dozen. She relished the partial intimacy. Sharing his enjoyment heightened her own.

As her mouth worked him, heat pulsed between her legs. She pulled back to swirl her tongue around his salty tip. A heady sense of power filled her. This was his first taste of this kind of pleasure. Whatever the future might hold, he would never forget this night. Never forget her.

His hands moved restlessly over her hair, tugging and kneading. Her braids fell in untidy strands across his lap.

"Marana have mercy," he panted.

She pulled back enough to speak, making sure her breath blew over his damp, sensitized flesh. "Do you like that?"

"Yes," he hissed, his thoughts echoing behind the word. *Good. So good.*

As if in a dream, she could see herself on her back with her hair spread across a pillow.

Such a position wasn't possible in the confines of the steamroom, though she could offer him deeper satisfaction a different way. Unable to resist, she gave his cock one last suck, then rose up to kiss him.

His mouth was hot and eager under hers. His tongue thrust deep. The wild kiss sent desire spiraling through her body, tightening her breasts and dampening her core.

Em parted her knees to straddle him. The warmth of his skin against her inner thighs drove her passion to new heights, leaving her desperate for more. She reached down between them and clasped his shaft, breaking the kiss to stare into his eyes. She wanted to watch his face as he entered her for the first time. Her thumb circled the sensitive tip of his cock.

"Please." The word trembled on his lips, and in his mind. *Please, more, please.*

She stroked his cock and positioned it at her entrance. "Tell me what you want."

She expected him to answer mind-to-mind but instead he took a shuddering breath and spoke aloud. "I need you, Em."

"I'm right here," she answered, rattled by the idea that he might not know he was sharing his thoughts.

Need you. The longing in his gaze pierced her as he struggled to speak. "I want to be in you."

"As you wish." She shifted her hips and took him deep inside.

Satisfaction flashed across his face. With a guttural groan, he arched his back. *Perfect.*

She rose off him and then slid back down. His hips matched her rhythm.

Pleasure and awe played over his features with every thrust. The time for conscious thought was over. Flooded with tenderness, she slowed her pace to draw out their enjoyment. All too soon she could feel her climax tightening her skin. She increased the tempo, riding him in earnest.

"Em, oh, Em!" Straining to bury himself yet deeper, he lifted her off the floor.

She captured his cries with a hungry kiss. Her body clenched with her own release as he pumped his essence into her.

She slumped boneless against him, nuzzling the soft skin between his neck and shoulder. His musky scent filled her senses.

Crushing her to his chest, he threaded one hand into her hair. *I need you forever. Marry ME!*

His voice was so clear in her head she almost thought he had spoken aloud. She smiled against his neck, ready to say yes.

No, idiot! No!

Shocked by the vehemence of his inner denial, she raised her head. Disgust flashed across his face. Was the prospect of marrying her really so horrible?

Gripping her hips, he lifted her from his lap. His limp flesh exited her body with a painful pull.

She flinched at the strange, postcoital sting.

He tensed. "Are you all right?"

She wasn't sure she'd ever be all right again. The air in the room suffocated her with heat, yet she felt chilled to the core.

"That hurt," she admitted. Why did her body ache from his loss?

"Sorry, I've never done this before." He eased away from her and retied his queue. "I was trying to prevent a babe. I didn't mean to pain you."

"Oh. Thank you," she said, though she didn't feel very grateful. His caution proved how desperate he was to sever all ties with her.

He might have wanted her in one brief moment of weakness, but his common sense had all too quickly silenced the impulse.

After all, she was a thief. A Hand could not marry an outlaw. The very idea was preposterous. As her anger flared, she welcomed its heat. And hated him a little for being sensible. Why did he always have to be so practical? She would have said yes. Eagerly, joyfully, without hesitation or reservation, she would have sworn to spend her life with him.

But he had not asked her to, the prig.

She wanted him to be as lost in love as she was.

Her heart faltered and then beat double time.

I love him. Heart, body and mind.

And it meant nothing. Nothing.

Chapter 37

"I should leave." Quintin scrambled to his feet and pushed open the steamroom door. He had to get out of there before he said something irrevocable. Or repeated his embarrassing confession of love.

Elkart whined unhappily while Quintin struggled to get dressed.

Em leaned against the doorjamb and made no move to help him.

Thank Fermena for her restraint. He couldn't handle her touching him right now. Not when he felt so raw and on edge.

Finding her deed chain with his things, he held it up reverently. She was free now, and he would do nothing to spoil that. Unable to resist, he slipped the chain over her head. She was so beautiful it hurt.

"I wish you well." His tongue felt thick and clumsy as he struggled to say good-bye, without saying too much. "In all you do."

She clutched the stones and met his gaze, a spark of something fierce in her eye. "Be happy, Quintin."

He nodded but made no promises. He didn't want his last words to her to be a lie.

His waccat's concern pressed against his mind as they walked home. Uninterested in sorting through his jumbled emotions, Quintin kept his thoughts to himself.

Mercifully silent, Elkart led him down the darkened path with his superior night vision. Quintin's head throbbed from the mind-sharing with Madi and the help of his second sight wasn't worth adding to his pain.

Numb and exhausted, he stumbled into his room, found his rumpled bedroll mostly by feel, and fell into it, too tired to turn onto his back.

Burying his face in his musty pillow, he waited for sleep to come. Pain hammered his head in time to his heartbeat.

You not happy.

Quintin groaned, in no shape for a philosophical discussion with his waccat.

Lady tell you, be happy. You not happy.

I'm tired, Elkart.

The waccat sniffed at his fingers before flopping down next to him. *You sad.*

Quintin draped an arm over the great cat, taking comfort from the warm furry body. In the privacy of his darkened room, alone with his waccat, he could admit to the depression gripping his soul. *Yes. I'm sad.*

Why? You mate with Lady. It good, yes? You like mating?

Oh, yes. It was . . . soul-shattering, earthshaking, glorious beyond his wildest imaginings . . . *good, very good.*

So why sad? Not like cubs?

There won't be any cubs. When they had separated, he used his limited water gift to pull his essence out of her body. He hoped it worked. Marana knew, he'd never practiced the technique.

No cubs? Then why mate?

Because I wanted to. Humans don't always make babies. Mostly it feels good.

She wanted also?

I think so, yes. He pressed his cheek against the waccat's fur. Sadness dragged at his soul. *Maybe. I don't know.*

Had she wanted him, or just wanted to please him? Everything they'd done had been for him. To satisfy his needs. Even now his body stirred at the memories of their coupling. Joining with her had been glorious but guilt gnawed at the edges of his thoughts. He couldn't shake the feeling she'd acted out of relief rather than genuine desire. A more honorable man would have resisted her given the circumstances.

At least he had stifled the urge to propose marriage. She might have said yes out of a misplaced sense of gratitude. He would have been devastated when she came to her senses. He shuddered. Or worse yet, she might have gone through with it, bound by a sense of duty and obligation.

He had not helped her escape from the tangled nets of her family only to snare her in an inauspicious marriage. She deserved better, to live the life of a Lady that should have been hers six years ago.

What's marriage? Elkart asked. *You want?*

Quintin's heart lurched. It didn't matter what he wanted. Em had made it perfectly clear that day in the cacao vault, how she didn't consider him marriage material. *Marriage is like bonding, only between humans,* he answered, focusing on the less painful half of the waccat's question. *Without waccat's abilities, humans can only tie their lives and their futures together, not their souls.*

Many humans do this? Bond without bonding?

Most people do it before making children. It's how we become family.

Pack good. Elkart's chest rose and fell with a sigh. *Lady good for pack. You marriage her?*

It's marry, and no, I won't do it again.

Again? You marriage already?

No. Quintin's brow wrinkled as he puzzled over his thought. *You bonded with me out of obligation. I won't have Em marry me for the same reason.*

Elkart's tail beat an irritated tattoo against the floor. *Obligation? What is this obligation?*

Quintin tightened his arm around the waccat, remembering how desperate he had been to bond. His mother had planned to beg his half-brother for the funds to send Quintin to school in the capitol. Distressed by the plan, he had gone to sleep in tears, pleading with the gods to save him from debts to a man he despised. In the night he dreamt of waccats. He spent the next week skipping school to hang around the Troika Hall. In the end, Elkart took pity on him and made him a Hand.

Not true. Elkart nuzzled his hair. *Waccats have no pity.*

Are you saying it's a coincidence you bonded with me right after I told you about my troubles with going away to school?

No. You say you leave soon. I not want you to leave. The waccat swiped a rough tongue over Quintin's arm. *So we bond and we stay.*

Quintin dug his fingers into the soft fur behind his waccat's ears. *Or at least stay together.*

Elkart's tail twitched. *Exactly.*

Quintin could not deny bonding with his waccat had led to the greatest friendships and opportunities of his life. He would do it again in a heartbeat, but he could never shake his gratitude to Elkart for taking a chance and bonding with a scrawny eleven-year-old he barely knew. The idea of entering into a marriage with Em on the same unequal footing left a bitter taste in his mouth.

He would rather be alone than love a woman who did not love him back with equal fervor.

~ ~ ~

The next morning Em took the steps two at a time as she entered the manor house at Merdale. Heavy silver links rubbed against her skin with every step, reminding her of her victory. The deed chain was hers. All of Violet's schemes were about to end. She should be glorying in her triumph, but it all tasted like ashes.

She wanted to crawl into bed and not come out for a month. Though if the night before were any indicator, even curling up in bed wouldn't lead to restful sleep. When sleep proved impossible, she tried to focus on the future and what she needed to do next to reclaim her lands. Instead, her mind kept circling back to Quintin and his aborted proposal.

Nothing would ever come of it, he had told her that fateful day in the jungle. She had known, even then, forgetting the truth would lead to heartache and pain.

But forget it she had, for one brief shining moment when their desires had aligned. In the ecstasy of perfect harmony, hope had given her heart wings.

Until cruel reality intruded. Dwelling on her grief, she blindly crossed the family courtyard.

"Emmie, you're home," Isabel called from a seat near the fountain. Em's brothers, along with Lord Evan and his daughter sat at a table laden with fruit and honeyed treats.

Em paused to bow at the gathering. "I hoped to change out of my riding clothes before any of our guests awoke. A thousand pardons for my appearance."

"Think nothing of it. I like to think we are more like family than guests." Lord Evan smiled at Em and gestured for her to join them. "Besides, you look quite fetching in a kaftan."

Em bristled at his familiar tone, reminded of his insulting scheme to marry her. The deed chain around her neck took on new weight and importance. She no longer had to entertain thoughts of an odious marriage for the sake of Aerynet.

"Come have some mango. I know it's your favorite." Jon dished up a plate and set it in front of the open seat next to him.

Em sighed and joined them.

Isabel wagged a finger at her. "Your father has been far too indulgent, letting you live at your temple this past week. Do you know about the celebration we have planned for today?"

"Father told me to return today. He didn't say why."

Isabel snorted softly. "Typical."

"We are going to honor your bravery, my dear." Lord Evan grinned broadly. "A pair of Hands representing the Novenary and the Mortarary will be coming up from Trimble, while I will represent the Luminary. I thought it only fitting the Troika thank you for saving one of their Hands, and Mistress Isabel has been most indulgent in letting me put together this little ceremony."

Isabel made a dismissive noise. "I'm happy to help."

"Qui—I mean, the Han-Auditor is coming here? This afternoon?" Her stomach churned. How could she face him again so soon?

"I'm afraid Han-Auditor Quintin won't be there," Isabel said. The calculating look in her eye countered any relief Em might have felt at the reprieve.

"I did invite him, but this is a very busy time for tax collectors." Lord Evan patted Em's hand. "We'll still have a very nice feast, my dear."

"I'm not your dear," Em said before she could think better of it.

Jon forced a laugh. "What?"

Lord Evan raised his brows. "I meant no disrespect."

Em tilted her chin up. If she'd slept better the night before, she would have had the presence of mind to confront Lord Evan in private. There was no help for it now. Since she'd started, she might as well speak her piece. "I know you mean to marry me."

His jaw dropped. "Marry you?"

"I overheard you talking about the marriage settlement with my father."

"And you thought I intended to marry you?" Lord Evan pressed a hand against his chest with a wheezing laugh. "Marana have mercy, no. You are far too young and headstrong for an old man like me."

"Then what—?"

"Catherine has done me the great honor of agreeing to become my wife," Jonathan said. He bumped Em with his shoulder. "Now you've ruined the surprise, Emmie."

Isabel clasped her hands together, her eyes sparkling. "Is this true?"

Catherine blushed, looking simultaneously embarrassed and delighted. Her hand rested on Jon's. "It is."

Isabel squealed and jumped up to give Catherine a hug. "A wedding! How wonderful!"

Gregory pounded Jon on the back in hearty congratulation.

"Now, now." Lord Evan raised his hands over the hubbub. "We are in mourning until Allgoday. There will be no announcement until after the festival."

"What a way to start the new year!" Isabel's dimple flashed. "This will be a Fermenasday to remember."

The celebratory chatter floated around Em like tendrils of mist, obscuring her sight without ever touching her. Crushing loneliness hollowed out her chest, leaving no room for anything else. She couldn't even muster up a spark of embarrassment for believing Lord Evan wanted to marry her. Why would he?

If a man who professed to love her was horrified by the prospect, how could anyone find her suitable?

"Em?" Catherine leaned in close. "Are you crying? Have we upset you?"

"No, no, I'm very happy for you." Em grabbed her brother's betrothed in a fierce hug, willing her tears to go back where they came from. If she gave them free rein, they might never stop. "Though I'll have you know Jonathan doesn't deserve a woman as good as you."

"I know I don't, Em," Jon said quietly. "I'm trying to do better."

Em's arms tightened around Catherine. Her deed chain dug into her skin.

Catherine pulled back and rubbed her chest. "Are you wearing a necklace?"

"Sorry." Em wiped her eyes before pulling the chain out from under her kaftan.

Jonathan gasped. "Is that a deed chain?"

"It's Mother's." Gregory grinned, delight filling his voice.

"Not Mother's. Mine. I have my own plans for the year of Fermena." While none of them were as joyful or lovely as a wedding, they were good plans nonetheless. She caught Gregory's eye. "For too long I've let my temple be grounded in the past. I want to start living in the now and would beg your assistance with bringing my goal to fruition."

Gregory poured himself a goblet of wine. "What might I do to help?"

Em toyed with her deed chain. "Well, first I need a new grounds-keeper."

Chapter 38

Three hours later, after a quick and satisfying trip to her temple lands, Em hurried to her room to prepare for the visit by the representatives of the Troika. Her mind on her lands and newfound possibilities, she allowed a maid to wrap her in a fresh sari.

"Hold a moment," Em instructed, before the maid pulled the end of her sari over her hair. She unwound the deed chain from her wrist and slipped it around her neck.

The maid's eyes darted to the chain and a frown wrinkled her brow, though she said nothing as she pinned the sari to Em's hair.

Em fingered the rough pumice stones. "My father doesn't care for my deed chain, yet it seems only fitting to acknowledge my place as a Lady entrusted by the Novenary when being honored by the Troika."

The maid's face cleared. "'Tis a pity it is so unsightly. No wonder I've not seen it before."

"Unsightly or not, I have resolved to wear it more often in recognition of my station."

"As well you should, my lady."

Once the sari was folded and tucked to her satisfaction, Em slid all the bangles she owned onto her wrists in an effort to hide the abrasions from the stocks. Finally garbed like a proper lady, she made her way through the family wing to the public courtyard to await the Hands. A crowd had already gathered, as their guests had little other entertainment before the Allgoday festivities.

"Here, Lady Emmanuella." Isabel's mother beckoned her to a raised platform in front of the central fountain.

Em approached the cluster of guests but balked at getting on the dais. "This is too much."

Lord Harold thumped his hand against the wood. "It is a fitting tribute to your bravery."

"You will look as beautiful as a goddess up there. I vow you are the loveliest Lady here." Isabel's mother perused her with a wide smile, though her smile faltered when it reached her neck. "What an . . . interesting necklace. Is it a deed chain? It's not in the usual style."

Em touched the silver links, marveling at its solid weight, proof of her daring success. "It is very old."

Lord Harold's eyes bulged. "How—"

"I know it's not very flattering." Em interrupted quickly with a warning smile at her father. "Yet I should take pride in my station when being honored by the Troika."

"You're wearing your deed chain?" Violet edged close, craning her neck to peer at Em. "I don't recall ever seeing it before. One would almost guess you didn't have one."

Lord Harold recovered enough to glare at Violet. "She is a Lady of the Realm with all the rights and responsibilities that entails."

Violet gave a languid shrug. "I'd heard rumors she'd lost it."

Gasps and whispers echoed Violet's words. Guests circled closer, attracted to scandal like vultures to dead meat.

"You heard wrong." Em pitched her voice to carry. She held the chain away from her sari so Violet, and the other guests, could see it clearly. "I never misplaced it."

Isabel's mother sniffed. "Obviously not! You wouldn't be so careless with a gift from your Novenary."

"A deed chain is more than a gift. It is a holy trust. One my family takes very seriously." Lord Harold pinned Violet with narrowed eyes. "I expect more from my honored guests than to be slandered by baseless lies."

Violet's nostrils flared, but before she could speak, her mother grasped her elbow.

"My daughter meant no offense." Aunt Florence bowed low, forcing Violet to do the same. "It was an honest mistake given how infrequently Emmie wears the chain."

"I'm not in the habit of displaying it," Em conceded with a nod. "I was so young when I inherited, it has taken me time to grow into my role. As I enter my third cycle, I vow to attend to my duties more closely. Why, only this morning I replaced my grounds-keeper."

Violet straightened so fast she yanked her mother up with her. "You can't do that."

Em stroked her deed chain, empowered by the rough stones. "I can and did."

"But, but," Violet sputtered. "The old grounds-keeper, he'll—"

"He'll be quite comfortable working on one of our other properties," Gregory broke in smoothly. "He has been well-rewarded for his loyalty to our family. It is a pity the only position we have is on an estate far from here, though he was eager enough to take it."

"You can't," Violet protested again, her lips bloodless.

"You are too kind, worrying so about the fate of a grounds-keeper. I assure you, we have no intention of punishing *him*." Em smiled at her cousin, making sure to show all her teeth. "This year of Fermena is going to be good for me and my temple. We are all starting fresh."

Isabel's mother nodded approvingly. "Changes are auspicious at this time of year, especially for a temple of Fermena."

A gong sounded at the front of the house, scattering the guests. Violet's shoulders slumped as her mother dragged her away, whispering furiously in her ear.

Em schooled her features to keep the triumph off her face. Aunt Florence would surely keep Violet in line, and her cousin would never be a threat to Aerynet again.

Isabel's mother clapped her hands. "Hurry now, Lady Emmanuella. You must be in position before they arrive."

Feeling a fool, yet seeing no help for it, Em allowed her father to help her onto the dais. Crossing her legs, she sat on a silken pillow, then straightened her sari to cover her feet and better display the beaded and embroidered hem. Proper and demure, she smiled politely at the entrance, ready to be rewarded for acting in a most unladylike fashion.

Isabel entered the courtyard, followed closely by the representatives of the Troika in wedge formation. Lord Evan took the center position while a man in a guard's uniform and a woman in a green sari flanked him. A pair of waccats completed the entourage. As they drew close to the dais, Em recognized the woman. Quintin's lovely year-mate.

Em's smile turned into a brittle mask, as the way Quintin said *Ophelia* echoed through her mind. He'd welcomed her like a man dying in a desert welcomes water. This graceful woman was the year-mate he professed to love in his youth, Em was sure of it. Obviously, his love had not faded.

Em knotted her fingers together to keep her hands from rubbing the painful ache in her chest.

Quintin would not recoil in horror at the thought of marriage to his beautiful, honorable friend.

Isabel presented the trio with great fanfare, introducing Lord Evan as if he had not been living at Merdale for the past week. The guard, a Trimble Han-Captain, made his bow crisply.

Finally, Isabel turned to the beautiful Hand in green. "The Novenary has sent Han-Mystic Ophelia d'Marana, Hand of Destin and Seer of Trimble to give her blessings to your future."

The Han-Mystic pressed her hands together and bent in a low bow. "I requested the honor of representing the Novenary in this, for Han-Auditor Quintin is one of my year-mates and well known to me. I thank you personally and from the bottom of my heart for your bravery and skill in vanquishing the bogbear and saving my year-mate's life."

Em's fingernails dug into her palms. This woman's flowery gratitude irritated her in a way Ulric's blunt bartering hadn't. "Only by the grace of Ferel my arrows flew straight and true and I was able to frighten the creature off. The Han-Auditor engaged the beast hand-to-hand. The Troika should be proud, for their Hand serves well and is a credit to them."

She swallowed against the pain rising in her throat. Quintin served so well, he scorned an outlaw such as herself even as he desired her. Lust stood no chance of overcoming his sense of duty and honor.

Ophelia raised her eyebrows. "Han-Auditor Quintin is a man without equal, which is why we thank you, as an instrument of Ferel's will, if nothing else."

"Indeed, the Troika are well aware of the value of each and every one of their Hands," Lord Evan interjected smoothly. "For saving someone so dear to them, we present you with this."

With a flourish, he pulled away the cloth draped over his left hand to expose a detailed carving of a rearing bogbear.

The crowd gasped and murmured. Bells jangled as women stomped the floor in approval.

Lord Evan held the statue high as he spun in a slow circle. When he faced Em once more, he bowed low and held the statue out to her. "For your service to the Troika."

"It is an honor to serve. I will treasure this always." Em curled her fingers around the smooth wood and placed it on her lap.

Lord Harold clapped his hands together. "Bring out the beast."

Servants carrying trays of smoked bear meat and other delicacies entered the courtyard along with a troupe of musicians and mummers who reenacted the battle with the bogbear. Lord Evan's approval of her unladylike behavior had changed her father's tune from stricture to celebration.

With the crowd's attention diverted by the food and entertainment, Em studied the carving on her lap. She ran one finger down a groove in the wood. The statue was less useful than a pouch of beans and less dear than the cloth Quintin had given her the first night they spent together. Still, she would keep it in remembrance of Quintin and his hopeless declaration of love.

"If I might have a word with you, my lady?"

Em glanced up to find Ophelia had moved close enough to speak privately. Her stomach rebelled at the thought of an intimate conversation with Quintin's friend, though she would endeavor not to make a scene. "What is it?"

The mystic leaned close enough for Em to smell her flowery perfume. "Thank you for sending the messenger to take me to Nadine. I was so relieved to see her again."

"The child is well?" Em held her breath against the answer.

"Yes." Ophelia's eyes unfocused as if she was looking at something no one else could see. "For now. Her future was grim, but I'm convinced the estate you sent her to was not the source of her troubles. To be safe, I've brought her back to Rivara and petitioned for her to become a novice under my guidance."

"I'm glad," Em said sincerely. She didn't need the girl's fate weighing on her soul along with all her other sins.

A pair of guests approached to congratulate her on defeating the bogbear. Em turned from Ophelia to greet them and accept their well wishes. After the guests drifted away, Em was surprised the Han-Mystic lingered nearby.

"I wanted to repeat my personal thanks for saving Quintin's life. He truly is as dear to me as a brother."

Em gripped the statue, its carved ridges biting into her fingers. Jealousy gnawed her gut, useless and idiotic. Quintin had curled against this woman like a lovebird. There was nothing fraternal about their embrace. "You needn't hide the truth from me."

Ophelia's smooth brow furrowed. "I beg your pardon."

Waving a hand to dismiss her words, Em tried to sound nonchalant. "I shouldn't have spoken out of turn, yet a blind man could see brotherly love is a poor descriptor for the affection you share."

The pretty mystic's eyes sparkled as she laughed. "It is true we are year-mates, a bond which is in many ways stronger than blood. Though if you think Quintin has any romantic notions about me, you are quite mistaken."

Em gritted her teeth, the woman's tinkling laughter grating on her ears. "I was there. I saw him greet you, and the way you two snuggled together on the divan. You cannot deny—"

"I have a water gift."

Em frowned. "Then you have no excuse for dissembling."

"I mean my gift is why Quintin was so happy to see me." Her smile softened, and her tone turned earnest. "He had been seriously injured, and his water has never been strong. He was glad to have me take over the task of keeping his blood in his body. We snuggled together, as you say, because physical contact makes water work easier."

The back of Em's neck itched with warmth. "Oh."

The mystic cocked her head. "I wonder why you were watching so closely."

Heat spread over Em's face. "He had been injured in my stead. Naturally, I was concerned for his welfare."

"It's a pity he's not here for you to thank personally for

his gallantry." Speculation gleamed in her eyes. "If you like, I could arrange a private audience at a later date."

"That won't be necessary." Em's throat closed as she remembered their last meeting. Her gaze dropped to the wooden statue in her lap. "Nothing would ever come of it."

"Worried your Trilord father won't approve?"

"If my father knew what we had done . . ." Memories of their kisses and exploits curved her lips into a secret smile.

"Then is Quintin not worth fighting your father over? Do you find a mere auditor shameful?"

Em lost her smile. "It's more like he is ashamed of me."

Quintin's year-mate raised an elegant eyebrow. "Ashamed of a Lady of the Realm?"

Em's lips tightened. She had said too much.

Chapter 39

The next day Quintin stared at the pile of quipus on his table without seeing them. Instead, his mind was back at Aerynet, experiencing again that perfect moment of completion and wishing—again—it didn't have to end.

"Quintin, come to my chamber." The Bursar stood in the doorway to his office, slapping his staff of office against his meaty palm. The buzz of conversation filling the main room died at his tone.

"Yes, Bursar." Distracted, he jostled his table as he stood. With his inability to focus, he would be lucky to be done in time to meet his friends for their weekly repast.

As Quintin navigated the maze of tables, the bustle of auditors finishing up their work resumed. In four days, once the new year had begun, the landholders in the area would be presented with what they owed, and the hard work of collecting tributes would begin.

Leaving the chaos behind, Quintin pushed through the curtain into the Bursar's office.

Fredrick sat behind the lone table in the room and motioned at the mat opposite. He tapped a fat finger on a quipu on the table. "Do you want to explain this?"

"It looks like the Merdale account." Quintin leaned closer to study the quipu. His brow furrowed and he poked a lumpy knot at one end. "Why have these knots been undone?"

"This is the quipu you made," Fredrick said, "though it's true your knots have not been as precise since your injury."

"I was done with the Merdale account before my injury."

Quintin ran his fingers over the loose knots and tried to recall the original.

"She must have been very persuasive to convince you to drop the Merdale tribute by so much in one year." Fredrick tsked. "Such an obvious ploy! Yet you are young, and so naive. I can understand the temptation to please a lovely woman. I am willing to overlook your weakness yet again, but this time it's going to cost you."

Finally registering the import of the Bursar's words, Quintin jerked his head up. "You're accusing me of altering the Merdale accounts to lessen their tribute?"

"It is patently obvious you did so, and not hard to guess why." Fredrick lowered his voice. "Have no fear, we can come to some other, shall we say, mutually satisfying solution."

"This quipu has been tampered with." Quintin straightened his shoulders, his back as stiff and unyielding as the Bursar's staff of office. "I did a fair and honest audit of the Merdale Estate as befits a Hand of Destin and a trustworthy Collector for the Luminary."

"Do you think anyone is going to believe you?" Fredrick tapped the table. "Your quipu tells a different story. While I do not want to expose you, I will if you do not cease in this nonsense."

"Did you tamper with it?"

The Bursar flushed. "There has been no tampering."

"You wanted to use this Merdale audit against me all along. How disappointed you must have been when I turned in an honest account of their holdings."

"You alone have touched this quipu, this I vow."

"Really, Fredrick," Quintin said in his most patronizing tone. "You and I both know your vow is worth nothing. You haven't the slightest notion of honor. This entire conversation has been a ploy to blackmail me. It won't work."

Fredrick snatched the quipu off his desk. "I was going to help you to save your reputation, your job. Now I am forced to report you to the Luminary, along with all the sordid details of your affair with Lady Emmanuella."

At the mention of Lady Em, Quintin's irritation burgeoned into a dark pressure on his lungs. After all they had been through, after all he had done to restore her to her rightful place, this contemptible worm's threats were intolerable.

He hurt Lady? Elkart's outrage mirrored his own.

Not if I have anything to say about it. Aware of the auditors in the next room, Quintin leaned forward and growled, "You will say nothing about Lady Emmanuella."

The Bursar's gaze turned calculating. "She'll be in big trouble, you know, for interfering in an audit. If you don't work with me, she could be thrown in the stocks—"

"I told you not to speak of the Lady." Quintin made a sharp pulling motion with his right hand, yanking the air out of the Bursar's nose with his gift. "To anyone."

Fredrick's eyes widened as he clutched at his throat. The quipu slithered forgotten to the floor. His mouth hung open as he tried to suck in air.

"Whatever issue you have with me, Lady Em is not a part of it." His stitches ached and pulled as Quintin moved his fingers, drawing the air away from the Bursar. "Do you understand?"

Fredrick nodded frantically. A horrible whistle emanated from his throat, while his hands clawed at his neck.

Quintin dropped his arm and released the air.

Coughing and gasping, the Bursar collapsed against the table.

Furious, Quintin leaned close to Fredrick's ear. "I will do a lot more than choke you for a pair of heartbeats if I ever hear of an unkind word about Lady Emmanuella passing through your lips."

Fredrick pushed against the table in a struggle to sit up. "How dare you!"

Elkart yowled from the other room, reminding them a Hand is never alone.

Fredrick turned sallow at the sound.

Quintin bared his teeth in a feral smile. "My waccat is very fond of Lady Em, you know. Imagine what he might do to someone who harmed her, either with word or deed."

"You can't threaten me." Fredrick's eyes flashed as he rubbed his throat. "I am your bursar."

"Not anymore you aren't." Quintin scooped up the quipu. "You can find yourself a new collector because I won't be back."

He swept into the main room, pausing only when he reached Auditor Sarah. He dropped the tangle of string on the table in front of her. "This will need to be fixed."

She flinched away from him.

"I'm sorry for my tone." He pressed his hands together and gave her a low bow, using the simple ritual to calm himself, though his pulse drummed in his ears at the threat to Lady Em. "You are the only one I trust for this delicate and important task."

Her spine straightened as she reached for the quipu. "Is this your Merdale account?"

His mouth twisted. "Yes and no."

"What are these clumsy knots? They're worse than mine. Surely you didn't make those."

"I did not. That's what needs to be fixed." His fingers itched to untangle the strings and retie the knots, but it wasn't his job. Not anymore. "You can use last year's account as a guide. They are very similar."

She stared up at him, her face troubled. "Why can't you do it?"

He squared his shoulders, feeling both frightened and freed. "Because I am no longer an auditor."

There was a collective gasp following this pronouncement.

Sarah dropped the quipu. "No."

"I will not work for a dishonorable man." Quintin gave her another bow. "I am sorry."

Ignoring the buzz of questions and whispers, he returned to his table and gestured for Elkart to follow.

There was a clatter of wooden beads as Bursar Fredrick burst from his office. He thumped his staff of office against the wall next to the door. "What is the meaning of all this noise? Get back to work."

Quintin's hands tightened into fists. He strode toward the Bursar.

"Is it true?" an auditor near the curtain asked. "Is Han-Auditor Quintin leaving?"

Fredrick raised the thick black staff over his head. "I said get back to—"

Quintin yanked the staff out of his grip and pitched his voice to be heard throughout the warehouse. "It is true I am no longer an auditor. I am no longer duty bound to obey the Bursar. Now I am only a Hand, whose duty lies in protecting and serving each and every citizen of the Troika."

He threw the Bursar's staff through the bead curtain before meeting the worried gazes of the other auditors. He was not abandoning them. Did they understand his duty as a Hand? "Once I tender my resignation at the Troika Hall, I can be found at the Salty Dog or my home should my services as a Hand be needed."

Fredrick hunched his shoulders and glowered at Quintin. "What are you saying?"

Elkart let out a low growl, his tail lashing.

Quintin wiggled his fingers, tickling the air in the Bursar's nose and reminding him of what his gift could do. "I'm saying you don't want to give me an excuse to come back here."

Fredrick cringed. "You'll have no cause to return."

Quintin gave a short nod. "In that case, I need a drink."

Chapter 40

The clerk at the Troika Hall pinched the bridge of his wide nose. "What do you mean, you resign? Whatever for?"

Quintin's stomach turned somersaults in his belly. To convince the clerk he was serious without implicating Em, he needed to select his words with as much care as when he persuaded Madi to free her. "I conceived an unseemly attraction to a member of the household I was auditing. My conduct has been most unprofessional."

The clerk's brow beetled. "You altered the accounts?"

"No, no. I did the audit to the best of my ability, but I was distracted." Quintin tugged at his queue. "I should have quit the case immediately."

"Well, why don't you do so now, then? Sending someone else out to redo the audit would be better than having you resign so close to the end of the year."

"It's too late. The Bursar knows of my attachment and holds my behavior against me. I must resign."

"The Bursar showed you the door?"

"No." Quintin flinched and bit his honest tongue. While confessing and quitting were the best ways to counter the Bursar's blackmail, the clerk didn't need to know that. "I resign. It is the only way to restore my honor."

"Well, there is no getting between a Hand and his honor," the clerk muttered. "Come back in the new year and we'll see what we can do about finding you a new position."

"Thank you." Quintin gave the clerk a low bow and exited the building. He headed straight for the Salty Dog, though it was too early to meet his friends. He ordered a pitcher of watermelon wine and hunkered down at a table in the back.

Elkart flopped next to him and rested his chin on Quintin's knee. *What we do now?*

Now we wait. Quintin took a swig of wine. A woman laughed, reminding him of Em. He hunched his shoulders. He was sure to get utterly lost in painful memories before his friends arrived.

His third cup was almost gone when Ulric thumped down next to him. "Boss let you off early before the big holiday?"

"I don't have a boss."

Ulric frowned. "What happened?"

"I quit."

"Quit? How can you quit? What are you going to do now?"

Quintin held up one finger. "First, I'm going to get drunk." He extended another finger. "Second . . . Second . . ." He stared at his cup. "I don't know what I'm going to do second."

"Well, you have to think of something." Ulric poured himself a mug of wine. "Never heard of a Hand without a job."

Quintin swirled the dregs in his cup. The reddish hue made him think of Em's hair, because everything made him think of her. He dropped the cup back on the table and buried his face in his hands.

"Still craving the nameless woman?" Ulric asked.

Quintin groaned. He was truly a wreck if *Ulric* could guess the source of his misery.

"You need a distraction." Ulric slapped his hand on the table. "Some fun on Allgoday."

"Or sooner," Terin said smoothly as he joined them. "Since the bogbear is dead, I have nothing to do. Finding a new lover would be amusing. You want to come with me?"

"Can't. Overseer wants the aqueduct finished by the new year." Ulric tipped his cup at Quintin. "Quintin needs a task, though."

Terin cocked his head. "Oh? Shall we seek out the fairer sex together?"

"No thanks." Quintin shuddered. Since poking Em, he hadn't been able to string two thoughts together without her in the middle of them. It seemed wrong somehow to pursue another woman when he knew he would only think of Em.

Terin shrugged at Ulric. "His standards are too high."

Ulric grunted. "Obsessed with a phantasm."

Quintin choked on a cough. Last week he had been dreaming about a stranger. Since then Em had become a real and complicated person in his life, as dear to him as any of his friends.

Terin swirled his cup. "Does Quintin actually find her so elusive?"

"Look, there's Ophelia and Madi." Quintin waved at the newcomers, grateful for the diversion.

Ophelia headed toward their table, but Madi stopped at the trill of a pipe player near the far wall. She pivoted and sashayed over to the handsome man whose delicate features marked him as Ophelia's twin, Jasper the Jubilant.

Terin chortled. "Well, Madi has found her evening entertainment."

Ophelia stopped next to their table and looked over her shoulder at their friend, who was leaning in to smile at her brother. "Marana's tears, I hope not," she said fervently.

"Hasn't she already dallied with him?" Ulric asked. "Why bother a second time?"

"I'm sure she's just being friendly." Terin's sly smile implied how far Madi's friendliness could go.

"Well, Jas won't object." Ophelia sat down and pressed a hand to her chest as if it pained her. "My brother is too accommodating by half."

The musician finished his tune and flashed a grin at Madi. She spoke to him a moment before giving him a cacao bean, the hand off involving far more contact than necessary. She'd already turned away, when he kissed the bean and slid it into a fold in his clothes. Then watched her walk away with hungry eyes.

Quintin's stomach clenched. Did he get a besotted look on his face when he thought of Em? It was too humiliating by half. How could his friends do it? Fall in and out of relationships without losing their hearts each time?

Terin poured Madi a cup of wine when she reached the table. "Dare I ask what you paid him for?"

Madi shrugged languidly and dropped onto a sitting mat. "A simple tune and nothing more."

"Which one?"

Madi grinned. "Guess."

As if on cue the minstrel began singing a mournful ballad about a dashing woman warrior.

Ulric groaned.

"Again, Madi?" Ophelia asked in a despairing voice.

"It's my favorite."

"Because your songbird wrote it for you?" Terin asked.

Madi rolled her eyes. "That's merely what Jas says to be charming."

"Are you sure?" Ophelia asked with quiet intensity.

Madi glared into her mug, all good humor gone. "Yes. I am."

"Madi—"

She turned abruptly to Quintin. "Sorry about Taricday."

"No, no." His heart beat double time at the painful prospect of delving into his lies. "Think nothing of it. Please."

Terin's gaze darted between them. "What did you do?"

"I arrested his lover."

Ophelia frowned. "Quintin has a lover?"

Ulric punched Quintin in the arm. "You sly dog."

Quintin rubbed his biceps. Three cups of wine wasn't enough to dull the effects of Ulric's affection.

Terin arched his eyebrows. "While unusual, fornicating with Quintin is not actually a crime."

"Idiot. That's not why I put her in the stocks." Madi drummed her fingers on the table. "It was an honest mistake. She looked like a laborer but had too much jewelry and beans on her. I pegged her for a thief, is all. Elkart sensed her distress and Quintin came and cleared up my suspicions."

"How do you know she wasn't an outlaw?" Ophelia pleated the edge of her sari. "As much as I respect and admire Quintin, a relationship with him is hardly proof of her innocence. If she had jewels that didn't belong to her—"

"The jewels were hers," Quintin interrupted flatly. If only he hadn't confessed his attraction to Em when he thought she was a mere thief. Would Ophelia be able to guess the truth?

"I know better than you the lengths people will go to in order to free their loved ones from the stocks," Madi told Ophelia, her voice dripping scorn. "I made Quintin speak mind-to-mind. He explained she was a Trilord's daughter in disguise. She'd snuck out to meet him. Nobles are so strange about sex. A grown woman shouldn't have to resort to such tricks to see a man."

"Ha! I knew it." Terin slapped the table. "I offered her the greatest pleasures a woman can experience, and she put me to work scrubbing bird shit off the statuary."

Ophelia blinked at him. "What are you talking about?"

"I thought she might be shy, or merely have tender feelings for you. Now it all fits." Terin wagged a finger at Quintin. "You are fornicating with your fair savior."

Ulric sprayed a mouthful of wine all over the table. "Your lover is La—"

Terin cuffed him. "Don't besmirch the name of a Lady in public."

Ulric rubbed his head while Madi laughed. "You're the one bragging about propositioning her."

Acid clawed the back of Quintin's throat. Had Em truly resisted his charming friend? His fingers cramped around his mug. "I sent you there to help her."

"Which we did." Terin waved his elegant fingers dismissively. "Stop glowering at me. I told you, she turned me down flat. You must have unknown talents to inspire such loyalty in your lover."

"When did you become lovers?" Ophelia frowned at Quintin. "I thought you met at the bogbear attack."

"No, I audited her father's estate in the days prior."

"He's been sleeping with her even longer," Terin added. "Since I saw her leaving your house the first day of the bogbear hunt."

Quintin shifted in his seat. Did Terin have to bring that up?

Ophelia narrowed her eyes. "You saw her in his rooms before the bogbear hunt?"

"Took her back to your house for a romp, did you?" Ulric grinned and shoved Quintin's shoulder. "What did your mother say?"

"By the blessings of the merciful Marana, my mother didn't see her."

Ophelia rubbed her forehead. "But Terin did."

Quintin hunched over his mug. "Much to my regret."

Terin spread his hands wide. "I never would have guessed she was a Lady. As Madi said, she was dressed like a charmaid. I was half convinced she was a prostitute."

"Wait, then who is the mystery woman?" Ulric's brows drew together. "You hadn't slept with her. Said you didn't know her name."

Quintin sighed and tugged his queue. "I certainly wasn't going to tell you. We were trying to be discreet, though we've made a mess of it."

"Because Madi arrested her?"

"And Terin walked in on you?"

Quintin shuddered. "The Bursar caught us kissing as well."

"No!" Madi leaned forward. "When?"

Quintin waved away the question. "It doesn't matter. What matters is he recognized her and sent me to audit her father's estate out of spite."

Ophelia bit her lip. "How awkward."

"You don't know the half of it." Quintin sighed and fiddled with his mug. "He tampered with my accounts and tried to blackmail me."

"What?" Madi straightened in her seat. "Should I put him in the stocks?"

Terin raised his eyebrows. "It's your day off."

"I don't care."

"I showed him the error of his ways," Quintin said shortly.

"You quit." Ulric buried his fingers in his beard. "Will it stop his blackmail?"

"I also nearly choked him to death."

Terin whistled. "Finally putting your air training to work?"

"If ever a man deserved it, the Bursar did."

"What will you do now?"

"I need to report to the Troika Hall next week. I hope work can be found for me here in Trimble." He closed his eyes and tried not to panic. "You'll look after my mother, won't you? If I have to leave?"

"We certainly will." Ophelia covered his hand with hers. "I'll pray it doesn't come to that."

"In the meantime, you can start your Allgoday celebration early." Madi flagged down a barmaid and ordered another pitcher of wine. She raised her mug. "To Quintin, for standing up for what's right, and damn the consequences."

Quintin groaned as his friends joined her toast. The conversation moved back to Terin's plans to find a lover, which was nearly as distressing as discussing his own love life.

Elkart's hot breath sighed against his knee. *You still not happy.*

No. Would he ever be happy again, or would he forever be tormented by a fleeting moment of perfection?

Eventually Ophelia stood and motioned for Quintin to join her. "You've been sitting here stewing long enough. Walk me home and get a breath of air."

He nodded, grateful to leave the boisterous talk of lovers behind.

Once they were well away from the tavern, Ophelia took his arm. "I have something for you."

"Oh?"

She handed him a colorful braided cord. "I didn't want to give it to you in front of the others. I wasn't sure how you would react."

He stroked the woolen strands, familiar knots catching at his fingertips. "These are Merdale's colors."

She nodded. "It is my great honor to formally invite you to celebrate Allgoday at Merdale."

The cord dangling from his hand trembled. "Who gave this to you?"

"Mistress Isabel. She's in charge of the festival, and so any invitation would have to come through her. She said if you want to come, you should wear the cord."

"Does Lord Harold know?"

"Maybe, maybe not. Many of the guests were asking after you at the feast celebrating Lady Em's triumph over the bogbear. Isabel was disappointed by your absence."

His jaw clenched. "The Bursar forbade it."

"He can't stop you now."

"I have no desire to be gawked at."

"Not even for the chance to see Lady Em again?"

He stopped walking and closed his eyes. "I promised her father I would stay away from her."

"Yet you sprang her from the stocks." A thread of disapproval laced Ophelia's voice.

His eyes popped open. "She was innocent. The jewels were her own."

"She is the thief, isn't she?"

His chin jerked in a short nod. "You must never tell anyone. After last night, she is putting her sneak work behind her."

Ophelia's eyes narrowed. "She wasn't disguised in order to meet with you, was she?"

He sighed. "No."

"However did you lie to Madi mind-to-mind?"

"By sticking as close to the truth as possible."

"Lady Em is your lover? Or was it a ruse?"

"It has mostly been a ruse."

"Not entirely?"

He could feel her body closing around him again. Warm and wet and wonderful. His hand fisted around the cord. "No."

"When I spoke with Lady Em, well, it didn't all make sense to me at the time, but I think she has some very strong feelings about you."

"You must be mistaken. She is very grateful for my aid, but . . ." His voice trailed off as he remembered exactly how grateful she'd been. "She thinks I'm kind."

"Well, she would. You are honest, trustworthy, and compassionate." Ophelia ticked off his qualities on her fingers. "Those things do add up to being kind."

"And none of them lead to strong feelings. Kindness is not as attractive as Terin's smile or Ulric's strength, as you well know."

"I'm sorry I hurt you," Ophelia said quietly. "All those years ago, when we were both so young and foolish."

Quintin sucked in a breath. Did they have to revisit his embarrassing puppy love? "It doesn't matter now."

"It does if it is preventing you from seeing the truth." Ophelia squeezed his arm. "There was no future for us, Quintin, and I knew it. I didn't dare dally with you like I did with Terin, for fear I wouldn't have the strength to leave you as I did him. It would have been a disaster."

"What are you saying? You treated me like a little brother. You always have."

"Yes. Because it was safest for all of us. And your friendship has been more precious than a few kisses ever could be. I made the right choice in not going down that path with you." She shook his arm. "It does not mean you aren't appealing. You heard what Terin said. Lady Em has no use for his charms. When she spoke of you . . . There is something there, Quintin, if you wish to pursue it."

Quintin's heart beat faster at the thought. Did he dare entertain such dangerous dreams? "She deserves more."

"Do you love her?"

Quintin opened his mouth to deny it but could only gape like a fish through the pain in his chest.

"Then you must go to the festival. You cannot waste this opportunity."

"I promised her father—"

"I only spoke five words to the man, and even I know her father is a buffoon."

"What can I possibly say to her? I have nothing to offer her."

"You've spent far too much of your life watching the rest of us fumble around searching for happiness and finding only heartbreak. You have a chance at love, Quintin. Don't squander it."

Chapter 41

The wooden railing slid under Em's fingers, worn smooth by generations of grounds-keepers spiraling up the trunk of the kapok tree that dominated Em's little patch of land. What a novel and freeing thing it was, to have land all her own.

"It's a bit of a climb," the new grounds-keeper said over her shoulder. "Though the view is worth it. You can see the whole half parcel from the house."

It seemed a stretch to call the one room building a house. Perched in the branches at the top of the stairs, it was so tiny Em couldn't see it during most of the climb. Yet the grounds-keeper had declared herself quite happy with it as an abode. In truth, Em envied her a little, for living in complete privacy high above the jungle floor.

By the time they reached the top of the stairs, the exertions of the climb had washed away her traces of envy. Breathing heavily, she leaned against the railing of the wraparound porch.

The grounds-keeper waved at the ground below. "Isn't the view worth it?"

"It is spectacular," Em agreed. The tops of bushes and low-lying tress rippled like a carpet below while the canopy trees arched overhead, enclosing them in layers of green. Parrots cawed from the branches, louder here amongst the trees. Tears pricked at the back of her eyes. The beauty of the jungle was doubled by the freedom it represented.

If only Quintin could be here to share in her triumph. She touched a finger to her deed chain. In less than a week her life had completely changed, all thanks to him. He truly had been sent to her by the Goddess to aid her in her hour of need. But Fermena was the Goddess of Now. Her gifts didn't last forever.

Em's fingernails dug into the wood of the railing. She would never see him again. It was for the best. *Really*.

Now to just convince her heart.

The grounds-keeper pointed a callused finger toward the jungle floor. "I want to put the kitchen garden there."

Em leaned over the rail, unable to distinguish one patch of land from any other. The plot was devoted almost entirely to cacao, which made the grounds monotonous.

"Those cacao plants aren't flourishing. It's too bright." The grounds-keeper gestured at the tree rising behind them. "With a bit of trimming, we could get enough sunshine for melons."

Golden light gleamed though the leaves of the kapok tree soaring above as Em tilted her head back, dizzied by the distance. Or perhaps it was all the new information making her mind spin. Queasy and trying not to show it, she refocused on the woman beside her. "Can you trim branches so high up?"

"I can, though I'd rather hire an expert if you think we can spare the beans."

Em rubbed her forehead. She hated making these decisions without knowing how many beans the lands usually produced in a month. And how would removing plants affect the total? Growing their own vegetables seemed like the best plan in the long run, but she wasn't a farmer. She longed to ride to Jardin and beg Hannah for advice or at least pour her woes into Quintin's sympathetic ear. She swallowed hard.

How could someone she'd known for such a short period of time leave such a gaping hole in her life?

The grounds-keeper cleared her throat and drummed her fingers against the rail. "I've been thinking about getting a flock of numididae to fill an old coop behind the house. I'd enjoy the eggs myself, and it'd be a way to add productivity to the land without any drastic changes."

"Eggs would be welcome at Aerynet as well." Surely the beans she had pilfered from Violet's room could pay for a few hens. "And maybe we can get one last harvest from the cacao plants before we make room for the garden. Could that pay for trimming the trees?"

"No sense letting beans go to waste." The grounds-keeper nodded her approval. "Now come around this way to see the shadier side of the plot."

Their feet clomped on the boards of the porch as they circled around the house. Em's mind spun with all the possibilities in her future. With so much to learn about gardening, she anticipated seasons of working closely with the grounds-keeper, until she could provide for Aerynet herself. Then she might be able to move into the little tree house, become her own grounds-keeper, and cease to depend on her family at all.

Em shook off a pang of loneliness at the prospect. It would not be a luxurious life, but it would be an honorable one.

~ ~ ~

"Quintin, are you awake?"

"I'm resting, Mother," Quintin called from his bedroll. He was lying on his back worrying the cord from Merdale. In the day since Ophelia had passed the braid to him, the wool had gotten smooth and shiny with handling.

His stitches itched like chiggers burrowing into his skin and every time he closed his eyes a breeze brought the scent of jasmine in from the garden to torment him with memories of Em. Better to lie in his room and pretend to sleep than to face his uncertain future.

"There is a woman here to see you," his mother said from the other side of the curtain.

He sat up, his heart pounding with foolish hope. If it were Em, his mother would have said so, yet who else could it be?

Elkart raised his head and sniffed. *Tax-woman, not Lady.*

"I'll be right there." Quintin threw off his sheet and tucked the cord back into the pouch at his waist. The Tribute Office was closed for the day, so Sarah could not be seeking justice for further abuses by the Bursar. After losing his temper in defense of Lady Em, Quintin didn't expect to see any of the other auditors again.

He tightened his queue and shook the wrinkles out of his kaftan, before stepping through the curtain.

Auditor Sarah smiled at his appearance. "I have the most wonderful news."

Bursar jumped in river? Elkart asked eagerly.

Quintin cuffed his waccat, though his face cracked in a smile. "Have you been promoted in my absence?"

"Not exactly." Her gaze flicked over to his mother. "Can we go for a walk?"

His stomach turned at the thought of walking through the woods where he had kissed Em. Would memories of her ever stop haunting him? He sighed and gestured outside. "Perhaps we can tour the garden."

At her nod, he offered his arm and escorted her through the rows of vegetables. He tried to focus on Sarah, though the jasmine blooms brought another woman to mind. "What is your news?"

Her fingers squeezed his biceps. "After you left, no one could stand the idea of working in those conditions any longer."

Quintin scowled, bringing his other hand up to cover hers. "The Bursar didn't threaten any of you, did he?"

"No, no, you thoroughly cowed him, but we knew it wouldn't last, and he did start to bluster once he realized our plan."

"What did you do?"

"We walked out, all of us." She waved her free arm in enthusiasm. "The whole lot of us followed you down to the Troika Hall and turned in our resignations. We weren't going to work under a cheating tyrant anymore, either."

Quintin pressed a hand to his head. "All of you?"

She puffed out her chest and grinned. "All the auditors in Trimble."

"But the audits, the accounts . . . it will be impossible to replace you all at once, and what will happen to the tariffs, the tributes? How will the guards get paid?" He grabbed her arms. "What about your own salary? You've told me time and again your family depends on the beans you send home."

She shook off his hands, standing straight and tall. "It was worth the risk. If you could forgo your salary to stand up for justice, so could the rest of us."

"I didn't intend—" He struggled for the right words. "I wasn't trying to close down the Tribute Office."

"Which is probably why you got promoted."

"Promoted?"

"The Speaker for the Luminary realized pretty quick an empty tribute office would not be an auspicious start to the new year. He offered to remove Fredrick if we kept working. We agreed, which raised the question of who should be the new Bursar. That's why the Speaker sent me to come get you, so he can offer you the job."

His shoulders straightened, opportunity unfurling like a flower in the sun. "I could be Bursar?"

Sarah nodded. "It's what the other auditors want. You've always been the one to bring balance to the office, plus done half of Fredrick's work besides. The Speaker wants you to pick up your staff of office at the Troika Hall. If you're willing he'd like you to start tomorrow so everything is in readiness for the new year."

"Thank you, Sarah. I'm touched by your support." He smoothed a hand over his wrinkled kaftan. "Let me wash up. Then I'd be honored to accompany you to the Speaker."

She threw her arms around him in a quick hug. "Congratulations, Han-Bursar. I can't wait to tell the others."

Chapter 42

"I have your new sari," Isabel sang out as she entered Em's room two days later.

Em stroked the vibrant red cloth folded over Isabel's arm. The flawless fabric flowed like water under her fingers.

"What do you think?" Isabel draped the sari on the bed, displaying golden embroidery with tiny jewels and feathers sewn into the pattern. "Isn't it lovely?"

"It is beautiful," Em agreed. She had never owned anything finer, but due to the color she wouldn't wear it again after the Allgoday celebration tonight. Would Isabel pitch a fit when Em sold it to buy seeds for Aerynet's garden?

"It is going to be perfect with your hair." Isabel smiled and handed Em a bundle of brown silk. "Here, put this on."

"What is it?" Em asked. She held up a garment similar to a choli, though it was cut far too small.

"It is for under your sari, Em," Isabel said in a tone usually reserved for idiots.

"Your seamstress must be blind. This won't fit me."

"Snug cholis are the latest fashion." Isabel's bangles chimed as she gestured at the choli. "They make the drape of the sari much smoother and more flattering."

Em pulled at the unforgiving fabric. "Will I be able to lift my arms?"

"As much as is needful," Isabel replied.

"In other words, no."

Isabel waved an impatient hand. "Just put it on."

Em's fingers squeezed the brown silk. She had always been aware of her blessings as the daughter of a Trilord.

Lately she had begun to count the costs. It was too much, and she refused to give any more. "I won't."

"You won't what?"

"I will not wear clothing too tight to move in." Em thrust the fabric back at Isabel. "I can wear an old choli or none at all. I'm not wearing this."

Isabel crossed her arms, refusing to take it. "You're being absurd. You can't wear a sari without a choli and your old ones will clash with your new sari."

Em shrugged. "I can wear an old sari."

"Don't be obstinate." Isabel stabbed a finger toward the bed. "We had this sari made particularly for tonight. You're wearing it."

"Then I can forgo the choli. It might take a little extra wrapping, but the sari will cover me well enough." Em tossed the choli at Isabel, forcing her to catch it. "I'll go in right after the bonfire and avoid any embarrassment."

The fabric crumpled in Isabel's fists. "If you go in at sunset, you'll miss most of the celebration."

"I'll have done my duty and made the rounds. You won't have any reason to be embarrassed, and I doubt I'll regret leaving early."

"I've worked very hard on this festival."

"And it will be wonderful. Stop worrying about me." Em gestured at the new sari. "Why don't you send a maid to help me dress and go get ready yourself?"

Isabel narrowed her eyes. "Promise me you'll wear the red."

"I will, without the choli."

Isabel heaved a sigh and threw the wrinkled brown cloth on the bed. Muttering in Verisian, she left.

Em had time to finish brushing her hair before a harried maid bustled into the room.

The maid picked up the sari and folded it with quick,

efficient hands. Em stripped off her clothes and set her deed chain on her jewel box.

Frowning, the maid held up the pleated sari. "Where is your choli?"

"No choli," Em said, raising her arms out of the way.

Clucking in disapproval, the maid set to work wrapping the long cloth around Em's body, ending with the heavily decorated pallu draped over her shoulder.

Fussing more than usual, the maid straightened and tucked the fabric, before fastening it with a nosegay of red flowers and feathers. Then she braided Em's hair and tucked more feathers and flowers around her face. Stepping back, the maid gave a nod of satisfaction and a low bow before hurrying from the room.

Once she was alone, Em crossed to the table serving as her vanity and picked up her deed chain. She had not let it out of her sight since Quintin placed it around her neck, and tonight would be no exception. She ran her thumb over one of the pumice disks. Dull gray in color and rough to the touch, the holy stones would clash with her sparkling sari. While Isabel would surely prefer she wear the chain unobtrusively around her wrist, there was value in flaunting her chain and further squashing any rumors Violet might have started.

Someone stomped outside her door, interrupting her internal debate.

"Come in," she said.

Her father pushed through the curtain, already dressed for the party in an elaborately embroidered himation. He smiled fondly. "You look more like your mother every day."

Em ran a hand over the smooth red silk of her sari. Had her mother worn the colors of Taric to honor Lord Harold, her husband? Or had she held her pride and her place as a Lady of Fermena in her own right? Em's heart twinged as she couldn't dredge up a single memory of her mother healthy enough to celebrate Allgoday.

Lord Harold cleared his throat. "I brought you a little something I've been saving until you were old enough." He held out a delicate gold necklace.

"I already have a necklace." Em dropped her deed chain over her head. She had no use for gifts from her father, not anymore.

Lord Harold stared at the deed chain, the necklace dangling forgotten from his fingers. "That thing always was uglier than a pile of ash."

"Was there anything else you needed?"

He sighed. "I know you are angry with me, Emmie."

Her shoulders tensed at his words. She wasn't ready for an apology. She wasn't sure she could forgive him. Not yet.

"I know you aren't impressed with your marriage prospects here. We should have gone to the capitol long ago, and I'm sorry I delayed the trip after your mother died."

Disbelief stole her breath, while anger churned her stomach with renewed vigor. Her life would have been very different, probably for the better, if she had made an acquaintance with the Novenary. Her father was right about that, even as he was utterly wrong about everything else.

"I'll make it up to you this year," he continued, oblivious as always. "It's time for us to finally find you a proper husband, and there is no better place to do it than the capitol. The Han-Auditor suggested the journey, and he's right."

She gasped at this new betrayal. How could Quintin be party to her father's matrimonial schemes? Did he have no feelings for her at all? "You talked to the taxman about finding me a husband?"

Lord Harold toyed with the gold necklace. "Yes, well, I was concerned after the business with the bogbear. I wanted to make sure he knew his place."

Her spine straightened. "You put a Hand in his place, moments after he'd risked his life for me?"

"Don't you take such a tone with me, Emmie. It was patently obvious you'd met in the forest for a tryst, and I wanted to put an end to it. We all know you've got better prospects than a simple tax collector. Hell, the taxman himself grasps that."

"Let's see if you can grasp this." Her fingernails gouged into her palms and she welcomed the pain as a focus for her thoughts. "My life and my marriage prospects are none of your concern."

"You are my daughter. As long as you are unwed and living under my roof, your marriage certainly is my concern."

"I have lands of my own. I am a Lady in my own right. It is time I started living like one."

His brow furrowed. "I know you are a Lady."

"I will go to this festival tonight. I will smile and dance and bring honor to your household, because I promised Isabel I would. But this is the last thing I will ever do for you. Any of you." Her blood sang with a heady mix of fear and triumph. She had not intended to move out so soon, yet she could not stay at Merdale any longer. "Tomorrow I will move to my temple and trouble you no more."

"There is no need to be so rash," Lord Harold protested. "Better to let the lands support the temple, while your family cares for you."

"My family stopped caring for me six years ago. It's only taken me this long to realize how completely you cast me aside."

He puffed up his chest. "I never cast you aside."

"Oh, really? I can think of a dozen times you and Gregory discussed some minor point of agriculture in front of me. Not once did you turn to me and mention if the technique was something I might want to try on my lands, or to simply ask how my land was faring. Jonathan's perfidy couldn't have happened, or would have been caught much sooner, if you had lifted one finger to help me. I was twelve years old, and I guess I was old enough to be on my own."

"Your mother had a perfectly capable grounds-keeper."

"Whom you never bothered to introduce me to."

"That's not true! I'm quite certain I pointed him out at your mother's burning."

"Oh, I'm sorry, I must not have understood," Em snarled. The day of her mother's funeral pyre had passed in a fog of pain and grief. "Later, when I begged you for guidance, you were too full of bitter jealousy to help. You wanted Aerynet to fail. Guess who you actually hurt? My temple is fine, but I'm not sure I will ever recover from what you did."

Her cousin's schemes, her brother's complacency, and her father's neglect had all combined to narrow her options and steal her honor. Under the circumstances, she did not regret the sacrifices she made for her temple. If only her past hadn't cost her a future with the man she loved.

She could never forgive her family for that.

Chapter 43

"What are you doing tonight?" Hannah asked as she joined Quintin for their evening meal.

He fingered the pouch containing the Merdale cord. "I don't know."

His mother's brow wrinkled. "It's Allgoday and with your promotion, this coming year means big changes for you. Aren't you going to celebrate with your friends?"

"I've been invited to celebrate at Merdale," he confessed. He stirred his curry, unable to take a bite.

"Well, now," his mother said in a pleased voice. "I can understand why your usual plans hold no appeal."

He toyed with his spoon. "I don't know if I should go."

"Why ever not?"

"I'm only invited as a novelty. It might be wiser to stay here alone with you."

She sighed heavily. "I've had my chance at happiness, Quintin. I loved your father mind, heart, and body. So yes, now I'm alone and have been for a long time. What I shared with your father was rare and precious and I'll not settle for less."

"Can you blame me for wanting something true and lasting, too?"

"I can blame you for letting it slip through your fingers." She threw her hands in the air. "You told me once you loved her. Was it only a passing fancy?"

He stared down into his bowl, his mouth dry as ashes. "No."

"People like your friend Terin get involved with only their bodies to spur them on. I figured there was no harm in you being more discerning, in waiting until your whole soul was engaged. Now you say you love this woman, and yet ignore an invitation from her family to spend Allgoday with her."

"I'm not invited to be with her."

She spread her hands wide. "They won't stop you either. Allgoday is a time for romance. You can't miss this chance."

"My heart is engaged, true enough, and my body." He cleared his throat, pushing aside memories of what Em's touch did to him. "My mind though . . . my mind tells me to stay away."

She frowned. "Does your reason tell you this or is it fear?"

His fingers tightened on his spoon. "I am afraid of what will happen if I go to the festival, but it's more than that. Logically speaking, she would be foolish to accept my suit when she has so many better prospects. What is the sense in following my body and my heart when my mind says nothing will ever come of it?"

"Lady Emmanuella is not indifferent to you."

"I am still an unacceptable suitor."

"You are not merely a vegetable seller's son," Hannah argued, her voice shaking.

"I am not ashamed of you, Mother." Quintin gripped her fingers. "That's not what this is about."

"You are a Hand and the son of a Lord." His mother pulled away from him and left the table.

Frowning, Quintin followed her into the house. He stood behind her as she rummaged through a trunk in her room.

Extracting a blue bundle, she stroked the folded linen. "This is your father's himation from our wedding. I've been saving it for you to wear when you make your own vows."

He swallowed. "I never knew."

"Perhaps you need it sooner. Perhaps you need it not for your wedding but for your courtship." Her eyes gleamed with determination. "Because you are a worthy suitor. Even to a Lady."

Her hope buoyed his own heart, daring him to dream.

"I'll go to the festival."

~ ~ ~

An hour later Quintin's sandals crunched on the gravel lane leading to Merdale. This close to sunset, the arboreal arch cast thick shadows over the drive. A pair of okapis trotted past, forcing Quintin and Elkart to jump to the side.

The draping end of his father's himation slipped, revealing his shoulder. Quintin pulled it back up and fussed with the herbal brooch holding it in place. No matter how he adjusted his borrowed finery, the unfamiliar wrap felt ready to slither to the ground and leave him naked. When properly draped it left his arms and an embarrassing expanse of his chest exposed.

Elkart nudged his bare knee. *Lady this way.*

Resting his palm on the waccat's head, Quintin drew courage from his furry companion. With Elkart at his side, he stepped forward, out of the shadows into the sunset-kissed clearing.

Glittering nobles crowded the garden paths. Drums and bells added a cheerful rhythm to the celebration while servants in towering headdresses circulated platters laden with dainties. At the heart of the garden a massive cone of branches stood ready to burn at sunset.

Quintin tugged at his himation. Dressed more lavishly than ever, he was merely a drab chicken joining a flock of peacocks.

Elkart nudged him again. *Lady there.*

Lady Emmanuella chatted with her brother and a few other young guests, all of them gleaming with jewels and rich fabrics. Her sari glinted gold in the fading sunlight, while the feathers in her hair shivered as she laughed. She was radiant.

"Han-Auditor! I'm so glad you were able to accept my tardy invitation."

Quintin spun to face Mistress Isabel. The edge of his unadorned himation slid off his shoulder. His face hot, he pulled the fabric back in place.

Mistress Isabel dropped into the supplicating pose of a hostess. "Be welcome and at ease on this most joyous Allgoday. The delights of Merdale are yours to enjoy."

Quintin bowed awkwardly, trying to keep his clothes in place. "You honor me greatly."

As he selected a dumpling, Isabel rose to smile at him. "My mother is interested in making your acquaintance. Come along."

Careful not to look in Em's direction, Quintin followed Isabel to meet a statuesque older woman.

Isabel's mother looked him up and down with embarrassing thoroughness. "There is not much to you, is there? No wonder Lord Harold's daughter had to come to your rescue."

He twitched with the desire to cover his chest from her predatory gaze. "Lady Emmanuella was most brave," he stammered.

"You've got nice form. I've always been partial to strong arms." The woman ran a finger down his biceps. "I would be happy to provide any protection you might need tonight, you know, after it gets dark."

"Mother!" Isabel slapped at her mother's hand. "He's here for Em."

Quintin's heart surged. "Did the invitation come at her request?"

"No, it was my doing." Isabel grinned and clasped her hands. "As a little surprise for her, so the evening will not be too dull."

"A surprise," he echoed, his excitement fleeing as quickly as it came.

"She's talked so much about your bravery facing the bogbear, I thought she might enjoy your company." Isabel's eyebrows wiggled suggestively. "Especially after the bonfire."

Heat spread from his face down his neck. "Surely more eligible men are already here."

"You don't need prospects to provide Allgoday fun. We'll be traveling to the capitol to find her a husband soon enough. Before we go, I thought you could give her a little needed experience with men since she scorns proper suitors."

"If Em should scorn you as well, it would be my pleasure to help you forget the insult," Isabel's mother offered.

Isabel laughed. "Mother! Do I need to find you some harmless fun of your own?"

Quintin backed away from the women, his stomach churning. His one night of mindless sex haunted him. He had no interest in a similar encounter.

It had been a mistake to come.

Chapter 44

"There you are, and with feathers in your hair this time."

Em turned from Catherine and Jon to greet Curtis with a cold smile. "Blessings of all the gods to you." She held out a platter of spicy treats. "Please enjoy what Merdale has to offer."

Curtis selected a date, his gaze oozing over her bare shoulder like a slug. "And what exactly is Merdale offering?"

Em pointed at the items on her tray as she listed them off. "We have candied ginger, cinnamon dumplings, stuffed peppers, wine-soaked dates—"

"Do you want to hear what I'm offering?" He stepped closer and touched one of the feathers framing her face.

She jerked her head away from his hand. "I'd rather not."

"Oh, come now. It's Allgoday and you're not wearing a choli. Don't tell me you aren't interested in a little fun."

"Not with you, I'm not."

Curtis popped the date into his mouth and grinned. "Well, I'm going to stick close to you. The bonfire is about to burn, and I wouldn't miss watching you toss those stunning red flowers on the flames for anything."

Em gritted her teeth and shifted away, gripping the edges of the tray, ready to smack him with it if he touched her again.

"Leave Em alone and go enjoy the fire behind the barracks," Jonathan suggested, cocking his thumb at the other side of the gardens.

Curtis smirked. "You should be glad your half-dressed

sister has distracted me. I had planned on following you and the young miss after the bonfire."

Catherine shrank back with a gasp.

Jonathan planted his hands on his hips. "Go to the second fire, Curtis. Violet and some friends are going to be rolling the bones for clothing as soon as the sun goes down. Their entertainments will be much more to your taste than anything out here."

Curtis snorted. "The bones always love Violet."

"Which only means you'll be out of your himation faster."

Curtis chuckled. "What do you think, Emmie? You want to lose your sari on a roll of the bones?"

She sniffed. "I've never had much interest in gambling."

"Violet is always more fun than you," Curtis tossed over his shoulder as he swaggered away.

Em narrowed her eyes at her brother. "What about you, Jon? Are you going to try your luck behind the barracks?"

"No." He captured Catherine's hand for a kiss. "I'm through with gambling, especially with the likes of them."

His betrothed sighed dreamily. "Thanks for chasing him away."

"Hey, I can't let anyone talk to my sister like that." Jon winked at Em. "Even if she is half-dressed."

"I haven't got a knife to eviscerate him with, so your gallantry was appreciated." Em's teasing tone masked the sincerity of her words.

"Come on." Jon tugged Catherine's hand. "Father will be lighting the bonfire soon. We don't want to miss it."

As her brother and his secret betrothed scampered away, Em returned to her duties with a heavy heart. She politely offered the blessings of the day to any nearby guests yet remained untouched by the celebration all around her.

Holding out her tray to yet another pair of guests, she

noticed a man slipping away from the crowd. Her fingers bit into the platter. Was it Quintin?

As he disappeared into the trees, she banished the fanciful thought. Her father would never invite a lowly taxman to the festival. In her loneliness, she saw him everywhere.

"Now where did he go?" Isabel said from at Em's elbow. "Vexing man."

Em pointed her chin toward the unlit bonfire. "Gregory is over there."

"Not Gregory. Your Hand, Quintin."

Her heart jumped. "Quintin is here? I thought I'd imagined him. Did Father invite him?"

"No, I did."

Em gaped at her sister by marriage. "What? Why?"

Isabel shrugged. "A woman deserves a little fun on Allgoday."

"You plan on finding him at sunset?" Em's stomach rebelled at the thought of the beautiful woman alone with Quintin.

"Not me, silly. You." Isabel nudged Em with her elbow. "I've seen the way your eyes sparkle when you talk about the heroic Hand who fought the bogbear. Allgoday is the perfect excuse to indulge in a romance."

The trees cast thick shadows where Quintin had disappeared. Em's heart pounded at the idea of following him into the darkness, though whether in fear or excitement, she did not know.

"He doesn't want me," she murmured, giving voice to her fear.

"Then why did he come?" Isabel sniffed. "He spurns this august company and was quite forlorn you had not instigated the invitation."

"He thought I invited him?"

"He hoped as much and was downtrodden when I told him the invitation came from me." Isabel elbowed Em again.

"Why don't you follow after him and see if you can cheer him up?"

"Why are you doing this? Don't you want me to stay here and flirt with more eligible men?"

"As if you ever would." Isabel snorted. "As I predicted, you're glowing at the mere mention of your Hand. Who knows, maybe you'll manage to spare us a trip to the capitol."

Em stilled. "He will never marry me."

"Then best to get over him with some Allgoday fun." Isabel swooped the welcome platter out of Em's hands. "It is almost sunset. If you want to catch your Hand, you'd better be quick."

Em left Isabel behind to slip between the trees after Quintin. She paused to get her bearings and let her eyes adjust to the twilight gloom under the canopy. Where could Quintin be? Stumbling around in the dark held little appeal, though it was better than mingling with the revelers while the bonfire burned.

An animal appeared between the trees in front of her.

Em froze, her fingers itching for an atlatl.

As the animal moved, she let out a gusty sigh of relief. She pressed her palms together and bent in a deep bow. "Joyous Allgoday to you, Elkart."

The waccat rubbed his head against her hip, emitting a rumbling noise suspiciously like a purr.

She scratched his ears. "Can you lead me to Quintin?"

The waccat bobbed his head in a gesture eerily like a human nod before heading between the trees.

She focused on tracking him in the darkness and scarcely noticed where he led her until they broke through the trees at the ridge of a hill. She was surprised to find herself in the clearing where the bogbear had attacked. It seemed like a lifetime ago, though it had been less than a week.

Quintin sat on the fallen trunk, his back to her as he faced the festive gardens. Adorable in a loose himation threatening to slip off his shoulder, he tugged at his queue in a familiar nervous gesture.

Her heart swelled.

In this very spot, he had protected her from danger and confessed his love for her. A love she couldn't let him walk away from. Not without a fight.

With careful steps, she crossed the clearing and sat down next to him.

He reared back in surprise. "Lady Emmanuella! What are you doing here?"

She braced her hands on the rough bark of the fallen tree. "Aren't we past you calling me Lady? At least when we're alone?"

"I suppose." He turned back to the view of the garden. "Why aren't you down there where you belong?"

"I don't care for crowds. Normally I would have returned to my room by now."

"So why didn't you?"

"You're here."

He sucked in his breath with a hiss. "And you wanted to have a little fun with me?"

"What else is Allgoday for?"

Before he could answer, a great cheer rose from below as the bonfire grew from a merry little blaze to a roaring inferno. Torches all around the garden sprang to life, casting a magical glow on the festivities. Colorful sparks shot into the sky as the burning sticks caught fire. Elegant revelers laughed and danced around the bonfire, tossing herbs and bouquets onto the flames.

"Give me your nosegay," she said, holding out a hand to Quintin.

"What?"

"It's sunset and time to honor the gods for the gift of fire. I assume you can't burn it yourself."

"No." He fumbled with his brooch. "I've never done the ritual like this before."

She carefully unpinned the flowers from her sari. Without a choli underneath, her sari threatened to slither off her shoulder and expose her breasts. This was why Allgoday festivals got so rowdy after sunset. Everyone's clothes started falling off. Though Quintin's himation needed no encouragement. The old-fashioned garment left one of his shoulders and half of his glorious chest bare.

Her body quickened with longing.

Clutching at his clothes, he handed her a clump of herbs tied with a woolen cord in Merdale colors. "Do we need to say some prayers?"

"If you wish. I'll be saying my own prayers to call the fire." She cleared a spot for their offerings and added a few dried leaves and twigs. With his voice rumbling prayers beside her, she begged all the gods to bless her with heat. Giving off a pungent aroma, the offerings smoldered before bursting into flame.

Careful to hold her sari in place, she turned from watching the flames, and gazed at his face. As difficult as they were to see in the fading light, his features were as dear to her as her own breath.

A bawdy song rose through the night air from the festivities below.

Em smiled, struck by an impulse to join in and celebrate the pure magic of being alive.

She shifted her body into the pose of welcome. Her mother always told her, when she complained about the strict formality of hospitality, that there would come a time when she would want to welcome a man into her heart as well as her home. Instead of drowning them both with emotion, the ritual would act like a boat, allowing her esteem to float above the heat in her blood.

Em had never known exactly what her mother meant until now.

She held up her hand with the end of her sari trailing over her fingers. "Joyous Allgoday to you, Han-Auditor Quintin of Jardin. May you savor all I have to offer."

Chapter 45

Lightheaded with desire, Quintin gulped in air and struggled for sanity. Em knelt at his feet with the end of her sari held out to him. Her meaning was perfectly clear. If he took hold of her pallu, she would be naked before him in short order. His loose wrap meant it would be the work of a moment to free his burgeoning member from the folds of his clothes. He could almost feel her lips closing around him again. His cock twitched at the thought.

Wasn't this the kind of reckless, impulsive act Allgoday was supposed to inspire?

His hands curled into fists. Allgoday or not, he could not bring himself to touch her.

As the silence after her offer lengthened, she slowly raised her questioning eyes to his.

"I'm sorry, Em."

She tucked her sari back over her shoulder, covering the swell of her breast. Hurt flashed across her face.

His gut twisted. If only he could be the careless lover she wanted. Instead his heart bled from their encounter in the steamroom. It couldn't take another beating tonight.

Her eyes narrowed, her gaze fixed on where his arousal tented his clothes. "You do want me."

"Always." Quintin resisted the urge to cover himself with his hands. He could give her his honesty if nothing else. "Touching you is like touching the stars."

"Then why turn me away?" she asked. "On Allgoday no less, when you can have what you want with no regrets, no expectations."

"Allgoday does not have the power to change the way I feel." The depression dogging him squeezed fresh pain out of his heart. "I barely managed to walk away from you once. I can't do it again, Allgoday or no."

"Then don't."

"What?"

"Don't walk away." She drew her knees up and wrapped her arms around her legs. She looked less like a Lady and more like a child playing dress-up. "Starting tomorrow, I'm going to spend a lot of time on my temple lands. You could visit me there whenever you want."

His heart twisted. A prolonged affair would only drag out his heartache. "You don't understand. If I lay with you, I'm going to want to marry you, Em."

"I know," she said, her voice a study in agony. "And a Hand can't marry an outlaw. I thought, or hoped, a Hand might be able to fornicate with one. Discreetly, of course."

"What do you mean, an outlaw? Your sneak work is over."

"It could come to light at any time. You can't risk the scandal of associating with me—"

"I freed you from all that." He slashed the air with his hand. "You were never caught and now you never will be. No accusation could stand against you as a Lady. You can go to the capitol and find a husband without worrying about your past coming back to haunt you."

She shuddered. "It will always be a part of me, like a stain on my soul."

"You're not tainted! Your family put you in an impossible situation." He squatted in front of her and peered at her face. "You were brave and clever and did an admirable job of tending to your temple in very trying circumstances. Never forget it."

Her chin rested on her knees. "Wouldn't marrying an outlaw, even a reformed one, be against the vows of a Hand?"

"While we do promise to uphold the laws of the land, we're also supposed to practice mercy and forgo revenge." Unable to look at her beloved face, he poked a stick into the dying fire, and pushed the necessary words past his closed throat. "If you find a Hand worthy of you on your trip to the capitol, don't hesitate to marry him for the sake of his honor or yours."

With a distressed sound, her face crumpled. She buried her head in her knees, while her shoulders shook with sobs.

He dropped the stick, stymied by misery and confusion.

Elkart paced back and forth, his tail lashing. *You make Lady sad.*

I didn't mean to. Her cries tore at his heart. He had plenty of experience comforting women after men had done them wrong. He'd just never been the man in question. Tentatively he reached out to rub her back.

Without lifting her head, she leaned toward him like a plant stretching for sunlight.

He took her in his arms, though he felt helpless before her tears. He pressed his lips against her hair. "I'm sorry."

When she spoke, her voice was so low he had to strain to hear her. "I told myself you couldn't stomach the idea of marrying an outlaw. That your vows as a Hand held you back. Instead it's me who appalls you."

"No, Em, no. I love you." He squeezed her tight. "All I've ever wanted was to help you. When you opened your mind to me and shared your fear, your desperation . . . I wanted to save you. Finding out you were a Lady did complicate things, but I still wanted to set you free."

"You wanted to marry me. I heard you, in my mind." She turned her head, bringing them nose to nose. "When we were together."

"Yes." He breathed in her air. Swirls and eddies in her thoughts blew through his own barrier. While they were not bonded like waccats, their shared connection would only grow stronger with use.

When we made love, when I was inside you . . . He didn't have the words to describe how it felt, even mind-to-mind. *I didn't want to let you go. Ever.*

I would have said yes. Her breath hitched. *If you had offered to marry me, I would have said yes.*

I know. That's why I didn't ask.

"Wait." She pulled her head back and sniffed. "You knew I would say yes, and so you kept silent?"

"I couldn't trap you, Em. Not again." His lungs emptied in a sigh, shame twisting through his gut. "After the stocks, you were nearly delirious with gratitude and relief. I took advantage more than I should have as it was."

"You think that's why I made love to you? Because I was grateful?"

"I hope you got a little comfort from it as well."

She rubbed her hands over her face, wiping away her tears and breaking his embrace. "Why do you think I offered to make love to you right now?"

"It's Allgoday." He tossed another twig on the embers. "Isn't it what people do on Allgoday?"

She straightened, regaining some of her Ladylike bearing. "I don't."

"Only because you're usually surrounded by potential suitors."

"What?"

"You only take lovers from the lower classes, remember." He snapped another twig in half. "To prevent them from getting any foolish ideas about marriage."

Her hand shook as she straightened a feather in her hair. "Is that how you see yourself? From a lower class?"

"I used to be the son of a lord, but I've been plain old Quintin of Jardin for a long time now." A muscle worked in his jaw. "Besides, it's obvious you think of me the same way. From the first time we touched you've treated me like a lover, which means I was never marriage material."

"You've always been a man apart, Quintin, beyond the simple labels of lover or suitor." She cupped his cheek. "I didn't make love to you because I was grateful, and I'm not looking for a temporary diversion tonight."

"Then why did you offer me your body?"

"Because I thought it was all I had to offer you." She kept her gaze steady though her voice wobbled. "Because my heart leaps at the very sight of you, because my body yearns to touch yours. I wake up weeping for you and what might have been. I thought at least we could have this moment together. It won't be enough, it would never be enough, but I'm not as strong as you, able to resist the lure of today because of the price to be paid tomorrow. I love you, Quintin, and I want to be with you whenever and however I can."

She loved him?

"Oh, Em." He reached for her and pulled her tight against his chest.

She kissed him, passionately, desperately.

She loved him, and it changed nothing. His heart ripped in two. Would his pain and regret tomorrow truly be worse if they made love?

She broke the kiss to gaze into his eyes. "I love you, Quintin. Say you'll marry me."

He slowly shook his head. "I can't do that to you, Em."

She pushed away from him. "Marriage is not some disease you inflict on me."

"You've spent the last six years haggling with fishmongers and bartering away luxuries. All I can offer you is a lifetime of the same. You deserve better."

"Do I? And exactly what is it I deserve?"

"You deserve delicacies dusted in cacao and saris covered in jewels. You deserve servants to cook and clean and care for you. You deserve okapis and palanquins, or at least a home of your own, none of which I can promise you."

She tilted her head, her eyes flat. "And what about love?"

"What?" His heart pounded. He could tell she was furious, though he didn't know why.

"Do I deserve love? Or respect? Or understanding? Am I unworthy of such things?"

"Yes, you deserve love," Quintin said with quiet conviction. "I have no doubt you will easily find a man who both loves you and has the title and wealth you deserve. You shouldn't settle for a landless taxman. All I can offer you is love, and it isn't enough."

"You're right, I don't think love is enough for me." she said.

He nodded, glad she understood.

"Though I don't need to wed to have all you say I deserve. My father gives me cacao and servants and saris dripping with jewels, like this one." She stood and twirled, her red sari gleaming in the firelight. "What do you think, Quintin? Do you like my sari?"

He frowned. Was this some kind of trick? "Do you want my honest opinion?"

She softened her stance and lost her brittle edge. "Yes, Quintin. I always want your honesty."

He studied her for a moment. The firelight and the red sari brought out the unusual color in her dark hair. It reminded him of how she had looked sitting atop her okapi after defeating the bogbear, a moment that personified beauty and strength. Yet, if she wanted him to be honest . . . "I don't like it."

"Why ever not? It is jeweled, is it not? And the fabric was quite expensive. What else matters?"

"It is very fine, and you are enchanting in it, of course. But it's the wrong color. You are a Lady of Air. You should be wearing white or lavender, not red, even if it is Allgoday.

Or maybe especially on Allgoday. Fermena is ascending tomorrow, and as a patron of one of her temples, it is only fitting for you to acknowledge her."

She folded her hands together and stared at him with serious eyes. "And that simple statement holds all the reasons why I love you, Quintin."

His brow knitted. "Because I think you should wear white?"

"Because my title, my patronage matters to you, more than they have to anyone I've ever met who wasn't directly tied to Aerynet." One side of her mouth curled up in a smile. "It doesn't hurt when you call me enchanting in such a casual way as if it is almost too obvious to be noticed."

"You are enchanting. Always."

"Because you love me."

"Well, yes."

"But more than that, you respect me. You honored and valued me when you thought I was nothing more than a common thief. My father gives me fine saris. He doesn't give me respect." She ran a hand over the glittering edge of her pallu, her face pensive. "I'm leaving here tomorrow, turning my back on servants and okapis and all those other things you say I deserve, because I would rather have my pride and self-respect."

She stepped closer and pressed her palm against his bare chest. "We can argue until the moons set about whether I could ever find a man I love half as much as I love you, Quintin."

His heart pounded as if trying to leap through his skin into her hands. Did she really love him so much?

"It is remotely possible there is someone else in this world who can fill me with fire the way you do." She lifted her hand to wave at the decadent festivities in the garden. "You'll never convince me a man of titles and wealth will honor and respect me as you do."

Quintin glanced at the distant revelers. She could be down there with them, her appalling family, where he told her she belonged. Instead she was here with him.

Because some things mattered more than wealth.

"I deserve to be honored and respected, Quintin. I deserve to be loved and cherished." She again took the end of her sari in her hand and held it out to him. "I deserve you."

Epilogue

Half of a season later, during Fermena's assent in the first cycle of the Troika of Peace

Raucous cheers greeted the bridal couple exiting Aerynet. Em's cheeks ached from the size of her grin. Shouting her praises to the Goddess, she released a pair of lovebirds with her new husband. The colorful birds filled the sky, matching the creatures stitched into the sari she wore, a pattern echoed by the embroidery Quintin had added to his father's himation.

Quintin raised their hands to his lips and kissed the marriage braid tying them together. Fragments of his thoughts teased the edge of her mind.

She dispersed her air defenses with a sigh and thought loudly, clearly. *I love you, my husband.*

And I you, my wife.

The appellation sounded both sweet and strange. She relished a lifetime of getting used to hearing it.

They clattered down the temple steps and were soon engulfed by a crowd of well-wishers.

A mystic of Ferel pressed his thumb against their foreheads in an air blessing. "What a beautiful wedding ceremony. Much more intimate and moving than the grand affairs at the Marana temple."

Em had insisted, with Quintin's full support, that they make their initial vows on Fermenasday, rather than the more traditional Maranasday. Though Lucy had been anxious about asking Patricia to perform such a seldom called upon ceremony, the mystic had recited the prayers flawlessly. Surely Fermena herself smiled on their union. "Thank you for coming and giving us your blessing."

"It is an honor to serve the Novenary." Nine mystics had come to the wedding to represent not only the nine deities but also as emissaries for the Novenary and her goodwill. The mystic bent low in a respectful bow. "I'll send her a full report, later this week. For now I must beg your pardon. I have other duties to attend to and cannot come to your wedding feast."

As if on cue, the Merdale guards in attendance blew their horns and cleared the way for a procession to Jardin.

Soon Hannah's tiny garden overflowed with guests from all walks of life, from humble neighbors to Lord Harold and his cronies. Fortunately, the wine flowed freely, and no one was standing on ceremony.

Quintin and Em circulated among the guests, accepting blessings and well-wishes from one and all. They paused where Quintin's year-mates clustered together.

Ophelia clasped Em's free hand, while Ulric and Terin thumped Quintin's back.

"You will come to the temple to receive the blessing of the Magus on Maranasday, won't you?" Ophelia asked.

Em smiled at the woman who had fast become a friend. "Yes, we're planning a full wedding week."

"Good." Ophelia threw her arms around the wedding couple. "I'm so happy for you both." Her voice choked with tears.

As she stepped away, Terin bent over Em's hand. "You are a vision. Quintin is the luckiest of men."

Ulric loomed beside his friend. "Lady or not, you treat him right, you hear?"

"Ulric—"

"I will," Em promised quickly. Her husband deserved no less, and his friends had reason enough to be suspicious of her.

Speaking of which, one of them was missing. As much as Em dreaded encounters with the guard who had arrested her, she would hate for any of Quintin's friends to miss their wedding. "Is Madi here?"

"Madi's busy making a new friend." Terin jerked his head at the other side of the garden.

Em stiffened to see Curtis standing a little closer than was proper to the striking guard. "Oh, no."

"What's wrong?" Ophelia asked. "Is he the sensitive type? Likely to be hurt by her flirting?"

"Quite the opposite. The man she's with is a lecherous cad."

Ulric grunted. "Sounds like the kind of arse Madi likes best."

"Don't worry about Madi." Quintin squeezed their joined hands. "She's in no danger of a broken heart."

Em couldn't help flinching as Madi laughed and leaned toward Curtis. The woman looked smitten. "Are you sure . . . ?"

"I'm sure I want more wine." Ulric clapped a hand on Terin's shoulder. "Brave the nobles with me?"

Quintin smiled at his friends as they moved away. "Thank you all for coming."

"It is a pleasure to serve." Ophelia gave a proper bow, though her serene smile held a hint of mischief. "Though you might think differently when you find the gift Terin insisted on."

It was traditional for the guests of the wedding feast to hide their gifts around the newlyweds' domicile, though Em hadn't spotted any yet.

Quintin groaned. "I don't want to guess, do I?"

"You'll know it when you see it," Ophelia promised.

"Now I'd better get some refreshments before Ulric devours them all."

Quintin tugged Em away from the gathering. "Come on. For once no one is looking at us."

"I'm sure someone else will want to talk to us soon enough," Em protested, as Quintin led her around the corner of the house.

"We can always tell them we're searching for gifts."

"What are we actually doing?"

"Taking a rest from all the people." Quintin leaned against the wall.

She played with his queue. "I hoped you had a more specific purpose in mind."

"Oh?" His fingers tightened convulsively on hers. "Like what?"

Em stroked the shoulder left bare by his himation. "It's been months since I've seen your gorgeous body, and now it is on display for everyone."

He fussed with his clothes in an ineffectual attempt to cover his chest. "Sorry. Mother insisted."

"I'm only teasing. It was a fine concession to my family as well, since I refused to wear what they wanted." Instead of the lavish, wildly inappropriate red sari, Em had fashioned her sari out of the length of cloth Quintin had given her when they first met.

She leaned forward to kiss the corner of his mouth. "We should get back to our guests before I give in to temptation."

"I need a little longer." Quintin pushed away from the house to drift closer to the door of the room they would share at Jardin. "We haven't found any gifts yet."

Em glanced back at the garden as her husband pulled her along. "We shouldn't abandon our guests."

"Em! I found a wedding present."

She spun around to see him peering in the window. "What is it?"

"Come see." He urged her to the window. "I assume it's from your family."

She peeked into their room and groaned. An enormous bed crowded the space, leaving all the other furnishings stacked against one wall. "How inappropriate! What was my father thinking?"

"I like it." His brow furrowed. "Unless it's your old bed from Merdale. That would be insulting."

"It would be most indecorous to have a family bed in a maiden's room. No, I've never seen it before. Gregory and Isabel inherited my parents' family bed so it's probably new."

"Which means your father had to have it custom made or imported." He slipped an arm around her waist, his thumb tracing an embroidered bird. "It took planning and effort. Getting it in here as a surprise must have been challenging. This is a very thoughtful gift."

"Thoughtful? It's ridiculous." She waved a hand at the window. "We won't have room to turn around in there."

"I'll admit it isn't the best use of space. Yet I'm gratified your father eagerly anticipates grandchildren from us and wants them to have the best."

She smiled at Quintin and touched his cheek. She had not completely forgiven her father for his neglect, though his support of their marriage plans had softened her heart. The traditional gift of a family bed did demonstrate his acceptance. "I'm glad, too."

"I very much look forward to filling our bed with children." His eyes darkened as he turned her in his arms to face him. "I've always dreamed of spreading your glorious hair across a pillow, and where better to do it than a proper bed?"

She moaned and pressed against him. "I agree we should put my family's gift to good use as soon as possible."

The corner of his mouth curled up in a wicked smile.

"But not yet. You'll have to wait a few hours more to have your way with me."

"It is pure torture waiting." She slid her palm down his bare chest.

He chuckled and captured her hand before it could stray into dangerous territory. "Tonight, my love, tonight. And for all the nights to come."

THANK YOU for reading TAXING COURTSHIP, Book One of *The Hands of Destin.* I hope you enjoyed Em's and Quintin's story.

The series continues with Book Two, DEADLY COURTSHIP:

Can a minstrel with a knack for predicting the future help a warrior face her painful past?

In a world rife with elemental magic, Han-Triguard Madi's earth gift strengthens her body, but makes her distrustful of fluid emotions. When her former lover Jasper, a water gifted empath, begs her to protect his brother's orphans, Madi struggles with unwelcome tenderness even as she tracks down a murderous Lord.

Then the Lord unmasks her shameful past, forcing her to risk her career—and her heart—to avenge a ghost and save the love she and Jas once shared.

Please enjoy returning to Trimble with this excerpt from DEADLY COURTSHIP:

A thick cloud passed over the full face of Terlune, the largest of the three moons, blocking its reddish light.

Han-Triguard Magdalena, Hand of Destin and Protector of Trimble, cursed.

The torch she held in her left hand barely illuminated the brick road under her soft leather boots, while the elegant two-story houses lining the avenue were entirely shrouded in darkness. She had been relying on the light of the moon to aid her patrol of the wealthy district neighboring the Reeve's sprawling villa at the peak of the city Trimble.

Ordinarily Madi wouldn't mind a little darkness, but the day of the week honoring the Earthen God Taric was always stressful. The two men in Madi's usual triad spent Taricday in prayer. As did all the other male guards. With the women in the guard spread thin, the city was ripe for mischief.

To make matters worse, her captain had assigned her normal Taricday partner elsewhere, leaving Madi solely responsible for ferreting out danger in every dark alley she passed.

A large furry head nudged her hip, reminding her that a Hand was never truly alone. She buried her fingers in her waccat's gray and black striped coat, grateful for the great cat's company. Verona's senses were sharper than her own, and the waccat's strength and speed gave her an advantage against any miscreants they might encounter.

Having the waccat at her side improved Madi in every way. In truth, her captain wouldn't have sent her to patrol alone if she weren't a Hand, blessed and honored by her bond to the cat.

Madi gave Verona's pointed ears one last stroke before gripping the hilt of her sheathed bronze sword and resuming her patrol. It was not such a bad night really, with two of the three moons spilling pearly light over the peaked roofs of the villas. They hadn't run into any trouble, at least not of any seriousness. She hadn't hauled anyone to the stocks all evening, hadn't seen anything suspicious.

Yet her instincts were on edge.

Verona tensed at her side.

"What's wrong?" Madi hissed, though the waccat would not be able to answer her in so many words. A talent in the element of earth blessed Madi with strength and a few dirty tricks when fighting. Communicating clearly with her waccat was not part of her gifts.

Verona took a sharp turn toward the center of the city. Madi tightened her grip on her torch as she followed, trusting the waccat's guidance.

They were entering the Temple district, far off their normal route, when the sound of sandals slapping bricks reached Madi's ears. Verona broke into a trot, and Madi lengthened her stride to keep up with the large cat. They turned a corner to encounter an elegant woman wearing a blue sari in the severe style of the devotees to the Water Goddess Marana.

"Ophelia!" Madi hurried toward her friend and year-mate, a pretty mystic who lived at Rivara, the High Temple to Marana in Trimble. "What are you doing out at night? On Taricday?"

The nearby cloister had very strict rules, and Ophelia wasn't the type to flout them, not unless her gift for foresight compelled her.

"It's Jasper," Ophelia gasped between heaving breaths. Whining in distress, Ophelia's own waccat hovered like a golden shadow at her side.

Alarm trailed icy fingers down Madi's spine. "Is Jas in trouble?"

Ophelia's charming brother should know better than to wander around on Taricday. The musician's delicate good looks tended to attract the wrong sort of attention.

"I don't know." The mystic rubbed her hand against her breastbone, her breath short. "I smell death."

"You've had a vision?"

Ophelia was the most powerful seer in Trimble. If she foresaw her own brother's death . . .

Madi's entire body went cold. She groped for her waccat's support, fingers clenching into a fist around the soft fur behind Verona's ears. Verona made a keening noise. Compassion and grief surged through her bond with the waccat. A grief matched by Madi's own sense of loss and disbelief.

"Is Jas going to die?" Madi's voice sounded high and thin to her own ears.

"I . . . I'm not sure." Ophelia's face twisted in pain, her cinnamon brown eyes focused on something only she could see. "It wasn't a proper foretelling, merely a horrible, horrible dream."

"Where is he?" Madi grabbed her friend's arm, creasing the blue silk pallu Ophelia wore draped over her hair. If Jas yet lived, she had to help him. "Take me to him."

Ophelia's gaze sharpened and focused on Madi's face. "He needs you. That's why I came looking for you. You can save him."

Thank Marana! Some of the tension left her body. "Good. Now, where is he?"

"Give me a moment," Ophelia murmured. Her eyes unfocused again, and she swallowed hard. With her powerful water gift, she should be able to track her twin through the emotional bonds of blood.

Madi let go of the seer to tug at the stiff leather jerkin covering her knee-length gray chiton. Urgency compelled her to move, to fight. While it had been weeks since she had last seen Jas, and years since they had been lovers, she would still stand between him and any danger. He was her year-mate's brother if nothing else.

"This way." Ophelia started drifting toward the center of town. Rubbing her breastbone as if soothing an ache, her speed increased with every step. "Such pain. Sorrow. Death."

Ophelia's hasty steps became a run.

Easily matching strides with the smaller woman, Madi fought to remain calm, even with the seer's dire mutterings echoing around her. Silent as ghosts, the pair of waccats kept pace with their Hands. Ophelia led them to a towering structure at the edge of the market. Three stories high and built of imported stone, the Troika Hall symbolized Destinese law in Trimble, and served as a nexus for the city guard.

Madi slowed. If Jas was in the Hall, he was either already dead or in the safest place in Trimble.

Clutching Madi's arm, Ophelia dragged her toward the front entrance. "Come on. He needs you."

They hurried up the wide stone steps to a pair of oversized double doors designed to intimidate. Madi pulled open a smaller door and led Ophelia into the familiar triangular hall. The open space felt cavernous in the dark, with the light from Madi's torch unable to reach the pillars and arches lining the walls.

Voices, muffled and indistinct, sounded from the Mortarary's corner at the far side.

Ophelia hesitated in the middle of the space. "Jas is below us."

There was only one thing below the floor. The cold room. A shiver raced across Madi's skin. "Is he alive?"

Corpses were stored in the cold room until they could be claimed by relatives or burned on the paupers' pyre.

"Yes!" Ophelia snapped, a comforting confidence in her answer.

"Then we need to talk to my captain." Madi headed toward the voices, trusting Ophelia to follow her light.

The voices got louder and more clearly agitated as they approached.

"You need to burn him!" The unfamiliar voice sounded young, cracking painfully on the last word.

"I'm not throwing anyone on a pyre without due cause," Captain Tess replied, ever the voice of reason. She turned and squinted at Madi. "Han-Triguard? What are you doing off patrol?"

Madi bowed deeply, the sign of respect conveniently hiding her embarrassment at the rebuke. "My apologies for abandoning my post. Han-Mystic Ophelia d'Marana foresaw an urgent need for me here."

"I smell death," Ophelia said, her serene voice making the words somehow more chilling.

"There was a murder in the Old Market district," Tess admitted.

Madi's fingers clenched around the leather grip on the torch. Jas rented a room in that shabby part of town.

"Uncle Bernard is dead and Uncle Jas killed him," the youth cried. "He killed his own brother."

"Absurd," Madi said sharply. Jas was the gentlest soul she knew. He would never kill anyone, even if they deserved it. To accuse him of fratricide was inexcusable.

"I found him, with blood all over his hands." The young man turned wild eyes on Captain Tess. "Throw him in the stocks until the burning."

Ignoring the overwrought youth, Madi addressed her captain. "You've a touch of water. Have you tasted his heart?"

Tess sighed and rubbed her face. "I have. His guilt nearly choked me."

WHERE TO FIND JAYCEE JARVIS:

Website: www.jayceejarvis.com
Facebook: https://www.facebook.com/AuthorJayceeJarvis
Twitter: @JayceeJarvis
Goodreads: https://www.goodreads.com/user/
show/35163453-jaycee-jarvis

Be the first to know about author events and new
releases by signing up for my newsletter: https://www.
subscribepage.com/y2c4x6

I always enjoy connecting with readers!